HELM OF AWE

ANCHORESS SERIES BOOK THREE

D. L. ARMILLEI

Diamond Cove Publishing

First edition, February 2022
ISBN 978-0-9986720-8-3 [digital]
ISBN 978-0-9986720-9-0 [softcover]
ISBM 978-1-7379179-0-8 [hardcover]
Library of Congress Control Number 2022900772

Diamond Cove Publishing, LLC,
P.O. Box 2292, Palm Harbor, FL 34682-2292
DLA@DiamondCovePublishing.com

Helm of Awe

I Ching #50 - The Sacred Vessel

"Serve as an example to others by sacrificing your ego and accepting the guidance of the Creator."

— The I Ching or Book of Changes

ONE

Vanessa Cross slammed her back against the aged chestnut tree, muttering over her cursed life, angered at the Elementals—no, the Creator—for holding her lineage against her.

She hid among the tree's low-lying branches with their spiky, curved leaves to catch her breath. Her heart, determined to burst from her chest, distracted Van as her eyes scanned the surrounding woods. Sweat beaded across her brow. She couldn't risk wiping it. The movement might catch the eye of her enemy.

Van's heart calmed, and her breathing slowed. She assessed her situation. Her teammates had screwed up and gotten themselves captured. Irritation burned in her gut over them leaving her alone to win the Jaychund games.

Her inept team, including her best friend Paley Ash and Van's ex-boyfriend Brux Lake, had let her down. Losing the games meant bringing dishonor and shame to her classmates at Canterbury Bells, and would lower Van's graduation status. Failing wasn't an option.

Making the situation worse, everyone on Providence Island, including her classmates and step-mother, watched the final game on the big screen, broadcast through the media feeds placed among the trees. The audience didn't miss a trick. Not a twitch, not a blink. Nothing.

Van remained still, her back pressed against the wart-like bark of the chestnut tree. She breathed softly, careful not to disturb the silence that echoed back at her. She knew from her training classes in the reservation program that by staying in one spot, she'd be found. Be the hunter, not the prey.

She took a step and froze as leaves rustled overhead.

A spiked, round husk, the kind that holds a single chestnut inside, tumbled down from the branches above like a falling star, making soft noises as it hit the twigs and leaves. The bur landed in the dirt by her foot with a thud that rippled through the silence.

Van braced.

An explosion came from the branches and leaves above her. A figure dropped and landed directly in front of Van.

The girl stood tall, looking natural, wild. Her brown skin, taut with the toned muscles of an elite athlete, shone from her sleeveless, midriff vest that looked like it was handmade with care from an animal skin. From the girl's exposed navel dangled a silver ring with tiny multi-colored jewels.

Suixsha. Unfairly brought to the island by Van's mentor, Uxa Huxatec, to challenge Van in the final game.

The girl's fist rammed into Van's solar plexus.

Van doubled over and gasped for breath, smoldering with embarrassment. Her bad luck made good content for the viewers.

Suixsha rummaged through the pockets of Van's uniform like a shrew burrowing for a mealworm.

Van's searing gut pain wasn't enough to block her boiling ire. This... *intruder* was not better than her. She snapped upright with her elbows held in square formation and struck Suixsha under the chin. Seizing the advantage of Suixsha's backward momentum, Van used her leg to shove her nemesis to the ground.

She straddled her rival and used her arm to push down against Suixsha's chest. Her free hand foraged the girl's pockets.

"This is over. Where's your token?" growled Van, all too aware the girl's punch had caused the throbbing in her stomach.

Taking another player's token eliminated that student. Sent them to spend the rest of the game in a holding area called "jail." Van couldn't find Suixsha's token and wondered if the girl had swallowed it. Van doubted it since, according to the rules, it would disqualify the unsportsmanlike player from winning.

Suixsha's necklace rested on her chest, strung with charm holders, each filled with a token taken from one of the other players. The girl obviously brought the necklace with her before entering the final, confident she would fill the holders. The pride—*the audacity*— of Suixsha wearing such a necklace infuriated Van.

In one seamless move, Suixsha shifted her hips and twisted using significant force. Van's grip loosened, and she got knocked to the side.

Suixsha contorted her body like a wild animal freeing itself from a trap and lifted herself off the ground, onto her feet.

She pounced on Van with powerful physical strength and dexterity, like no average teen. She possessed a skill level Van had yet to come across on her missions in the Living World or in her training classes with the Grigori.

Suixsha pinned down Van and methodically searched Van's pockets like a machine designed to do only one thing. Get the token.

Using precious seconds, Van assessed her enemy for weaknesses. Suixsha had made a mistake in not tying back her waist-length, spiral curls. Van grabbed a handful and yanked.

Suixsha's chin jutted toward the sky, causing her silver headpiece to tumble to the ground and exposing her necklace. Paley's token tauntingly dangled in Van's face. Yet, the girl didn't budge.

"You have no right to be here," said Van through gritted teeth as she struggled to get free.

Her rival's prying fingers got close to the pocket where Van hid her token. Van wriggled her hip.

Suixsha's sharp hazel eyes noticed the motion.

Van slammed her fists against Suixsha and kicked her legs so hard the muscles in her body strained to the point of bursting. Her impending loss—in her *senior year,* no less—made Van furious and left her frustrated, desperate to win. She needed power.

And power she had. The magical Anchoress bloodline she inherited from her mother. Using this advantage was, of course, against the rules. Van would be in trouble with Uxa and the other Elders if the onlookers who knew nothing of the island's secrets viewed Van using her substantial, otherworldly power.

Suixsha's frenzied fingers found the pocket hiding Van's token and dug in.

Not about to let this newcomer beat her, Van pushed her hip into the ground harder, trying to block the girl's fingers from reaching her token. The insult of losing to Suixsha reverberated down to Van's soul. She allowed the resulting fury to connect her to her inner magic, fully expecting to feel the tingling of her blue eyes as they turned violet, a mark she had engaged in her powers. Van waited.

Her eyes didn't change.

Van's connection shorted out. The drain of trying to access her magical Anchoress bloodline made every muscle in her body feel weighted, causing her to exert extra energy just to move and breathe.

Why can't I access my power? Suixsha must've cast a spell on me! Van gathered her last shreds of strength and clenched her fists.

Suixsha used her knee to force Van onto her side.

Van pounded her nemesis's arms as Suixsha's fingers dug deeper into Van's pocket.

Suixsha released Van and rose to her feet in victory, eyes locked on the token she raised between two fingers.

Van laid on the ground, fuming so hard she thought steam might come from her ears.

Suixsha peered down at her. "Your anger cause you lose energy," she said, not in pride, but as an undeniable truth.

"Shut up, you loser," spat Van, fully aware it wasn't her finest moment.

"Only one loser here," said Suixsha in the monotone of a cold, hard fact. "You."

TWO

Van gathered the resolve to sit upright, long after her rival had departed.

She grunted from the effort of lifting her body from the ground. Her muscles burned with strain. Her bumps and bruises throbbed. Although Massachusetts had beautiful weather and leafed out trees in June, despondency plagued Van. Head down, shoulders slumped, she dawdled along the winding path through Providence Island's nature preserve.

Ahead, the after-game tent peeped through the trees.

Van pulled aside the door's flap and entered, smoldering with dread over the thought of facing her teammates and Uxa. She glanced at the players and medics busily performing their after-the-final tasks. Her stomach knotted as she saw the Elders attending to their duties—like assessing each player's performance, along with the students' written final exams, to determine each student's class rank and career track placement. For seniors like Van, the Elders determined their permanent career placement.

Paley descended on Van and chattered in her trademark rat-atat-tat manner. "You did great! That girl definitely cheated some-how. Did you see Brux take Drew's token? I heard Mark got..."

Her voice faded as Van noticed a dark purple bruise on her friend's forehead and frowned. "Are you hurt?"

Paley rapidly shook her head. "I'm glad you're not hurt. You're not hurt, are you? Not seriously hurt?"

"Just my pride," said Van, with a half-hearted grin.

"That was one tough game. Bringing in that girl..." Paley lowered her voice. "From *off island*. We know what that means."

Van cocked her head. "What?"

"This year's miss—*task*—must be a doozy."

Van shrugged. "Finals get tougher each year." She squinted at Uxa holding a clipboard and chatting with Suixsha in the after-games medical area. "You think her win will affect my placement?"

"If it does, totally not fair." Paley flipped her dyed-blond hair over her shoulder. "I hope I still get placed in Advanced Studies Grigori Support. So I can be there for you, always."

"ASG Support?" Van raised her brow. Paley had earned it. The program allowed terrigen involvement in operational aspects of the Grigori. "Congrats!"

Paley cast her eyes downward and blushed, "See, sneaking me over two years ago paid off."

One of their schoolmates, who had competed in the final game, rushed past, presumably hurrying home to get ready for the evening's formal Placement Ceremony. He gave Van a quick pat on the back and muttered, "Great job." Van doubted he meant it. Her gut wrenched again as she recalled her failure to win the final.

"What's with the pouty face?" Brux's grin stretched his split lip.

Van's heart lurched at seeing pink splotches of blood smearing his teeth and his mud-splattered black, combat-ready clothes. "You okay?"

"The medics put birch tar tincture on my sore spots." Brux stretched his bruised hands in front of him and flipped them up and down, as if checking to make sure all his fingers were still there. "See. I'm already healing. How're you two? You see the medics yet?"

"We survived," said Paley, grinning.

One of their teammates, Brooke, stopped by and said to Brux, "Great job in the game."

Van narrowed her eyes at Brooke's oh-so-casual sweep of a hand across his back.

"You all did." Brooke briefly cast her gaze at Van and Paley before landing her eyes back on Brux. "How's your sister?"

Daisy, a year younger, had won her year, but her team had been eliminated early in the final.

"Fine. They've already cleared her from the after-game tent," said Brux, and the three of them chattered away.

Van scowled as she watched both Brooke and Paley jockey for Brux's full attention. Just because she couldn't be with Brux didn't make it open season for Brooke or Paley to date him.

"I wouldn't let the final upset you," said Brux, misinterpreting Van's facial expression. "Suixsha was a fierce opponent. You did your best."

Van's eyes darted away, and she mumbled, "My best wasn't good enough, it seems."

"Here you are," a medic said to Brux. "You haven't been cleared yet. Please come with me back to your cot."

"You left without being cleared?" Brooke playfully swatted him on the shoulder.

"Blame Van, it's her fault." Brux grinned. "She lured me away."

"Yup," said Van, lightly, to hide how irked she felt over the painful truth behind Brux's casual words. "Everything's my fault." He held her responsible for his life circumstances instead of placing blame where it belonged—on the Elementals. They chose Brux as her assigned protector, not Van.

After Brux left with the medic, Brooke wandered away.

"Want to leave early?" Van asked Paley, sizzling with a new-founded sense of urgency to get going on this year's mission. "Skip the Placement Ceremony?"

Paley turned pale, even through her tanning-booth bronzed skin. "The Alignment doesn't happen until Sunday night at midnight." Her eyes widened. "What about that—that..."

"It can't cross into the boundary of Salus Valde." Tiny shivers erupted on Van's skin over the thought of encountering the monstrous Quasher again. It existed for one reason, to hunt Van down and snuff out her light. The Alignment, or Luxta as the ancients called it, provided a thirty-day window in time based on celestial configurations that allowed the Anchoress to safely enter the Living World without being hunted by the wolf-like shadow-beast. "We'll stay at Lodestar until the window opens."

"Uxa won't allow it. Not outside the Alignment."

"I'm entering the Advanced Studies Grigori program in the fall," said Van, hoping it was still true despite losing the final game. "I'll be there all the time."

"But... I really want to go to the ceremony." Paley pouted. "And the festival. It's our senior year."

During the ceremony, Uxa announced career track placements for each student to all the islanders, and nerves ran high. After the formalities, the islanders began celebrating the three-day Jaychund festival.

Paley shook her head. "Unh-uh. No. It's too risky. Uxa makes you live on the island for your own protection. The Balish and the Quasher can't get through the portal to get here."

"What do the Balish have to do with it?" snapped Van.

"You know." Paley leaned in and whispered, "Because a lot of them want to kill you."

"I'm dating the Balish prince. He doesn't want to kill me." Although Van hadn't heard a word from Ferox since they had parted at the end of last year's Alignment. "I don't want to be here to watch Pernilla—" Van shook her head over her misspeak. "I mean, *Suixsha* to get awarded my All-Grades Trophy."

Van knew what caused her to associate Suixsha with Pernilla. Losing the final had made Van doubt her abilities. Pernilla had been better than Van in school work and athletics. If Pernilla couldn't survive last year's mission, what chance did Van have this year? She soothed her anxieties by telling herself she went on the same mission as Pernilla. She had survived then and would again now.

An intern medic dressed in a white robe with a red insignia on the chest came over and said to Van, "Time for your medical look-over and debriefing." She ushered Van away from Paley and over to a private cot.

As the medic examined and treated Van, her stomach churned at the thought of rehashing her time in the game.

After the medic finished her exam, Van's dread escalated when Uxa approached, looking forbidding in her customary sky-blue and silver, tunic-styled uniform of the reservation Elders.

"So," Uxa's icy-blue eyes flashed, made more dramatic by the contrast of her light-brown skin and dirty-blond hair worn scraped back into a long straight plait. "Let us talk about what happened in the final."

"I lost. That's what happened." Van shifted her weight. "Suixsha must've cheated."

"She did not." Uxa held a clipboard and pen, ready to take notes.

"She's not from Canterbury Bells. She shouldn't have been in the games."

"Paley also took part. Some would say she did not earn her place in the games," said Uxa. "That she was there because of her friendship with you."

Van's cheeks flared in exasperation. "Twice Paley went on missions in the Living World. For *you*."

Uxa scribbled something on her clipboard.

"She proved her dedication to the Grigori's cause by training off hours with me and some of my classmates in the reservation program." Van's jaw hurt from gritting her teeth. "That's why I picked her to be on my team in the final."

Uxa continued making notes without looking up.

"Why does everyone have a problem with Paley? Who cares that she's an orphan? She's earned her place a million times over."

Uxa stopped writing and stared at Van. She paused, as if considering how to respond. Or, more likely, calculating her words so not to expose any high-level Lodian secrets or hidden agendas.

"When the negativity emanated by the mainland terrigens increases, it affects our little community here on the island, not just the Living World," said Uxa.

"I know that."

"It is much worse than you know."

"Like, how worse?" Van's mouth went dry.

Uxa subtly shifted her eyes, as if checking to make sure no-one overheard them. "Soon the terrigens' violent tendencies will escalate to the point of a world-wide war."

CHAPTER

THREE

"World War Three?" said Van, mouth agape. "Are we sending out more Grigori? Will the magic hiding Providence Island still work to keep us safe?"

"The Lodian Consilium and I have a plan in place," said Uxa. "It is not something for you to worry about."

Van glared. "So why bring it up?"

"I am simply explaining to you why your peers are not changing their attitude toward Paley. The negative vibrations coming from the mainland have locked their mindsets in place."

Van snorted. "How's that fair?"

Uxa tilted her chin down and peered at Van with a "you need to think about what you've done" look.

"What?" Van feigned innocence.

Uxa held her gaze.

Van flipped her hand in the air. "Okay, fine. I tried to access my Anchoress powers. I wasn't cheating. Grigori training taught me to use all resources available during an encounter. That's what I did."

"As is your right. However, you acted out of anger at Suixsha for besting you."

"My powers didn't work... I couldn't connect." Van raised her eyes to Uxa's. "Why?"

"What were you feeling in the moment?"

Van contemplated Uxa's question.

"I... I wanted to beat Suixsha. Nothing else mattered."

Uxa made a quick scribble in her notes. "Mastering another brings strength. Mastering yourself brings power." She peered at Van again. "What made you choose to access your power?"

"I can use my power as I see fit." Van crossed her arms. "*I'm* the Anchoress."

Uxa appeared unimpressed. "When ego takes over, it causes you to act from a place of selfishness, for your own benefit, to win for your own self-gratification, not for the team."

"If I win, the team wins, too."

"Ego is an illusion of power," said Uxa. "It caused you to make the wrong choice. Trying to access your powers drained you of energy and you lost."

"I've been training non-stop. I'm physically stronger than ever before."

Being the Anchoress designated Van as the warrior destined to fight—and win—in the prophesied Dishora, a time when darkness rises from the mud seeking to destroy all light. Van needed to stay fit so she could access her power. Although, right now, her body still ached from the games. She pushed her pains aside and raised her eyes to meet Uxa's. "It was worth a try. A win is a win in my book."

Uxa paused and then said, "The Creator recognizes and rewards actions only when you behave in an upstanding and fair manner. When you try to gain advances by questionable means such as aggression and anger, you will always fail."

Van slumped. "It's the curse." Her ancestor, Amaryl, inadvertently placed a curse on her own bloodline, the Anchoress bloodline, which caused Amaryl's heirs to suffer a life of misfortune. "It always wrecks things."

Uxa's pen scratched along the clipboard, making more notes.

"You are to meet Fynn at Marble Hall at six p.m. on Sunday. He will escort you to my office in Lodestar, where you will be briefed on this year's task."

Van leaped to her feet. "I want to start this year's mission now. Ask the Brotherhood if I can leave today?"

The Brotherhood of the Magic Circle, a covert group that controlled most governments in the Earth World, worked closely with the Grigori to keep the demon problem under control. Van suspected the Brotherhood also had authority over operation of the Lodian Consilium.

Uxa pursed her lips. "I do not need the Brotherhood's permission to send out my team. We stick to the plan. Fynn will escort you over on Sunday." She gave Van a brisk parting nod and walked back to the other Elders gathered at the far corner of the tent where they discussed grades and career placements.

Van plopped her butt down on the cot, grumbling about wanting to finish pleading her case to Uxa. She glanced around the tent, looking for someone to share her gripes. All the other players, including Paley, had left except for one.

Suixsha paced in front of her cot like a caged animal.

Van scowled. She had Suixsha all figured out. Lingering to bask in every bit of glory that came with being this year's winner. "Your pacing is annoying."

Suixsha stopped and directed her attention to Van. "Big ego is weakness in warrior."

"Wrong," said Van. "It's a strength."

Suixsha pushed her thumb to her chest. "I win."

"You got lucky."

The glint from the tokens dangling from Suixsha's necklace sparkled in Van's face like a bundle of little trophies. Van figured Suixsha would wear the prized tokens until death. To Van's surprise, Suixsha had already replaced them with talismans.

"Anger get best of you. It cause you make poor choice and you lose." Suixsha continued pacing, apparently done with their conversation.

"Bad choice? You mean, doing everything I can to win?"

"Glory by cheating mean no glory at all," said Suixsha.

"Agree to disagree." Van rose from the cot with a sudden urge to move her body. She stretched her arms over her head and eyed Uxa, still chatting with the other Elders.

It didn't matter. If Van couldn't get Uxa's go-ahead, she would head to Lodestar anyway. Not getting Uxa's permission to do something had never stopped her before. She had waited all year to confront Ferox for ghosting her. Long enough. Now she needed to head home, get cleaned up, and pack.

Van left the tent and followed the windy path in the woods. Voices emanated through the trees as she neared Hopping Hill Road.

Paley and Brux were waiting for her.

"Did you talk to Uxa about leaving early?" asked Brux.

"I still have to pack." Paley flipped her hair with a smirk, as she had little to pack, other than her plethora of crazy colored contact lenses, and could be ready in minutes.

"It's unclear," said Van, disgusted with herself for failing again, although she appreciated Paley's sense of humor.

"I'm taking that as a no," said Brux.

"Yay!" Paley clapped her hands together. "We can go to the festival!"

Paley and Brux turned and meandered down the road. Van trailed behind. They looked like a couple, strolling happily along, gabbing, laughing, oblivious to the world around them. Van sighed, remembering how solid and warm Ferox's chest felt against her fingertips. His kindness, coupled with his ability to take command, made Van's heart flutter. She ached to see him in person. It was the only way she could learn the reason for his silence.

To be fair, Van hadn't reached out to him either, not wanting to seem needy. She had an unspoken rule that if a guy was interested in her, he would attempt to keep in touch. *Where'd I get that stupid rule?* Not Genie. Her step-mother lived and died by male attention.

Perhaps the strict Elemental-enforced guidelines on who Van could marry scared Ferox away. He was only sixteen, a year younger than Van. They were much too young to think about marriage. Still, it could've given him cold feet about dating.

Ferox was an unacceptable choice for her in the eyes of the Elementals. Her ultimate duty as Anchoress would be to pass on her bloodline to her daughter, always the firstborn and likely to be the reason for her death, thanks to the curse. A fact made more likely by mixing Balish and Lodian bloodlines were she to choose Ferox as the father of her child.

Maybe Van could ease Ferox's concerns by finding a counter-curse. Her father gave his life searching for one in the Living World. She intended to follow up on his lead.

Brux and Paley continued chattering as they strolled ahead of her.

Van had broken up with Brux because of the Elemental's rules. He was her assigned protector, which meant the Elementals forbade them to become romantically involved. Now he had to witness Van pine after the Balish prince.

She hoped it wouldn't hurt Brux if she and Ferox got back together. Like, it was okay for Van to break the Elemental's rules for Ferox, but not for Brux? That's not how it would be, but... Again, Van sighed. The world was cruel, and she had no power to fix it.

"The whims of the Creator control everything," she muttered to herself, watching as Brux bent down and scraped his sneaker with a twig after stepping in dog poo.

CHAPTER

FOUR

Van entered Mt. Hope Manor her usual way, through the back door leading into the kitchen.

She dashed down the hallway of her blissfully silent house, listening for signs anyone was home. Luma, their housekeeper, took the long weekend off and, so far, her step-mother, though most likely home, was nowhere in sight or sound.

She careened up the main stairway and zipped into her bedroom on the third floor, focused on getting to the amphitheater at Community Gardens. Van intended to grab Uxa before the Placement Ceremony began. Then, she would coax Uxa into letting Fynn take her to Lodestar tonight.

Van threw back her lemon-yellow curtains and peered outside as if hoping to see Uxa crossing the rich, green lawn of the manor. She hastily closed the curtains, almost ripping them from their rods, and dashed into her bathroom for a quick shower.

Then she changed into jeans and sneakers, tossed her hair into a ponytail, and shoved clothes and essentials into her mustard-colored backpack.

"Mwwrp eep rrrrpt."

She turned to see a glowing-white critter that looked like a bunny-cat mix sitting on her bed.

"Wiglaf!" cried Van, pleasantly surprised her magical pal had stopped by for a visit.

Van dropped her backpack and sat down on her queen-sized canopy bed next to her bunfy.

Wiglaf scooted onto her lap.

She scratched behind his long, pointed ears, the way he liked. His purrs soothed her soul. She took a moment and closed her eyes, breathed deep, and relaxed her muscles.

A familiar amaranthine glow entered her mind's eye. Another otherworldly friend had arrived.

"Greetings, my little warrior." The woman's white-gray, waist-length hair and light-blue eyes came in clear as her image hovered above the floor.

Jacynthia! Van cried in her mind, delighted.

"You are troubled?" asked Jacynthia.

I'm cursed. I lost the Jaychund games because of that interloper, Suixsha. Uxa won't let me go to the Living World early, and Ferox has forgotten me.

"Passion gives fuel and engages our will. But one must wield it with mastery," said Jacynthia. "When our passions are fixated on that which is not manifesting, our power becomes depleted. Energy can be regained by letting go of the attachment. Break attachments that are not serving your ownership of energy."

Instead of calming Van, her spirit guide's words irked her.

What attachments? Wanting to see Ferox?

"Your frustration is taking you away from me." Jacynthia flickered, almost disappearing.

I'm sorry. I... I just feel like Uxa is keeping me away from Ferox by not letting me go over early. I know, stupid, right?

"You are confronted by the results of your actions, good or bad. Nothing is given to us and nothing is kept from us. We alone carry the responsibility for everything we receive and experience. The ability to effect change comes from the awareness of power within the Self."

So, by leaving for Lodestar right now, with or without approval, I can empower myself to set things straight?

"When unable to achieve goals, our ego becomes inflamed and we are at risk of hardening into anger and bitterness, to lash out and aggressively grab control over the situation. Ego becomes the enemy of one's mind when it keeps you out of touch with reality. It often prevents one from hearing critical but necessary assessments, resulting in an overestimation of one's abilities and under-estimation of the effort and skill required to achieve one's goals."

I also want to go over to make sure Uxa doesn't get any ideas about Suixsha taking my place on the mission. I need to make sure that cheater doesn't get my glory for a job well-done, assuming she can even complete the task.

"Anger incites ego. Without control of your anger, any move is premature and will bring disaster. Anger is not a source of power. To act in accordance with the Creator, you must learn the true source of power."

Which is what?

"Genuine power comes from your connection to the infinite spirit of the Creator. You must release your anger. Only then will you achieve a state of peace, think clearly, and make correct choices. Reconnect to your divine source and you will persevere."

Got it. Thanks.

Van shot open her eyes, forcing herself back to consciousness and breaking her connection to Jacynthia.

She scooped Wiglaf off of her lap and dropped him next to her on the bed. "Time for me to go."

Van leaped up, grabbed her backpack, and sprinted down the stairs. She stopped short on entering the kitchen.

"Ah, Vanessa," said Genie. "There you are."

Dammit. Van avoided speaking to her step-mother as much as possible, which proved challenging since they lived in the same house.

Genie hovered at the butcher's block table in front of two chilled martini classes, a jar of green olives with the little red peppers stuffed inside, a box of long toothpicks with a curl on one end, a large bottle of Royal Dragon vodka (the swirling dragon design on the bottle reminded Van of her step-mother's pelvic tattoo), and a classic silver cocktail shaker.

Genie perused Van's attire. "And where do you think you're going?"

"I wanted to—"

"Not dressed like that, you're not," said Genie. "Go upstairs and change. We're leaving soon."

Her step-mother wore a soft-yellow, form fitting dress designed with fiery-orange, rose, and gold-colored swirls reaching upward from the hemline. The dress clung to her toned body like flames wrapping around a campfire log. She looked smoking hot, as usual.

"No need to let yourself go just because you lost the games." Genie clasped the jar of olives with her delicate, manicured fingers. Her nails were painted in the same yellow color as her dress. "Uxa only selects winners to go on—work on her summer projects."

Her boyfriend, Uncle Rummie, had to be nearby for Genie to watch her words.

Van's step-mother grabbed a toothpick and slid green olives onto it. "I wonder if you'll even be invited this year."

Van watched Genie's full lips move, not really listening to her step-mother's words, instead distracted by how her pink lipstick perfectly matched her rose-colored stiletto heels and the rose-colored swirls on her dress. No wonder Genie expressed constant disappointment in Van. Her step-mother set an impossibly high standard for her—or any female—to follow.

"Suixsha will most likely take your place." Genie stopped fussing with the drinks and looked at Van, as if waiting for a response.

"What are you talking about? Do you know something?" Van snatched an olive from the jar before Genie could slap her hand.

"No need to feel threatened, dear," she said, in a tone that implied the opposite.

Genie confirmed Van's intuitive fear that Uxa or the Brotherhood, or both, might replace her with Suixsha on the mission. Worse case scenario, Van wouldn't be going to the Living World. Her hopes of confronting Ferox for avoiding her all year went up in smoke.

"There's my beautiful girl!" boomed Uncle Rummie. He entered the kitchen with the distant sound of the hall toilet flushing. He opened his arms wide and headed toward Van.

"Abort, abort." Van grinned as she playfully ducked his hug.

"Hoo, hoo, hoo," bellowed Rummie with a belly laugh. "You're a feisty one!"

"Hi Uncle Rummie," said Van, practically blinded by the sparkle of his excessive gold jewelry—rings, bracelets, necklaces—against his sun-kissed skin. She imagined, hidden under his jersey, hung a big gaudy family crest medallion dangling from one of his chains.

"Great job in the games, girl." He patted Van on the back with his meaty hand.

Genie and Uncle Rummie got caught up in their own conversation. Van kept quiet so neither would engage her in their discussion, and perhaps her step-mother would forget about making Van change and go to the ceremony.

Genie giggled like one of Van's classmates after being asked on a date to the school dance. Van noticed her step-mother's skin had the faint glimmer of a tan… and her hair, darkened from its usual slivery white-blond.

Van frowned.

Demimondaines were skilled in magic and often used it to alter their appearance, making themselves more pleasing to their man. She figured this accounted for Genie's new look. Van recoiled over the extent Genie would go to snag a man, certain this one must meet her step-mother's criteria of possessing great wealth and or power.

Van wondered what her father would've thought about Genie's behavior.

She turned her attention to Uncle Rummie. "Why'd you always wear so much jewelry?"

"Vanessa!" cried Genie. "Stop being rude."

"Sorry," said Van. She couldn't help it. Uncle Rummie's chains reminded her of her mother's lost necklace. Her father attempted to get that locket to Van by handing it to Genie as one of his last acts before dying. Her step-mother, instead of passing it to Van, lost it. Or rather, she hid it in the hollow of a tree trunk where it disappeared.

So, who took the necklace from the tree? Why would someone take it? For its intrinsic value? The solid gold could be melted and sold. Or did others know something about the necklace that Van didn't, like magical properties that Van strongly suspected resided in the locket?

"Stop frowning, dear," said Genie, breaking Van from her thoughts. "You'll get wrinkles."

"Young people don't have to worry about wrinkles," said Van. Genie's appearance rarely changed. She always looked around thirty years old thanks to her magical, demimondaine-inspired potions. Van eyed the martini.

Genie noticed. "Get upstairs and change or we'll be late."

"I don't want to go to the Placement Ceremony," said Van. "I want to—"

"We're going," snapped Genie. "I'll hear no more of it."

"Both of you?"

"No, no," muttered Uncle Rummie. "Not feeling well..."

"It's still not appropriate for me to be seen dating," said Genie.

"Too soon after your dear departed father, I'm afraid," said Uncle Rummie.

"It hasn't been three years yet. I can't even imagine what dreadful chatter would come of it." Genie shook her head.

"Fine." Van darted up the stairs back to the third floor, stomping on each step as hard as possible, knowing the noise would irritate Genie and underscore Van's lack of desire to go to the ceremony.

Wiglaf had hung around and was nestled into the puffy, yellow-and-white comforter on her bed.

"Rrrp?" He sat upright, stretching his long ears.

"I wish my father was here," said Van, surprised at her surging, heated emotions. "Nothing ever goes right in my life. Now I'm stuck going to the stupid ceremony when I should be going to see Ferox."

Instead of changing, she paced her bedroom. "It's the Elementals, or the Creator. One of them is blocking my path... or it's the curse, giving me bad luck."

Wiglaf's dark blue eyes moved back and forth as he watched Van tread and mutter.

"Why hasn't Ferox gotten in touch with me? He has feelings for me. Why wouldn't he? What did Jacynthia mean about breaking attachments? With Ferox? So, I'm not supposed to be with anyone?"

The more aggressively Van stomped, the more Wiglaf hunched into the bedspread like a tiny white pillow. He pulled his ears down around his body, his round eyes opened wider than usual.

"Ugh!" Van threw her hands in the air. She paused and looked at Wiglaf. "I need to punch something."

In a blink, Wiglaf disappeared back into his magical animal realm.

Her eyes darted around her bedroom, searching for the bunfy who was nowhere to be seen. "I didn't mean punch *you*. I would never..." She tossed her hands in the air again. "Oh, I give up!"

Van stormed into her walk-in closet, grabbed the first dress to reach her hand—a bright yellow chiffon—and wiggled into it. She yanked off her ponytail holder and gave her hair several rough brushes, which was way more effort than she felt like making. Then, grabbed her backpack and headed downstairs.

Genie had a taxi waiting in the driveway at the foot of the grand stairway to the manor. She stood beside it with the door opened and looked daggers at seeing the backpack slung over Van's shoulder. She opened her mouth to speak.

Van held up her palm. "Choose your battles." She zoomed into the backseat, as if moving faster would save time, despite knowing there was now little hope of running into Uxa before the closing ceremonies began.

The taxi sped away. After a quick trip, a sharp hit to the brakes jostled Van and Genie as the taxi came to a stop outside the entrance to the amphitheater at Community Gardens, the location of the ceremony and festival.

Tradition dictated the entire community celebrate Jaychund together and a throng of islanders headed into the amphitheater, all wearing their best dresses and suits for the formal occasion.

Brux and Paley were waiting outside the entrance and greeted them.

"Any word yet?" Brux asked Van.

She shook her head. "I'll try to get to Uxa after the ceremony. If not, I'm going either way."

Customarily, families sat together. The orphans from the Gables counted themselves as one big family and did so, except Paley, who always sat with Van. Brux departed to sit with the Lakes.

With Paley next to her whispering funny anecdotes about how certain classmates would fare in their placements, Van endured the ceremony. When Uxa announced Paley's permanent placement in Grigori Support—which the islanders knew as a coveted placement in a secretive division of Homeland Security—there were some grumbles, as expected.

Van heard comments like, "Fixed." And, "Not fair." She wanted to scream out that Paley had earned her place and exactly how her friend had done it. But, of course, she couldn't. Their missions in the Living World were classified.

Brux and Van got awarded permanent placement in the Grigori program. No surprise there. Brux's sister, Daisy, remained on the Grigori track. Also, no surprise.

More and more classmates got their placements. Van tapped on her heel, counting the minutes until the ceremony ended. She scanned the audience, noticing grimaces and frowns from the students disappointed in their placements. Some got mouthy about it. Other students' faces lit up with big smiles. Same thing happened every year.

The audience exited the amphitheater after the ceremony ended, most of them in a rush to carry on with the festivities. Genie, in a hurry to get home to her secret boyfriend, bid Van and Paley farewell.

Van watched her step-mother slide into the waiting taxi, hoping she wouldn't see her again for thirty days, after Van returned from the Living World.

"My placement sucks. I'm not doing it," said an angry voice, loud enough for anyone in the vicinity to hear.

It was Wade, a spiky-haired kid in Van's year, gathered with a handful of peers on the road outside the amphitheater.

"Screw Uxa." Wade clenched his fists. "Screw the Elders."

"Shh," said Brooke. "Watch your words."

"Uh-oh," muttered Paley, as she and Van gaped at him, wide-eyed. This didn't happen often, and, like watching the tragedy of a house burning down to ashes, they couldn't turn away.

Some in the exiting crowd turned their necks to catch the commotion as they kept moving, not wishing to get involved. Most of the teens and kids wanted to stop and gawk like Van and Paley, but their parents shuffled them along.

"What do they know, anyway?" asked Wade, through a clenched jaw.

They know a lot, thought Van. The Elders observed student's abilities from the time they entered Canterbury Bells in kindergarten through high school graduation. They matched each student's skill set with careers essential to the community and required graduating seniors to fulfill their final placements. Seniors could refuse—as it looked like Wade was about to do—but, as a result, were excommunicated and sent to live on the mainland.

If someone changed their mind after leaving, the magically hidden island made it near impossible to find your way back. Without luck, the only way for an excommunicated islander to return was if an Elder sent someone to the mainland to "find" them.

"I'm not going to spend my life working as a marine electrician on this crappy island!" shouted Wade.

"But, that's a good placement," said Deacon. "Better than mine in culinary arts."

"Or mine in mechanical engineering," said Amber, rolling her eyes. "Snore."

"Who are they to tell me what I'm supposed to do with the rest of my life?" cried Wade.

Brooke held a finger to her lips, trying to shush him again. "They'll think you're refusing your placement."

Wade huffed, red-faced. He pursed his lips as if mulling over the idea.

Island security assigned to monitor the event had taken notice. Several moved closer to Wade and his classmates, causing a crowd of mostly adults and teens to gather around, curiosity getting the better of them.

"Think about your parents, your sister," Deacon said to Wade. "They'll have a fit if you leave."

"It will reflect poorly on your family," said Brooke, as if it were the worst possible thing.

Wade looked as if he were about to erupt.

"Don't," warned Amber.

Wade shouted, "I refuse my placement!"

Island security rushed over. They grabbed Wade and shoved him into one of the nearby parked security buggies.

Brooke and Amber clutched each other, their eyes watering.

Deacon stretched his arm and spread his fingers, as if reaching to bring Wade back. "Buddy..." he said meekly, knowing what happened next was out of his control.

"We're never going to see him again," Paley muttered to Van.

"It doesn't happen that fast," said Van. "He has to sign stuff and so do his parents. It's a whole process."

"He'll be held in the Complex until he's excommunicated." Brux had wedged through the crowd of onlookers to join them. "Paley's right. We're never going to see him again."

Paley gnawed on her cuticles.

Brux wrapped his arm around Van's waist. "Let's get you out of here, in case there's more trouble." He glanced at Paley. "Both of you."

Van wriggled out of Brux's grasp. "No, I need to talk to Uxa."

"We should go to the festival to cheer us up after that fiasco," said Paley.

"Why don't we talk to her tomorrow?" asked Brux.

"You guys go." Van stretched her neck to peer over the mob of people jostling her as they left the amphitheater. "Try to have some fun. We'll catch up later." Van glimpsed Uxa and President Sterling, the top Elder in the Lodian Consilium, and began making her way through the departing crowd.

Uxa and President Sterling were speaking to Deacon, Brooke, Amber, and Wade's parents and little sister who had been brought over by island security. A handful of guards surrounded them, several were breaking up the crowd of onlookers.

Van pushed her way through, headed straight for Uxa, when she heard a male voice calling her name from behind.

CHAPTER

FIVE

Van halted her pursuit of Uxa.

She turned to see Ken Rose, her former boyfriend. His lips tight, cheeks flared with pink splotches.

"Hey, what's up?" asked Van, concerned about his flushed appearance. For a brief flicker, she thought the demon virus had returned.

"No wonder Pernilla died." He held his arms straight by his sides, fists clenched. "You can't even win the games."

His anger bombarded Van, making it hard for her to breathe, as if she was being suffocated by his very presence. The multitude of attendees, occupied with gossiping about Wade refusing his placement, moved around them without a glance.

"You always hated her." Ken trembled with each word. "You never got over it. That I left you for her. That she was better than you at everything. Nilla won the games, she beat you and you hated it."

Pernilla had won the All-Grades Trophy in Van's sophomore year, earning her top career placement. Her skills, along with meeting other criteria for a mission, like developing ichor in her blood, secured her a place on the team Uxa sent into the Living World last summer to check the second seal. Pernilla never returned home. She died bravely, battling a sea monster.

Ken didn't know the true story. He only knew the rhetoric told to the townies by the Elders. That Pernilla, along with Van and other hand-selected peers, had taken part in a summer internship with Homeland Security, Grigori division.

"There's no way you had her back." Tears seeped from the corners of his eyes. "You hated her. You let her... you let her die."

Ken paused. He let out a huge sob.

Van reached for him in a gesture of comfort.

He crumbled into Van's arms. His wet cheeks soaked her shoulder. She wrapped her arms around him and let him bawl, holding back her own tears.

"Pernilla still lives on in our memories and in our hearts," Van said, caressing his back. Her heart ached over his pain, worsened knowing he would never understand the selfless sacrifice made by his girlfriend. "I find comfort believing there is no death, only continuity of life through our eternal soul. She still exists in a happier place. She wouldn't want you to be upset over her."

It was wrong to keep the details of his girlfriend's death from him. But Van had no power to correct the situation.

Some time passed as Ken clutched Van. While comforting him, she watched the mindless lingerers disperse from the amphitheater, occupied with their own lives, smiling and chatting on their way to the nearby festival.

Once pacified, Ken released Van.

"S-sorry." He used his knuckles to wipe his eyes. With slumped shoulders, he ambled away.

A bit stunned by Ken's explosion of emotion, Van almost forgot about catching Uxa. She glanced at the spot where Uxa and President Sterling had been standing. They were no longer there. She scanned the stragglers. Most people had already made their way over to the festival. Van didn't see Uxa anywhere.

She hurried into the nearest public bathroom, tore off her dress, shoved it into her backpack, and changed into jeans, a tank top, and sneakers. Then left the amphitheater and rushed out of Community Gardens.

Ken's guilt laid heavily on her. She couldn't shake it.

Dammit. Van changed her trajectory. As a courtesy, she decided to find Brux and Paley before going to the reservation to see Uxa, since, after that, she planned on going straight to Lodestar.

Ken blamed Van for Pernilla's death. Was he right? If Van couldn't protect Pernilla when she had access to her magical Anchoress abilities, what made her think she should go on a mission when she couldn't access them? Van shook off the thought. It wasn't enough to snuff her burning desire to confront Ferox.

Van hurried through Community Gardens's fields where the festival was in full swing. She passed a bunch of booths offering carnival games—ring toss, needle in a haystack, balloon darts— and remembered the days when she and Ken were dating and he would keep trying until he won a prize for her. It felt like a lifetime ago.

She saw the Ferris wheel towering high in sky and followed it, knowing she would find the food court at its base. Paley, Brux, and a handful of their classmates were hanging around one of the picnic tables, chatting, drinking Blood Orange Rickeys, and, thankfully, smiling.

"Hey Van," said Paley cheerily, Wade's fiasco a thing of the past. She had stars and hearts painted on her face and stared at Van's clothes. "I see you're ready for action."

"I see you hit the face-painting booth," said Van. Next to Paley on the picnic table lay a briefcase-like box that had rows of a distinct piece of jewelry set inside. "What is that?"

"Here's to Paley's entrepreneurial adventure," said Deacon, raising his drink. The others raised their cups and hooted, except Brux.

Paley beamed.

"What are those?" asked Van, knowing full well the answer.

Brux hustled around the picnic table to get closer to them, so he could whisper, "I know. I tried to tell her."

"Tell her what?" asked Brooke.

Van's eyes met Paley's. "Why?"

"I like the design." Paley shrugged. "It's selling well."

Van picked up a gold, snowflake-shaped jewel with spokes and forked ends that resembled the feather end of an arrow.

"I made them at the orphanage," said Paley. "We get lots of craft donations and—"

Van grabbed Paley by the elbow and roughly pulled her away from the others.

"It's the Runestar," said Van. "You made replicas of a relic from the Dark War, a valuable piece of jewelry highly sought after in the Living World?"

Paley shrugged. "No one knows it's that."

Van glared at Brux, who had followed them over. "You let her do this?" she snapped at him. "Of all people, I thought you would know better."

Van stomped back to the picnic table and tossed the replica back into the box.

"What's the problem?" asked Brooke. "Are we about to get more drama? I can't take any more drama tonight." She raised her cup into the air and then took a gulp.

"Nothing. It's just... I don't think the Elders would like you having an unauthorized business," Van said to Paley.

"Pffft," said Deacon. "Let her have her side hustle. Take control of her destiny." He took a chug from his cup.

The drinks served in the food court didn't have alcohol in them. Van suspected her friends had rectified that oversight.

Ixl Huxatec sauntered over to their table. He stared at the jewelry box. "What do we have here?"

Everyone became silent and still.

Paley blinked rapidly. Her shoulders tensed.

No surprise, thought Van. Ixl, being Uxa's son, made him de facto in island security, and Paley had made a poor choice last year that resulted in serious injuries to him.

Van hadn't seen Ixl since the accident. "Where's your mother?" she asked, hoping to distract him from the dreadful memory for Paley's sake, plus she really wanted to know.

"Where's *your* mother?" Ixl asked Van, flippantly.

He picked up a piece of jewelry, turned it back and forth, scrutinizing it. Then, snorted at the fake Runestar and tossed it back into the case with the other replicas. He glanced at Van. "Nice outfit. You get that at Ropa Moda?"

His glib comment made Van feel sorry for him, for the suffering he experienced after the accident, and for his current appearance. She inwardly cringed at the horrific burn scars on his face and hands, and figured they continued under his clothes onto his body.

"What are you staring at?" Ixl snarled at the group. "Haven't you ever seen portal burns before?"

Everyone scattered from the picnic table, except Paley, Van, and Brux.

Even wearing street clothes, Ixl looked like a Latin military action figure. His scars made him look like his face was partially melted. Although a year younger than Van, he emanated the energy of a survivor and a warrior, ready to take-on the worst of any situation.

"I'm so sorry," said Paley, on the verge of tears.

"How's your pal, Myles?" Ixl asked her. "I heard you've been visiting him quite a lot."

Paley's eyes darted to the ground.

Van gaped at her friend. Unable to comprehend why on earth Paley would visit Myles Dinkle.

Last year, Myles, a mainlander terrigen, had, with great luck, navigated his speedboat to the island. He intended to blog about finding it on his conspiracy theory website devoted to uncovering the hidden island and exposing its secrets. Island security snagged him and tossed him into a holding cell. The island didn't welcome surprise callers.

Paley had visited Myles when he was initially being held. He manipulated Paley by using her desire to find her birth parents, and talked her into breaking him out and sneaking him through the portal into the Living World. The stunt resulted in serious injuries to Myles and two other people—Ixl and the Brotherhood's Agent Brad Davis. The latter two received more severe injuries from the blowback.

"How is Agent Davis?" asked Brux.

Ixl sneered-talked at him. "He couldn't come to the festival because his brain got fried when your friend here," he jabbed his thumb at Paley, "helped that terrigen jump through the portal with us. He's in long-term care now."

Paley's cheeks grew moist from her tears.

"Why is Myles still being held here?" asked Van. She half suspected Myles didn't want to leave the island, not while there were more secrets for him to uncover.

"The Brotherhood believes he'll cause problems if they release him back to the mainland," said Ixl.

Van glowered with disapproval.

"It's true. He knows too much," said Paley. She opened her eyes wide at Ixl, as if hoping to win his favor. "Myles says his mother and sister are going to be searching for him."

Ixl raised his brow.

Paley, seeing she gained his interest, leaned in and whispered to him, "The magic cloaking the island is faulty, he said, that's how he found it. His family will find it soon enough too."

"Humph," said Ixl, as if only mildly interested. The glint in his eyes told a different story. He said to Paley, looking at the jewelry box, "Put that away before I report you."

She snapped the box closed and dropped it under the picnic table.

Ixl sauntered back into the crowd.

The trio released a collectively held breath.

After a beat, Van said, "I stopped by to let you know I'm going to the reservation. I'm leaving tonight."

"Can't we wait until tomorrow?" asked Paley.

"I think we should stick to the rules and wait for Uxa's go-ahead," said Brux.

"It's the same old thing every year," said Paley. "We go over, get next Item of Creation, almost die..."

Of course, Paley wouldn't be as interested in getting the Items as Van. They were magical weapons that belonged to the carrier of the Anchoress bloodline. Retrieving them secured Van's status as a future leader of the Lodian people and gave her validation that she deserved her place on the island. Having them in her possession would also release rule-abiding Brux from his duties as her protector, something Van desperately wanted for him.

"Paley has a point," said Brux, with a liquor-induced, sloppy grin.

Van had no desire to waste time at the festival. The celebration held no fun for her. What she wanted to do was see Ferox and then get the next Item. "You guys meet me at Lodestar." She did them a favor and slipped away before they could object.

She grabbed one of the taxis waiting outside the festival and headed to the reservation. Van marched up the front steps of Marble Hall, entered the building's stately lobby, and took the wide, center staircase up to the third floor.

She burst into the waiting room of Uxa's office, startling Creenelia, Uxa's secretary.

"Oh—uh, Van," said Creenelia, leaping from her seat.

Van swept by Creenelia, to the door of Uxa's office. "Is she in?" Van opened the door and peered into an empty room.

Creenelia hovered next to Van, wringing her hands. "No, no. Uxa's at Lodestar."

"Oh." Van hadn't expected Uxa to be gone. She stood there wondering what to do next.

"You know, you really shouldn't just barge in here. It's—"

"I'll wait." Van dropped her backpack on the floor by a couch in the waiting area and took a seat.

Creenelia huffed at Van's brazenness. "You might be waiting a long time."

Van shrugged.

"It's possible Uxa won't be back until Sunday night at six o'clock to collect you and the others with Fynn."

Van raised her eyebrows. "Yet you're still here. Working tonight. On a holiday weekend."

Creenelia straightened her spine. "Well, I'm just leaving." She grabbed some papers off her desk and locked them in a drawer. Snatched her purse, marched to the door, and yanked it open.

She paused. "You coming?"

Van crossed her arms. "Nope."

Creenelia shook her head at the sassiness of kids these days. "Fine." She stormed out of the waiting area.

Time ticked past. Van noticed the softness of the couch cushions, way too inviting for a waiting room, unless they expected people to sleep there. She curled her legs underneath her and got into a snuggly position...

VAN'S EYES were still closed when she woke. What she slept on didn't feel like the comfy, high-quality mattress in her bedroom...

She used her hand to wipe drool from the side of her mouth and her muscles felt stiff—then it all came roaring back. It was Saturday morning, and she was still in the waiting room in Uxa's office.

Her eyes shot open. She bolted upright. Van scanned the waiting area to make sure she was alone, then got up, stretched, and inspected the office. *I guess Creenelia told me the truth.* Uxa wouldn't be back until tomorrow night. *Now what?*

She had an idea. Van grabbed her backpack and left the office, bounded down the stairway, and dashed out of Marble Hall.

She didn't know how to get into the House of Lacus from Uxa's office without a passcode, but she knew another way into the transportation building. She skirted the outside perimeter of the Complex and entered the transportation building through the main door. The building's circular atrium was empty because of the holiday weekend.

Van hurried under the high, domed ceiling in the House of Lacus. She couldn't help staring at the magnificent statue in the center of the atrium titled Queen Amaryl of the Dark War. In that moment, she appreciated her ancestor, the Anchoress of a time long past. She took in the details of the statue. The water pouring into the fountain from an urn carried under Amaryl's arm, sword sheathed in her belt, and coin pendant necklace dangling from her neck.

Van paused.

In Amaryl's right hand, she held what Van had always thought of as a torch. But, for the first time, Van noticed a long handle and realized it wasn't a torch. It was a rod with a blazing fire atop. *Goustav's Staff of Fire!*

Van's body responded with a pull toward the real Staff hidden somewhere in the Living World. At one time, this Item belonged to her ancestor, Goustav Moor, the prince who betrayed his brother, Manik, and took over the Balish kingdom more than a thousand years ago.

Even on Providence Island, the lure of the Item affected her, called to her, tugged at the essence of her life-force, igniting a desire within her to find it. Van assumed her mission would be to retrieve the next Item, now sure it would be Goustav's Staff. If Uxa planned on changing the mission this year, Van needed to know. Now.

She tore her stare away from Amaryl's statue and continued across the atrium. She passed the grand pillars and dashed up one of the two curved stairways that led from the floor to the platform in front of the portal.

Van stood in front of the enormous black disc, waiting for it to activate so she could transport to Lodestar.

Nothing happened.

The granite stone band surrounding the disc didn't move. There were no swirling sparkles of silver in the blackness of the portal's entrance. Nothing.

In the past, Van either used the Twin Gemstones to transport, or a Grigori in the control room activated the portal. She didn't have either of those things.

She headed back down the stairway, confident she could figure out how to activate the portal from the control room. When she reached the floor, her peripheral vision glimpsed the elevators located under the dais that held the portal.

Ah-ha! She remembered another way through the portal that had slipped her mind.

Van traveled by elevator to her reservation program classes held at Lodestar. Her teachers didn't have a code, they simply pushed the button, same as in Earth World elevators. She tried it.

The doors slid open.

Van scooted in.

CHAPTER

SIX

As far as Van knew, the elevator only opened onto her classroom floor in Lodestar.

She saw a panel of buttons and pushed all of them. Only one lit up, meaning the rest were inactive, or more likely you needed a key or passcode to activate them.

Van traveled upward. The elevator came to a stop, and the door slid open.

Now to find Uxa's office.

On her prior trips, Van remembered seeing rows and rows of floors while standing in the lobby of Lodestar Station. She figured the office would either be on the same floor as her classrooms, or near it, since Uxa regularly monitored the students' progress.

Van scurried down the hallway, opening doors one by one and peeking inside, not worried about coming across any workers. If she did, she'd ask them where she could find Uxa. Most of the employees in Lodestar probably knew of Van, and seeing her wouldn't alarm them.

She passed her eerily silent classrooms and tried door after door until she came across one that opened into a stairway. Van ducked inside, went down one flight, and tried the door. *Locked.*

She turned around and dashed back up the stairs to the floor above her classrooms.

Van clasped the handle—it opened! The hallway looked similar to the one below and was just as quiet. She became disheartened by the deserted offices and unoccupied conference rooms until voices emanated from behind a nearby door.

She cracked it open and peered inside.

"Vanessa," said Uxa, startled. She stood in front of her desk next to Suixsha.

The room had a formal flair, similar to Uxa's office in Marble Hall. Not like Uxa's home office, which was messier, more casual, and had the weird grandfather clock. The one that haunted Van's thoughts on her missions by counting down the time she had remaining before the Alignment ended.

Suixsha shifted her eyes to the unexpected intruder, looking ready to pounce. Her hands moved to her hips where she had a tomahawk on each side, secured by specialized looped holsters made to give the ambidextrous easy access in combat. Her fingers dangled near the handles.

She had changed into what Van thought of as her everyday wear: sturdy halter top made from animal skin, fitted leather pants, and calf-high suede boots. Clothes not bought in any store where Van had ever shopped. A feather with several strands of multi-colored beads hung from one side of her long cornrows.

Van unwittingly placed her palm over the spot on her stomach where Suixsha had punched her yesterday. It pulsed with a dull residual ache.

Although Suixsha relaxed her stance once she recognized Van, her hands remained close to her tomahawks. A clear sign Suixsha considered her a threat. A rush of pride rippled through Van despite the feeling being mutual.

Finding Uxa and Suixsha deep in private conversation gave Van a forbidding feeling that Genie, and her own gut instinct, might be right. Uxa planned to replace Van with Suixsha on the mission.

Uxa gathered her wits and said, "What brings you—"

"I want to start now," said Van. "I'll stay here until the Alignment. Do research, gather my gear, get the details. You know, the stuff you usually wait until the last second to give me."

Van expected Uxa to be furious about her early, unauthorized arrival. Instead, Uxa said, "It is good that you are here. We have some adjustments to discuss regarding your summer project."

The hair on the back of Van's neck prickled for two reasons. One: Uxa used the official title of "summer project" for what Van did over break, rather than calling it a "mission." Two: Van had broken the rules by showing up at Lodestar, and Uxa acted as if it were no big deal.

"What *adjustments?*" asked Van, as she smashed her backpack down on the floor.

Suixsha remained silent, though her eyes told the story she absorbed every nuance of the exchange.

"I'm getting the next Item, right?" asked Van. "I've been training all year. It's in the southern region, I can *feel* it."

"I was briefing Suixsha on the Items of Creation when you arrived," said Uxa.

"Four magical relic belong to Lodian Anchoress heir." Suixsha's presence filled the room with a fierce energy that annoyed Van.

"Yeah, *me.*" Van thumped her thumb against her chest. "I'm the only one who can retrieve them from their hiding place. So don't go getting any ideas."

"There is Coin of Creation—"

"Which *I* got two years ago," said Van.

"Cup of Life," Suixsha continued. "You retrieve last year," she quickly added.

"Then there's Goustav's Staff of Fire and then there's a sword. What's the point of this?" Van asked Uxa. "I can fill her in on the details while we prep over the weekend. Is that why she's here? She's on the team?"

Tussel Fynn, Uxa's first assistant, bounded into the room, waving a parchment. He wore a similar tunic-style uniform, like his boss, Uxa, but in a darker shade of light-blue, the same color as his eyes.

"Uxa, I just got word—" Fynn noticed Van and halted.

She inwardly groaned seeing him. His disapproving attitude toward Van served as a constant accusation—she didn't deserve the exalted status of being the Anchoress heir.

"What're you doing here?" Fynn looked down his nose at her. "I'm scheduled to meet you in Marble Hall tomorrow at six."

"I came early to prep for the mission," said Van.

"Not one for rules, are you?" Fynn's eyes turned to Uxa. "I take it you haven't told her yet?"

"Told me what?" huffed Van.

"I am honoring you with an unfamiliar task," said Uxa. "I have assigned you to the mainland to fight demons with the Grigori. Being in the Earth World makes the Alignment irrelevant. You can start early, as you requested, and stay on the internship for the entire summer."

Van gaped in disbelief. Although she suspected something was up, hearing it, having it thrown in her face, made it a cruel reality. She deserved to get her next Item, to go to the Living World, to meet up with Ferox. She was the Anchoress, *for light's sake!*

"Suixsha will go on the mission—"

"What? *No!* No way!" Van stomped her foot. She glared at Suixsha, who gripped the handles of her tomahawks.

"This task will take longer than thirty days as it is more complex—"

"I'm going. I can handle it!" said Van.

"I win game. I go," said Suixsha, placidly, though her eyes remained sharp.

"Suixsha is an elite warrior from a tribe outside of Salus Valde," said Fynn. "We held special games this year, here, using students in the Advanced Studies Grigori program against teen warriors from other tribes."

"Suixsha won," continued Uxa. "I brought her to Providence Island to test her against you."

"You need a royal bloodline to use—*even touch*—the Items without going mad. *She's* not a pure-blooded Lodian, like *I* am." Van fumed.

"Last year you asked for placement in the Earth World so you could fight demons on the mainland," said Uxa.

"That was—I want—I've been training for this all year. I need my Items. I *need* to go." Van stopped short of saying, *so I can confront Ferox* and instead said, "I'm the only one who can retrieve the next Item. It's the Staff of Fire."

Retrieving the Staff felt more personal for Van than the prior Items. A thousand years ago, the Balish Prince Goustav, her ancestor, had used the Staff to kill her other ancestor Queen Cordelia, Amaryl's mother, and then later to kill Amaryl.

"Suixsha's mission is not to retrieve another Item," said Uxa, attempting to calm Van. "I am sending her to check the third seal."

Van glared at them.

She understood the importance of the three seals that secured the invisible membrane-like veil separating the Living World from the Earth World. Last year, Uxa feared a crack in the second seal, a cenote at the bottom of the bottomless sea, and had sent Van and her team to check it. Van also retrieved the Cup of Life on that mission, which was in the same location. The second seal had no crack.

Neither did the first. The seal Uxa had inspected. The portal that connected Lodestar Station to the House of Lacus on Providence Island.

"Is the third seal a portal like the first?" asked Van.

"Pfft," said Fynn. "If it was, don't you think we would've already transported Suixsha there?"

"No." Uxa shook her head, answering Van's question. "There is only one portal."

Van narrowed her eyes at Uxa's false claim. They both knew that Van's birth mother, Aelia, had a private portal in the manor's basement. One that her father used many times after Aelia's death. As far as Van knew, no one had used it since the night her father died. She didn't know why Uxa wanted this kept a secret from Suixsha, but was glad just the same.

"It's a shame part of Manik's law restricts us from sending adults out of Salus Valde," said Fynn. "We could really use some on these tasks. And Van, have you forgotten you're restricted too?"

"Vanessa not adult," said Suixsha, as if Van's immaturity were a well-established fact.

Van snorted at Suixsha, as if that would prove her maturity. Then said, "The Elementals don't allow me to be tracked by the Balish squawkers. It's an honor system."

Van fondly remembered getting caught outside the boundary last year. Breaking the law didn't result in a political nightmare since Van ended up dating her captor, the Balish Prince Ferox.

"King Nequus repealed that restriction late last summer," said Uxa.

Van mulled over their concerns, and then asked, "Why not let Suixsha check the seal and I can get the next Item?"

Uxa stared at Van, looking grave. "You are having trouble connecting to your power. It is not a good time to send you outside the boundary of Salus Valde. There is no need for you to risk your life."

"It's Ferox's territory, his people," said Van. "Maybe he can look after me."

"No." Fynn shook his thick blond curls. "Not even he can protect you from the rioters."

CHAPTER
SEVEN

"What rioters?" asked Van. "Is Ferox okay?" Her stomach churned with worry.

Uxa nodded. "He and the royal family are safe. But when the Balish citizens discovered their council had allowed a Lodian-made magical potion put into their water supply without their knowledge or consent…"

"Pockets of riots broke out around the countryside," said Fynn. "And on Balefire Palace grounds."

"Many of their citizens have stopped drinking water," said Uxa. "Those ill are refusing treatment."

"They attack water storage facilities daily," said Fynn.

"That's awful." Van ran a jerky hand through her hair. Her idea of putting the cure in the water supply had caused the revolt.

"Sickness return," said Suixsha.

"But, the Cup of Life… you made the cure, the vaccine." Van turned to Uxa. "Isn't it working anymore?"

"We eliminated the illness in Salus Valde and on Providence Island," said Uxa. "But not in Balish and Balish-occupied territories.

We've trained a special squadron of their soldiers to handle people who turn into demons."

"What a disaster," muttered Van. Grigori learned to kill demons without generating additional negativity over years of schooling. Now Balish soldiers were running amok, slaying them in their districts. "We need to treat the sick, get people vaccinated."

"The lingering illness means we can't rule out that Solana cracked a seal when she brought demons to this world to... you know..." Fynn lowered his voice to a whisper. "Kill your father."

Van almost growled at Fynn for so callously mentioning her beloved father. But she realized the true culprit for her anger was...

"Solana," spat Van. The Balish princess had murdered Van's father and also killed her own twin brother, who was the heir to the Balish kingdom. "She's still working with her dark master. I know it."

"Suixsha's mission also involves gathering intel on Solana," said Uxa. "The royal family took their princess back under agreement that she does not use magic or communicate with demons."

"And that she honors her engagement to her first cousin, Prince Merloc Moor," said Fynn.

"Is she under surveillance? Drugged? Locked up at night?" asked Van.

"In public, Solana appears as a happy member of the royal family," said Uxa.

Van's gut told her the Balish princess desired the throne. With Ferox alive, there was no way that would happen. His life was in danger. "I have to go there. See for myself what's going on."

"The last thing Balish citizens need right now is to find you poking around in Aduro," said Fynn. "Their council will assume you're after the next Item. They're still worried we're planning to attack Balefire with a bunch of terrigen-turned-demons and cause their Solmor."

Uxa pursed her lips and gave a brief nod. "The Balish Council is on edge more than ever since you retrieved two of your Items. They are looking for any reason to void the part of Manik's law that protects us from an invasion by them."

Van furrowed her brow. "But Ferox has the Coin of Creation and we have the Cup of Life. Each of us has one Item. We did it that way to maintain the balance of power between our tribes. To keep the peace."

"Their council thinks we have both," said Fynn.

"It is not safe for you outside Salus Valde," said Uxa.

"I go," said Suixsha. "I watch Solana and check seal."

Van would be damned if Suixsha took away her prestige by completing a mission for Uxa, especially after already eroding Van's status by winning the games. "I can handle myself."

"Losing to Suixsha proves you cannot," said Uxa.

Van spun toward Uxa, cheeks blazing. "She's *untrained* and incapable of completing this mission. I don't care if she won the games. She tricked me. It won't happen again. Believe me."

Suixsha observed Van, as if unaffected by her rant, even as Fynn snorted in disbelief at Van's comment.

A look of concern etched across Uxa's face. "The Anti-Manik Rebels are taking aggressive action to find Goustav's heir. They wish to put this person on the throne as the rightful ruler to the Balish kingdom."

"Since that heir is you, it's an additional risk," said Fynn.

"They are spreading rumors that Ferox does not have the fortitude to take the throne after his father," said Uxa. "They are laying the groundwork in anticipation of finding you. Many citizens have taken to the idea."

"And with Solana hanging around the palace," said Fynn. "Despite her trying to be a good girl and fit back in with the royal family, your presence at Balefire might provoke her given she seems to hate you."

"The feeling's mutual," said Van.

"She tries to murder you every chance she gets," said Fynn. "If the Anchoress bloodline dies out before you have an heir, our world loses its light. We'll have no way to fend off the coming darkness of Dishora."

Van glowered at each of them.

Uxa's shoulders tensed. Fynn clenched his jaw. Suixsha appeared unruffled.

Silence hung in the room.

"I think Van should go on mission," said Suixsha, breaking the tension.

Van blinked, unsure she heard correctly. Uxa and Fynn turned their heads and stared at Suixsha.

"Destiny not waited for. Destiny achieved." Suixsha passively peered back at them. "Van go with me."

"That was unexpected. Thanks," said Van.

"I not do for you," said Suixsha. "I not do for me. I do what best for tribes."

"At least now you don't have to go alone," said Van, feeling benevolent.

"Well..." Fynn flicked his hand for emphasis. "Not *alone*."

"Meaning?" Van glared at him.

"The third seal is in Pusiel, in the deep south," said Uxa. "Close enough to Balefire for King Nequus, with Ferox's encouragement, to agree to send their own men with our team."

"Near the Staff of Fire, I'm sure of it." Van perked up, liking what she heard so far.

"That's why you can't go, to make sure you don't retrieve it," said Fynn. "The prophecy says Dishora is four years away. Retrieving the Staff can wait until next year."

"Suixsha is familiar with the area," said Uxa. "Pusiel is where her tribe lived before..."

"Balish kill them." Suixsha shifted. She tightened her hands into fists, then released them.

"Balefire Palace will allow Suixsha in as part of the team," said Uxa. "The royal family will welcome her to make amends for what happened in the past."

"Our priority is for Suixsha to check the third seal," said Fynn. "And to covertly observe Solana while building relations with the Balish royal family. We need to make sure they keep administering the cure and don't void Manik's law and start a war with us."

"Suixsha, are you okay with this?" asked Van.

She nodded.

Her calm, level-headedness incensed Van. "Why aren't you mad? The Balish obliterated your tribe, your family."

"We all have dragon inside," said Suixsha. "It either protect you or harm you. When anger burn bright, mean dragon eating you."

Van glanced at Uxa. "You sure Suixsha has all her logs on the fire? If you know what I mean."

Uxa threw her a look that Van interpreted as disappointment mixed with watch-your-manners.

"Temper anger, temper dragon," Suixsha continued in her characteristically serene tone. "I use fiery determination of dragon to burn away obstacle that keep me from truth. Dragon is reptile, cool inside. Cold. I cool inside, mean dragon now guard me."

Uxa knitted her brow. "Vanessa, there is something else you should know..."

Fynn shifted his eyes toward Van. "Get ready to poke that cool dragon."

CHAPTER
EIGHT

Uxa came right out with it. "Ferox volunteered to be on the team."

Van concealed the enormity of her shock. *Why wouldn't Ferox tell me?*

She came up with one reason. He didn't tell her about being on the team for the same reason he hadn't contacted her all year. He wasn't interested in being with her. This disempowering realization hurt worse than Suixsha's punch to her gut during the final game.

"Suixsha will accompany him and his men to check the seal," said Uxa.

The air hung heavy in the room. Nobody spoke, their eyes locked on Van.

Van took a breath, mentally pieced together her broken heart, and said, "If I'm needed to fight demons in the Earth World, then that's where I'll go."

Tension broke and Fynn blurted, "Great!"

"We must decrease the amount of demons being generated in the Earth World before the seriousness of the situation leaks to the

Balish," said Uxa. "Currently, our Grigori reports are down-playing the circumstances."

"If they find out, they'll use the situation to void our protection from Manik's law," said Fynn. "We still don't know who's the traitorous spy in Lodestar. How much they know, or what they've already told the palace."

"Fynn, you mentioned Solmor," said Van. "Ferox told me it's a prophecy written in their *Sanctus Novus*." Remembering her time with the prince caused an ache in Van's chest so intense it smothered her breathing. "Is their text right? Are terrigens morphing into demons?"

Fynn wrung his hands and turned to Uxa, who paused in contemplation.

"Information I extracted from Myles Dinkel helped validate my suspicion," said Uxa. "There are probable non-terrigen-generated demons in the Earth World."

"New evil," said Suixsha.

"Morphed terrigens?" Van asked again, alarmed. She had many terrigen friends, including Paley.

Fynn's lips turned downward. "Possibly a mutation of the virus."

Van gasped. "The original demon illness was bad enough. Now this?"

"You must uncover what is happening so we can put an end to it," said Uxa.

Van rubbed her temples to lessen her emerging headache. "This is a lot to take in."

It was important for her to check out the demon situation. But going to the mainland meant she wouldn't be able to confront Ferox. How could she focus on hunting demons while he was a world away, checking the third seal with Suixsha?

Her breathing became labored. Objects in the room took on their own noisy presence—the blocky wooden desk, the several high-back chairs... couch... coffee table... bookshelves filled with aged books.

"I need a moment. Excuse me." Van dashed from the room. She hurried down the hallway and ducked into a nearby ladies' room.

She rested her hands on the counter by the sinks, head down, and took a deep breath.

It made no sense for Ferox to exclude Van, Brux, and Paley from going on the mission, not with their skills and experience. Unless he didn't want to be around Van at all, not even as a friend. Or be with people who reminded him of her.

Her head continued to throb. She turned and rested her backside against the counter, closed her eyes, and relaxed her muscles.

Jacynthia. Van called without using words.

She waited…

Her shoulders ached with tension. She consciously loosened them and forced herself to take a deep breath.

Jacynthia.

Van expected the amaranthine haze to fill her mind's eye. It didn't come.

"Jacynthia!" Van shouted, her voice echoed off the cold, hard bathroom tiles. Her eyes shot open. "Ugh!"

She twisted around and smashed her fists on the bathroom counter. Her eyes darted, searching for something else to hit.

The bathroom door swooshed open.

Fynn—of all people—popped his head in the ladies' room.

He appeared wild-eyed and flushed with either terror or excitement. Van couldn't tell which.

Still hurting and looking to take out her anger on something, Van thought about punching him. He deserved it for, well, being him, and for peeking into the *ladies'* room. I mean, *hello.*

He spoke rapidly, "Come quick." He waggled his finger, pointing down the hallway. "The parade. He's on his way."

"Who?" Curiosity replaced Van's anger.

"Prince Ferox." Fynn grinned, clearly delighted. "He's here, in Salus Valde. He's on his way to Lodestar!"

Van's heart skipped a beat. *Ferox! Here!* She tore out of the bathroom. A faint glimmer of hope flickered inside her.

Uxa and Suixsha joined them in the hallway, and they hurried down the corridor.

Uxa looked flustered. "I would have appreciated some advanced notice."

Fynn appeared stricken. "That's what I came into your office to tell you." He turned to Van and Suixsha and said, "Manik's law allows the Balish Council to send inspectors to Salus Valde under the guise of Living World security."

He acted both apprehensive and enthusiastic about meeting Ferox. With Salus Valde being a democratic republic, his apparent fascination with meeting royalty surprised Van.

The four of them assembled on the top landing of the marble staircase that led to the grand doors of Lodestar. From their raised position, they could see the approaching parade.

Rows of sleek, stylish black horses came toward them, taking up the entire road. Their graceful yet brisk, four-beat, prancing gait carried riders dressed in black, tunic-styled military uniforms. Instead of the balaclavas that Van had seen Balish soldiers wear in the past, they wore black triangular caps that, upon squinting, had a flap hanging down the back. Van also noticed red-and-gold crests on the soldier's chests. The insignia designated the riders as men enlisted in the Royal Balish Military.

The parade route veered to the right, passing by the main stairs where Van and the others stood.

After the horses came a section of men dressed in black-and-gold uniforms with red aiguillettes. They animatedly blared upbeat music by playing woodwind, brass, and percussion instruments. Women dressed in shimmering, gold-sequined unitards did aerial cartwheels, split leaps, roundoffs, and other gymnastic moves around them.

Van gaped in awe at the passing parade. Marchers waved banners with the royal Balish crest, others tossed sparkling round balls that gave off flames and glitter as they soared through the air. A group of dancers swirled long ribbons tied to a handle as they flipped and leaped.

Behind the dancers, riding high on a decorative platform pulled by eight white horses, rode... not Ferox, as Van expected, but a stately man who appeared to be the main attraction in the parade.

With a big smile, he waved to the crowd gathered along the sidewalks to watch the spectacular event. Even from a distance, Van noticed his nose. A protuberance with several bumps, so enormous it looked like a mountain growing out of his face, an unfortunate feature enhanced by his slight build. He wore curled objects around his ears that looked like coiled ram's horns.

The float carrying the man with the enormous nose stopped in front of them and he climbed down from the platform. As he stepped onto the sidewalk, several soldiers flanked him.

"What part made you think Ferox was here?" Van asked Fynn.

He answered her with a scowl.

"Greetings," cried the man as he approached the steps, arms opened wide. He looked at each of them with dark-brown eyes that held a natural squint. "I hope you don't mind our little entrance."

"Not at all." Uxa waited while the man and his soldiers climbed the steps. Once he reached the landing, she said, "Good to see you again, Alden," in a tone that made Van certain his unexpected visit irritated Uxa.

Alden and Uxa clasped their hands around the other's wrist in greeting.

"May the light of our king illuminate your path," said Alden with a warm smile.

Uxa introduced him as Alden Goodchild, the right-hand man of Prince Ferox.

"To what do I owe this pleasure?" asked Uxa.

"No, no," said Alden, good-naturedly. "No need to worry. This is just a tiny, friendly diplomatic visit."

"Will King Nequus be joining us?" she asked.

"No, but Prince Ferox will be."

Van's stomach did a flip.

"Fynn, please see to our parade guests," said Uxa. "House them in the southern guest wing."

Fynn gave a curt bow and departed.

Alden beamed. "Your hospitality is much appreciated."

Van nervously scanned the street, anxious about coming face to face with Ferox. The crowd began to disperse now that the fanfare had died down.

"Come, let us go inside," Uxa said to Alden.

"Just a moment, if you will." Alden turned to face the street, hands clasped behind his back, a position that meant he was prepared to wait.

Van and the others stared at the near empty street, waiting along with Alden for a more grand entrance by Prince Ferox.

A pop, snap, and bang came from the road to the left. All heads turned in that direction. A puff of smoke billowed upward from a vehicle hidden by the trees lining the street.

A yellowish-brown... *turd?* No, a vehicle that looked like a giant dried fig large enough to hold five people stopped in front of Lodestar. It had a windshield and port-hole like windows, but instead of wheels, it hovered several feet above the ground. When it parked at the bottom of the stairs, a plume of smoke rose from the pointed roof and several sparks flared from the rear muffler. The triangular rind slowly lowered until it rested, hovering a few inches above the street.

Suixsha took a step down, ready to defend Alden, their honored guest, from this miscreant. She paused, startled by the emerging passenger.

Van immediately recognized those strong shoulders, and that cropped brown hair. She had been daydreaming about them for a year.

Ferox had arrived.

Her entire body tingled with excitement, even as her brain filled with dread over the inevitable conversation they would have about why he bailed on their relationship.

Dressed in a casual, tunic-style garment, he leaped up the stairs before anyone could rush down to greet him. He stopped to take Suixsha's wrist in greeting.

"What that thing?" asked Suixsha.

"Mo-rind," said Ferox. "I call it a fig. Runs on thermal energy."

Uxa welcomed Ferox. Then he greeted Van.

Van couldn't deny her elation over being near him. Her joy at having him standing in front of her, gazing at her with those almond-shaped, amber-yellow eyes. He stood close enough for his body heat to warm her. Or was it her passion for him heating her body? She wanted to be mad at him. Instead, she hoped he would give her an explanation that would make everything okay between them and they could get back to dating.

"Not one for grand entrances, are you?" asked Van, not knowing what else to say. It certainly wasn't the right time to put him through an inquisition about the possibilities of continuing their relationship.

"Not my style," said Ferox, pleasantly enough, though Van perceived a hint of coolness underneath his mannerisms. "I leave the flashy stuff to Alden."

"Oh," Alden humbly swooshed his hand as if to brush away the idea, then chuckled. "Okay, okay. Yes." He raised his hands in surrender. "Guilty."

Ferox and Van paused for a moment, gazing into each other's eyes.

"Why did you—what are you doing here?" asked Van, inwardly cringing over her challenging tone.

It made her feelings for him obvious. Giving him the upper hand by letting him know she was hurting from his disinterest in her. Then she decided she had a right to her feelings and shouldn't be embarrassed by them. She also had a right to be upset with him. Van squared her shoulders and stood her ground.

"Let us make our way inside," suggested Uxa. She threw Van a glance that sickened her stomach.

A look of pity? Disapproval? Whatever it was, it worked. Van's bravado melted away and the doom of her ancestors—her cursed life—clouded any hopes she had for a future with Ferox.

CHAPTER

NINE

After having a quiet dinner alone in a small break area, Van shuffled back to her assigned room in one of the guest wings. It reminded her of hotel rooms on the mainland back home. Two queen-sized beds, a desk, nightstands. The only difference being no television or phone.

She flopped backside-down on one of the beds. Ferox knew where to find her, or could figure out how, if he wanted to.

Van wished she could talk to Jacynthia. Why hadn't her spirit guide appeared when Van called to her in the ladies' room? Maybe Van's ill temper blocked their connection. Or had Jacynthia already given Van the advice she needed?

She yawned...

WHILE WALKING along the lush field in Astrid's Hollow on Providence Island, the moonlight cast its rays on a blond girl facing Van, about the age of five, wearing a simple golden dress that matched her wavy blond hair. She paid no attention to Van, instead her round, blue eyes gazed up at the night sky. The girl stretched her arm upward. Her tiny hand clasped and unclasped, as if wishing she could reach high enough to grab one of the twinkling stars from the sky.

One of the brilliant golden flecks dropped from the dark blanket of night and fell directly at the girl, who caught it. Or more accurately, the star landed smoothly in her hand.

The little girl giggled, gleeful at her luck. She joyfully opened her fingers and saw a gold snowflake-shaped piece of jewelry in her hand. The girl squealed in delight, excited to show her mother this wonderful find.

She stepped forward as if to dash away and halted. Her eyes opened wide; her smile faded. The girl watched, terrified, as the brooch disappeared into her palm. She shrieked.

VAN WOKE, startled she had fallen asleep. She got up, shaking her head to clear the lingering echoes of the little girl's scream, and peaked behind the curtains to see the soft yellow rays of the morning sun.

Under Uxa's directive, Van would leave for Providence Island after lunch. To pass the time, Van went down to her classroom floor and into the gym.

Hands up, chin tucked, and barehanded, Van began her workout using the punching bag.

Punch. *I deserve an explanation from Ferox.* Punch. Punch. Kick.

Pivot, elbow. Punch. *When I'm alone with him.* Punch. *I'll make him tell me why he ditched me.* Punch. Punch. Kick.

Yet the thought of confronting him made her queasy.

Punch.

She lowered her fists, chest heaving from exertion.

Hearing his explanation would break her heart, this she already knew. He would say something like, he could see deep inside her soul and knew she was a loser. Or, he saw a dark thread and knew there was no redemption for her.

Van wiped the film of sweat forming on her brow, then sunk her forehead into her palms and scrunched her eyes.

She couldn't do it. She couldn't face Ferox. The thought of it fried her nerves. Van changed her mind about trying to run into him by hanging around the halls at Lodestar to a new plan of hiding from him.

"Hey," called a female voice, delicate as a flower petal.

Van looked up.

Daisy and Kopius sauntered into the gym, both grinning and wearing t-shirts and sweatpants.

"Hey!" Van rushed over and gave them big hugs. "What are you guys doing here?"

"We made the cut," said Kopius. "Looks like you're stuck with us again this summer."

Van's spirits plummeted. She didn't have the heart to tell them she *hadn't* made the cut.

"I didn't get to talk to you after the games," said Daisy, perceiving Van's dip in enthusiasm. "You did a great job."

"Thanks." Van began pounding her fists against the bag again as Daisy and Kopius started their pre-workout stretches.

Daisy sat on a nearby mat and extended her legs. "I saw Suixsha. She's on the grounds, training." Her fine white-blond hair fanned her knees as she reached for her toes.

"Who would train outside when we have this gym?" scoffed Kopius, standing as he twisted his body from side to side.

"I would." Daisy peered up at him with her pale-blue eyes. "I think I'd like that."

"You would," said Kopius. "My little wildflower." His flirty tone made her grin.

Daisy raised one knee and twisted to the side, using her elbow. "Brux is having a fit being away from you," she said to Van, as if trying to cheer her.

"He's stepping up as a man." Kopius bent one leg, grabbed his foot and pulled it to his butt in a quad stretch. "Trying to do his duty protecting you, working hard to get an early travel-through."

"Paley won't let him come here without her." Daisy shifted knees. "They're waiting for Uxa's approval."

"I wonder what's the holdup." Kopius switched legs. "They definitely made the team this year. I would think."

Van stopped punching and grabbed the bag to keep it from swinging back and hitting her in the face. "She's not allowing it because I've gotten orders to head back later this afternoon."

Through her peripheral vision, Van saw them both pause their stretching routines and gaze at her.

Van held her eyes on the bag and reiterated. "I didn't make the team this year."

"I'm so sorry," said Daisy. "Maybe we can help. Kopius is like a magician with fixing things."

Van shook her head and began pounding on the bag again.

Daisy and Kopius respectfully backed off from continuing the conversation and began sparring, leaving Van to sulk and process her disappointment by working her body against the bag.

Van wondered if Daisy knew the mission required her to stop at Balefire Palace, the place where Merloc held her as a prisoner for a short time before transferring her to Windermere Castle. Van doubted she would want to go back there.

Seeing Daisy holding her own against Kopius changed her mind. Her growing strength showed in her form and moves as she sparred with her brawny Adonis boyfriend.

When Van's muscles pleaded for her to stop, she ended her workout and said goodbye to Daisy and Kopius. They offered to speak to Uxa on her behalf. Van thanked them but refused their help.

As she ambled down the hallway, the impact of observing the loving playfulness between Daisy and Kopius caused Jacynthia's words to come booming back. Particularly, her spirit guide's advice about fixating on passions that weren't manifesting and the enormous amount of energy regained by letting go of the attachment.

Van concluded she wanted peace between the Lodians and Balish. If sending Suixsha to Balefire would help tribal relations, then so be it. She prepped herself to live with the nagging pull of the Staff, at least until next year's Alignment.

And if Ferox wanted nothing to do with her, then fine. She decided to let him go and redirect her energy to her assigned task of hunting the new type of demon in the Earth World.

"Oh, hello," said Alden, yanking Van out of her reverie.

"Hey, hi," said Van. "Are you enjoying your time here?"

"Oh, yes," gushed Alden. "We're overjoyed by the wonderful accommodations in the presidential suites. Always a lovely time visiting Lodestar."

Van grinned. She enjoyed his company and his curly horns. His personality exuded a rainbow of color.

"And what have you been up to today?" he asked, being too polite to comment on Van's matted hair and sweat stained workout clothes. "Enjoying yourself?"

She chuckled. He probably knew this wasn't her usual standard of appearance. "I've been training all morning."

"Sounds lonely," said Alden.

"My friends, Daisy and Kopius, were with me."

"I'm familiar with Daisy, lovely girl," said Alden. "Such a complex soul wrapped in such simple beauty. Her purity gives her great strength."

His bright eyes clouded a bit as if despondent over recalling a particular memory of when he had met Daisy in the past. Likely from when Merloc had held her captive in the dungeons of Balefire.

"Do anything fun since you've been here?" asked Van, knowing a change of topic would brighten him again. And perhaps she could find out what Ferox was doing. Old habits die hard.

"The prince has been occupied in meetings since we arrived. Most of which I have accompanied him."

Score! Ferox hadn't come to her because he was busy with work.

"All a day in the life of a prince," said Alden.

His gestures became more lively and his eyes sparkled when he spoke of Ferox and his duties to the prince. Van could tell he held great passion and respect for his placement as Ferox's confidant.

"Tonight you'll be briefed on the mission's details," said Alden.

"I'm being sent back—" Van hesitated. She wasn't sure if he knew about Providence Island. Then remembered Ferox knew, so did Solana, and the spy in Lodestar. That meant Alden knew. In case he didn't, she said, "home."

"No, no, my dear." Alden swooshed his hands. "You are mistaken. You're going."

"Going?" asked Van, not daring to reignite her hope. "Going where?"

"You're scheduled to accompany the prince back to Balefire. From there you'll proceed with the mission to check the third seal."

Van stopped. "Since when?" She peered at him, trying to detect if was lying or, worse, making a joke to tease her. "Nobody told me anything about a change in plans."

"Oh, I'm quite sure," said Alden, pleasantly. "Under the prince's strict orders. Without you, there is no deal of cooperation between our tribes."

Just when Van had given up on her and Ferox being together, a revitalizing shiver of exhilaration flickered through her body. She hardly dared to believe it.

Alden bid her adieu, and they parted ways.

Van dashed back to her room, elated.

On her coffee table lay a scroll. She tore it open and squealed in delight. The diplomatic mission to Balefire now included Van, Brux, and Paley.

CHAPTER

TEN

Van had an idea where the presidential suites were located and headed in that direction. She found them and tapped on the door. "Ferox?"

No one answered.

She tried the handle. The door opened into semi-darkness. Van's "flashlight eyes," an Anchoress ability, allowed her to see in the dark. It made sense that Ferox had a suite rather than a room. She crept into its open living area.

As she walked farther inside, faint streams of moonlight filtered in through the floor-to-ceiling windows along the far wall, illuminating three closed doors Van assumed were bedrooms.

"Ferox," murmured Van, unsure why she whispered.

Next to the kitchen area, a ray of light filtered from an ajar door. A study or office? She tiptoed toward the light and peered into the room.

Ferox sat hunched over a desk filled with scrolls and parchments, his back to her. He gazed at an unrolled scroll, deep in concentration. Van realized that's why the door to his suite was unlocked. Ferox hadn't yet gone to bed.

He made no sign of hearing Van's approach. She wasn't trying to be quiet. It just didn't seem right to shout his name and startle him.

She reached out to lay her hand on his shoulder... in a snap, Ferox twisted around and leaped from his chair.

He grabbed her wrist and held a knife to her throat. "*What do you —*Van?" Ferox lowered the blade and relaxed his stance. "I could've hurt you." He tucked the knife into his belt. "Why are you sneaking up on me?"

Van gawked at him. She thought he would confess on the spot why he didn't want to be with her. Now she didn't know what to do.

"What's with you saying I can go on the mission as *part of the deal?*"

"You snuck into my rooms to ask me that?"

"I'm not sneaking. Your door was unguarded and unlocked." Van straightened her spine and looked him in the eye. "Anyway, I wouldn't have to sneak if you hadn't avoided me all year."

"Oh? *I* avoided *you?*" Ferox raised his brow. "You're the one who never responded to my letters. You denied my request to visit you over—"

"I did no such thing! Wait..." Her tone softened. "You tried to visit me? When?"

"Over Luana," he said.

Gleefulness mixed with a tinge of disbelief surged in Van. Ferox had attempted to visit her during the terrigens' Christmas season! *And* he had written to her! "I didn't know you came by. I never got your letters."

He looked relieved. "So, you're not blowing me off?"

"No!" said Van. He thought *she* had dumped *him*. "No way." Her misgivings about their relationship faded as every cell in her body giggled in delight.

Ferox grinned and reached for her. "Well, then. It's good to see you."

They hugged.

Van pulled back. "Wait, then who's been keeping us apart?"

Ferox shrugged. "Could be any number of people."

They moved into the kitchen to talk. Over a soothing blonde-leaf tea, they caught up on what each had done over the past year. Van told him about her Grigori training, the issues she's having with her step-mother and the annoying new boyfriend, and confessed she had never stopped thinking about him.

"I sent my guards away, hoping you'd stop by." Ferox grinned.

"You know me so well." Van grinned back, even bigger. Leaving himself unguarded in enemy territory proved the rumors about Ferox not having the fortitude to rule were unfounded.

"I'd like to get to know you better. Maybe meet your mother sometime."

"Step-mother." Van didn't offer to make plans. Although thrilled with his suggestion, the thought of Ferox meeting her ditzy step-mother was bad enough, but throwing in Genie's boyfriend would prove too embarrassing.

Ferox shared stories about helping his father run the kingdom. He mentioned Solana's return to Balefire and his sister's re-integration into the family.

"She really has changed," said Ferox. "She's no longer under the influence of a demon. It made her do terrible things, like... what she did to you. I'm sorry that happened."

Van held her tongue. This wasn't the time to tell Ferox his sister was rotten to the core, would never change, and most likely wanted to kill him so she could take over the Balish kingdom.

She changed the subject before she said something to provoke him. "Did you bring the Coin?" In Uxa's office, Fynn had implied Ferox never gave it to the Balish Council.

"I..." His eyes dropped to his teacup. "I have something to confess."

Van's stomach flipped. She knew their reunion was too good to be true. The Anchoress curse struck again.

"I used the Coin to find the Staff of Fire."

"What?" Van shot up from her chair. An acute awareness of

Ferox's Balish heritage made her doubt his intentions. She hated herself for it.

"For you! To help *you*," said Ferox. "I found its general location, but I didn't go any farther. I backed off."

"I can't believe you did that." Van slid back into her seat after getting over the initial shock.

"Alden agreed it was a good idea, and, Van, I was doing it for you. To save you from risking your life and to give it to your tribe as a peace offering."

"I really like Alden. But…" Van crossed her arms and shrugged.

"I trust his advice."

"Didn't Alden know you needed me to get the Staff? Or did he plan on getting you killed?"

Her neck muscles tensed at the thought of Ferox jeopardizing his life trying to retrieve the Staff. He knew only the Anchoress heir could retrieve an Item from its holding place in time and space and that it only appeared in the physical plane during the Alignment. Something Alden would know too, as Ferox's confidant.

"That's Lodian lore," said Ferox. "No one knows for certain if you're the only one who can retrieve an Item."

Van knew for certain. Based on thousand of years of Lodian history. Ferox hadn't been harmed, so she saw no point in pressing the issue.

Ferox remained pensive for a moment, then said, "When I was a child, I accompanied my mother to a run-down village to help her do charity work. I snuck away from the royal guards and wandered off, almost got run over by a horse-drawn wagon. The near-miss with the wagon landed me on my butt in the muddy road and badly shaken."

Van imaged a young Ferox muddy and confused sprawled in a puddle on the road. She kept her grin in check, sensing he was opening up to her about an impactful story from his childhood.

"The driver and his passenger could see that I had manicured nails, a neat haircut, expensive clothes. Things only allowed to the wealthy. They stopped, but not to check if I was okay... they roughed me up and rifled through my pockets to rob me." Ferox held a vacant stare as he recalled the memory.

Van reached across the table and clenched his hand in comfort.

"*Why you?* They asked me," continued Ferox. "Why did I get riches and not them? They... I thought they were going to kill me. Alden risked his life to intervene. He didn't know me from a hole in the wall, yet he saved me."

Ferox paused, overcome with emotion.

"Alden was just another homeless teenage scruff from the streets, ignored by society. A child dumped into the gutter at the age of seven, same age I was when he saved me, by parents who couldn't afford another mouth to feed. They regarded him as useless because he had a learning disability with numbers and math."

"Dyscalculia?"

Ferox nodded. "Along with significant hearing loss. That's why he wears hearing-horns on his ears. I begged my mother to take him in, told her the story. She got really upset that I had wandered off." He gave a dull chuckle, in the way of recollecting a poignant-memory. "But she agreed, thankful to him for saving my life. Now I realize Thuxeor had cast a protection spell on me. My mother would've seen to that."

"Who's Thuxeor?"

"The palace wizard."

Van remembered seeing him, along with Ferox, when she passed through the Skeleton Coast last summer. She flushed, remembering the moment she first set eyes on the handsome enemy prince now sitting before her.

"Alden had been living on the streets for thirteen years by then, scraping by," said Ferox. "He saved me just the same. Even with his disabilities and life treating him so poorly, he knew it was wrong to sit by and do nothing."

"I'm so glad he did." Van gave his hand a squeeze, feeling closer to him for sharing such a touching story from his childhood.

Ferox flipped his hand to clasp Van's. He raised it to his mouth and gave her a soft kiss.

They continued chatting until just before dawn.

Van gave him a parting kiss and then scurried back to her room to grab a few hours' sleep before they left for Balefire.

She laid in bed, elated about getting back together with Ferox. Then, nagging thoughts eclipsed her happiness. She had forgotten to ask Ferox the location of the Staff, and he never answered her question about the Coin.

CHAPTER

ELEVEN

"Please tell me this is not my team." Ixl's strapping body towered over his mother.

It was five a.m. on Monday morning in conference room F. The Alignment had begun at midnight.

"This is why I privately briefed you," said Uxa.

"Just because you've had me in Grigori training since diapers doesn't mean I can carry this band of misfits through a mission."

Van watched as they continued bickering back and forth, as do mothers and sons. Ixl's disappointment in his team didn't diminish the optimistic after-effects resulting from her talk with Ferox. Van's glee would be complete, if not for one tormenting caveat. The Anchoress curse. With her relationship progressing nicely, finding a counter-curse moved up on her to-do list.

Ixl ignored his mother's reproving glare and sneered in disgust at the meager scraps he had been challenged to team-up with, namely Van, Paley, and Brux. Daisy and Kopius hadn't yet arrived in the conference-turned-prep-room next to the main lobby in Lodestar.

"At least I have you," Ixl muttered to Suixsha, who stood alert

69

facing the opened, double-doors, staring into the lobby as if waiting for someone.

Van frowned at Ixl. He voiced being let down by his mother's choice in teammates, yet Van couldn't figure out why *he* was on the team, other than being Uxa's son. His arrogant and annoying personality alone should've ruled him out for teamwork. She suspected Uxa might have an ulterior motive for sending her son on the mission. Van decided to keep a close eye on him.

"He scares me," whispered Paley.

"A bit gruff," said Brux. "But he's okay."

Van relaxed her scrunched forehead. If she didn't stop frowning, she'd get wrinkles.

Kopius sidled up next to her. "I heard he placed highest in the South American games. Suixsha beat him overall though."

"I thought Providence Island was the only place vichors lived," said Paley.

"There're other Grigori outposts in the Earth World," said Kopius.

Van narrowed her eyes. "How do you know that?"

"Because I'm amazing," said Kopius.

"Where's Daisy?" asked Brux.

"She's dawdling in the hall, fighting for justice." Kopius bent down and grabbed his backpack.

Paley titled her head quizzically. "Huh?"

Suixsha's eye caught something. Whoever she had been waiting for had arrived. She dashed into the lobby.

Van nudged Paley and they, along with Brux, peered from the doorway. Kopius stayed to re-check his and Daisy's already packed backpacks.

Van saw six men dressed in Royal Balish Military uniforms marching into the lobby from a hallway. On their shoulders, they carried a large cage with a big cat pacing inside. The animal had two long fangs and a hairy orange coat with black stripes.

Ferox arrived with the soldiers and the big cat. Followed by a tense, red-cheeked Daisy.

As they came into the expansive lobby, the magnificent creature let out a roar so loud it rattled the opened double-doors next to Van.

"Set that animal free. This instant!" shrieked Daisy, in her sweet, yet powerfully commanding voice. "How would you like to be ripped from your lush forest home and stuffed in a cage?"

"What do you think it is?" Paley asked Van and Brux, as they watched the scene unfold from a safe distance.

"I don't know," said Van. "It's bigger than the tigers from our world."

The animal snapped its tail let out another agitated roar.

Paley clutched onto Brux's arm.

"I agree with my sister," said Brux. "Let the poor thing out of the cage."

Suixsha slowly stepped farther into the lobby. Her eyes held steady on the cat.

This time, when the animal howled, it did the most amazing thing. Its fur stood on end, wavered, and burst into flames.

Van and Paley gasped and jumped back.

Brux cringed and raised his hands to shield his face from the furious blast.

Suixsha didn't flinch.

The cat swatted its fiery paws through the bars of the cage, trying to catch a soldier in its claws.

The soldiers dropped the cage. It crashed to the floor in the center of the lobby. They backed away, patting themselves to put out minor flames.

The animal's fiery coat generated so much heat, Van wondered if the initial blast had singed her. She ran trembling fingers over her eyebrows.

Ixl dashed into the lobby, followed by Uxa. They both used their hands to shield their faces from the flaming beast.

"What's going on here?" Ixl asked.

"He angry in cage." Suixsha moved closer to the cat, unaffected by the animal's heat.

The cat calmed when Suixsha approached. His fiery coat turned back into fur as if turning off a gas flame on a stovetop.

"If I was in a cage, I'd be angry too," Van said to Brux and Paley, wishing she had the authority to release him.

Uxa and Ferox conferred for a moment.

Daisy glided over to the cage. The animal shifted his attention to her. Van winced, certain Daisy was about to become burnt toast. Instead, her presence soothed him.

"Let him out. Or I will," Daisy shouted at Ferox and Uxa.

Uxa nodded at Suixsha.

Suixsha unlocked the cage's door. Then stepped back, giving the cat room to exit.

He lumbered out and shimmied his head and body as if to shake off the bad vibes from being trapped in the cage.

Van braced, expecting the entire room to burst into an inferno.

The animal strolled to Suixsha and rubbed his head against her shoulder like an enormous domestic house cat. She reached up and scratched him behind the ears.

He sauntered to Daisy next, who appeared much more serene after the cat's release. The animal sat in front of her and looked down, eye to eye. He reached his nose forward.

"Hello." Daisy allowed him to sniff her face. They communicated with each other without using words.

Curiosity got the better of Van and Paley and they made their way over, along with Brux, who went to his sister.

"What is it?" Paley asked Suixsha.

"Tyger," said Suixsha. "T-y-g-e-r. Different from yours."

"What's his name?" Paley reached to pet him. Van clasped her arm to stop her.

"I not give him name. I not own him. He stay with me because he choose to."

"What do you call him, then?" Van asked.

"Tyger," said Suixsha.

"You named your tyger—Tyger?" Paley giggled.

Suixsha shifted her hazel eyes at Paley and gazed at her like she had come across a curio at a yard sale.

Paley's expression shifted to one of wistfulness. "I wish we had animals like this on the island."

"Magical creature free to enter Earth World," said Suixsha. "They choose not to. Terrigen harm them."

"Animals would be crazy to risk it." Van thought of her brave little bunfy. She missed Wiglaf and hoped he wouldn't hold a grudge against her much longer.

"The tyger is worshipped in her tribe, or was," Ferox had come over and whispered to Van. "Suixsha is the only survivor of the Genetrix, and Tyger is the last of his kind. She claims they're kindred spirits."

Van knew the Balish had attacked Suixsha's tribe, and Suixsha's "cool dragon" kept her from being vengeful. But the sole survivor? She couldn't image what Suixsha must've gone through and re-evaluated her stance on being so disagreeable to her teammate.

With Tyger freed and everyone getting use to the savage beast, Suixsha redirected her attention to the room, ready to start the mission now that she was reunited with her companion.

"We leaving?" Kopius sauntered into the lobby wearing his backpack and holding Daisy's. He halted and gaped at the sitting tyger towering over his girlfriend. "Fascinating."

Ixl ran his eyes up and down Suixsha. "You going to put some clothes on?"

She glanced at her body, forehead scrunched.

"Covering the belly button is considered rude in her tribe," said Ferox.

"Correction. It shows they're not a good fighter," said Brux.

Suixsha said nothing, seemingly unbothered by them talking about her customs in front of her.

"I'm headed to the guest wing with my men," said Ferox, mostly to Van. "To see my people before they leave for Balefire."

"Are you going to travel with them?" Van hoped the answer was no.

Ferox shook his head. "Our team is going together, separately from them, for safety reasons. See you soon."

As Ferox and his men departed, Ixl's voice caught Van's attention.

"I should've been able to pick my team," he said to his mother. "Van's not on her game. It puts us at a disadvantage."

Paley stormed over and jabbed her index finger at Ixl. "Listen. Van survived the last two missions when some of our other teammates didn't. *She* saved my life. *She* retrieved two Items of Creation. What have you done?"

"What have I done? How about getting spit out of the portal thanks to you!"

"Enough," cried Uxa. She patiently began discussing the merits of everyone selected for the mission with Ixl and Paley.

Tyger, smitten with Daisy, allowed her to pet him while she stood on her tiptoes and murmured into his ear. Suixsha appeared pleased with the relationship. Kopius kept a wary eye on them, ready to take action if the animal acted out.

"Attention, if you will," shouted Uxa.

They gathered around.

"This mission is more dangerous than those in the past," she said.

The room grew so quiet Van swore she could hear the strange grandfather clock ticking in Uxa's home office miles away.

"There is something I must tell you before you go..."

CHAPTER

TWELVE

"I sent out a team a few months ago to check the third seal." Uxa paused, as if bracing herself for what she said next. "They never returned."

"Well, that certainly heats things up," said Kopius.

Uxa shifted her eyes to glance at each one of them as she spoke. "Your mission is clear. Check the third seal, find out what happened to the other team, and gather any information you can about the affairs at Balefire under the guise of diplomacy."

Van squirmed at the last directive, especially since Uxa mentioned it while Ferox and his men were absent from the lobby. Spying on Solana was one thing, but what would happen to her relationship with Ferox if he caught Van snooping around his family matters?

"Are we allowed to bring the Cup of Life?" asked Brux.

"The Cup stays," said Ixl. "The Elders might need it to make more of the cure. Besides, Van might lose it."

"Really, Ixl?" Van steamed. "I appreciate the vote of confidence."

Paley put her hands on her hips and glared at Ixl. "She wouldn't lose it. More likely, it would get stolen."

75

"If we took it with us, we could use it to treat people infected with the virus," said Brux.

"And heal our own wounds," added Kopius. "So there's a better chance of us not dying."

"I do not fear death," said Suixsha and Van in unison. They turned and stared at each other.

"We've all taken the cure, vaccination, potion, or whatever you want to call it," said Paley. "So we're immune to the virus. We don't need it for that."

"I don't need it at all," said Van. "Or anything else to check the seal. I can do it on my own. Like I did last summer. That mission ended with me retrieving the Cup."

Uxa hardened her gaze. "Do not retrieve the third item."

Van huffed and crossed her arms.

"If you come across the Runestar in your travels," said Uxa. "Bring it back here. Our consilium would like to present it as a gift to the Balish royal family. Word of our generosity would spread to their citizens, creating a feeling of benevolence."

"What is Runestar?" asked Suixsha.

Paley perked up. "It's a really pretty pin!"

Van half-expected Paley to whip out her jewelry case with the replicas inside to see if Suixsha wanted to buy one.

"A brooch," said Daisy. "The Balish want it, not only because of its intrinsic value but as a cherished relic from the Dark War. It's known to have magical protective properties."

"Remember," said Uxa. "If you find the Runestar, do not let the Balish know and do not give it to them. Bring it back to Lodestar."

Uxa halted her speech as Ferox and his men returned to the lobby.

"The Alignment's begun," said Brux. "We're on the clock. We need to get moving."

"Then let's go," said Ferox. "I'm ready."

Ixl's face brightened when he learned Ferox's physically fit soldiers were joining them.

Suixsha moved next to Van. She leaned in and said, "If time run short, you go back. I finish mission."

Van narrowed her eyes, unsure if Suixsha was being confrontational or helpful. Either way, Suixsha's comment irked her.

Uxa nudged Van. "I need to speak to you alone. It will take but a moment."

Van let out a breath she didn't know she was holding, relieved to get some uplifting and motivational words.

"You are not yet powerful enough to defeat your enemies," said Uxa. "Stick to the mission of building peaceful relations between the tribes and mending the seal. Do not risk your life trying to retrieve the Staff. There is time for you to get it next year, when you are stronger."

Van's hopes of getting encouragement from her mentor fizzled.

"As your Anchoress abilities grow, the Elementals will make certain your trials become increasingly challenging. They will get darker and more personal with each passing year until you access your full power."

"Wonderful." Van's tone burned with sarcasm. "Don't get the Staff until next year. Got it."

Uxa looked stern. "If the third seal is broken and you are unsuccessful in mending it..."

"I know, I know—it will give demons in the Earth World a doorway here. They'll rise, run amok, and cause Dishora. Don't worry. I got this."

"There is a difference between bravado and courage," said Uxa with a probing gaze. "Use this time to connect with your inner light, gain clarity, and build your power."

Ferox called the group to attention from the opened doors to the main steps. He nodded at Uxa as if they had something planned.

Van and Uxa rejoined the group.

"For Van's safety," said Uxa. "Alden will publicly state that Ferox and Van are traveling with the procession from the parade and will reach Balefire in two days."

"But Van, and all of you, will leave with me and my men," said Ferox. "We'll get there tomorrow morning by taking the figs."

"Awesome." Paley bobbed her head.

"Royal etiquette dictates that my family sponsors a welcome dinner when we arrive at Balefire," continued Ferox. "We'll do that before word gets out to the citizens of Aduro that Van is in the palace. Again, for her safety."

"You will leave the following morning to check the seal," said Uxa. "Questions?"

No one spoke. Anticipation filled the air.

"To the figs!" cried Ferox.

The group bounded down the staircase of the main entrance to Lodestar. They hastened along the sidewalk and rounded a corner. Parked on the street were three mo-rinds hovering a few inches above the road.

"Van, you're with me," said Ferox.

Brux marched forward. "I'll go with Van, too."

She braced for an altercation. To her relief, Ferox nodded in agreement.

Van stepped in first. The fig dipped as the hovercraft adjusted to her added weight. Then Ferox, Brux, and one of Ferox's three men climbed aboard. Van sat and then leaned forward, stretching her neck to see out the door.

Paley, Daisy, Kopius and one of Ferox's men jumped into a fig. Ixl and the remaining soldier leaped into another one.

Suixsha stood motionless on the road, Tyger by her side.

"Suixsha," said Van. "Any day now."

"I walk," she said. "Other travel weaken warrior."

Van sighed. "Stop being difficult and get in a fig."

Suixsha bent down and tugged off one of her boots.

Van threw her hands in the air. "What are you doing now?"

"I walk, bare feet." Suixsha pulled off the other boot. "Get energy from ground."

"Suixsha." Ixl stuck his head out of his fig's door. "Get in. Let's go." He wrinkled his brow at Tyger. "I don't think the cat will fit though."

"I'm done." Van sank back into her seat and crossed her arms.

Ferox flicked his head at his man inside their fig. The soldier rose from the driving chair.

Brux leaped up and blocked him. "I'll handle this."

The soldier looked to Ferox for direction, and sat back down.

Brux stepped out of the fig. Tyger let out a low, rumbling growl, causing him to stop. He met Suixsha's eyes. "Tell me what I can do to help."

Tyger held his gaze on Brux and snapped his tail.

"We don't have time for this," said Ixl. "Ticktock." He got jostled aside as Ferox's solider wedged his way out.

Suixsha glanced side-eyed at the approaching soldier. Tyger shifted his gaze.

"You can come in ours," shouted Paley.

"Too crowded," said Suixsha.

"Too crowded?" Ixl snorted. "I'm the only one in mine."

The soldier picked up Suixsha's boots and clasped her by the elbow.

"Whoa." Brux held up his palms. "Hold up."

Tyger stared down Ferox's man and blared a furious roar. His fur wavered, stood on end, and burst into flames.

The soldier released his grip, dropped Suixsha's boots, and leapt back from the fiery beast.

Tyger moved between Suixsha and the soldier, snarling.

The soldier and Brux backed away, using their arms to shield their faces from the heat.

"Suixsha." Ferox leaned out the door. "I'd be honored if you would be my guest in our fig. I'll have my man ride in another. It will just be me, you, and Van."

He nodded to his man in the driving chair, indicating it was okay to travel in a different fig.

Suixsha, unaffected by Tyger's blazing coat, spoke to her cat in a language Van didn't understand. The animal stopped growling, his coat returned to fur. Suixsha and Tyger locked onto each other's stare, then he trotted away as if in understanding.

Daisy popped her head out of her fig, looking saddened. "Where's he going?"

"He travel by woods," said Suixsha. "He free."

Suixsha turned to Ferox and nodded. She picked up her boots and tugged them on.

Brux twisted around. "Van..."

"It okay," said Van, peeking her head out. "Ferox is with me."

"I'll look out for her," Ferox said sincerely.

Brux clenched his jaw, looking aggrieved. He pulled back his shoulders, ready to do the right thing, even if it meant sacrificing his position as Van's protector to Ferox if it would get the group moving.

Suixsha hesitated as she peered in the door of Van and Ferox's fig. Her eyes ran over every detail of the vehicle's interior. Apparently, she deemed it suitable enough for travel and climbed aboard.

Ferox took command of the fig by settling into the worn, cushioned driving chair. He pulled a metal lever that revved the engine. The vehicle lifted higher. With a snap and a bang, the mo-rind shuddered and moved forward, hovering several feet above the ground.

The other two figs followed and the three mo-rinds zoomed down the street, headed south to Balefire, Aduro. Deep into the fiery eye of Balish territory.

THIRTEEN

Chit-chat in the fig kept to a minimum.

The soft murmuring of the engine's machinery attempted to lull Van into a relaxed state against her will. But fears about seeing Solana again and meeting Ferox's family simmered in her thoughts like water in a kettle, ready to come to a boil at any second, making it difficult for her to rest.

Suixsha stared out the window as if trying to comprehend the advantage of the fig's speed over walking.

Eventually, the sky grew dark, and Van drifted into sleep.

THE COMFORTING VIBRATION of the fig reached Van's awareness. She opened her eyes to see daylight filtering through the small, round windows.

Sunbeams shone through the windshield, highlighting Ferox in the driving chair. Suixsha continued to gaze out the window in the same position as when Van had fallen asleep.

"Do you need a break from driving?" Van asked Ferox.

"Thanks, but I took a break. One of my men drove for a few hours last night." Ferox twisted around and threw her a grin. "You slept through the whole thing."

Van blushed and glanced at the floor, unsure why she felt embarrassed about sleeping.

"How about you?" Van asked Suixsha. "You get any rest?"

Suixsha shook her head.

"You're not tired?" asked Van.

"I fine," she said.

Van peered at her, wondering if the girl's lack of sleep had something to do with being in Balish territory, or being in confined quarters with the prince. Ferox's family, or the council, must've ordered the attack that destroyed her tribe. Did Suixsha's cool dragon stance keep her from resenting Ferox by association? Van held both Suixsha and Daisy in awe at being brave enough to return to hostile territory for the good of the tribe.

Come to think of it, why did Suixsha agree to the mission? And what made her accept Uxa's offer to enter the games held in Salus Valde?

"Do you go to school in Lodestar Village?" asked Van. "I know they take refugees... I'm sorry. I'm not sure if that's the right word."

Suixsha glanced at Van, shook her head, and returned to staring out the porthole-shaped window.

"How'd you hear about the Jaychund games?"

Suixsha turned her attention to Van. "Word come to me in forest."

She couldn't tell if her questions bothered Suixsha, so Van kept asking. "Like, where? Where do you live?"

"North Tipereth Forest. Near Mt. Altithronia."

"It's beautiful up there." Van remembered seeing the purple-pink leafed trista tree fields, and it made sense Suixsha would pick that area to make home. People journeyed to bury deceased loved one's possessions under the trista trees, believing it brought healing to those suffering from grief. Sadly, Van's father had gone there after her mother's death. She looked vacantly out the window, her heart now aching for both herself and Suixsha.

"We're almost there." Ferox glanced over his shoulder. "I wanted to thank you, Suixsha, for agreeing to help us check the third seal. I'm happy for you to be my guest at Balefire."

Suixsha shifted in her seat to face his direction and gave him a nod.

"I'm sorry our past is so..." He hesitated, unsure how to finish the sentence. "Just want you to know I don't hold you personally responsible for the Alga massacre. I'm willing to let it go. Leave the past in the past."

Suixsha fully twisted around and gaped at Ferox.

Van gave him a quizzical look. She figured the Alga massacre had to do with the Balish attack on the Genetrix Tribe, meaning Suixsha should be the one forgiving Ferox, or, rather, his family.

"Only when you speak in truth can you be true leader," said Suixsha.

"What does that mean?" Ferox held his stare on the road, his shoulders tensed.

Although Van wanted to know more about what happened in their tribes' past, Suixsha and Ferox's growing ill will worried her. "Maybe we should talk about how we're going to find the seal?"

"No, no," said Ferox. "I think it's good to get this out in the open. Clear the air."

Suixsha appeared weary and wisely said nothing.

"Say your piece," urged Ferox. His tone had changed from friendly to adversarial. "I'd really like to know why your tribe murdered my grandparents."

"Wait, your tribe did what?" Van asked Suixsha.

"Go on. Tell her." Ferox allowed Suixsha a courtesy pause of maybe half a second, then continued. "A group of warriors from the Genetrix infiltrated Windermere Castle. They massacred my grandfather King Xavier and my grandmother Queen Elisha, who were visiting at the time."

"My tribe peaceful, sun worshipping." Suixsha's nostrils flared. "Until your people decide they want our sacred land, rich in mineral."

"Our council made the Genetrix a generous offer for surrendering their land as a contribution to the kingdom." Ferox's knuckles whitened as he gripped the steering wheel. "What I don't understand is why your tribe killed my grandfather? He protected indigenous people, including yours."

"Genetrix falsely blamed," said Suixsha. "They not behind Alga massacre."

"Oh, really? Then who?" asked Ferox. "Who committed such a heinous act against my family?"

Suixsha hesitated, and then said, "Your father."

Ferox slammed the brakes. He turned around and shouted, "You speak of treason!"

"I speak of truth."

Ferox rose from the driving chair. Hunched under the curve of the fig's roof, he towered over Suixsha. "You must've been a baby when this happened. How would you know anything? My father would never do such a thing."

"Truth of story burn bright in heart of those affected," said Suixsha.

Ferox tore open the door and stepped outside, as if needing air to clear his head before he breeched protocol and went to blows with his welcomed guest.

Van followed Ferox out of the mo-rind. When her foot hit the ground, she sunk down to her ankle in sand. Her hand snapped to her eyes to block out the blaring sun. She tried to swallow, but the dry air had siphoned all her saliva. Droplets of sweat coated her skin, making her forever grateful the figs came equipped with air-conditioning. Without a doubt, they had left the southern Tipereth Forest and reached the dry region of Aduro.

Vast reddish-yellow mounds filled the landscape, looking like baked waves in an unmoving ocean. In the distance, heat from the earth blurred the horizon. The desert landscape held no paved roads. A route they took on purpose, Van assumed, for her and the prince's safety.

Suixsha, not one to run from a fight, stepped out of the vehicle into the scorching desert.

"My father wanted to leave your tribe alone," said Ferox heatedly. "He petitioned to the council to extend our agricultural land to Kezef rather than go after the Genetrix in Pusiel. He felt it more important to increase control over our food supply rather than minerals. It's in our records."

"Your council rule against it," said Suixsha. "That in record too."

Ferox's three soldiers surrounded him, hands clasping the handles of their holstered DEW handguns, ready for the slightest signal from their prince to take down his adversary. Van's teammates exited their figs.

"It's hot as the devil's crotch out here." Paley wiped her brow with the back of her hand.

Brux protectively moved next to Van.

Ixl gripped his blade. "What's going on?" His eyes darted from one person to the next, ready for a fight, just trying to figure out against who.

Kopius sharply eyed the situation. "Nothing we can't work out friendly like." He kept Daisy and Paley shielded behind him.

Suixsha and Ferox glared at each other, jaws clenched.

"We're talking about the Alga massacre," Van said in a moderating tone. She swore every one of them, except Paley, winced.

"Your father wanted prove worth," said Suixsha. "Secure future kingship. While your grandfather and council focus on how take land from my people, your father went behind back. Attempted make pact with mule in Kezef."

"With the Tarcs?" asked Van.

"Hinnys," said Brux. "They're a mule-like race that look similar to the Tarcs but are a passive, agricultural tribe."

"Hinny decline," said Suixsha. "Offering land mean being slave for Balish profit. Same reason my tribe say no. Your father decided take command of situation, impress council with control over region. He use influence and power to secretly fund off-book mercenary, use taxpayer money."

"That's ridiculous," huffed Ferox.

"The mercenary got money, border pass, weapon," said Suixsha. "With own agenda they wipe out Balish in Windermere Castle in East Alga instead of Hinny."

"That blunder must've scared Nequus out of his mind," said Kopius.

"With his father's death, he ascended to the throne," said Ixl. "Talk about looking guilty of patricide."

Suixsha paused. It was the first time Van had seen a semblance of emotion other than aggression on her typically placid face. "To keep secret, new king, Nequus, order Genetrix Tribe die because they know truth."

"The Alga massacre outraged my people," said Ferox. "My father's swift response to the attack established him as a powerful leader. A king who would do anything to protect his people. They respect him for it to this day."

"What happened sounds like a horrible mistake," said Daisy.

"One that if known would force King Nequus to default the throne to his brother Mador Moor, and in succession, Mador's eldest son Merloc," said Ixl.

"There's no way this could've happened without me knowing about it," said Ferox, cooling down some. "My family would've told me."

"After, confidence leave your father," said Suixsha. "Guilt eat soul, make him weak, cause him drinking."

"My prince." One of his men stared at the nearby ground.

They all turned to see what caught his attention.

Van thought she might be hallucinating, or maybe the heat waves played a trick with her eyes. The sand appeared to shift as if something large slithered underneath like a serpent swimming in a desert ocean.

"We need to leave," said the soldier. "Now."

"What is it?" asked Paley, as they headed back to their respective figs.

"Tatzelwurms," said Ferox. "Not something we ever want to encounter."

As Ferox's man ushered him back into his fig, Brux whispered to Van and Suixsha, "King Nequus won't like knowing there's a Genetrix survivor."

"He'll be terrified you know the truth, Suixsha," said Van. "You'll need to be careful in the palace."

"Palace need be careful of me." Suixsha leaped into the fig. This time, she allowed Brux to ride with them.

Ferox's man refused to leave the prince for security reasons, and, with a packed fig, they continued their journey to Balefire. The other two mo-rinds followed behind.

Van contemplated what had transpired. Suixsha and Ferox both believed their side of the story. Van wasn't sure who spoke the truth. She wouldn't put it past Solana to hire mercenaries to do her dirty work like obliterating Suixsha's tribe. But Ferox's father? If it were true, that meant his whole family was rotten.

In the past, Van had peered into Ferox's soul and saw no dark thread, only white light. Could she trust her instincts, or did Ferox use his magical connections to cloak his true essence?

What Van really wanted to know, does the darkness fall far from the tree?

CHAPTER

FOURTEEN

On the horizon, the tops of turrets and domed skylights of Balefire Palace peeped into view through the fig's port-hole-like window. As they got closer, the palace became obscured by a massive stone wall enclosing Balefire City.

Ferox veered the fig toward the main gate. "There's only one entrance into the walled city."

Van's apprehension about meeting Ferox's father, facing his sister again, and staying at his home in hostile territory faded compared to what Suixsha and Daisy must be feeling.

Through the windshield, Ferox signaled the sentinels in the guard houses flanking the entrance. The thick wood and iron gate rumbled upward.

Brux strained to see the top of the wall. "How high is that?"

"A hundred feet. It's a remnant from the Dark War, built to keep out invaders," said Ferox. "Now it just keeps the wind from blowing sand into the city."

They traveled past boxy, multilevel, ground-stone houses lining the city's paved roads. Some had a small courtyard. The buildings, roads, people were clean and well-groomed in their predominantly thawb-inspired clothing. Not a speck of dirt, grime, or trash in sight.

They passed through what Van thought of as the downtown area. The citizens moved about running errands and getting on with their daily routines. Vegetation not native to the desert provided the town with a cooling shade and decorative landscaping. Curly ferns, shrubbery, palms, and oak trees imported from other parts of the world like Tipereth Forest lined the streets and filled the yards. A beautiful green foliage crept up the sides of most buildings.

City dwellers gathered at outside cafes and restaurants, looking relaxed while eating sandwiches or kabobs and drinking iced beverages. Like most of the Balish population, the people had varying shades of brown skin, from sun-kissed to dark brown. Van saw no blonds like herself, but some men wore turbans, and many women wore stylish head scarfs, so she couldn't see their hair color.

As they left the bustling urban area and got closer to Balefire Palace, foot traffic died down and the stone houses became more upscale. Homeowners had laced the outer walls with elaborately detailed gilded designs, the most popular being a variation of scrolling curves, bursts, and suns.

Many houses had gold statues of animals that looked like Living World versions of lions, lizards, and rams decorating their meticulously landscaped courtyards. Some properties were enclosed with five-foot walls.

Foot traffic picked up again. Families and groups of friends strolled along the sidewalks headed toward Balefire. Van intended to ask Ferox about them, but forgot the moment she got a close-up view of the stunning palace.

High on a hill, the colossal residence sparkled like a jewel rising from the center of Balefire City. Van thought of it as a compound more than a palace, or its own town within the city.

A ten-foot sandstone wall with a gated main entrance surrounded the palace grounds.

Van's emotions struggled between apprehension and exhilaration as they hovered past the lion gargoyles guarding the road leading to the Balish royal family's ancestral residence and Ferox's home.

"The gate's opened for the festival," said Ferox.

Van gaped at all the people wandering about the festivities. She caught glimpses of the courtyard's rich grassy areas and a giant fountain with water spurting from the mouths of various gold aquatic animals.

No one paid any attention to the three figs driving along the perimeter road usually used by servants, maintenance people, and other workers that led to the back entrance of the palace.

The cheery festival-goers ate meat off sticks and stuffed fluffy golden tuffs into their mouths that looked like cotton candy made of spun gold. Van ogled the multicolored tents, mostly orange, yellow, and red-and-white striped that offered food or items for sale. There were jugglers, magicians, and swirling rides that defied the laws of physics and most certainly involved magic, including one that looked like a futuristic Ferris wheel. The Balish Council obviously picked on a whim when to enforce their rules about magic.

For a split second, Van thought the celebration might be in honor of her arrival. Then, she noticed a huge papier-mâché sun decoration. "Is this Kupalle?" she asked Ferox.

"It is." Ferox beamed.

Van puffed out her chest, proud of herself for retaining information about his customs.

"Balish celebrate the time of year when sun hours are at a maximum," said Brux. "Takes place on the same weekend as our Jaychund."

"That's right, sort of," said Ferox. "Our ancient tradition celebrates the time of year when the sun is at its strongest, able to keep the darkness of night at bay for the most hours in a day. Over the millennia the significance of the holiday changed to celebrate the light within our king."

They passed by a group of children playing a game where a

handful of kids dressed in black were being chased by one wearing a hat in the shape of the sun and a bright yellow robe.

"I've read the Balish royal family has a piece of the sun within," said Brux. "Giving them the power to bring warmth and life to the lands."

Van raised her eyebrows. Impressed Brux had studied Balish traditions.

"And the strength to conquer any darkness thrown our way." Ferox's amber-yellow eyes sparkled against his sun-darkened skin as if on cue.

As they passed by the main entrance to Balefire Palace, a group of protestors had gathered at the foot of the grand stairway. They held signs that read, "Our water! Our lives! Our choice!" and "Magic is a curse, not a cure!" and the word magic surrounded by a red circle with a slash.

"Speaking of darkness," muttered Van.

Ferox scowled. "I'll have my people monitor them."

As they rounded the palace, the festival faded, and they passed a holding area containing probably a hundred massive black horses, and another corral with four-legged, hyper-muscular beasts that looked like a cross between a bison and a camel—*allocameli.*

Van took in a sharp breath.

"You okay?" asked Brux.

She widened her eyes at Brux and subtly shifted her gaze to the window, giving him the hint to look outside the fig.

He did. Then turned back to Van, jaw slackened.

Brux caught the meaning of the allocameli. Tarcs were at Balefire.

They had the displeasure of encountering Tarcs on a past mission. Their leader, Lord Godreel, had saved their team from hungry trolls, only to hold them captive. Godreel promised to set them free for gold. Van and her team paid his fee, but Godreel broke his word and tried to force them into slavery.

Ferox brought the fig to a stop outside the modest back entrance. They piled out.

The desert heat hit Van full blast again. Her lips throbbed and with each breath, her throat burned from the dry air.

Paley sauntered over, squinting. "Should've brought my shades."

A handful of palace guards waited at the entrance, apparently aware of their prince's low-key arrival. As they entered the palace, one of Ferox's men said, "Place all weapons in the bin." He pointed to a nearby table.

"I don't think that's in our best interest, mate," said Kopius.

"I'm sorry," said Ferox. "It's palace protocol."

"You're the prince. Can't you help us out?" asked Ixl.

Brux brushed past Ixl and dropped his dagger in the bin. "He's not the king, his father is."

Suixsha placed her tomahawks in. She glanced at Ixl and Kopius and said, "Path least resistance."

The team complied, although Ixl and Kopius continued to grumble about it.

Ferox's men departed and they followed the palace guards up the stairs. As they snaked through the servants' hallways under the upper floors, Van's stomach jumbled in anticipation of meeting Ferox's family and seeing his dreaded sister again.

They came to a spiral stairway and went up three flights.

Ferox maneuvered himself next to Van and whispered, "It's best for us to keep our relationship quiet for now."

"What? Why?"

"It's a bad time for us to announce it," he said. "It would cast more doubts in the minds of my people about my ability to lead."

"Did the protestors spook you, or was this planned?" Van fumed. "I thought you wanted me on the mission so I could come to Balefire and meet your family?"

Ferox clenched his jaw. Two guards opened the double doors for him and he entered the foyer, saving him from discussing the issue further.

Van had no choice but to drop it for now and followed Ferox. She gasped at the beauty of the grandness of Balefire Palace. Polished sandstone pillars decorated the entrance hall with elaborate gold detailing that extended along the top of the walls. An expansive curved stairway with gold handrails dominated the room. The impressive decor predominately had black, red, and gold in their wall hangings and artwork. A spicy scent of bergamot filled the air.

"It's amazing." Van gaped.

"My mother decorated the palace," said Ferox.

"Queen Brigid?" The scar on Van's lower back tingled, a remnant of her mother's interaction with the queen.

Ferox nodded, a glint of sadness clouded his eyes. "She was a noble, well-regarded woman. I wish you could've met her."

"At least I'll get to meet your father."

"He isn't here." Ferox cast his eyes downward. "He's traveling the countryside to monitor delivery of the treatment and vaccine. To build trust with the masses about the cure. You'll meet him next time."

Van's heart whirled in delight at his mention of "next time," meaning there would be one. Still, despite being intimidated, Van had hoped to meet the Balish king. She thought winning him over might help her standing with the Balish people and subsequently solidify her relationship with Ferox.

Van soon discovered there were plenty of Ferox's other relatives and officials for her to meet. Cousins, aunts, uncles, wellborns, council members... Ferox led Van down the receiving line, followed closely by Brux, then Paley.

Suixsha and Ixl trailed next. To Van, they looked like the oddest couple in history. Then came Daisy and Kopius, the legit most gorgeous couple ever. Out of all of them, Suixsha appeared the most uncomfortable, like she hated every second. Paley appeared to love every minute.

Van couldn't blame Suixsha. Besides being more comfortable running barefoot through the woods with her giant tyger, Suixsha was being forced to mingle with the people who believed her tribe had murdered their former king, while she believed these people wiped out her entire tribe.

Although overwhelmed by it all, Van thought she handled herself well. Genie would've been proud.

Then Van saw them.

Standing in a separate receiving line by the stairway, flanked by a line of servants. Solana and her cousin-fiancé, Merloc, along with, who Van assumed were, Merloc's parents.

She glanced at Daisy, sending vibes of strength to her friend and praying Daisy would be okay with coming face to face with her captor.

Van whispered to Brux, "Maybe you should go to your sister and—"

"She's fine," he said, not taking his eyes off Solana. "She's with Kopius."

Van turned her attention back to Ferox, and he led their way to the royal family, none of whom were smiling. Their manner appeared stuffy and oppressed.

All except one.

Solana.

As the Balish princess laid eyes on Van, her lips curled at the edges into the most venomous smile...

CHAPTER

FIFTEEN

"May I introduce you to Underqueen Sybil Moor and her husband Underking Mador Moor," said Ferox. "Also known as Aunt Sybil and Uncle Maddy. This is Vanessa Cross."

Van greeted them with a small curtsey.

"Underking?" asked Paley, stretching her neck around Brux.

"There's only one king," said Mador, jovially. "My brother Nequus. All other kings rule their regions as underkings. We use the title of king outside of Aduro and then only when the true king is not in the same region."

Brux and Paley met the underking as Ferox moved Van to the next person in line.

Dread lit Van like a flame.

"Princess Solana Moor," said Ferox. "I believe you have met Vanessa Cross."

"Yes." Solana grinned.

Van glowered, half-expecting fangs to extend from Solana's canines. The Balish princess had ditched her trademark skin-tight catsuit for a formal, low-cut, tunic-styled dress. Her glossy jet back

95

hair was styled in an elaborate braided up-do instead of falling down her back.

"Lovely to see you again, Princess Vanessa."

"I'm not a princess—well, I mean, I am, but we don't have a—um, just call me Van." Her cheeks flared, annoyed with herself for letting Solana throw her off her game.

"Of course, my apologies. *Van.*" Solana, cool and collected, smoothed over Van's babbling.

Van tried, really, really tried, to detect sarcasm, but couldn't. She noticed a stunning rock on the ring finger of Solana's left hand. The diamond ring had a gold chain attached, leading to a wrist band made with red, white, and black diamonds.

Ferox smiled smugly. Pleased Van and his sister were making their best effort to be cordial.

"This is my cousin, Underprince Merloc Moor," he said. "Merloc, this is Vanessa—Van Cross."

Van gave a nod to the most fearsome man she had ever met. His towering form made Van think he might be part Tarc. Merloc seemed made of solid muscle and resembled a human wall.

"It is my honor to meet you, *princess,*" cooed Merloc. He had dark black hair and sun-bronzed skin along with eyes that stole their color from the sun, common to Balish royalty. His facial skin appeared scarred, not from battles but from acne as a teenager. He extended his palm to Van.

She placed a trembling hand in his, assuming this was one of their customs, and hoped he wouldn't crush her bones.

He bent down and kissed the back of Van's hand.

Her skin crawled. He was the least cuddly human she had ever met. A perfect match for Solana.

Next, Ferox introduced Van to Thuxeor, the palace wizard.

Van had crossed paths with the wizard last year and immediately recognized him. The meticulously groomed, raven-haired wizard still sported a stylish goatee and wore the same elegant purple and gold robe.

"My dear," he bent at the waist and kissed Van's hand. "Enchanted to see you again."

Van's gaze darted to the floor... wall... anywhere but him. Last time she saw Thuxeor, Ferox was holding Van and her team captive in a basement. Being reminded of those circumstances emphasized the precariousness of her and Ferox's relationship, and how much Van and the others didn't belong there.

She let out a sigh of relief when Ferox moved her down the line, meeting other members of the Balish Royal Court and their families. Their names, lineage, who lived where, who ruled what, and who was married to whom merged, making Van's head spin with information overload.

After meeting what felt like everyone in Balefire City, Ferox introduced Van and her team to their personal butler, Ebus, and housekeeper, Efore.

"They're your point of contact and will handle all your needs during your stay," said Ferox. "I've put you in the gold wing. It's the main guest area reserved for VIPs." He leaned toward Van and whispered into her ear. "And closest to my quarters."

Van's heart whirled, loud enough to squelch her doubts about their relationship.

"This way, if you please," said Ebus.

"I'll catch up with you at dinner," Ferox said to Van. "Your backpacks are already in your suite. Get some rest and settle in." He dashed away as Ebus and Efore shuffled Van and the others up the grand staircase.

Van glanced at Daisy. "You okay?"

"I'm fine," said Daisy, not looking fine at all.

Kopius kept close to her.

"Seeing Merloc again must've been upsetting," said Van. "Understandable."

"My time with him... it gave me a gift," said Daisy.

"A gift?"

"The gift of strength." Daisy and Kopius picked up their pace and moved away from Van.

Ebus and Efore led the group through a gold-decorated archway into a hallway wide enough to be considered a lobby.

"Ladies, if you will follow me," said Efore.

Ebus extended his arm. "Gentlemen, this way, please."

"Wait." Brux popped up his hands. "I don't like the idea of us being separated."

"Me either," said Kopius.

"We are guest. We stick to rule of house." Suixsha stood in the hallway looking out of place like a majestic tree hacked down from the forest and dragged inside the palace.

"The girls can handle themselves." Ixl strolled toward Ebus.

Van pulled Brux aside and whispered, "I'm not sure when I'll see you again. Keep your eyes out for someone familiar. Someone you've seen at Lodestar or on the reservation. It could be the spy. Pass it along to the guys."

Brux agreed, and they rejoined the others.

Ebus led the guys to their suite, and Efore led the girls to one across the hall.

Inside, Van loved the open concept. Lots of space with comfy, round-arm chairs and sofas. A small kitchen to the side of the larger dining area added a homey feeling to the suite. As much as a suite that slept twelve could feel homey.

"Nice." Paley plunked down on the sofa under an enormous oil painting of a desert landscape in a fancy gold frame.

"It's wonderful," said Daisy. "Thank you, Efore."

Efore smiled graciously, then suggested they unpack, rest, and get dressed for dinner. "I will call for you at eight."

"Dress for dinner?" asked Van, relieved she still had her yellow chiffon dress from the Placement Ceremony stuffed in her backpack. "Is this formal?" *Duh.* Stupid question since they were in a palace.

Paley bolted upright. "I didn't pack anything."

"My dears," said Efore. "The closet is full of clothes of all sizes." She extended her arm toward the large double doors inside the suite.

Paley dashed over and swung them open. Before her was an enormous walk-in closet. Elegant dresses and gowns, in an array of colors, hung from the wardrobe bars.

Van rubbed the fabric of one between her fingers. *Very high-end.* She gave the dress an approving nod.

Van, Paley, and Daisy explored deeper inside and saw another several rooms with rows and rows of shoes, boots, and other wardrobe accessories. The never-ending closet even had a dressing room with several vanities.

They came back out, and Paley exclaimed, "Wow, it's as big as the suite!"

"I already dress for dinner," said Suixsha. "I need no rest."

Efore glanced at Suixsha. "What's most important to us is our guests' comfort. Dress as you will." She nodded in parting and left the suite.

Van, Paley, and Daisy burned time trying on multiple dresses. Suixsha left to do pushups and crunches in her bedroom.

Van and Daisy settled on beautiful full-length ball gowns. Van's with blue and orange lace accents, and Daisy's yellow and white. They sat on the couches, waiting for Paley to choose her dress.

Paley peeked her head out of the closet. Her contact lens colored eyes had changed to a deep red and her hair was in a simple up-do. "Suixsha, come look at this," she cried. Paley's eyes darted to Van and Daisy. "You ready?"

Suixsha, appeared looking curious and a bit sweaty.

Paley came twirling out the of closet in a stunning, drop-dead-red corseted dress with a bustle skirt and ornamental trimming. "This is the one!"

Van clapped. "Bravo."

"You look gorgeous," said Daisy.

Paley's twirl stopped short. She stared at Suixsha. "You need to change. It's almost eight o'clock."

"I wear this. Comfortable."

"Wasn't it you who said as guests we should stick to the rules of house?" quipped Van.

Suixsha turned to Daisy, searching for a better response.

Daisy tossed up her delicate hands. "Oh, I agree with Van. Or, rather, *you*. As guests, we do as the hosts wish. You should change." She gave Suixsha a cheeky smile.

"Come with me." Paley grabbed Suixsha by the hand. "I'll help you."

Suixsha grimaced as Paley dragged her into the closet. Van and Daisy giggled. Van couldn't wait to see Suixsha in a formal dress.

By the time Efore returned to the suite, all four were dressed and ready. Their housekeeper escorted them down a side stairway and into a small-for-the-palace atrium.

Efore held open a window paned door. "You'll wait in the sitting room until called for dinner."

The four gaped at the crowded room, in which, ironically, no one was sitting.

"What are we supposed to do?" asked Van.

"Mingle with the other guests," Efore replied.

The gorgeous room fit in with the rest of the palace, with its crisp decor heavy on the gold and with accents of red and black. Harpists strummed over the murmur of the crowd and drinks clinked and sloshed. Staff dressed in crisp black kitchen uniforms served hors d'oeuvres.

Van surveyed the crowd as she wedged her way inside.

"I see Kopius." Daisy dashed away into the throng.

Suixsha unabashedly positioned herself by the door like a comely sentinel in her modest, earth-toned tunic dress.

The air crackled with electricity. Van's pulse quickened. "Let's find Brux and Ixl."

Paley stuck close to Van, quietly absorbing the unique event, her widened-eyes taking in all the glamor.

Van stopped, causing Paley to step on her heels. She tilted her head to direct Paley's attention through the crowd to Solana, chatting with a group of people.

"Whoa. She looks beautiful," said Paley.

Van disagreed. If she had to pick an adjective to describe Solana, it would be *dangerous*.

Solana smiled and laughed, exuding confidence and charm, as she chatted with dignitaries. Several were humanoid creatures that looked like a mix of bovine and homo sapien, with their flared nostrils, tiny ears on top of broad foreheads, and elongated faces. *Tarcs*. Van had seen none of them before, though she admitted it difficult to distinguish them from one another, other than by their clothing and jewelry.

"Maybe we should go talk to them," said Paley. "You know… mingle."

Van didn't want to and when it came down to it, Paley couldn't muster the nerve. The dignitaries and terrifying Tarcs intimidated her. So they continued weaving their way through the guests and settled in a corner.

"It's weird no one we met earlier is talking to us," said Paley.

"Cross your fingers it stays that way." Van glimpsed Ferox, and it caused a flutter of excitement in her stomach.

Clearly, he was the main event, surrounded by members of the Balish Council and Balish Royal Court. She had learned earlier, all the court's members were Ferox's relatives, most of whom Van had met in the reception line. She also recognized a few council members.

"Look." Paley tilted her head. "It's the palace wizard. He's the most stylish one here."

Van saw Thuxeor through the crowd. "Hm. Yeah." She narrowed her eyes.

As the person who trained Solana to become a sorceress, she placed him on Solana and Merloc's side. He also helped Merloc nurse Solana back to life after Van nearly killed the princess using the power of the Coin. Before making a conclusion about Thuxeor's alignment with darkness, she peered into his soul.

Startled not to see a dark thread, she made a mental note to visit with him later.

A lumbering figure obstructed Van's line of sight. *Merloc.* His amber-colored eyes locked onto her from across the room. His soul, pure black.

A chill rippled down Van's spine as his massive form strode through the crowded room toward her.

CHAPTER
SIXTEEN

Paley saw Merloc approaching and yelped. She disappeared into the plethora of party guests.

"Princess Vanessa," said Merloc. "Excuse me. *Van.*"

She didn't respond. She couldn't. It took all her energy not to punch him in the throat for what he did to Daisy.

"I have something to discuss with you."

"Go on," croaked Van. The words stuck in her dry throat. From the weather, she told herself, not from fear.

"I was not happy to hear about your and Ferox's relationship. Well," He shrugged. "My cousin is entitled to his whims."

Van lifted her eyes to his. "You don't scare me."

"Your existence is causing problems with our people." Merloc sneered. "You used *magic* to create a cure for the demon illness."

"Using magic to create medicines is allowed under Balish law." Van held his stare. "So why would Ferox, or the council, or anyone have a problem with it?"

"You..." Merloc's hands trembled. "You and your *dirt-loving* pals in the consilium... put it in our water supply. Against the will of *my people.*" Spittle flew from his lips when he said the last word.

"*Your* people? More like, *Ferox's* people."

Solana slithered over. "Now is not the time," she murmured to her fiancé, then stared at Van. "I hope you're enjoying your welcome dinner. Always nice to have such *diversity* in our halls."

"Yes." Merloc lifted his upper lip, showing his teeth like someone who had failed smiling class. "Enjoy yourself. While you can."

Van's eyes darted to nearby guests, irritated that no one had witnessed their encounter, especially Ferox. She glowered at Solana and Merloc as they disappeared back into the party.

Brux rushed over. "You look upset. What happened?"

Van recounted her conversation with Solana and Merloc.

"You have to tell Ferox." Brux's nostrils flared.

"No," snapped Van. "I don't want to mess up our relationship now that it's going well."

Brux tightened his jaw. "If you don't, I will." He stormed into the crowd.

"Brux... don't!" Van called after him.

She tried to follow and kept bumping into people, eventually losing track of him. Her eyes swept the room, searching for either Brux or Ferox. As she moved about, Van overheard several Bales use the derogatory phrase "dirt lover" regarding Lodian people, a dignitary talking about raising taxes on the poor and chuckling about it, and a wellborn (Ferox had told her wellborns were the wealthy elite that didn't have royal blood) complaining about the "lack of quality help these days."

Van stayed still, hoping it might help her locate Brux, or someone from her team. A server wandered over holding a tray of chilled, triangular-shaped glasses filled with a rose-colored liquid with gold flakes floating in it.

She took one. "Thank you." Van wondered what made him choose to work in the palace. It was probably a desirable occupation, one of high standing and with significant benefits. "How's your night going?"

"Excuse me?" His tone sounded pleasant, yet his eyes widened in fear.

"How's your—how long have you worked as a server here?"

He rocked from side to side like he wanted to dash away. "I—I—don't understand. I'm sorry. My position is not server."

"Oh, what's your title then?"

"He slave." Suixsha appeared next to Van.

"A what?"

With Suixsha distracting Van, he scurried away.

"Slave."

Van gripped her glass so tight she thought it might crush in her hand as the hot fingers of anger rose from her core. She knew slavery existed among the savage tribes in the Living World, like the Tarcs, and the gnomes were used to mine gold in Yesod for the Balish. But human slavery? In the palace? How could Ferox allow this injustice?

Van stared at Suixsha, who looked cool and collected. "How can you be calm about this?"

"Whoever make you angry control you," replied Suixsha.

"This tulle is so flipping itchy." Van tugged at her dress. She got no response from Suixsha, so she asked, "What took you away from your vigil by the door?"

"Mission." Suixsha wandered into the crowd.

Van saw her lingering within eavesdropping distance of Solana. To gather intel, no doubt.

"Humph." She resumed her search for Ferox and Brux.

A sudden coldness hit Van's gut as she glimpsed a Tarc wearing a distinctive gold nose ring. Lord Godreel. Accompanied by a handful of his men, all looking sharp, wearing formal tunic-style outfits popular with the royal Balish and wellborns. Van abruptly turned around, terrified of catching his eye and being forced into a conversation with him.

She wandered near several men who were members of the Balish Council and did her own recon.

"Demons cannot rise to our world by human hand," said one

man. "They gain strength from the negativity of the terrigens. Then they use their corruptive powers to morph terrigens into demons. That's how they grow into many. Only then can demons gain the collective power needed to reach our world."

"I beg to differ," said another. "I read ancient scrolls in the Hall of Records that said demons can enter our world with a key."

"By human hand?" said the third, visibly disturbed.

One caught Van's eye as she lurked, and she ducked out of sight behind the nearest gathering of people. All this mingling unnerved her. The guests were so prejudiced against Lodians that no one struck up a conversation with her, not even at her own welcome dinner pre-party. It didn't bother Van. She found it a relief.

With that in mind, Van didn't want to stay in one spot for long in case a brave soul decided to be friendly and talk to her. She searched the crowd for *any* of her teammates and saw Daisy and Kopius chatting by themselves. She marched over. As Van reached them, so did a bearded, middle-aged man.

"I know you." He waggled a finger at Kopius. "You look really familiar."

"No, we haven't met before," said Kopius. "I'm great with faces. Sorry."

"If you'll excuse us." Daisy clasped Kopius's hand and led him away. She turned her eyes to Van. "Come on."

"Who was that?" asked Van as they weaved their way through the crowd.

Kopius shrugged.

"Let's find a quiet place until we're called for dinner," suggested Daisy, apparently done with pre-dinner socializing, too.

"Great idea," said Van.

They roamed near the walls until coming upon French doors. They were unlocked and opened into an unoccupied alcove.

"Perfect," said Daisy.

Compared to the rest of the palace, the small room's decor appeared simple. The furnishings were immaculate, as expected, and every item had its place: the couch, coffee table, vases, bust of a man on a pedestal. The walls were lined with shelves filled with books.

"This is nice." Kopius leaped over the back of the couch and landed perfectly on the cushions in a reclined position. "Too many people out there." He shuddered comically. "Yuck."

"Not very pleasant ones either," said Daisy.

"Exactly." Van perused the cozy room. "The scar on my back has been tingling since I got here."

"Really? Why?" Daisy sat in a chair across from the couch.

Van mumbled something unintelligible, not in the mood to rehash her mother's tragic past.

"Why aren't you hanging out with the love of your life?" asked Kopius.

"Ferox is tending to his duties as prince," said Van. "Not babysitting me."

Daisy shot Kopius a furious look. "Their relationship is none of our business."

"Hey, don't start the fire if you can't tend the flame." Kopius twisted his neck to glance at the stuffed bookshelves. "I hope they have permits for all these books."

He was kidding, of course. The Balish regulated all print and media in the kingdom, leaving little doubt these books met all legal requirements.

"Displaying books is a sign of wealth and status." Daisy rose from her chair, pulled a book from the shelf, and began flipping through its pages.

Van peered at the bust. The plaque read, "King Goustav Moor." Her pulse quickened as she scrutinized the features of her ancestor's face. His eyebrows, lips, cheekbones. Her gaze moved to a full-body oil painting of Goustav grasping a staff with intricate detailing on the tip. It looked like an original work of art, made over a thousand years ago. The young king stared from the canvas with haunted eyes.

"This room has a lot of Goustav memorabilia," said Van.

"You're not kidding." Daisy held the book open. "From what I'm reading, I don't think we should be in here."

"What is it?" Curiosity got the better of Kopius and he got up to check out the room's items, too.

"It's an account of Queen Cordelia's death during the Great War," said Daisy.

"You mean the Balish version of what happened?" Van gave her an eye roll.

Daisy closed the book, using her finger to mark the page. "You don't want to hear about it, then?"

Van grinned. "I didn't say that."

"I'm all ears." Kopius peered at a gold statue of a ram on an end table.

"The Balish wanted control of the lands, including Lodian-occupied territory. They didn't fear the Lodians or their mythical Anchoress-in-waiting and desired access to the portal. So they could clean-up the lesser world by killing the terrigens."

"Sounds familiar," said Kopius.

"Balefire received news that the Lodian's Anchoress-in-waiting, Queen Cordelia, was headed to Mt. Altithronia to retrieve her weapons from the Elementals. This would allow her to come into her full power and take her place as Anchoress. She could end—*win*—the war."

"You just said the Balish didn't believe in the Anchoress," said Van.

"Mmhm," said Daisy, her eyes glued to the pages. "Before this news, the Balish King Meli, father to Manik, his twin sister Magdalene, and Goustav, didn't believe in the Items of Creation, or the Anchoress. Though familiar with Lodian lore, King Meli thought of it as nothing more than foolish beliefs. After hearing about the retrieval, the king couldn't risk taking the chance that his enemy's folklore was true. If the Lodian's Anchoress truly existed and she possessed those weapons, he would lose the war."

"He sent Goustav to intercept Cordelia on her way back down

from the mountain," said Van. "He also sent Manik. That's when Manik met Zurial and they fell in love."

"Aw, how sweet." Kopius's words smoldered with sarcasm.

"The Moor brothers and their men had dressed as travelers, not soldiers, so not to raise suspicion," continued Daisy.

"Goustav killed Cordelia and took the Staff," said Kopius. "That's a no-brainer."

"This is King Meli's account," said Daisy. "Goustav returned to Balefire with the Staff of Fire, but the other Items were lost when Cordelia's people scattered during the attack. Manik eventually returned to Balefire with the sword... there was a problem..."

"Yeah, he fell in love with the enemy." Kopius glanced pointedly at Van.

She scrunched her face at him. Then, turned to Daisy and said, "We know Zurial had the Cup of Life. Rowen had the Coin of Creation and gave it to his wife, Amaryl, who had become the Anchoress-in-waiting after her mother Cordelia died. Goustav had the Staff of Fire and Manik the sword. I'm not sure what it's called..."

Daisy peeked up from the book. "Sword of Swords."

"Way to be creative with names," said Kopius.

"It balanced the power between the opposing tribes, each had two Items." Van gazed at the painting of Goustav. The Staff prominently displayed by his side, his chest raised, showing off his treasure and succumbing to its power. Van assumed, later in his life, the corruption caused by misuse of the Item ended up damaging his soul, as it had with Amaryl and Zurial.

"Oh, this is interesting," said Daisy. "King Meli and Goustav knew nothing about the properties of the Staff, including how to use it. One of their palace staffers couldn't control his desire for the Item and touched it." Daisy looked up at Van and Kopius. "He went instantly insane." She put her nose back in the book. "He killed Queen Helena, King Meli's wife, with it."

"Karma's a bitch," said Kopius.

"It devastated King Meli," said Daisy.

"And Goustav? Manik? Magdalene?" asked Van. "Did any of them care that their mother got killed?"

"King Meli talks about his own grief, about how his wife's death changed him. Manik hadn't yet returned, and their sister, Magdalene, was away fighting in the war."

"Manik wrote in his text that only people with royal bloodlines can touch the Items without going crazy," said Van. "Now we know the origin of that belief."

Daisy bobbed her head. "They concluded royals had different upbringings. They have all they need so are less likely to become corrupted by the Items' power."

"Demons rose to this world during the Great War, causing it to turn into an even greater war, the Dark War," said Kopius. "Balish propaganda says that's when Goustav saved the day using his Staff."

"We know that's not true. Amaryl used her Items and won the war." Van wondered what part of Goustav's eventful life he was experiencing at the time the artist painted his portrait.

She lifted her hand, compelled to touch the painting... to run her fingers over Goustav's cheek, a futile gesture intended to soothe the troubled expression on the young king's face... Van's hand inched closer. The heat of his emotions reached her fingertips. Anger, jealousy, sadness emanated from the painting...

"No! Don't touch it," cried Daisy.

Kopius leaped over and grabbed Van's arm. "The last thing we need is for you to pass out from getting a memory engram. We're deep inside enemy territory."

Her friends were right. However, it didn't lessen Van's desire to learn more about her ancestor.

"The palace is the perfect place for me to use my abilities to learn more about Goustav and the Staff." Which Van now had every intention of getting, despite what she had told Uxa.

"How about not right now," said Kopius.

A bell chimed from the sitting room. A muffled voice filtered into their alcove and declared, "Dinner is served."

"Ask your boyfriend about Goustav over dinner." Kopius tugged Van's arm to tear her attention away from the painting. "We'll need something to talk about with these people."

"This isn't the best place for her to mention Goustav," said Daisy. "You know, because of her being his secret ancestor."

"Oh, this is gonna be great." Kopius rubbed his hands together with blatantly false enthusiasm.

The trio left the alcove and rejoined the gathering. Ready to endure a cordial dinner with the enemy.

CHAPTER

SEVENTEEN

The dining table seemed to stretch a mile long. Guests began taking their seats.

"Look, there's a seating chart." Daisy pointed to a table by the entrance.

"We better be near each other," said Kopius, as he and Daisy looked it over.

Van bent over the chart. "Where am I?"

"Hey," said Paley from behind. "Where'd you go?"

"She was in a side room with Daisy and Kopius," said Brux.

Van turned to face them, bristling at Brux's comment. She appreciated him doing his duty by keeping an eye on her, but felt like he had invaded her privacy. She crossed her arms. "Did you talk to Ferox?"

Brux shook his head. "Couldn't get anywhere near him." He lowered his voice. "I overheard talk that the Anti-Manik Rebels are here, in the fairgrounds."

"So?" Van shrugged.

"Ferox knows you're Goustav's heir. You're a threat to his throne. It makes him a danger to you."

They apparently lingered by the seating chart for too long. The palace butler bounded over and suggested he escort them to their seats. He led Van to the head of the table and placed her at "the seat of honor" to Ferox's left. As he moved on to seat the others, she wondered if he, too, was a slave. Van considered confronting Ferox about the palace using slave labor, but this wasn't the time or place.

The seating alternated between males and females, except in a few places where there were more males than females.

Van squinted at the far end of the table and noticed an unoccupied chair. "Who's sitting at the foot of the table?"

"We keep that seat empty in honor of my mother," said Ferox. "My father would normally take this seat, but, as you know, he's away."

Van saw Underking Mador seated to the left of the empty seat. Next to him sat Solana. Merloc sat directly across the table from his intended, with Underqueen Sybil to his left. Van breathed a sigh of relief. Solana and Merloc were nowhere near her or Daisy, who sat in the middle, along with Suixsha, Kopius, and Brux.

Van cringed when she saw the butler seat Paley to Merloc's right, a pairing that could be troublesome. Her heart went to her stricken-looking friend.

"Why's Paley sitting so far away?" Van noticed Ixl seated close enough to Paley, Solana, and Merloc, to monitor their conversation. Hopefully, he could mitigate any issues.

"The host seats guests as he chooses," said Ferox. "Usually based on personal accomplishments, social prominence, and mutual interests shared by seat mates."

"Who's hosting this?" It hadn't crossed her mind until now.

"Uncle Maddy, in place of my father. He allowed me to sit at the head of the table." Ferox smirked. "As crown prince, I outrank him."

He introduced Van to those seated around them.

The only name she remembered was Hutriel, the menacing-looking Tarc seated to her left. He smelled like rotted meat.

A handful of servants—Van couldn't bring herself to call them slaves—brought out platters of food.

"Highest rank picks the menu." Ferox grinned.

Van doubted Mador, Solana, and Merloc were okay with Ferox outranking them.

The main staple of most dishes were chunks of meat and a grain that looked like red rice. Leafy green vegetables and squashes filled some platters, others offered carved slices of light and dark meats. Jugs of mountain rum appeared to be a favorite of the Tarcs and were plentiful, along with chilled pitchers of mead. The staff had also placed rockwine carafes generously around the table. Van saw a servant pour Diamonfitz for a guest and inwardly gagged, remembering her past unpleasant experience with the drink.

She chose a dish made with red rice, squash, and beans that tasted so delicious she wanted to focus on eating and nothing else. Etiquette ingrained in her by Genie forced Van to turn her attention away from her meal and to the conversation going on around her.

"I don't care about those with weak immune systems," said Hutriel.

"Easy for you to say," said Ferox. "Since the Tarcs show immunity to the demon illness."

"We're not immune," said Hutriel. "We fight all. Even disease." He flexed his biceps, almost elbowing Van in the face. "Fighting is the way. Fighting is always the way."

Since Van was seated next to Hutriel, she politely asked him some questions about himself.

"Where are you from?"

Hutriel took a long gulp from his cup, then answered. "The mountains."

"Where's that?"

He didn't answer.

"Is this your first time at Balefire?"

He shoveled a scoopful of meat into his mouth.

"It's spectacular, don't you think?"

"I think... I need more *rum*," he bellowed, then engaged in a conversation with Ferox and other nearby male guests.

Van remained pleasant, despite the boorish behavior by the Tarc. She couldn't wait for dinner to be over.

The guests pounded drink after drink. Mead, wine, rum, Diamonfitz. The dinner party that began as stuffy and reserved turned into an all-out tumultuous affair. Including loose lips speaking about topics normally taboo, like religion and politics.

Ferox rose from his chair.

"Where are you going?" asked Van, terrified he would leave her there alone with the horrid dinner guests.

"It's necessary. No one may get up or leave until I'm finished eating. The proper way for me to show I'm done is to leave my seat and circulate." Ferox smiled at her. "You'll be fine." He excused himself and began meandering around the table, chatting with guests.

Some men, probably other royals related to Ferox, followed Ferox's lead and rose from the table.

Eventually, more guests left their seats. Some accumulated by the fully stocked bar. Others went to the tables set up along the wall serving extra desserts and a hot, dark liquid that reminded Van of coffee.

Feeling drained, Van stayed seated. She overheard several guests mention the games and thought it odd for people at Balefire to speak about Lodian customs. How did they even know about the Jaychund games?

Merloc and Solana interrupted Van's musings by coming over to "be social."

Merloc and Hutriel chatted with each other, leaving Van to pick up a conversation with Solana. Instead of asking her what murderous plot she had planned, Van said, "This was a lovely dinner."

"Really?" said Solana. "Then you weren't paying attention."

"Meaning?"

"If you had a brain, you'd be more observant," she said with a smile, so any onlookers, like Ferox, would think they were exchanging pleasantries like good friends. "There's more here than meets the eye. As you will soon find out."

Everything the princess said sounded like a threat. Of course, Ferox wasn't around to hear it. But... now that Solana mentioned secret goings-on in the palace, Van became aware of the unusual amount of visiting royals, wellborns, and Tarcs. She originally thought the evening's event was because of protocol for her visit. Now, she realized not all the guests were at the palace for her welcome dinner.

Van's cheeks flared. "Why don't you just tell me what's going on?"

"What fun would that be, silly girl?" drawled Solana.

"Does Ferox know?"

Solana shrugged, meaning yes, but she wouldn't say so.

"Hey, you. Girl," Hutriel barked at Van. "Are you contaminated by the filthy terrigens your kind protects?"

"What?" For a second, Van thought he was asking her about the secret at Balefire.

"You have no reason to fear terrigens." Brux had left his seat and come to the head of the table. He said to Van, "Some Bales are afraid they'll become polluted if they set foot in the Earth World."

Van was thankful to see him and also wished Ferox would return.

"I, for one, fear nothing," said Merloc. "It is our duty as Bales to control all creatures, even terrigens."

"I will join you in the Earth World, my friend," said Hutriel. "We will take care of the filthy terrigens together."

"They aren't bothering anyone," said Van. "Just leave them alone."

"Terrigens will get sick of living in their miserable world," said Merloc. "They will morph into demons and rise here. Attempt to kill our beloved king and take over our lands."

Brux shook his head. "That won't happen."

"It's written in our *Sanctus Novus*," said Solana.

Ferox rejoined the group, bringing Ixl with him.

"We're all interconnected," said Brux. "Causing harm to the terrigens will cause harm to us, to you."

"Both the Lodian's *Victus Opuseulus* and our text claim there is one power," said Ferox. "We have similarities, let's focus on those."

Van's insides swirled with happy tingles at both Ferox's knowledge of the Lodian's belief system and his timely return to support her.

"One power means we don't exist individually," said Ixl.

Merloc snorted in disagreement. "That kind of talk means you're soft."

"The one power is that of our great king, King Nequus!" Hutriel banged his cup on the table. "Our Creator chose him to carry the light with the responsibility of sharing it with all. The light of the sun runs through his veins!"

"There is only one power," said Ixl. "That of the Creator."

"We believe in maintaining a balance with all things," said Brux. "Elementals, terrigens, vichors… all tribes. Living beings must work together as one to please the Creator."

"Let us think about that as we enjoy our time together," said Ferox.

No one dared counter the crown prince. Instead, Hutriel, Solana, and Merloc glared at Van. Their intense stares told Van they suspected she had poisoned Ferox's mind with her Lodian magic. Tension thickened the air, despite the party-induced camaraderie.

Van considered their reactions, trying to figure out what was going on with them. Merloc, being upset that Van might have poisoned Ferox's mind, meant he was okay being an underking, marrying his cousin Solana, and letting Ferox inherit the kingdom. Solana, on the other hand, should be glad Van had poisoned Ferox's mind, because it would make him easy to usurp.

She drew one certain conclusion about their reactive pause.

Ferox talking about Lodian beliefs made him look weak in the eyes of the people closest to him.

"I agree with my brother," said Solana, cheerily raising a glass of rockwine. "Let us enjoy the night. It's not like we live forever."

Solana's fake reform didn't fool Van. She hadn't forgotten the princess's deepest desire. To become immortal and rule the worlds for eternity.

Hutriel took another chug of rum. Solana threw him a look.

"Enough." He slammed the cup on the table. "Time for some celicap." He lumbered over to the side table with the dark liquid.

"Excuse us for a minute, will you?" Ferox put his arm around Van's waist and led her away from the others.

"How are you doing?" he asked. "Are you having a good time?"

"Yes, of course," lied Van, not wanting to spoil his good mood. "Thank you for the wonderful dinner."

"You're so welcome. I'm glad you got to meet most of my family. They really like you."

Van found that hard to believe. "I was happy to have met them."

Ferox told Van about all the great things his relatives were doing for their citizens. He talked about their generosity and how they were living up to their duty, upholding the Moor name, honoring his father. They were doing right by their people with infrastructure projects, technological advancements in energy, charity work.

While she listened to him excitedly share insider details, her pulse quickened as a profound realization struck her. Solana wasn't the one causing problems between them. *It was his entire family.*

Raised voices came from the head of the table, prompting her and Ferox to rejoin the others. Tempers flared.

"Bales are susceptible to falling into the shadows," said Ixl. "Evil tempts you because you don't know how to handle the darkness of night, you fear it."

"Both tribes believe in the light as a reflection of the Creator," said Ferox, trying to calm things down.

"Yes, the light of the moon," said Ixl, his voice rising.

"The light of the sun," barked Merloc.

"How can you reflect the light of the Creator?" asked Ixl. "When your people are constantly trying to break Manik's law so you can invade our land and kill the terrigens."

"Terrigens are demons in the making," said Hutriel. "We must eliminate them for the safety of our world." He refilled his cup from a tin kettle on the table in front of him. The liquid was so thick and dark it looked like espresso mixed with chocolate syrup.

"They're innocent and we must protect them," said Brux.

"Innocent?" drawled Solana. "They're so violent and out of control they morph into demons."

"That's not true," said Ixl through a clenched jaw.

"Terrigens' negative energy generates demons," said Ferox. "That's a fact of nature."

"Whose side are you on?" asked Van.

Ferox frowned at Van. "There are no sides."

"Bah! The best way to lead is by firm rule." Hutriel chugged another celicap, the official coffee of the Living World. He had to be on his tenth cup, at least.

"The Creator speaks through our mighty king," said Merloc. "It's in the people's best interest to be told what to do by us."

"Prophets talk about a split among royals, signifying the coming of a new cosmic cycle," said Ixl. "It begins with a battle between blood, perhaps cousins. Despite your talk, maybe you're not okay with Ferox ascending to the throne instead of you."

"How dare you question my loyalty!" Merloc slammed his fist against the table, shaking glassware to the far end. He lunged at Ixl.

CHAPTER

EIGHTEEN

Efore appeared at the door to the dining hall, wringing her hands.

The head butler ushered Van, Suixsha, Daisy, and Paley to the doorway immediately after the room burst into an all-out brawl.

Crashing of furniture, breaking of glass, and angry shouts echoed throughout the hall. A mob of women and a few guys made a mad dash for the exit.

"I want stay and fight," said Suixsha.

"No, no. This is no place for ladies." Efore shuffled them into the departing crowd. "We must get back to the suite."

Ferox, Brux, Kopius, and Ixl stayed to either help break up the fight or join in.

"Aw." Paley pouted as the girls dashed up a back stairway. "I was enjoying my forest jelly bonbon."

"We can't fight in these dresses, anyway." Van glanced down at her puffy skirt.

"I think that's done on purpose," said Daisy. "To restrain us."

"I had fun until the brawl. Didn't you?" asked Paley.

"It was interesting," said Van. "But not fun."

"What caused it?" asked Paley. "Was Ixl being a jerk?"

"Balish ego caused the fight, no doubt," said Daisy.

"Yup, to both," said Van.

"Good warriors willing to fight if need be," said Suixsha. "But fight is last resort."

"Not when there's free-flowing rum," said Van.

Efore opened the door to their rooms and made sure they had everything they needed. "Due to security concerns, please stay in your suite." She gave them a curt nod and left.

"I train as spiritual warrior," Suixsha said to Van. "I willing to stand ground. Protect sacred within. Gain balance through harmony with surrounding. Maintain power in firm and quiet way."

"Yup. It's all about power." Van punched the air like she was boxing. "The power of fists."

"Brute force is never match for spiritual strength." Suixsha disappeared into her bedroom.

Van looked at Daisy and Paley, hoping for some conversation. "Solana practically told me outright there's something strange going on in the palace. Anyone else pick up weird vibes?"

"Nothing weirder than normal." Daisy yawned. "It's been a long day. I'm going to bed." She excused herself and went into her bedroom.

Paley yawned, too. "Night."

Though exhausted, Van was too antsy to sleep. She went to the bathroom in her room, thrilled it had a big shower. One with a sliding glass door, and could fit about ten people.

As water sprayed her body from the multiple shower spouts, she imagined it cleaning away the evening's negativity. She worried about Brux and how he, Kopius, and Ixl were faring against the Tarcs and the Balish. Despite Efore's request for them to stay in the suite, Van considered going back to the dining hall to check on them. The sweet rose scent of the soap and the warm shower stream lured her into a calmed state and the idea faded from her thoughts.

After her shower, she found a silky nightgown in the walk-in closet, threw it on, and tucked into the luxurious, king-sized bed.

Her head rested on the fluffy, over-sized pillow, and she drifted into a light sleep.

A NOISE WOKE VAN. Someone was creeping around her bedroom.

The intruder's footsteps inched closer. Her untouched backpack lay on the floor near the bureau. No matter, it held nothing she could use to defend herself. The palace guards had confiscated their weapons on arrival. She tensed, ready to unleash her hand-to-hand combat skills.

"Van," whispered a male voice.

She snapped upright. "Ferox?"

"Shh. Yes." He sat on the edge of her bed. "Let's not wake the others."

"What's wrong? Why—"

"I came to see how you're feeling about what happened at dinner," he said. "I wanted to make sure you're okay... that we're okay."

"The fight... are *you* okay?"

He nodded. "So are your teammates."

His musky scent amplified his masculinity, igniting Van into a state of frenzied desire. She wanted to wrap her arms around him and kiss his gorgeous face. Instead, she recalled her conversation with Solana and reeled in her passion. "Is something going on in the palace I should know about?"

"Like what? Balefire is the working administrative headquarters of our monarchy. There're lots of state, local, and municipal issues that are being dealt with on any given day—"

"Why are so many Tarcs here? There's a bunch of your extended family and officials in the palace, too. I know they all didn't come to welcome me."

"Is that what's upsetting you?"

Van shrugged.

"They're here for the games. Been here for months."

If the Balish wanted to copy their Jaychund games, Van thought it a compliment. Why would Solana think it would upset her? As long as Van didn't have to compete, she could live with it.

"It's a Tarc tradition. They usually hold the games in Kezef. This year we're honoring their tribe by holding them at Balefire. It's for Tarcs only. No humans are allowed to play, the matches are too rough."

"Sounds lovely." Van gave him an eye roll.

Ferox chuckled. "I've never seen any. The crowds love 'em, I heard. Other tribes travel to Kezef to watch them. Tarc warriors practice for nine months, hoping to be chosen. Games last for three. It's considered an honor to compete. The winner moves up in status, gets his pick of breeding partners."

"Again, lovely tribe."

"My father insists we build an alliance with them." He peered at her. "You sure that's the only thing bothering you?"

Van paused before answering, allowing herself time to choose her words. She decided not to bring up her concerns about his sister because it might cause too much friction between them. "Why do you trust Merloc? How do you know he and his father aren't planning a takeover of the throne?"

"My father vouches for him and Uncle Maddy," said Ferox. "Says they're keeping a family secret. About something that happened a long time ago, but one that could hurt my father." Ferox held up a palm. "I don't know what it is. My father didn't tell me."

Van stared at him.

"Come here." Ferox enveloped her in a hug.

All Van's worries faded once his warm, solid body pressed against hers.

"As confident as I might seem," Ferox whispered into her ear. "I was a little nervous about you meeting my family. I'm pleased it worked out."

"Mmhm," murmured Van, lost in the woodsy scent of his skin and hair.

"I'm so grateful you're in my life," he said. "I want to arrange permanent rooms for you here so you can visit whenever you want. If you'd like that."

"Oh, I'd like that," said Van.

Ferox released his arms just enough to make room to press his lips against hers.

His kiss set Van's body aflame.

They broke apart and silently gazed into each other's eyes through the darkness.

Van could no longer fight the fiery passion burning inside her. She reached for Ferox, and he reciprocated.

They wrapped themselves in each other. Van wanted to be as physically close to him as possible, to push away all outside interference. In a steamy burst, they created their own intimate microcosm.

Afterward, they lay in bed cuddling, skin dewy and flushed.

Van lazily ran her fingertips back and forth over Ferox's bare chest. "I really wish I got to meet your father."

"Next time." Ferox tightened his arms around her. "I wish I could've met your father. From what I heard, he was a good man."

"He was," said Van with the familiar heartache that comes from the loss of a loved one. It made her anger at Solana burn hot again. "You know... my father and your brother were both in Tipereth Forest when Solana's demons attacked and killed them. She manifested them by connecting to a master demon."

"Yeah," said Ferox. "My sister was lost for a bit. She's redeeming herself."

"The magic Solana used that night might have cracked the third seal," said Van.

Ferox took a deep breath and let it out slowly, as if taking the time to prepare his response. "Solana admitted to dabbling with dark magic. She made up the master demon, trying to make herself sound important. *But,* if it's real, my soldiers will deal with it. Let's just check the seal and take it from there."

"Should we bring the Coin?" Van half-suspected Solana had already stolen it and delivered it to her dark master. "Where is it anyway?"

Ferox gave her a side-glance. "Safe."

Against her will, his short answer made her question his loyalty. Her insecurities came rushing back. If it ever came down to a choice, Van still wondered if Ferox would choose Van and love, or his family and power.

"When we head out to check the seal," said Van. "We need to search for our missing team."

"Yeah, Uxa told me about that." Ferox rolled onto his side and gazed at her. "It's awful. I'll help in any way I can to find them."

"Thanks. I want to keep my eye out for the Runestar, too." Van still hoped to wrap up the mission quickly and spend the rest of the time strengthening her connection with Ferox, his family, and the Balish people.

He raised an eyebrow. "The rebels believe the charmed Runestar will return to Goustav's true heir."

Van thought hard, combing through every piece of jewelry she owned, and shook her head. "Well, I don't have it, so we know that's not true. Anyway, if I find it, I'll return it to his heirs... your family."

"No." Ferox shook his head. "You're his true heir. No secrets. I want the Runestar to point to you in front of the rebels and the council."

"Why? It would mess up things between our tribes, including us."

Ferox grinned. "Because then we could openly declare our relationship and my people would support it."

Van's heart whirled. She gave him a lingering kiss and made a mental to note to let Brux know he was wrong about Ferox being a danger to her.

"Come to think of it," said Ferox. "I heard rumors the Runestar is in Aduro."

CHAPTER

NINETEEN

Ferox slipped from Van's bedroom at the first light of dawn. She would've preferred he left before anyone else had woken, but the murmurings of conversation between Suixsha, Daisy, Paley, and Ferox reached her ears. Then, the soft close of the suite's door as Ferox left.

With her teammates awake and starting their day, guilt made Van want to get up and join them. She stretched and yawed... just needed to shut her eyes for a bit first.

VAN WOKE AN HOUR LATER. She had dreamt about the little blond girl again. The one who reached to the night sky and caught a falling star. She shrugged it off and wandered into the kitchen area. Paley and Daisy sat at the dining table, chatting.

"Well, good morning!" said Paley with a knowing smile. She had changed her contacts to yellow cat's eyes. "And how was your night? Sleep well?"

Van blushed and refused to meet their eyes. She also couldn't wipe the stupid grin off her face.

127

"I'm so happy for the two of you," said Daisy.

Paley winked at Van. "You can tell me later."

"There's oatmeal and fresh fruit. Efore brought it up early this morning." Daisy waved her hand at the kitchen area. She had a fruit stone in front of her that looked like a peach pit. Not a filling breakfast.

"Something up with you and Kopius?" Van asked Daisy. Her gut told her something was off with them.

Daisy cast her eyes down, causing her fine white-blond hair to cover part of her face as if using it to hide. The ends brushed against her thighs as she shook her head.

"Suixsha went outside to work out," said Paley.

"In this heat?" Van opened the refrigerator looking for something to drink.

"Hey, Van." Paley came into the kitchen area. "I want to talk to you about something."

Van threw her a look.

"No." Paley shook her head. "Not about you and Ferox."

"Okay, talk."

"I want you to know I have your back."

Van closed the refrigerator door and turned to give her friend full attention. "What?"

"I wanted to make it clear because of... you know, all the stuff with Brux and my weird behavior when I was sick last year."

"Yeah... okay." Van never once considered a demon-free Paley not having her back.

"I haven't forgotten about finding a counter-curse, either," said Paley. "I'll help you with that."

"What brought this on?"

"I just feel like..." Paley shrugged. "I don't want you to have any doubts about me, is all."

"Thanks," said Van, feeling closer than ever to her best friend. She made a bowl of cold oatmeal with some nut milk, grabbed a peach, and sat at the table.

"Did Ferox mention what time we're leaving?" asked Daisy.

Van had to think about it. "Not really. He said he needed to take care of some things and gather his men."

Paley threw her shoulders back. "I'm ready."

"Ready for what?" Kopius entered the suite and kissed the top of Daisy's head. "I came to check on my baby."

Brux trailed behind Kopius. Van caught his eye. "Did you come to check on your baby, too?"

"Not funny," said Brux.

Paley giggled.

Ixl barged into the room, half dressed with a gleaming, freshly cleansed, bare chest. A towel hung around his neck, partially covering the portal burns on his torso.

"It's day three. The clock's ticking." Ixl sat himself down at the dining table like he owned the place. "So what's the game plan?" He propped his bare foot on his opposing thigh, pulled a kitchen knife from his back pocket, and began cleaning his toenails.

"Um, couldn't you have finished that in your room?" asked Paley.

"And miss this parche? No way." Ixl ran the blade under the nail of his big toe.

Instead of being repulsed, seeing his quirk caused a pang in Van's heart. It reminded her of Jorie and how much her former teammate had loved Zachery, her war axe. Jorie had hated when Van called Zachery an axe. "It's a labrys," she would say. The memory of Jorie's words and her subsequent death made Van's chest ache more and underscored the dangerousness of their missions.

"When we heading out?" asked Kopius.

"After lunch, I think," said Van.

"We have some time then," said Brux. "Let's use it to explore the palace."

"Yay!" Paley clapped her hands. "Let's go snoop around."

"We can meet back here for lunch," said Brux. "Grab a quick one and then head out with Ferox."

"Maybe we can find clues about who the spy is," said Daisy. "Or what happened to the other team."

Van quickly finished her oatmeal. "Shouldn't we get Suixsha first?"

"Nope. She's not here, that's on her." Ixl smashed the used knife down on the table and leaped from his chair.

"Where do you think Suixsha's tyger is?" asked Paley.

Daisy closed her eyes and breathed in through her nose. "He's nearby. I can sense him."

Ixl gave her an eye roll that, by the look on his face, didn't sit well with Kopius. Ixl sauntered back to his suite across the hall to finish getting dressed.

"We can split into teams of two," said Brux. "I'll go with Van."

"You forgetting something, mate?" asked Kopius.

"You have to stay with Paley because of the Twin Gemstones," said Daisy.

Brux's face tightened. "Then the three of us will go together."

They squabbled long enough for Ixl to return, dressed and ready to go. "Teams of two make more sense. We can cover more ground. We're doing that."

"I know you feel the need to protect Van," Kopius said to Brux. "But Paley's your girl this time."

Brux snorted in frustration, then accepted his assignment with a curt nod.

"Keep a low profile in case the Bales are no fresco with us wandering about," said Ixl.

Paley and Brux paired off, as did Van and Ixl, and Kopius and Daisy. The three teams left the suite. Van overheard Paley say to Brux, "The palace has a room filled with records. Maybe there's a list of all the babies lost to the Janus monster. I can find something about my birth parents."

Brux grunted his approval, and the teams headed in different directions.

Ixl and Van passed through several atriums and wandered down hallways.

Every time someone passed them—palace guard, person, or Tarc —Ixl instructed Van to duck and hide.

"Why are you so paranoid?" Van found his behavior irritating. "We don't have to hide from every single person who walks by."

"My mother's training. Ingrained in me since birth," he said, unabashedly. "One of my skills is strategic military maneuvers."

"We're safe here, under Ferox's protection."

"Maybe," said Ixl, as they continued exploring the hallway.

"I don't think we'll need military strategies," said Van. "This mission is mostly diplomatic. And to check the seal."

"That would be a shame." Ixl peeked into a room to see if it warranted an investigation.

"And why is that?" asked Van, already tired of his company.

He grinned at her. "Because you wouldn't get to see my favorite tactic. Called the hammer and anvil."

"Oh, boy. Tell me more," deadpanned Van.

"It's usually confused with a single envelopment."

"I didn't mean for you actually tell me."

"Well, then you shouldn't have asked."

Ixl kept talking as they continued down the hallway, like he was testing himself to make sure he knew the answer. "It's an encirclement where one group keeps the enemy occupied, weakening them from the front, while the other group delivers a blowing force from behind."

Van didn't find the information useful or interesting. But Ixl gave her a glimpse of what his childhood was like being raised by his mom. She pictured Uxa feeding him nails for breakfast, molding him from birth to be militant through and through.

Ixl stopped. He motioned for them to duck behind a nearby pillar.

They crouched as a yoke of Tarcs passed by.

"Certainly a lot of them roaming about," whispered Ixl.

"They're here for their games, like a rougher version of our Jaychund," said Van.

They re-emerged from behind the pillar.

Van, being stuck with him, made the best of it. "Let's go outside to the festival. We can blend into the crowd. Sound good?"

Ixl agreed.

The closer they got to the main entrance of Balefire Palace, the hallways and atriums became more crowded, making it virtually impossible for them to keep ducking and hiding. Ixl and Van took the risk of being seen, and bounded down the outdoor main stairs and into the festival with no issues.

They walked past colorful concession tents. Van knew from her arrival yesterday that the festival sprawled all the way to the wall enclosing the palace grounds.

Townspeople, young and old, officials, both humans and Tarcs, dressed in neatly pressed tunic style clothes or in loose robes, wandered around in a well-behaved, orderly manner. Van saw little hugging, hand clasping, or touching of one another.

Sun replicas dominated the fair's decorations, and many vendors had variations of suns for sale. Stuffed suns, papier-mâché suns, metal or wooden suns. Suns on pins, wall hangings, pillows, sticks...

Venders also sold: dazzling handmade jewelry with gorgeous colorful stones set in gold; statues, mostly of animals or suns, to display in yards or smaller ones for home decoration; meticulously carved wooden boxes with detailed inlays; Balish flags with the red, gold, and black royal insignia.

They stopped in a tent to poke around. Every item Van picked up —mugs, pictures, pins, shirts—had an image of the current royal family on them, or one member separately. Some had depictions of the ancient King Goustav or of Nequus's deceased father, King Xavier. Many patrons happily parted with their coins to get the merchandise. If Van had any Living World money on her, she probably would've bought a mug plastered with Ferox's face.

"Most of their culture seems to be propaganda about how great the Moors are," Ixl muttered to Van.

They moved deeper into the fair and passed by tents offering food. Hunks of meat on sticks, colorful fruit kabobs, and sugary dessert treats were popular. One tent with a long line offered icy-cold snow cones.

"Hey, over here." Ixl called Van over to a tent selling sweets. "You want to get something?"

Van practically drooled over the flakey pastries, thickened milk puddings, fruit cake bars, and frosted cookies.

"Nah, I'm good." Van again regretted having no money with her. She wandered to the next tent and looked through their beautifully handcrafted blouses.

Ixl came over, in each hand he held a treat bag filled with bite-sized, crispy dumplings drizzled with a thick, yellow syrup.

They looked delicious. It didn't surprise Van he bought two for himself.

"Lokma." He handed one bag to Van. "They're great. Take it. I figured you didn't have any money, so... it's no problem."

"Thanks," said Van, touched at his unexpected thoughtfulness.

They meandered by an area where kids were playing a game. One was blindfolded and had to "hunt" the other kids, tagging them once found. Another play area had a large wooden board game on the ground where the kids took turns using their hands to slide discs into pockets, like an enormous version of air hockey.

The children's games were close to the mead hut, where many male adults stood drinking from mugs and chatting. Women gathered in their own area, sitting at tables, sipping an orange-colored liquid in tall glasses poured from icy pitchers. They talked with each other while casually weaving chunky strands of garland. Mostly with black, red, and gold threads, and one other color per strand. Van figured the garlands were used to decorate their homes for the holiday.

More than a few of them gazed at Van and Ixl as they meandered past the mead hut.

Ixl glanced at Van's head. "We need to get you a hat or scarf. Something to cover your hair."

"Why?" Van ran her hand over her fine, blond locks, paranoid the desert air made it look frizzy.

"We're getting too many stares. It's like waving a flag that you're Lodian."

"Oh, right." The Balish had a more swarthy appearance and the Tarcs, well, they were enormous and looked like humanoid oxen. "Your Latin vibe gets you by, but your blue eyes are a dead give-a-way that you're not from around here either."

He grinned. "We're two odd ducks."

They scooted into the nearest tent. Van breathed in the welcoming scent of ylang-ylang. Scarves, incense, oils, candles, and, impressively, books were displayed for sale.

"Happy Kupalle," greeted the proprietor on their entrance.

Noises from the festival filtered into the tent, but only a few other shoppers had wandered inside. Ixl walked past the scarf bins to bookcases set aside for what Van figured were rare texts based on the quality and age of their bindings.

"We fully register all our books with the Balish Royal Court. They come with papers," said the proprietor.

Van perused the pretty handmade scarves. She picked up a colorful rose and gold one. The luxurious material felt soft and fine against her fingers.

After looking through the scarfs for a few minutes, she decided on one with a blue thread weaved into it, to match her eyes. Then tossed it back, thinking it wasn't a good idea to enhance her Lodian-blue eyes. She settled on a more traditionally colored black, red, and gold scarf.

She wandered over to Ixl, who appeared absorbed in a book. The proprietor hovered, keeping a sharp eye on him to make sure he didn't damage, or steal, the valuable text.

"It's about war strategies," Ixl said to Van, flipping through the fragile parchment pages.

"Written in the language of the ancients, a thousand years ago," said the proprietor. "By our revered King Goustav. A hundred percent authentic."

"You can read the ancient language?" Van asked Ixl.

"My mother taught me." Ixl kept his focus on the book.

"Check to see if he mentions the hammer and anvil," teased Van.

Ixl pulled his attention away from the pages and stared at Van, grinning. "Hey, you paid attention."

"We have others," the proprietor said to Van, a potential double-sale gleamed in his eyes.

Van looked at the bookshelf. She pulled out a text that discussed symbolism in the *Sanctus Novus* and put it back. Then, flipped through another about King Nequus's insights into managing daily responsibilities.

"Written by the king himself," said the proprietor. "One of a kind."

Van tucked it back into the shelf.

"Do you have a particular interest?" asked the proprietor.

"Authentic stories about Goustav during the Great War," said Van.

"When he was a prince. Yes, of course." The proprietor beamed. "I have some books... ah!" He pulled one from the shelf titled *Sand Tribe: the Brethren of Purity* and handed it to Van.

"Also written in the language of the ancients," he said. "By Azamere, the palace wizard at the time."

As Van read the book, she learned that in ancient times, before the Dark War, the Balish were known as the Sand Tribe. It made sense, given that Aduro was mostly desert land.

Azamere's musings mentioned the properties of the Staff of Fire. No surprise, it provided troops with fire. Giving them warmth, the ability to cook food, and light so soldiers could see in the dark. A more subtle feature gave the user energy, physical strength, and increased will power. The holder could use the power of the Staff to ignite troops with the desire, passion, and perseverance needed to win each battle.

Van's pull to retrieve the Staff surged. She tore her eyes from the text and took in a deep breath. She paused for a moment, then read more.

Azamere advised never using the Staff against other people. He discouraged using its abilities in a battle against human enemies due to the Staff's shadow side, or negative attributes.

He wrote the Staff corrupts those not able to handle its power. When used incorrectly, against the will of the Creator, passion and desire turns to anger; energy to exhaustion; peace to war. Victory to defeat.

The wizard also warned about the destructive properties of fire. If used carelessly, flames will burn the wielder of the Staff. He compared its power to a raging fire. Both could get out of control, destroying everything in their path, with no distinction between good and bad.

Van glanced up to check and see if her immersion in the book bothered anyone. No one appeared to be paying attention to her, other than the proprietor. She flipped through the pages and found a reference about the seals that bound the worlds. It revealed the location of the third seal. In the deep south, a place called Muspell. She frowned at another passage. About three *somethings*... not seals... but related to the seals... Van couldn't interpret the translation.

She felt it important enough to have Ixl take a look.

"Hey." She kept her eyes on the book while stretching her hand to tap Ixl's shoulder. Her bare skin accidentally brushed against the text he was reading.

All faded to black as Goustav wrenched Van back to his time...

CHAPTER
TWENTY

Van felt the weight of the Staff as Prince Goustav gripped it in his hand.

He skillfully blocked the swing of an enemy's sword, pivoted, and smashed the bottom end into his opponent's gut. The man doubled over. Goustav twirled the Staff and drove its pointed top through his enemy's head.

Goustav surveyed the battlefield. Through his eyes, Van saw dead bodies blanketing the ground. Their blood filled her nostrils with the sickly smell of iron, sweat, and fear. Balish soldiers checked the wounded for survivors and drove swords through their chests to ensure they would not rise again. All those from the other tribe, the Silver Tribe, must die.

He clasped his prized war Staff, chest high, and gazed over his fallen enemies. Their deaths meant victory for him.

A buzzing sound came near his ear. An insect darted back and forth around this head. He swatted at the noise. The bug squeaked. A faery gnat. Not an insect, a messenger.

The tiny, black, insect-like human with wings of a fly whirred around his ear.

"Go on," growled Goustav.

The faery gnat crawled into his ear canal and spoke in his brother Manik's voice.

"Father is ill. I fear he may pass in the night. There are urgent family matters we must discuss. Return home posthaste."

After delivering the message, the faery gnat flew away.

Goustav shook his head in disgust and muttered, "Couldn't even tell me his whereabouts for the past several months. Now he calls me home."

The vision blurred, and Van found herself at Balefire Palace. It looked remarkably similar to present-day.

"Our father would never agree to such heresy." Goustav raged.

His heart ached over returning home to find his father had passed away. According to Manik, their father had died from a "broken heart" over the murder of his wife, their mother, Queen Helena.

"If Magdalene was here, she would understand," said Manik, his eyes red and swollen from tears over his father's death.

"Our sister would take your side as twins often do for each other," said Goustav. "Yet Magdalene stayed in battle, rather than come running home at your request like I did. Only to hear nonsense sputter from your mouth."

"In truth, father agreed to the truce between our tribe and Lodian Tribe," said Manik.

"Bah. You can use fancy words for the Silver Tribe, but it doesn't—"

"He gave his formal blessing for my wedding to Princess Zurial."

"Never would father betray us or his tribe in that way. It goes against everything he stood for in life."

"He changed after mother's death."

"Bah!"

Manik faced Goustav. "I am now king. I command you to comply with the terms of the truce. That includes welcoming Zurial into our family."

Goustav grunted, the best he could muster. His duty required him to accept the king's wishes. He learned Manik had recovered the Sword of Swords but his brother had let the silver witch Zurial take the Cup of Life.

If Manik had secured both the Sword and the Cup, the Balish could have swiftly won the war. Three Items against one. The Coin of Creation held by the Silver Tribe would pose no match.

Goustav listened to his brother blather on about balance and harmony between the two tribes, becoming more certain with every word that Zurial had cast a spell on Manik, bewitching his weak-minded brother. A more distressing thought occurred to him. Zurial's spell also might have compelled Manik to murder their father.

As Manik's brother and defender of the kingdom, Goustav took it upon himself to set things right.

The vision blurred again as Goustav carried Van forward in time.

Goustav paced, twirling the Staff.

"My king, what troubles you?" asked a man with a goatee and long black hair, wearing a purple and gold robe. The place wizard.

"Magdalene along with Manik's followers helped my brother escape from the dungeon," said Goustav. "I planned to hold Manik until we killed the silver witch, thus freeing him from her spell so he could return to his normal state of mind. Then we could have crushed the Silver Tribe and their allies out of existence." Goustav stopped pacing and stared at the wizard. "My sister claims my ego has led me to commit treason. What say you?"

"There are sacred writings that enlighten us about corruption to the mind caused by over-use of the Staff of Fire," said the wizard.

"Nonsense." Goustav snorted. "My siblings have sided against me, against the kingdom." He began pacing again. "My brother took the Sword when he fled. Now the Lodians have three Items of Creation. You must help me tap into the Staff's full powers. Help me win this war for the Balish kingdom."

"Only the Anchoress can safely access the Staff's full abilities," said the wizard.

Goustav swung the Staff and held its tip to the wizard's throat.

"L-let me check the Book of Instruction," said the wizard. "The ancient writings have many references to magical weapons."

"That's better." Goustav lowered the Staff.

The palace wizard scurried to a nearby shelf and grabbed a bound parchment book. He held it in the crook of his arm and turned pages with trembling fingers.

"Ah yes," said the wizard. "There is a key that opens the door to an army of dark creatures brought from the depths of the earth into our light. One can open the door using this spell with any Item of Creation."

"An army?"

"But." The wizard held up his index finger. "The writings warn against this. It says a horrible aberration will follow the army and seek to consume all light. To unlock this army of darkness... requires a blood sacrifice." The wizard met Goustav's eyes. "The very act of opening the door will further corrupt your soul. It is an incorrect use of the Staff's power."

"Further corrupt?" Goustav raised his brow.

"Misuse of the Staff is already compromising you. Starting when you used it to kill the Lodian's Queen Cordelia. It is my duty as advisor to the kingdom to tell you I believe the Staff is bringing out your dark side, your deepest insecurities, and is causing you to make rash decisions."

"I appreciate your advice," said Goustav with a tight-lipped smile. "And your bravery."

The wizard quavered under his unblinking stare.

"I can control any army." Goustav raised the Staff, gripping it with white knuckles. "And any aberration that follows them here. This army, along with my Staff, will make me invincible!"

"And the sacrifice?" The wizard's eyes belied the truth he didn't wish to face.

Goustav's stare turned even colder. He pointed the tip of the Staff at the wizard. "Do it."

Goustav's message ended, and he released Van.

She opened her eyes and sat upright, rubbing her head in the spot where it had hit the ground.

Ixl knelt next to her. "I don't really like you doing that."

"Right?" Van massaged her aching shoulder.

The proprietor and his wife hovered over them. The wife held a wooden tray with a tin teapot and matching cups.

"How are you feeling?" asked the proprietor. "Have something to drink. It's the heat."

"I'm okay," said Van.

Ixl helped her to her feet and kept his arm firmly wrapped around her waist.

Van stared at him. "You can let me go. I won't drop again."

Ixl snapped back his hand, acting as if she implied his touch had been inappropriate.

"Why don't you sit on the cushions for a while," said the proprietor, in a tone that indicated he wanted Van to leave as soon as possible.

"No, I'm good. But thank you." Van went to leave, then stopped and turned around to face the proprietor. "Tell me something, after the Dark War, why didn't Goustav kill his brother Manik?"

"What? Oh, of course." The proprietor wrung his hands, probably to keep them from pushing her out of the tent. "They had a binding magical pact, sealed with blood."

"A blood oath?" asked Ixl.

The proprietor nodded. "Then, our great King Goustav single-handedly battled the demons and saved our world."

"I want the real story." Van swooshed her hand toward the bookcases. "Having all these books means you've come across other authentic accounts of the Dark War."

Ixl pulled several gold coins from his pocket.

The proprietor looked at his wife. She nodded her approval and went to distract the customers in their shop. He snatched the coins.

"Not the Balish propaganda," warned Ixl.

The proprietor shuffled them over to a corner. "Once Goustav used the Staff of Fire to summon the army of darkness, it quickly became obvious that demons weren't controllable. They attacked Goustav's own soldiers. Those still alive retreated in fear. He used the

Staff to fight the demons but one Item of Creation wasn't powerful enough."

Van remembered reading a passage in Manik's text years ago. "Manik warned that evil incites fighting among humans to gain more power."

The proprietor nodded. "Fighting creates an atmosphere of lack and devastation, which galvanizes someone into using an Item to unleash evil, believing the demons will serve their agenda."

"Lesson learned," said Ixl. "Demons trick ignorant people into releasing them."

"Goustav sought help from Manik," the proprietor continued with his story. "He confessed his mistake and humbly begged his brother for forgiveness and help. Goustav had only wanted control of the kingdom, not to bring about Solmor."

"Knowing you're about to be defeated by an army of demons does that to people," said Ixl.

"Family bonds are strong," said the proprietor. "Manik forgave his brother. He believed the dire circumstances of Solmor had caused Goustav to gain clarity. Manik understood the seriousness of the situation and agreed to let Goustav join sides with him, but not before taking an oath of loyalty to their bloodline. Goustav accepted the terms and the two brothers took the blood oath."

"But he killed Zurial," said Van.

"Goustav was crafty, and the oath was easy for him to accept. He loved Manik. His primary goal remained killing Zurial to remove the curse she had cast on his brother. The oath only applied to their bloodline, not relatives through marriage. But to Manik, the oath solidified their unwavering loyalty and trust of each other."

"Big mistake," said Ixl. "So Manik, Goustav, the Lodians, along with their allies, and the Anchoress, banded together to fight the demon army in what became the Dark War."

"Manik wrote that evil is our own creation," said Van. "It's powerless unless we give it power. His point was not to fight in the first place. Every time darkness rises, the light of the worlds is at risk."

The proprietor glanced at the exit. "You're feeling better?"

Van nodded. "Let's go," she said to Ixl.

As they left the tent, the proprietor muttered to no one in particular, "Foreigners. They can't handle our climate."

"What happened to you in there?" asked Ixl.

Van told him about her ability to get memory engrams. "Proof positive the book you were holding was written by Goustav."

After getting her ancestor's message, Van worried about Ferox's family. She suspected Merloc, along with his cousin-fiancé Solana, were planning a rebellion, a takeover of the kingdom from Ferox, the same way Goustav did to Manik after the Dark War.

"I want to hear more about it," said Ixl. "But, let's get you out of this scorching heat first."

Van began telling Ixl about her glimpse into Goustav's life when they passed the water protestors.

One of them noticed Van, or more likely her blond hair.

"That's her!" screeched one protestor. He pointed at Van, causing everyone in earshot to turn their attention in her direction.

"Let's get her!" cried someone else.

The mob rushed toward them.

Ixl and Van took off in the opposite direction, running out of the fairgrounds and around the side of the palace, frantically searching for an entryway.

They dashed in a side door and stopped on the stairwell's landing to catch their breath.

"I was trying to help them." Van bent over with her hands on her thighs, breathing heavily, face flushed from anger and heat. "I gave them a cure so they wouldn't turn into demons. This is how they repay me?"

"People are idiots." Ixl raised a hand to place on her back in an offer of comfort, then thought better of it and pulled back.

"Can we lock this?" Van tipped her head toward the door. "They could get inside, right?" Her dry throat caused her to cough.

"Already done." Ixl checked the lock on the door handle, just to be sure. "Did you see those guys in the horde? The ones egging on the protestors?"

"Huh?"

"I think they were Anti-Manik Rebels," he said, full of adrenaline from their near escape. "They may believe Goustav's heir is Lodian, so..."

"Then why send the protestors to kill us?"

"I'm not sure, but I think they might've been following us around the festival." He paused for a beat. "Kinda weird, especially since you just got a memory engram from Goustav."

"More dangerous than weird." Van used the back of her hand to wipe sweat from her forehead.

"You seem beat," said Ixl, without derision. "I'll understand if you need to go back to the room."

Van shook her head and raised herself to her full height. "Which way?"

They were presented with two options. One, a large wooden door leading to the main floor of the palace. The other, a stone stairway going into the sub-levels.

"Let's go down," said Ixl, "If I were up to no good, that's where I'd hide stuff."

"Brux and Paley might already be down there," said Van, as they bounded down the stairs. "They mentioned going to the Hall of Records."

Ixl shrugged. "There's more than one restricted room, I'll bet."

Van welcomed the cooler air as they headed deeper into the sub-levels. After the fifth flight down, she thought of Daisy and her kidnapping. "I don't want to go into the dungeons."

Ixl nodded. "Let's stop on this floor."

They crept along a shadowy, tunnel-like hallway. Wall torches hung in sconces, giving off light rather than the elegant gemstones seen in the upper levels of the palace. The hallway dead-ended at an ominous wooden door.

Without hesitation, Ixl tried the handle.

It opened.

TWENTY-ONE

Van and Ixl entered a split-level room dimly lit by torches in wall sconces.

Upside down, painted triangles on the lower level walls reached from floor to ceiling. Several wooden tables had bottles in a variety of sizes spread across them, filled with varied colored liquids, some half-full, some foaming, others thick. Hard-cover texts and strange instruments appeared well used and placed here and there around the room. Some looked like Bunsen burners Van had used in chemistry class.

Several worn apothecary cabinets stood near the tables, most of their many drawers opened, or half-closed. A swirling globe encircled by gold bands hung from the ceiling, along with several massive, multitiered chandeliers that seemed out of place in the room Van now thought of as a lab. Shelves stuffed with books lined the walls along the upper level.

"Welcome to my humble abode." Thuxeor's purple and gold robe swooshed as he opened his arms wide in what Van thought of as a refreshingly friendly gesture.

She glimpsed an alcove off the main room with cushioned

benches and throw pillows. The colors of the room matched the decor of the palace: sand, oranges, gold, and black, with accents of red. Van realized they had entered Thuxeor's living quarters.

"You gonna rat us out?" asked Ixl.

Thuxeor shook his head. "I was expecting you."

"How?" demanded Ixl.

"The All-Seeing Eye." Thuxeor glided his palm toward a table holding a crystal ball with a multi-colored serpent made of smoke swirling inside.

When the wizard mentioned the crystal ball's name, the serpent morphed into an eye for a few seconds, as if it understood the wizard's words.

"You saw us coming?" Van hoped he used the crystal ball responsibly. Like, by not peeping into the bedrooms of guests in the palace. She blushed remembering her and Ferox's encounter last night.

"How may I be of service?" asked Thuxeor.

"What kind of distance you get with that thing?" Ixl glared at the Eye.

Van followed Ixl's line of thinking: the wizard could be the spy. With his All-Seeing-Eye he didn't physically have to be in Lodestar to uncover its secrets.

"Ah." Thuxeor gave them a knowing nod. "The Eye only shows me what I need to see. I can ask it to show me specific events or places, but the spirits who guide the serpent only show me that which is for my highest good. I obtain wisdom which aids me in offering guidance to the king and the royal family."

"So you're able to eavesdrop on Lodian Consilium meetings?" Ixl flexed his muscles, as if ready to drag the wizard back to Lodestar for an interrogation.

Thuxeor grinned. A serpent's smile, just like the one swirling inside the crystal ball. "Of course not. The Eye would never allow it. Also, I cannot see through the veil between the worlds."

Ixl threw him a skeptical grimace. "Use it to tell us who's the spy at Lodestar."

Thuxeor hesitated.

"We think it's someone here, in the palace," said Van. "If you tell us, it'll benefit the royal family by maintaining peace between our tribes."

"Very well." Thuxeor placed his palms on the crystal ball and closed his eyes like he was wordlessly communicating with it. After a moment, he opened his eyes and removed his hands. The smoky eye appeared for a moment and then transformed into a swirling mess that the wizard seemed able to interpret.

"I can tell you this," said Thuxeor. "The spy you seek is destined to bring about Solmor, your Dishora. You cannot prevent it. Any attempt to do so will offend the Creator and bring great misfortune."

"Trying to stop the Escalation to Dishora will cause harm to the royal family?" Van's curiosity surged.

Thuxeor nodded. "That is all I can tell you."

Based on her experience talking with Jacynthia, Van knew she wouldn't get anything more out of him on the subject. He seemed open to another question, so she asked, "A team was sent from Lodestar to find the third seal. Do you know what happened to them?"

The wizard gazed at the swirling smoke inside the crystal ball. "Yes."

Van held her breath, waiting for Thuxeor to elaborate.

"Well?" Ixl tapped his foot.

"The answer lies all around you."

"Why don't you cut the crap and just tell us," said Ixl.

"Your fate... it is set in motion," said the wizard. "It is your destiny to experience the answer, to uncover the mystery for yourselves."

"It would really help if you could at least give us a hint," said Van. "We're short on time."

"Time is irrelevant," said Thuxeor. "Past. Present. Future. All are woven into the tapestry of life, making them one. You already know what happened to the other team. To see it, open your eyes."

Ixl glared at the wizard as Van pondered his answer.

"May I help with anything else?" asked Thuxeor.

"Can you tell us where to find the Runestar?" asked Van. Using the Coin to find it seemed superfluous. Also, probably not a good use of time running around searching for a piece of jewelry instead of focusing on their mission.

Thuxeor sashayed to a table with a small terracotta bowl sitting amongst the vast array of other gadgets, papers, and ampoules. He tossed a few pieces of charcoal into the bowl, grabbed several glass jars, and sprinkled a mixture of incense over it. He struck a match and lit the charcoal.

The cloying scent of the smoldering incense tickled Van's already dry throat. She struggled to stifle a cough.

The wizard dramatically waved his hands to stimulate the rising smoke as he closed his eyes and breathed in. After a long minute, his eyes popped open. "The Runestar cannot be found."

"Why not?" asked Ixl.

"For it is not lost," said Thuxeor.

"Oh, brother," muttered Van. She had planned on asking him a vague *what's going on in the palace?*, but didn't because she knew it would yield no results.

"Let's go," Ixl said to Van, also fed up with the wizard.

Van turned to Thuxeor. "We appreciate your help. Thanks."

"At your service." Thuxeor honored them with a half bow. "Always."

Van and Ixl hurried out of Thuxeor's lab.

"I've had enough adventure for one day," said Van. "Can we go back to the suite?"

"At your service." Ixl mimicked Thuxeor's bow. "Always."

Van laughed and gave him a playful whack on the shoulder.

"It's almost lunchtime," said Ixl. "The others should be on their way back, too."

～

BACK IN THE girl's suite, Van discovered Efore had brought them lunch. All her teammates sat around the dining table, except Ixl, who had returned to the guy's suite, and Suixsha.

"Sorry we didn't wait before we tore in." Paley sat in front of a half-eaten dish of meat chunks and red rice. "We weren't sure when you'd be back."

Brux stood when Van approached the table. "Glad to see you."

"You too." Van noticed his plate was untouched.

"I waited." Brux pulled out the chair next to him for Van.

Kopius shoveled a bite into his mouth. "Didn't want it to get cold."

"Right now, cold sounds good." Van sat in the chair. "Thanks," she said to Brux, then asked the table, "Anyone else go outside to the festival?"

They all began talking at once.

Ixl barged through the door, startling everyone.

"Hey, figured you guys were in here." He carried a platter of what looked like oversized turkey legs. "We got a full spread in our suite too."

"What kind of animal is that?" Daisy eyed the platter and turned a shade paler than usual.

Ixl shrugged as he took a bite. "Dragon?"

Kopius and Paley chuckled.

"Your mother won't be happy about you eating that," said Van, given the Giorgi program required recruits to practice veganism.

"What she doesn't know won't hurt her." Ixl chomped on the meat. He rested the platter on the table and settled into a seat.

"So, Ixl," said Kopius. "You and Van explored outside?"

Ixl and Van recounted their escape from the protestors and their meeting with the wizard. Then Van told them about her memory engram from Goustav.

"He used the Staff to destroy a seal," said Brux. "That's how he released the demon army."

"Most likely the third seal, given its proximity to Balefire," said Kopius.

"Goustav caused the Great War to turn into the Dark War." Paley leaned back in her seat, hands over her full stomach. "See, I pay attention."

"With the war going on, the conditions were right." Daisy stuck her fork into a small scoop on her plate of red and black rice mixed with yellow squash. "The vibrational frequency was low enough for demons to survive here."

"But... who did Goustav sacrifice?" asked Paley.

"Azamere," said Van as several others said, "The wizard."

"They thought Dishora, the end of time, had come," said Daisy. "Or, Solmor, to the Balish. But it hadn't."

"For a true Dishora, demons have to gain the strength to rise here on their own without help," said Brux. "During the Great War, Goustav set them free."

"What about you two?" Van asked Kopius and Daisy.

"People in the palace seem excited about Kupalle," said Daisy. "And we heard more about the brutal Tarc games."

"The games seem a bit overkill once we found out the Tarcs are dying off," said Kopius. "Pun intended."

"*Were* dying off," Daisy corrected.

"Dying off?" Brux dug into his bowl of what looked like vegetable and potato stew.

"We overheard some Bales talking. Lack of offspring," said Kopius. "And you know, killing each other every chance they get. That's got to narrow the gene pool."

"Daisy, you said they're not dying off anymore?" asked Van.

"Part of their deal with King Nequus," explained Kopius. "When the Tarcs took over Kezef, Godreel claimed all the jennets, that's what they call the females of the Hinny race."

"Humph. Makes sense," said Ixl. "Hinnys are a mule-like race, peaceful. Similar to the Tarcs, but smaller. Jennets are strong enough to provide good offspring, to ensure continuation of the Tarc bloodline."

"What about the male Hinnys?" asked Paley.

"Tarcs don't need the male mules, called jacks," said Kopius. "They put the strong jacks to use in the fields and slaughtered the weaker ones for food."

"Food? Gross." Paley squirmed.

"How's that different from eating dragon or turkey?" asked Daisy.

"We didn't find anything that points to the spy," said Kopius. "And nothing about what happened to the other team."

Daisy glanced at the door. "Suixsha should be back by now."

"I'll go find her if she's not back soon." Kopius gently clasped her hand.

"Us next." Paley bounced, practically flying out of her seat. "We found tons of stuff, couldn't even get through it all."

"We went to the Hall of Records," said Brux.

"The place where my father stole Manik's text two years ago," said Van, getting choked up. It seemed like a lifetime had passed since then.

"It's a network of rooms filled with filing cabinets," said Brux.

"And rows of storage shelves stuffed with boxes, books, and stacks of papers," added Paley.

"We saw museum-quality glass cases in some rooms, displaying ancient artifacts from the Dark War. Weapons, statues, bowls, utensils, scrolls..." said Brux. "Some had ancestral items from the royal family."

"Cool," said Van, wanting to go there.

"Speaking of ancestral items, the wizard told us the Runestar wasn't lost," said Ixl. "You didn't see it in any of the cases, did you?"

Brux shook his head.

Paley put down her fork. "I found the Janus records. I got to search for my birth parents."

"You did!" exclaimed Van. "That's amazing!"

"I found nothing." Paley's shoulders slouched.

"I'm sorry," said Van.

"Me too," added Daisy.

"I read some of the ancient documents," said Brux. "I came across a mention about Amaryl's curse—"

"What?" screeched Van. "And you didn't lead with that?"

"No, no." Brux glanced Van. "Nothing about a counter-curse. The Elementals built something that has to do with the curse."

Van's head spun. She had to get down there. Or she could send Ferox. Or they could go together. The Hall of Records held the information that would set her free from the Anchoress curse. That's why her father had risked his life to get into those rooms.

"This is great news!" said Daisy.

"Not so great," said Brux. "I looked through all the related documents and found nothing more."

"We didn't stay long enough to go through even a millionth of what was down there," said Paley. "But we found something about the seals."

"And you haven't mentioned this yet... why?" asked Ixl.

"Because you and Van already found the location of the third seal," said Brux. "In Muspell."

"There was something else, though." Paley squinted as if trying to recall.

Brux shifted uncomfortably in his seat. "I found a passage about the three seals binding the worlds."

"So did I," exclaimed Van. "In the book at the fair."

"Hard to translate," Brux and Van said at the same time.

Brux added, "Something about their binding... didn't translate right..."

"What does it mean, if there's a problem with how the seals are bound?" asked Paley.

Brux looked grim. "Trouble."

CHAPTER

TWENTY-TWO

"**O**ur bellies are full. We know where the third seal is. So, let's get going." Ixl leaped from his seat. "Where are Ferox and his men?"

They all turned to Van.

Ferox hadn't made solid plans with her. *That's on him.* Van stood. "The clock's ticking. We need to get on with the mission. Ferox, or no Ferox."

Daisy rose. "We have to find Suixsha first."

"Ugh." Paley slumped dramatically. "Where is she?"

"Her last known location was the training area," said Kopius. "Wherever that is."

"I'll go find her." Brux marched toward the door.

Paley suddenly became energized and jumped up to follow him. "You go, I go, gemstone partner."

"Wait," said Van, aggrieved. She and her teammates didn't need the additional complication of Suixsha being MIA. "Searching for her will slow us down."

"You suggesting we leave without her?" Kopius raised an eyebrow at Van.

154

"We're more likely to get stopped and questioned if we hang around looking for her," said Van. "She could join Ferox and his men."

"Only if the prince sticks to his word about offering us a crew," said Kopius.

"This is more complicated than a jaunt about the palace." Ixl took a few steps toward Van and met her eye to eye. "We find Suixsha. We leave no teammate behind."

Van didn't find his approach accusatory or threatening. She had to admit; she liked this newfound shift in their relationship. And he was right. They were a team. She shook her head. "No, of course we're not leaving her behind. We'll find her together."

Brux let out a relieved breath. "I'm on board with that."

The team grabbed their backpacks from their respective suites and stormed down the hallway on a mission. Literally.

They didn't get far.

Alden came rushing toward them, along with a handful of guards. "I was on my way to see you. You must get back to your rooms," he said with a worried frown. "The palace is on lockdown. Someone spotted an assassin called the Magician masquerading as one of our guests."

Van caught her breath. "Is Ferox okay?"

Paley's finger shot to her mouth and she began gnawing on her cuticle.

"Rest assured, the prince is secured and well guarded," said Alden in a pacifying tone.

"What's he look like?" demanded Ixl, ready to go out and serve the assassin justice with his own two fists.

"Young. Old. Blond. Brunette. Unfortunately, he or she can change their appearance and blend into the crowd," said Alden. "They are skilled in murder, stealth, and deceit. Until we apprehend the person, please, get back to your rooms. If you get caught roaming the palace, the guards will place you under suspicion."

"We're not allowed to leave our rooms?" asked Brux, as Alden dashed away at a pace that suggested he had urgent business elsewhere.

"The palace is sequestering all guests to their rooms until further notice," Alden said over his shoulder. "Ebus and Efore will take care of your every need."

"Who's the assassin after?" asked Paley, as the palace guards escorted them back toward their suites. "Ferox?"

Daisy threw Van a worried glance. "You said the protestors saw you..."

"Maybe it's a good idea for you to stay in the suite," Brux said to Van.

"You think the protestors sent an assassin to kill me?" Van thought if anyone sent someone to kill her, it would be Solana. But a maneuver like that was way too overt for the princess.

"It's unlikely they had one hanging around that could get here that fast," said Kopius.

"Naw," said Ixl. "Van, you seem pretty easy to kill. No offense. But if someone wanted you gone, you'd be dead by now."

"It is offensive, coming from you." Brux scowled, though Van was only slightly miffed. "You've never been on a mission. Van's survived two."

"A hired assassin would've poisoned Van during dinner. Made it look like an allergic reaction," said Kopius. "Or, with the unguarded rooms, he could've easily slit her throat during the night. Also would've been easy to—"

Daisy placed her dainty hand on his arm. "Please stop with the graphic input."

The guards dropped them at the doors to their suites. "We'll be stationed outside your rooms," said one. "For security."

"What about Suixsha?" Paley twisted a strand of her hair around her finger. "She could be in danger."

"She could be the assassin," mumbled Ixl.

"We'll find your friend and bring her back," said a guard.

Daisy opened the door to the girl's suite. They all moved to go inside when a guard barked, "Hold up. In your own suites. Boys here, girls there."

"Is that really necessary?" Kopius stared the guard in the eye.

Daisy nudged him. "Let's just do what he says."

The rest of them grumbled a bit, and then complied.

FOUR DAYS HAD PASSED since Van, Paley, and Daisy had seen the guys, and Suixsha never returned to the suite. No one thought their sequestering would go on for this long.

On day two, they heard a commotion in the hallway. The three rushed over and whipped open the door. They found the guards wrestling with Brux, Kopius, and Ixl, blocking their attempted dash to the girl's suite.

After that incident, the guards locked their doors.

"No problem." Paley rummaged in her backpack and pulled out her trusty picklocks.

Van pressed her ear to the door. "It's quiet. I think the guards left now that they locked us in. Try it."

It took Paley less than a minute to open the locked door. She grinned at Van and Daisy as she opened it.

A massive guard stood at the threshold, facing Paley. He had heard her picking the lock and grimaced at her pathetic break out attempt.

"It's almost insulting," he said.

Paley reluctantly handed over her picklocks and closed the door.

"Of course it wouldn't be that easy." Daisy slumped back down in her chair.

From that point on, the suite's door only opened for food deliveries to their rooms. Nevertheless, on day three, Van screamed through the door for the guard to open it. One eventually complied.

"I demand to speak to Prince Ferox!" Van shouted in his face.

"I'll be sure to put in a request," said the guard sarcastically.

"The prince is on lockdown. For his security, he cannot leave his rooms or have visitors," said another guard. He tried to close the door.

Van wedged her foot against it and stopped him. "Then some other way. Like, a phone, maybe?"

"A phone?" asked the one holding the door.

"There are no *phones* here," said the first guard. He roughly prodded Van out of the way.

As the guard slammed the door closed, Van screeched, "I want to speak to the prince, *now!*"

By the middle of the fourth day, Van lacked the energy to join Paley and Daisy's conversation.

"A week has passed since the Alignment started," said Daisy. "I'm worried about completing our mission."

Paley chewed on her cuticle. "I'm sure they'll catch the assassin soon and we'll hear from Ferox."

Van yawned, although it was only early afternoon. Doing nothing was exhausting. "I'm going to my room to lie down."

She closed her bedroom door and flopped backside down onto her comfy bed. Her anger over the team's situation had drained her and her mood turned to frustrated boredom. She gazed at the furnishings in the room, studying each one to occupy her mind, to keep her from going crazy from the confinement and lack of progress.

The afternoon's bright light filtered through the sheer voile panels hanging under the red velour drapes with their detailed gold embroidery and tassel trim. The bulky gold lamp on the nightstand had an elaborate design, making it look more like a trophy than a light. The grand sandstone mantel on the fireplace depicted male warriors dressed in skirts and capes holding swords or spears fighting a battle against some unseen assailant. Above the warriors, peaceful maidens in togas held flowers and danced. The background, beautifully embellished with swirls and stars... Van bolted upright.

The design! It reminded Van of the stone wall carving in her father's study, the one that hid a private portal. She leaped from the bed and rushed over to inspect it.

The portal in her father's study needed a key to activate. Was this a portal? Given how many secrets Uxa kept behind tight lips, Van thought it possible. She ran her hands over the carvings and pushed the stars at random to see if anything happened.

She stepped back to better scrutinize it, hoping to find a pattern or clue.

Hidden among the decorative details, four distinct items popped out at her. A sword, a cup, a coin, and a rod. *The Items of Creation!*

Van indiscriminately pressed them. Coin, Cup, Staff, Sword...

The fireplace made a shifting noise.

It slid open, revealing a hidden passageway.

CHAPTER

TWENTY-THREE

Van peered down the dingy passageway. She took a step inside and her innate ability to see in the dark kicked in.

She tread forward. Narrow linear openings high on the wall near the ceiling would've been imperceptible except for the light streaming through. Enough to dimly illuminate the passage and made carrying a light source unnecessary for those without her "flashlight eyes."

Ahead, light filtered in from two eye-level holes in the wall. Van peered through and viewed an oversized master bedroom with more gold decorations than in her room. It also had a bigger bed, a three-tiered chandelier, and a sitting area with luxurious furniture.

She crept farther down the passageway, went by more peepholes, and then came to an up-and-down stairway. She went down, figuring it led to the main floor.

Van came across more dusty corridors and additional eye-holes that revealed common area rooms, all empty of people. No surprise given the lockdown.

She continued walking until she passed peepholes where male voices emanated from the room. Van leapt back, heart racing, as if she had gotten caught sneaking about. Hand on her chest, she took a calming breath. *They can't see me.*

She gathered courage and looked through the eye-holes, wondering who would risk breaking house lockdown rules.

Some men had gathered in a small library, or, perhaps, a high-end study. The perfect place to hold a clandestine meeting. Merloc, Lord Godreel, and Underking Mador were there, along with two other officials Van didn't know.

She held her breath as if it would make her more hidden, or allow her to hear better. She knew it wouldn't, but holding her breath as long as possible helped her to concentrate. She crossed her fingers, hoping the men would reveal the identity of the Balish spy in Lodestar, or confess to hiring an assassin to kill the prince.

"We cannot attack," said the stocky official with a hooked nose.

"Salus Valde must fall," said Merloc, causing Van's stomach to clench. To some relief, she noted Ferox wasn't in the room, neither was Alden.

"I am here to help you with that," drawled Godreel. "In exchange for my demands, such as making my people—"

Someone snorted.

Godreel glowered but continued, "Making my people full Balish citizens, equal tribes, along with the respect and rights they deserve. I also expect to gain title as Underking of Kezef."

"I agree with Meximuth, we must not attack," said Mador. "We can't risk the wrath of the Elementals."

"I speak for the council," said Meximuth, the stocky, hooked-nose man. "We must bide our time."

"Put our Lodian guests in the games," said Godreel. "Allow one of them to live, to go back to Lodestar with their story of mistreatment. This will provoke a Lodian response."

"Yes," said a salt-and-peppered haired man. "An attack by the Lodians would violate Manik's law. We could then take over their lands without fear of retaliation by the Elementals."

"We can't put them in the Death Games," said Mador. "Prince

Ferox will not allow it and neither will the king. They're interested in peace between the tribes."

"Well, it's a good thing they do not know about the—"

"The king is not here," said Godreel, cutting off Meximuth. The movement of his head when he spoke caused his gold nose ring to glimmer in the light. "We can handle the son."

Merloc turned to the salt-and-peppered haired man. "Sacerdos, what does the Magistrate of the Balish Royal Court say?"

"If we find cause. One the court could use to deem it necessary for our Lodian guests to enter the games in order to maintain peaceful relations between our tribes..." Sacerdos paused as if contemplating the consequences. "It could work."

"Not all are required to enter," drawled Godreel. "Only one." He raised his thick, bovine-like brow.

"The rebels are acting up," said Mador. "The protestors, too, are becoming more aggressive. All this threatens the safety of the royal family."

Godreel nodded. "Having that girl here poses a threat."

Of course, Van was *that girl*.

"Given the situation, I am not opposed to your plan of entering her into the games," said Mador.

Merloc snorted. "The Anti-Manik Rebels are no threat to us, father, nor are the protestors. Goustav has no heir. Manik's descendants are safe."

"I can easily take care of these troublemakers," said Godreel, in his gravelly voice.

"We must follow the rules of the court. In all matters," Sacerdos interjected. "We don't want another fiasco like the Alga massacre."

Meximuth winced at the mention of the Alga massacre.

Godreel gave a chilling grin. "That is how I became a favored ally of the Balish. I continue to provide you with a useful, problem-solving alliance."

"We helped *you*," said Meximuth, heatedly. "When we found you, you had nothing. No home. No organization, no policies. You and your heathen brethren were nothing but hired hands for sale to do anything for goods or money. We gave you land. *Kezef*. The title of *Lord*. And you... you had the *gall* to double-cross us."

Godreel leaped from the leather chair, surprisingly agile for such a bulky build. "Little choice did I have. For decades, I had been trying to gain social status for my tribe. Your Prince Nequus came along and offered me an opportunity. I took it."

Mador scowled. "He never hired you to attack Windermere Castle."

"Yes, only to wipe out the Hinny's," said Godreel. "I did something better. My tribe needed the jennets for breeding. As an oxen race, it suits my people to farm. We work the land better than the weak jacks. Your people continue to profit nicely from my tribe's labor."

"You attacked us and framed the Genetrix," said Meximuth. "You caused an innocent tribe's annihilation. For your own gain."

"Kill one tribe, kill another. It is all the same to me." Godreel rested back down in his chair. His voice carried a menacing undertone. "And now I am sitting here, in this nice palace in Balefire, having a civilized conversation with top Balish officials. In allegiance to our King Nequus, pledged to take his secret to the grave."

"It worked out in the end," said Sacerdos, attempting to cool things down after catching the meaning of Godreel's no-so-veiled threat. "Both our tribes benefitted. Let's let the past stay in the past."

Van's head spun with this new information. *Tarcs* were the mercenary army hired by King Nequus. Palace officials knew the truth about the Alga massacre. The Genetrix were innocent, just as Suixsha had claimed. Yet they kept it a secret from Ferox.

Weirdly, this made Van more trusting of Merloc. If Merloc wanted Nequus off the throne, he could easily coerce Godreel to tell the truth about the Alga massacre. Van pushed away from the wall and gasped. *This is the secret Ferox's father mentioned to him. The one kept by Merloc and Ferox's Uncle Maddy.* This was the reason Ferox blindly trusted Merloc. He just didn't know the story.

But he does know it. Suixsha had told it to him.

Van's mouth went drier than usual. Did the officials hide the truth about state secrets from Ferox to protect him with plausible deniability? Or because they had no intention of him ever becoming king?

Her attention went back to the peephole as Mador said, "The past has come back to haunt us, it seems. We've recently learned someone survived the massacre, and she's in the palace."

"She would've been a baby," said Meximuth. "What can she know?"

"Loose ends cause problems," drawled Godreel.

"The games will fix everything," said Merloc.

"We all want what's best for the kingdom," said Sacerdos. "And for our great King Nequus."

"Here, here," responded the men.

"So it's settled then," said Sacerdos. "Merloc will see to *one* of our Lodian guests being *legally* entered into the Death Games. The others will hurry back to Lodestar with the story of our war-provoking awfulness."

Several of the men chuckled.

"So, which one of the of two will it be then?" asked Meximuth.

Merloc snarled. "That obnoxious Vanessa Cross."

CHAPTER

TWENTY-FOUR

eath Games? Van pushed back from the peephole, trembling.

Wanting her dead seemed a recurring theme with the Balish. Still, hearing it spoken out loud by top officials unnerved her.

She took off down the corridor back the way she came, her thoughts racing.

Merloc would benefit from Van's death by solving two problems. First, it would free Ferox from Van's supposed love spell which posed a threat to the Balish Kingdom. Second, if the Lodians attacked in retaliation—and Van agreed they would—without her magical Anchoress powers to protect her people, the Balish had the manpower to take over Salus Valde. After a long, bloody war.

One good thing came from overhearing their clandestine meeting. Van got confirmation that Merloc supported King Nequus, and, therefore, Ferox as the crown prince. He seemed content with his place as future underking of East Alga, as long as Ferox upheld the Balish tradition of marginalizing the Lodians.

Although none of the men had mentioned Solana, Van still believed the princess wanted power, and the first step to get it

165

involved taking the throne. Solana being banished to East Alga as an underqueen? No way.

Van bounced ideas back and forth about how to best handle the situation. One thing became clear. She and her team needed to get out of the palace. To do that, she had to find a door leading to the outside. She slowed down her pace and searched for one.

She came to the end of a passageway. Instead of turning around, Van thought it odd the corridor simply ended. She ran her fingers against the wall, searching for a lever or latch. She found one, pulled it, and a door opened.

The glaring afternoon light crashed in, causing her to squint. Heat came at her like a blast from a furnace. She stepped outside to figure out her location in the palace and to see where it dropped her on the property.

Once her eyes adjusted to the light, Van saw an expansive yard with a plain three-foot sandstone wall bordering a packed-dirt ring. She went over to look. Scattered around were lead balls, jump rope, barbells. *The training area!* Her eyes darted the grounds, searching for Suixsha.

She shook her head. Suixsha wouldn't be training for four days straight. And the guards would've seen her and brought her back inside the palace. Speaking of guards, male voices reached her ears, telling her some were fast approaching.

Van twisted toward the door, now invisible against the outside wall of the palace, and too far away for her to make a dash before getting caught. Woods surrounded the training area and were much closer. She could hide there. Van slipped into the forest.

Shade provided by the trees cooled the air and refreshed her. So she kept walking.

A growl rumbled through the woods. Van froze.

Rustling came from a tree above. A mass rushed down and landed with a thump in front of her.

Having learned from the Jaychund games, this time she swung her fist as the person hit the ground.

Suixsha landed on her two feet and ducked, avoiding Van's punch. She rose and faced Van. "You much better this time."

Tyger strolled in from between the brush.

"Suixsha." Van placed a hand over her heart. "You scared the light out of me. Why didn't you come back to the palace? What've you been doing?"

"I more comfortable here, with Tyger," said Suixsha.

It made sense to Van. Being in the woods offered Suixsha a place to cope while being surrounded by the people who murdered her entire tribe.

"Trouble in palace, so I not go back. Stay in woods. Watch. Listen."

Van put hands on her hips. "Were you ever going to come back and finish the mission?"

"Yes."

Van narrowed her eyes. "What have you been eating?"

"I forage in wood. Eat with Tyger."

"Oh," said Van, taken aback.

She filled in Suixsha about the assassin and the lockdown. Told her about overhearing the Balish planning on forcing one of them to play in the Death Games.

"Me. If Merloc has his way," said Van.

"Death Game not good. You lose mean you die."

"That appears to be the plan. It would cause the Lodians to retaliate. Start a war between our tribes."

Tyger snapped his tail and peered at something in the woods. He let out a low growl and tread in that direction with his hackles raised.

Suixsha and Van crept behind him. They came to a clearing with a large barn and crouched in the landscaping to avoid being seen by the palace guards standing by the ground-to-roof red, wooden, double-doors.

Tyger growled again.

A roar bellowed from within the barn.

Van's stomach dropped. "What is that?"

Suixsha motioned for Van to follow.

Van and Tyger trailed behind Suixsha as she led them through the perimeter of the woods to the backside of the barn. The forest extended close to the structure, giving them the cover needed to get closer. Multiple roars echoed from inside.

"Wait here." Van rushed toward one of the barn's windows.

She stretched on her tippy toes, peeked through, and gasped. "For the love of the light!"

TWENTY-FIVE

Van hardly believed her eyes.

Suixsha shifted from foot to foot as she waited among the trees with Tyger, who huffed and shuffled his paws.

Van rushed back to them.

"Dragons," she said, catching her breath. "In cages. Three. And one of them is a baby."

Suixsha's typically placid face showed signs of despair.

"Why?" asked Van, on the verge of tears.

"Dragons here for Kupalle. Balish sport. Put in a ring with warrior. Fight to death. Dragon never win. No food, no water for month make them weak."

"I'm going to be sick." Van grabbed her stomach. "We have to save them."

"Mark of good warrior is be invisible," said Suixsha. "So is mark of good guest."

"You're saying I should sneak into the barn?" Van bit her lip in contemplation.

"No. I mean, not rescue dragon. It disrupt host culture."

A disagreeing grumble came from deep in Tyger's throat. He flicked his head and snorted.

"Tyger agrees with *me*." Van tapped her fingers on her chest.

"It your right to make choice." Suixsha's sharp eyes held steady on Van.

"What if Tyger was in one of those cages?"

"Dragon rescue harm Lodian-Balish relation," said Suixsha, her tone impassive.

Van considered what Ferox and Uxa would say about her freeing dragons bought to Balefire for the Balish Kupalle festival. She imagined herself in front of the Lodian Consilium, defending her actions.

If Daisy was here, she'd agree with me. The dragons were innocent and deserved to live their life. Van weighed the consequences of setting them free against her responsibility to best serve in her role as a peace ambassador.

Once Van becomes a full-fledged Grigori, her duty will be to protect the innocent. Might as well start now. "You do what you want. I'm not leaving them to get slaughtered for sport."

"I stay. Help."

Van blinked. "I'm sorry, what?"

"I proud you stand ground."

"Why'd you try to talk me out of it, then?"

"When you give up will, you give away power to another. Disable will, take away right to take action."

"You tried to trick me," huffed Van. "You planned on saving the dragons all along."

"Temper cause you lose power," said Suixsha. "Direct energy to will instead, use it to achieve goal."

Van scowled. "Save it with the lessons. Let's focus on the dragons."

"Take them out front door. We distract guards." Suixsha and Tyger dashed away.

Van went back to the window and maneuvered herself onto the

sill. She wobbled before balancing herself on the narrow plank. Then pushed open the vertical windows.

She jumped down, dropping at least five feet. Her knees buckled, and she toppled onto the hard floor, landing near the dragons' cages.

She expected her clumsy entrance to agitate the dragons. Instead, they seemed more intrigued by her presence than fright-ened. *Good.* It hadn't crossed Van's mind until then that they could've roasted her with their fiery breath.

The dragons stared at her through the bars of their individual cages. Three of them, two adults and one baby. The golden adult dragon appeared larger and more muscular than the other and had stubby legs. Van figured him for a male. The other adult was green and had softer features and long legs. Van deemed her the female or mother dragon. She concluded they were the parents of the golden green baby dragon.

Smoke billowed from the nostrils of the adult dragons as they flicked their heads and snorted. The claws of their forelegs dug into the hay strewn floor. Their wings pushed against the bars as they spread them as much as possible, given the restriction of their cages.

The softness of the baby dragon's features made Van think it was a girl. Her round, black eyes stared at Van, as if her youth still allowed for the expectancy of hope. The baby wrapped her wings around her body and let out a friendly, chirpy sound.

"Don't worry," cooed Van. "I'm getting you out of here."

But how? Her eyes darted around the barn. Bays… a loft… empty stalls. Suixsha told her to leave through the barn doors, wide enough to take up practically the entire entrance wall. The doors provided the only viable exit. Hopefully, Suixsha and Tyger were doing their job distracting the guards on the other side.

Van cautiously approached the golden dragon, praying he would understand and not fry her. "I'm going to open your cage." She slowly raised her hand to the cage's latch. "Shh…"

The dragon flicked his snout, agitated, untrusting. Or, perhaps, excited in anticipation of being freed.

Van swung open the massive cage door and stepped back.

"Go out the front." Van pointed to the barn's front doors, hoping he would crash through, knock out the guards, and fly away.

The male dragon emerged from the cage. He didn't eat Van, fry her, or take off. He snorted at Van and then stared at the other two cages.

She opened the mother's cage next.

The green female dragon exited, flicked her head, and snorted. She waddled to the golden "husband" dragon and nuzzled against him. They both turned their attention to Van.

Once Van freed the baby, the adult dragons let out monstrous roars that shot fire into the high-arched ceiling. Nowhere near Van, but her skin still prickled from the heat.

The loft burst into a blaze of burning hay.

The adult dragons stampeded toward the barn doors. The baby moved to follow and paused. She turned to look at Van and let out the cutest little squeak-roar.

"You're welcome." Van smiled.

The baby continued on, trailing after her parents.

With their torch-like breath cranked on high, the two adult dragons blasted the double doors, then smashed through them, shattering the wood to splinters.

The guards, away from the doors chasing Tyger and Suixsha, who had almost reached the woods, crouched down, startled from the burst.

The dragon parents made sure their baby took flight before they did. Then they stretched their wings, and the three flew into the sky.

Van sighed in relief, thrilled the dragon family made their escape. Off to live their life wild and free.

The guards scrambled to their feet, snatching their DEW hand-guns from their holsters. They took aim at the dragons.

"No," cried Van.

Beams of light flashed from the triangular heads of their Directed Energy Weapons.

A deadly ray nicked the mother dragon's wing. She screeched and twisted, dipping mid-air. The male dragon turned back and hovered over her, the baby followed. After gaining control, the female adult continued her flight.

Rays blasted from the guards' DEWs, even as the dragons flew out of range.

Flames grew in the barn.

Van relaxed as she watched the dragon family reach the safe zone.

Suddenly, the male looped around and headed for the guards.

"No! Don't!" Van ran forward, waving her arms at the dragon. "Just go!"

The mother and baby hovered far enough away to stay out of the DEWs' range. Both barked fear-based cries.

The male dragon darted and dodged the deadly rays. He dived and blasted the guards with his fiery breath. One yelped as the fire singed his body and sent him running. The other guard had a clear shot and took it.

Pewww.

Right in the eye. The dragon's skull exploded, the blow pushed his head and neck backward, his body jerked with it. His wings flapped less and less until his enormous body slammed to the ground. A cloud of dirt rose around him as if welcoming the dragon in a comforting embrace of death.

The mother and baby dragon screeched. In any language, any species, those sounds meant the same thing. Crushing, agonizing heartbreak. They turned and flew away.

The guards moved their attention to Van, who stood wide-eyed with the burning barn behind her. Paralyzed in sadness, she could barely breathe. She took on the excruciating pain of the mother and baby dragons' loss like it was her own.

"You're coming with us." The singed guard grabbed Van's arm.

"You'll go to the dungeons for this," growled the other guard. "You've ruined Kupalle. And the barn."

"Let go of me!" Van twisted her arm from the guard's grip. "I'm Prince Ferox's girlfriend."

"Humph," snorted the singed guard.

"My tribal beliefs require me to protect the innocent. I don't think the prince will be happy when I tell him about how you're treating me."

"The palace is on lockdown," said the other guard. "No one is authorized to be roaming the grounds. Not even the prince's *girlfriend*."

"Your little stunt near killed me," growled the singed guard.

"But it didn't. You killed *him*." Van's eyes burst with tears over the unjust death of the dragon.

As the guards dragged Van away, her only consolation was that the mother and baby dragons, Suixsha, and Tyger had escaped.

The singed guard cruelly grinned at Van and said, "You're gonna fry for this."

TWENTY-SIX

Van shuffled her feet as the guards escorted her back into the palace. She had destroyed intertribal relations. Worse, she had ruined her relationship with Ferox.

They led her down a musty, spiral stairway, similar to the one she experienced with Ixl days ago. Her heart picked up its pace with each descending level. Panic gripped her at the thought of being thrown into a dungeon, left to rot among the rats and sewerage.

When the guards tossed Van into a chamber, she swore she had entered the gateway to hell. She couldn't imagine how Daisy survived being in such a horrid place for an extended time.

Van wasn't there long when Suixsha got chucked inside with her.

Suixsha held a pained gaze at Van.

"I told them you had nothing to do with it." Van tilted her head to the side. "What's wrong?"

"They take Tyger."

Light footsteps echoed down the dungeon's stairwell.

"No, no, no." Alden swooshed his hands as he strode in under the stone archway. "This is all wrong. They are guests of the royal family. Release them to me at once."

"Under whose authority?" grumbled the head guard.

"Prince Ferox." Alden waved an official-looking parchment stamped with a royal crested wax seal. "He would've come himself but he remains on lockdown and cannot leave the secured area."

The guard tore open the letter. He nodded, and the others reluctantly released Van and Suixsha into Alden's custody.

"Where Tyger?" Suixsha asked Alden the moment she stepped out of the cell.

Alden's eyes darted to the floor. He shook his head and let out a long, inaudible sigh. "He's caged, I'm afraid. The prince is working on his release."

Suixsha stormed past them through the archway, shoulders tight.

Silence ensued as they climbed the winding staircase.

Van couldn't handle the tension, and said, "Thank you."

"Don't thank me yet." Alden's forehead wrinkled with worry.

No one said anything else as he led them back into the girl's suite.

Daisy and Paley leaped from their seats in the living area.

"What—how did you get out of the suite?" Daisy asked Van.

"Suixsha!" said Paley. "You've returned at last."

"You have a message from the prince." Alden handed Van a polished gemstone, roughly the size and shape of a multi-track, cut with a flat viewing surface. "It's red."

"So?"

"Red means he sent the message in anger."

"Red can also mean love," said Van, although her stomach knotted with anxiety.

"Pink means love," said Alden, going along with Van's banter despite their looming circumstances.

"No, pink is friendship." Van argued for no other reason than to calm her nerves.

Alden turned to leave. "Yellow. Yellow is friendship." At the door, he twisted around and said, "Now, stay put." He shut the door behind him.

Suixsha nudged Van. "Play message."

Van inspected the red gemstone, flipping it back and forth. "How do I turn it on?"

She swiped the surface with her index finger. Nothing happened. Then she shouted, "Play message," at the screen. Nothing happened. She pressed and held her thumb in a groove on the side, thinking it might be a fingerprint scanner so only the intended receiver could play the message.

Ferox's face floated into clarity on the screen. She braced herself for his red-hot, angry words.

"Vanessa," said Ferox, through a clenched jaw. "You've put me in a critical position. The officials asked you to stay in your suite for your own safety. Dragon fighting is a Kupalle tradition. When you set them free, my family, the council, and the court took it as in insult."

"Listen." His face softened. "I understand what lies in your heart. I just... it's a delicate balance trying to keep peace with the visiting dignitaries, my family, my citizens, and having you here. Grigori culture, your nature, compels you to protect the innocent. I'm in your corner. I really am. I'm doing my best to fight the prejudice my people have against your tribe. So we can be together, openly." He sighed. "It's difficult to accomplish when things like this happen."

His features hardened again, as if remembering his political obligations. "I'll contact you again once I smooth over this incident. No more burning down barns. Stay in your suite."

The screen went blank.

Van stared at the gemstone, still processing Ferox's words. The red faded, and the device became clear.

"You saw *dragons*? You *burned down a barn?*" Paley chuckled.

"What happened?" Daisy plopped down on the couch, ready for a long story.

Van recounted her adventure with the dragons. "Now, I'm stuck in this room." She paced. "I can't even talk to Ferox and tell him my side of the story."

"I'm glad you rescued the dragons. I would've done the same," said Daisy. "Lilla, the Elemental Guardian of All Animals, will favor you for doing that."

"We need rescue Tyger," said Suixsha.

"I'm so sorry," said Daisy. "We'll find a way to free him."

"If they want us to stay in the suite, it's for our own safety, right?" Paley twisted her hair.

"Pfft. Safety." Van filled them in on the secret passage and some of the conversation she overheard among the Balish officials.

"I don't like the sound of the Death Games," said Paley.

"By rescue dragon. You give them cause," said Suixsha.

"Yes," said Van, sharply. "I'm aware of that."

"Ferox mentioned nothing about Death Games in his message," said Daisy.

"I don't think he knows yet. They keep a lot of things from him." Flushed with the heat of anger, Van told them what she overheard about the Alga massacre.

Van met Suixsha's eyes. "You were right about what happened." She clenched her fists, thinking about the unfairness of it all. "How can you not be angry with the Balish over what they did to your tribe and now they have Tyger?"

"When anger consume you," said Suixsha. "You not find clarity until let it go."

"They want us both dead," said Van. "That's pretty clear."

Paley shook her arms to release nervous energy. "We have to break out of this joint." She began pacing. With her yellow cat-eye contact lenses, she reminded Van of Tyger.

"If I leave the palace again, it'll get Ferox into more trouble with his family," said Van. "It would do irreparable damage to Balish-Lodian relations. Mission fail." *Relationship fail.*

"If there's a crack in the seal, negativity will continue to seep into this world," said Daisy. "Evil thoughts and actions will increase and spread to more of the citizens. The virus will get worse." She looked at Van. "We need to talk this through with the guys."

"Follow me." Van took them through the fireplace in her bedroom and into the hidden passageway.

"I'm not sure which way is the guy's suite." Van led them down the dimly lit passage. "But I think... yes, here it is. Find a latch."

Everyone's hands ran along the wall. They bumped into each other in a frenzy to find the latch. Their interference annoyed Van. With great effort, she held her tongue.

A door into the master bedroom slid open, the girls tumbled into the room.

Paley giggled. "That was fun."

The guys almost took them out, thinking they were under attack.

"Paley's giggling saved you." Ixl relaxed his grip on the kitchen knife.

"This is most unexpected." Kopius lowered his fists. "And most welcome." He smiled at Daisy.

"Van," said Brux, looking thrilled to see her. "What is this?" He peered into the passageway.

Van filled them on her discovery. She got the guys up to date on everything that had happened so far.

"Ferox won't let them hurt Tyger," Brux said to Suixsha.

"Death Games don't sound like anything good," said Kopius.

"Of course it's not good." Ixl grimaced. "It has to do with the Tarcs."

"They plan on using the games to kill me and or Suixsha," said Van.

"They can try, they won't succeed," said Daisy.

The fury in her eyes startled Van. From the looks on the others' faces, they also seemed amazed that someone so refined could unleash such power. Except for Kopius, who proudly grinned.

"We can use the passageway to get out of here right now." Brux gestured at the door.

Everyone agreed. The guys grabbed their backpacks.

"I'm not leaving," said Van. "I can't do that to Ferox. You guys go."

Brux dropped his backpack on the floor, looking resigned. "Then I'm staying too."

"That means, so am I," said Paley.

"I stay," said Suixsha. "Tyger here."

"We're a team," said Ixl. "We all stay together."

"I need to talk to him in person." Van edged her way through her teammates to the fireplace. "Fix things."

"Do not let burning desire for Ferox get out control," warned Suixsha. "Will lead you to make bad choice for Self, and us."

Brux placed a hand on Van's shoulder. "I can go with you."

Van shook her head. "I need to do this alone. I'll be fine. Suixsha, I'll see what he can do about Tyger." She ducked into the passageway. "Back in a sec."

Van disappeared into the darkness.

Ferox mentioned his rooms were close to her guest suite...

The grand master bedroom she had seen earlier—*it must be Ferox's!* That's how he got into her bedroom the other night. He used the passageway.

Van found her way back to the peephole, pulled the latch to the sliding panel, and stepped through. She came out in front of his fireplace.

Shuffling sounds emanated from the adjacent room. The hair on Van's arms prickled. She could tell it wasn't Ferox by the sound of the person's movements, like they were searching for something. *The assassin?*

Her instincts prompted her to protect Ferox. Then Suixsha's warning haunted her thoughts. Van brushed the advice aside. She wasn't about to stand down and let someone harm Ferox. Not on her watch. Yes, she burned hot for Ferox, but an attack on him would be terrible for public relations. Blame would fall on the Lodians.

She tiptoed forward and glimpsed around the corner into the room. Her eye caught sight of glossy, waist-length black hair.

Van's internal alarm blared.

TWENTY-SEVEN

Van controlled her impulse to leap onto Solana and pummel the evil princess to death.

Instead, she remained crouched and hidden as she tried to figure out what Solana was searching for in Ferox's suite. Obviously, the lockdown didn't apply to the princess, who was free to roam the palace like the male officials Van had seen earlier.

Solana fanned through several books on the shelf. Then she yanked open an end table drawer and paused.

"What brings you to my brother's suite?" Solana closed the drawer and turned to face Van. "Here for a little tryst?"

"Where's Ferox?" Van emerged from behind the wall, hands curled into fists.

"Lovesick, are we?" Solana smirked.

Van marched forward, narrowing the gap between her and Solana. "It wouldn't surprise me if you hired the assassin to kill him."

Solana also stepped forward. Her smirk turned into a scowl. "That's a big accusation coming from such a little girl."

"I'm not fooled by your good sister routine," said Van, so tensely her neck muscles strained. "I caught you snooping around his room, looking for what?"

Solana flashed a furious look, then regained her cool demeanor. "I'm supposed to be here. You're not." She glanced at the suite's door. "Guards!"

The door burst open. Several palace guards charged in and pointed their DEWs at Van.

Solana dashed behind one of them as if she feared for her life. "This Lodian has no authorization to be wandering the palace, never mind trespassing in the prince's rooms. Thank the light I came to check on my brother or who knows what might've happened."

Two of the guards lowered their weapons and roughly grabbed Van by the arms.

"Wait—no—I—" Getting caught in Ferox's suite would get her in more trouble.

"She could be the assassin," said Solana. "A special interrogation by Merloc will uncover the truth."

"You won't get away with this," cried Van. "I'll make sure of it."

Solana snorted. "Assuming you're still around."

"Hey, hold up!" Ferox came bounding down the stairway and into the open living area. Apparently, his suite had multiple floors. "What's going on here?"

One guard said, "We caught this intruder—"

"I'm so sorry." Solana cut off the guard. Her eyes wide with innocence. "While I was waiting for you, I heard a noise. Van leaped out at me. Gave me a fright. The guards heard my scream and rushed in."

"Release Van at once," said Ferox.

"I will compensate you for your prompt action," Solana said to the guards, eyes sharp, tongue sweet.

"Are you okay?" Ferox asked Van.

Van nodded. She didn't like how the guards hesitated when Ferox gave the command to release her. She threw Solana a look blazing with fury, and mouthed, "Nice try."

"Sister, we will talk later," said Ferox.

"Of course." Solana dipped her head and left the suite, trailed by her guards.

Ferox turned to Van, fuming. "Why are you out of your rooms?"

"I just... I need to talk to yo—"

"I'm trying to protect you, and you do this," growled Ferox. "You come here—through the secret passage, no doubt—and get seen by Solana and her guards. You're in enough trouble already. We don't need to add more."

"The passage is not so secret." Van crossed her arms. "Why leave it open? It seems like a security risk."

"Only my father and I know about it. He never uses it." Ferox stomped over to Van, getting so close they were nose to nose. "Don't change the subject."

"Fine, I won't. You heard about the dragons... and the barn. So what happens now?"

"I'll take care of it." Ferox's anger became replaced by worry. "Promise me you'll stop breaking the rules."

Van hesitated, then gave a slow nod. Making this assurance to him meant she couldn't leave the palace with her team.

"When you admitted to acting alone, it kept Suixsha out of trouble," said Ferox. "She's in the clear, but Tyger is being held as a danger to the palace."

"You have to get him out," said Van.

"I'm working to help both of you. I asked the court to drop your charges. Or at least make the ruling time served."

"I was in the dungeon for less than an hour," said Van.

"No one outside a select few needs to know that."

"What about Solana seeing me here, breaking the rules of the lockdown?"

Solana would most certainly use the incident to underscore Ferox's lack of control to those who mattered in the palace.

"It's not her I'm worried about," he said. "I can handle my family. It's the loose lips of her guards. Solana is on our side."

"When I got here, she was rifling through your room searching for something." Van was barely able to contain her irritation. Why was Ferox so stupid when it came to seeing his sister for what she was, a conniving, black-hearted—

"She probably got bored waiting for me while I finished my gemstone meeting."

"Are you sure she wasn't after the Coin?" Van had no doubt Solana kept in touch with the master demon. It wanted the powerful Items of Creation. Solana had access to them.

"She wasn't."

"How do you know?" demanded Van.

"Because I told no one," said Ferox heatedly. "No one here knows I have the Coin."

Van paused for a beat to take in his confession. This meant Uxa and Fynn had gotten accurate intel about the Coin. "Well... that explains why the council is on edge about us Lodians. Why'd you keep it a secret?"

She wondered if it had to do with him gaining power. If he had told his father or the Balish Council about the Coin, they would've taken it from him.

"It's safer for my family if I keep it hidden," said Ferox. "Its energy can corrupt the weakest of minds, royal or not. With Solana's history... why take the chance?"

"I'm glad you don't a hundred percent trust her," said Van.

"Not with an Item of Creation. My sister... she has issues, but like I told you, she's working hard on developing her inner Self."

Since Ferox annoyingly placed hope in his sister, Van tried a different approach. "I'm pretty sure Merloc can't be trusted." Given what she had overheard, Merloc enjoyed causing trouble for Van, making him and Solana perfect for each other.

"I might not trust him with an Item either, but Merloc is loyal to the family," said Ferox.

Van told him about the conversation she overheard between Merloc and the officials regarding the Alga massacre.

Ferox glanced at the floor, truth sinking in. "That means Suixsha was right. I was wrong."

"It's okay." Van wrapped him in a hug. When he seemed to be all right, she let go and took a step back. "I understand Merloc is loyal to your family, but... he wants me dead, and to use my death to start a war between our tribes."

"It's Merloc's twisted way of protecting me," said Ferox. "I'll speak to him."

Van opened her mouth to tell him she heard Merloc and the others planning to force her into the Death Games, when a knock interrupted their conversation.

"It's my officials," said Ferox. "No one else is allowed out of their rooms." He shuffled Van into his bedroom. "Go back to your suite. I'll fix this, then send word to you."

As they reached the fireplace concealing the secret passage, Van asked, "What about the mission?"

"I had Merloc ramp up security. They'll soon find the assassin. Then the council will allow me and my men to go with you."

"And if the assassin isn't found?"

"Then I'll send my men to escort you and your team," said Ferox. "Give me a couple of hours. Either way, plan to head out at dusk."

"What if I leave now?" asked Van, in a rush. "I can wait outside the gates surrounding Balefire's grounds with my team and we can meet?"

"You won't make it. Guards are roaming the palace's perimeter from the increased security."

"What if we—"

"If you get caught out of your rooms again, it will create an inter-tribal relations nightmare, escalating the likelihood of a war. Making our being together impossible."

The knocking grew more urgent. A male voice called out for the prince. The door handle rattled...

Ferox gave Van a quick kiss goodbye, and she scooted into the passageway.

She fully intended to follow Ferox's instructions and go back to her suite. Until she passed the peephole into Ferox's living area. Curiosity compelled her to stop.

Van peered through the eye-hole opening and saw Ferox talking to two of the men she had seen earlier, Sacerdos and Meximuth, along with Alden, who appeared agitated.

"Your safety is our only goal," Meximuth said to Ferox. "We cannot allow you to run off on a fool's mission with the Lodians."

Ferox's eyes darted to Sacerdos. "My family agrees with this?"

"The court's main priority is to protect you and your family," said Sacerdos. "It is in the interest of the realm that you remain in your rooms."

Ferox turned to Alden. "You agree?"

"For the record, I most vehemently disagree," said Alden, with such force that Van expected flames to shoot from his ear horns. "Ferox and his team should accompany the Lodians to check the third seal as planned."

"We came to notify you of a change in program." Meximuth wrung his hands.

"Vanessa Cross has not only violated our restriction of the lockdown," said Sacerdos, taking a seat. "She has been charged with theft of dragons, arson, trespassing, aggravated assault on two guards, seriously injuring one. Now, we run into Solana's guards, who witnessed her again violating the rules of the lockdown and trespassing in your suite. I'm afraid she has multiple legal violations."

"We have determined Vanessa Cross poses a threat to your life," said Meximuth. "It is a serious offense and she must suffer the consequences."

"Vanessa doesn't pose a risk to me." Ferox threw back his shoulders. "She's my girlfriend."

Sacerdos cleared his throat. "We have determined that your relationship is not in the best interest of the—"

"You don't tell me who I can date." Ferox clenched his jaw.

Alden raised his index finger. "I also want to be on record opposing Lodians entering the games."

"The *games*?" Ferox turned pale.

"Your father has already been contacted and given his approval," said Sacerdos.

"How...? Humans aren't allowed in the games." Ferox stared him down. "I won't allow it and neither should the court."

"As prince, your power is limited," said Meximuth, continuing to wring his hands.

Ferox's tone deepened, and he turned to Meximuth. "Then I'll enter the match in Van's place."

"No." Sacerdos flapped his hand. "I'm afraid that's impossible. It's against the law to place any member of the royal family in harm's way."

"You are most certainly not allowed to play," said Meximuth.

"It is done." Sacerdos smacked his palms on the armrests of his chair as if they were courtroom gavels and stood. "As punishment for the repeated violations of Balish law, we will hold Vanessa Cross at Balefire until she enters the Death Games."

Van's stomach clenched.

As the men left, Ferox held Alden back for a moment and said, "Keep working on finding a solution to this disaster. Go see Uncle Maddy for help, Merloc too."

Alden gave him his word and slipped from the suite.

With the officials gone, Van wandered back in.

Ferox snapped his head toward her. His cheeks flushed.

Before she could tell him about overhearing his uncle and cousin scheming to force her into the Death Games, Ferox rushed over and clutched Van's arms.

His frenzied tone betrayed is lack of control over the situation. "Go on your mission without me and my men," he said, practically spitting on her. "Or just go back to Lodestar. Use the passage. It's not safe for you here anymore. *I can't protect you.*"

"I-I don't want to get you in trouble..."

"Leave the palace," said Ferox. "*Now*."

"But, I—"

"Van... your first match in the games... it's a fight to the *death*."

CHAPTER

TWENTY-EIGHT

Van dashed through the secret passageway back to her suite, breathing heavily, more from anxiety than exertion.

She stumbled into her bedroom and hurried into the kitchen area. Her teammates sat around the dining table, tense and still.

"Van!" Brux rushed over, looking panicked.

"It's..." She said, catching her breath. "It's a fight to the d-dea—"

"We know." Ixl waved a scroll with the royal wax seal broken. "A messenger delivered the official decree just before you came back."

"Oh, Van!" Paley walloped her in a hug. Daisy joined.

Suixsha stood in the open living area, muscles glistening. "I enter game with you."

"No need," said Brux. "I'm entering the match in Van's place."

"No." Van shook her head. She detached herself from Paley and Daisy. "No one is entering with me or for me."

Brux wrinkled his brow and said in a resigned tone, "You lost to Suixsha in the Jaychund games. You can't win, not alone."

"Thank the light for your Anchoress abilities. That will help us win," said Daisy.

190

Van's eyes shifted to the floor. "In Jaychund... I couldn't connect to my magical bloodline." She lifted her head and addressed them. "Yes, I tried to cheat. It didn't work... my powers didn't work."

"You didn't bother telling us?" Ixl took several short paces and ran his fingers through his hair.

"It's the curse giving me bad luck." Van threw her hands in the air. "Or the Creator blocking me."

"The game is a death sentence," said Ixl. "I'm entering for you. I can win this."

"Like I said, no one is entering anything," said Van. "We're leaving."

After a stunned pause by the group, Paley asked, "What about Ferox?"

"He wants us to leave. He can't protect us anymore." Van dashed toward her bedroom. "Grab your stuff. We're getting out of here. Where's Kopius?"

"He's in the guy's suite," Daisy called over her shoulder as she and Paley hurried to their rooms.

"We'll grab him," said Ixl. He and Brux darted past Van into the secret passageway.

Suixsha entered Van's room. "I stay, rescue Tyger. Meet you later."

"Come with us." Van heaved on her backpack. "You know the area. That's why you're here."

"I not leave Tyger," said Suixsha.

"We'll come back for him." Daisy entered the room wearing her backpack. "No matter what."

"Ferox won't allow anyone to hurt him," said Van. "For now, we stick to the mission."

Paley came in and placed a hand on Suixsha's shoulder. "I'll sneak back here with you. We'll set him free. Promise."

"We're a team," said Van. "We stick together."

Suixsha gave a pained nod.

"Kopius wasn't there." Brux stepped into Van's bedroom through the panel door.

Ixl entered behind him, carrying Kopius's pack. "Where is he?"

"Right here." Kopius bounded into the bedroom from the secret passageway. "Just scoping it out."

"Let's move." Ixl handed Kopius his pack. "We'll fill you in on the way."

As the team crept down the dim corridor, Van said, "Maybe with a little help from the Creator, we can get out of here alive."

"Creator not do for you what you can do yourself," said Suixsha.

Van scowled and brushed past Suixsha. She said to Ixl, "I know a way out."

She led them to the exit door she had found earlier, and they piled out of the palace. The smell of burned barn lingered in the air.

Paley scrunched her face. "I smell barbecue."

"Training area." Suixsha pointed at the ring. "We on back side of palace. Go into wood. Head south."

"Come on," urged Brux. "Before the palace guards make their rounds."

The team scrambled into the woods. After walking for some time, Ixl held up his hand. They stopped.

"We're not alone," he whispered.

Men dressed in plain jerseys with loose fitting leather vests appeared from behind the trees and surrounded them. They wore black eye masks and carried spears and daggers. Van lost count; there were too many for them to fight.

"Rebels," muttered Brux. "Watching the palace."

"That's right," said one of them. "We know from seeing that one,"—he pointed his thumb at Van—"at the festival with her bright blond hair, you're Lodians."

The rebels grabbed them, tied their hands behind their backs, and secured blindfolds. The rebels shoved them forward.

"Where are you taking us?" demanded Daisy.

"What do you want?" asked Brux.

They moved through the forest for some time before the rebels forced the team to stumble up several stairs.

Van heard their footsteps crinkle. She knew they had entered a structure and were walking on aged, fragile floor tiles. The air grew cooler and smelled mildewy.

Once deep inside the building, the rebels removed their blindfolds.

Van scanned the open room. It had several large in-ground rectangular pools, long ago dried, now cracked and spotted with black mold; a bathhouse. Magnificent in its day, now run down and abandoned.

One rebel opened an easy to miss, hinged, folding door that blended into the design of the wall. Van thought the door might disintegrate from the movement. After passing through, she noticed it had been reinforced on the backside.

The rebels led them down a crumbling stone stairway. At the foot of the stairs, they entered a cement tunnel about twelve feet in diameter with more mold and less air.

Van's eyes watered from the stench. "Is this an old drainage system?"

"Sewerage system," said Kopius. "Used by the bathhouse in its heyday."

"No talking," growled a rebel, as he shoved Kopius.

They moved deeper into the cement tunnels. A rebel lit a torch.

The fractured walls and stone fragments along their path gave Van a genuine fear the tunnel might collapse.

They entered a circular room with a decaying mosaic floor and cracked pillars that reminded Van of the lost temple of the Ming I, a place she came across while in the Caves of Wolfenden a couple of years back. This room, although spacious, was not as big as the temple and had nothing else in it, only dark archways every few feet in the wall encircling the room.

Torch lights flickered through each archway, coming closer.

Black-cloaked, hooded figures surged into the room, surrounding Van and her team. Most gripped war staffs.

As the cloaked figures silently scrutinized their Lodian captives, Van wondered why the rebels had brought them into the heart of the Anti-Manik Rebels' hideout.

Kopius took in a breath, about to speak. Before he could say anything provoking, Van said, "We're friends. We mean you no harm."

She realized how ridiculous that sounded while she and her team were surrounded by about fifty armed rebels, a hundred feet below ground, in an abandoned bathhouse somewhere in the woods of Aduro.

A rebel standing in the front, his face hidden by a hood, holding neither a staff nor a torch, said to one of the men who had captured them, "Explain."

"They're Lodians," said the rebel to his leader. "Important ones too, to be at the palace for Kupalle."

A figure standing next to the leader said in a rushed, low voice, "This is perfect. We can kill them and make it look like the Balish did it."

Paley whimpered.

Ixl strained against his captors, earning him a bop on the head by the blunt end of a war staff.

"What? Why?" asked Brux. A rebel smacked him on the head. "Ouch."

"To increase tension between the Lodians and the Balish," said another cloaked rebel.

"Silence," demanded the rebel leader.

"Why would you want to do that?" Kopius ducked to avoid getting bopped on the head too.

"We have no love for Lodians," said the leader. "Putting your magic in our water, against our will—"

"The Balish Council and King Nequus okay'd that," said Van. "Why aren't you mad at them?"

Brux nudged her, hinting for her to cool her jets.

"The Moors," snarled the leader. "Flaunting Manik's descendent on the throne. It's blasphemous!"

"It's the rightful place of Goustav's heir," said the rebel standing next to him.

"You want to start a war between us and the Balish?" asked Daisy, face slackened, eyes wide.

"You believe as the Balish do about Solmor..." said Brux. "Except you want it to happen because you think it'll draw out Goustav's heir."

"His heir will rise to the occasion," said the leader. "And defeat the demon army just like Goustav during Dark War." He turned to his people. "Kill them!"

The nearby rebels grabbed Van and her team, the other rebels rushed at them, staffs raised.

"Wait!" cried Van. "I'm Goustav's descendent! I'm the heir."

The leader raised his hand. "Halt!" He stared at Van in contemplation for what seemed like forever, then said, "Many people claim to be his heir. Prove it."

"How?" asked Van.

"Show me the Runestar," said the leader.

"We don't have it," said Paley. "But we can get it for you. Right, Van?"

"A witch created the Runestar after the Dark War in honor of the great King Goustav," said the leader. "A charmed gift. If lost, it magically returns to his bloodline. If you don't have it, then you're not his heir."

"She meant we don't have it with us," said Van. "Let us go and I'll bring it to you."

Mumbles erupted among the rebels.

The leader once again raised his hand. The others silenced.

"I'll let you go," said the leader. "Once you get the Runestar proving you are his heir, we won't kill any of you. On one condition. You will help us sneak into the palace."

"To what end?" asked Ixl.

"To kill the crown prince and the king," said the leader. "And any other royals blocking our quest to put the rightful heir on the Balish throne. *You.*"

Van gulped. She didn't expect this turn of events. What could she do?

With no other option, Van said, "Deal." Dreading that she might've just sealed Ferox and his family's fate.

CHAPTER

TWENTY-NINE

"You're free to leave," the rebel leader said to Van.

She let out a breath of relief.

"But... the others will stay," said the leader. "Bring us the Runestar by midnight in three moon's time. Or we'll hand over your friends to the protestors. Let them know these are the people responsible for corrupting their water supply. They'll seek justice. Tension between the tribes will increase after your friends' deaths. We win either way."

Before Van could argue, a rebel blindfolded her again. Several led her out of the ancient bathhouse and through the woods. When they reached the edge of the forest, they removed her blindfold.

Van smoothed her hair with her palm and glanced at each of them. "See you here at midnight, three nights from now with the Runestar." She hoped to leave the rebels with the impression it would happen so they wouldn't get antsy and hand her teammates over to the protestors early. Although Van had no idea how to find the Runestar, and according to Thuxeor, it wasn't lost.

She hurried across the palace grounds, so preoccupied with saving her teammates it didn't occur to her being near the fair posed a risk. She heard people shouting. A group of protestors came charging at her.

Van pivoted and sprinted in the opposite direction. She smacked into a palace guard, who, along with another, had been rushing over after hearing the commotion. The impact almost knocked her to the ground.

One guard grabbed her by the arm, and the three dashed into a side door of the palace. The other guard used a multi-track to notify their commander about the unruly protestors and then said, "We caught Vanessa Cross trying to sneak out of the palace."

They dragged Van back into the dungeons and tossed her into a cell.

"There's no escaping justice," said the guard she had bumped into, sneering.

"You'll face yours in the death match," said the other guard.

Van clasped the metal bars. "I want to talk to Ferox."

The guards meandered away.

Van shouted and banged on the bars. "I demand to speak to the prince! Right now!"

The guards twisted around. Fear of getting in trouble from the noise apparent in their scowls.

"Fine," said one. "Simmer down."

After some time, Alden glided into the dungeon. He wore a formal robe made of white, black, and red silky material trimmed in gold and a matching turban. He looked solemn as he handed each guard some coins. "Leave. I need to speak privately with the prisoner."

He hurried over to the cell and said in a rush, "Van, I'm so sorry the palace is still on lockdown. The prince is not allowed to leave his suite."

"It's okay," said Van, copying his hurried tone. "The rebels are holding my team captive. They need help."

"I'll tell the prince." Alden seemed pacified after seeing she wasn't hurt. He said, slower, "The prince and I brainstormed ways to help you win the match. I brought you something."

"I don't want the Coin." Van held up her hands. "I tried cheating in our Jaychund games. I lost. I don't want that to happen again."

"Even in the face of death?" Alden studied her. "My, my. I understand what Ferox sees in you. However, it's no matter." He flapped his hands. "You can't bring the Coin into the match. The surt is charmed. No magic and no weapons allowed."

Van took the news like a blow to the head. She had planned on trying to connect to her Anchoress bloodline to give her greater strength to fight the Tarcs, to make the match more even. Now, even if she could connect with her innate abilities, they were powered by magic and wouldn't work, anyway.

"Surt?"

"It's where you'll play the game. Listen." Alden lowered his voice, although they were alone. "The prince and I visited Thuxeor. He made a potion that will shield you." Alden took Van's hand and slyly placed an ampoule with gold flecks floating in bright-yellow liquid. "No magic, all power."

"No... I don't want to cheat—"

"It's unfair, you against the Tarcs," said Alden. "Take it. The prince cannot lose you."

Van trusted Ferox and Alden, not Thuxeor. Two against one. She grasped the ampoule.

Alden clasped Van's hands through the bars and said with a bleak half-smile, "Break a leg, as they say in your world." His robes swooshed as he turned away.

Van watched Alden disappear up the stairs and muttered, "Good luck would've sufficed."

She clutched the ampoule and anxiously paced her cell. *Calm down. Think.*

Van sat on the dingy cot. Pulled up her legs and crossed them. Closed her eyes and breathed deeply.

Scuffling of rats and a *drip... drip* of water distracted her. She relaxed her jaw muscles and shook her head to clear her mind, hoping to connect to Jacynthia.

Her spirit guide didn't appear.

Van huffed and flopped backside down on her cot.

"Those matches are brutal," said a dungeon guard, loud enough for Van to overhear. "She's gonna die."

"She's puny. I'm not betting on that one," said another.

They gawked at Van as they continued past her cell, making their rounds. Prattling on about bets they had placed regarding the winner and speculating how Van would die.

She closed her eyes. Somehow caught some sleep, though she tossed and turned all night. Again, she dreamt of the little girl catching a falling star. She thought the dream might mean something. But what?

Van figured it was late afternoon on the third day after they had tossed her in the cell when two palace guards arrived looking smug. As the days passed, Van had grown increasingly worried about saving her team. But, she still had time. Their meeting was tonight at midnight.

"Let's go," said one guard.

Van's stomach growled as they led her out of the palace. They offered her little food during her time in the cell, and today, no breakfast or lunch, starving her like they did the dragons. At least she still wore her traveling clothes. Black leggings and a black, ribbed tank with sneakers and her hair in a ponytail. She hoped her athletic attire would enhance her agility in the match.

She sweat profusely as they hiked for about a mile in the humid, hundred-degree heat through the contrived green landscape that appeared unnatural in a desert land. They entered a clearing with an enormous ten-foot high pit, walls made of thick clay. A myriad of multi-tiered tent-like accommodations on stilts occupied most of the area around the surt, along with stands on the far side, all high enough for onlookers to see into the playing area.

Men and women meandered around. The men dressed in tunic styled garments or robes. The women wore elaborate toga inspired dresses, their hair braided with ribbons or covered with head scarfs, some carried sun umbrellas. All the women appeared to be wearing as much gold and gemstone jewelry as possible, practically blinding Van with their reflective glittering from the sun.

The crowd had its share of Tarcs mingling among the humans. They were easy to spot, towering over the tallest man and three times a human's size. The Tarcs' attire didn't help them blend in. They dressed in red, black, and gold robes that made their bodies look even bigger.

The guards led Van down a sloping ramp. Before the stands disappeared from her line of sight, she glimpsed Ferox in a centrally located box surrounded by his family. Merloc, Mador, Sybil, Solana, and a multitude of guards on alert for the assassin.

Ferox smiled and chatted, looking relaxed, happy, and certainly not worried about Van. Maybe he trusted Thuxeor's potion or thought Van could access her Anchoress powers despite the magical restriction. She snorted. He didn't know she was having trouble accessing her powers. Even without the magical restriction, they'd be little help to her in the match.

Despite his indifference to her plight, his safety concerned her. Why would Ferox risk coming? The answer... to impress his family. This emphasized the reality that his family posed the biggest threat to their relationship. If Van survived, she'd be sure to address this with him.

If she died, Merloc and the other plotting officials, along with the rebels, would get their wish for an attack by the Lodians. An act that would break Manik's law of protection and ignite an all out Lodian-Balish war.

They came to the end of the ramp. A man stood in front of a wood door. He introduced himself as the gaming official.

"If you will follow me." He pushed a button on the wall and the door slid open horizontally. He led Van into the surt.

She entered the enormous ring. The stench from the packed-dirt floor blazed in her nostrils. The bright sun beat down on her. Her heart beat so hard it smashed against her ribcage. The intense humidity made her breathing difficult. Or was it fear? Her stomach did a flip.

Around the surt, doors slid open. Through each one entered a Tarc dressed in full combat uniform—sans weapons—alongside a gaming official.

Van and her official paused about twenty yards inside, as did the others, who appeared far away inside the massive arena.

"There are a few rules," the official said to Van. "This is a fight to the death. There will be one winner. Magic is not approved for use during this match. The surt has been charmed so magic, if used, will be ineffective. Weapons of any kind are not allowed. Do you have any concealed weapons on you?"

Van shook her head, legs trembling.

"If you do not abide by the rules and somehow circumvent our security measures and sneak in weapons or use magic and you win, you will be executed. The match will be nullified and no winner declared. The munerarii, the wealthy individuals sponsoring the match, will be most upset. They will take their disappointment out on your friends and family after your death. Do you understand what I have just explained to you?"

"Y-yes." Van wanted to vomit. How could she fight the massive Tarcs without magic or weapons?

At the gaming official's urging, Van forced her rubbery legs to move forward into the center of the surt. Ready, or not, to face the bovine-like creatures who prided themselves as mercenaries, a para-military tribe that handled dirty deeds for the Balish regime.

Pitted against her.

In a fight to the death.

CHAPTER

THIRTY

Twelve massive Tarcs faced Van from across the surt.

Yeah, totally fair.

An ear-shattering shriek came from the head gaming official's whistle. He ducked out of the arena.

The Tarcs rushed at Van.

Her mind blanked, and her body became paralyzed.

One galloping in front of the yoke twisted around and swung. He punched the Tarc behind him in the throat with so much force it made a crunch sound. The injured Tarc flew backward and smashed to the ground. Blood bubbled from his mouth.

The other Tarcs slowed down and glanced questioningly at the incident. Then a free-for-all busted loose and they began smashing fists into each other.

Van sighed in relief until several picked up their pace and barreled toward her.

With a jolt, she turned and ran. She came to edge of the surt and skidded to a stop, gasping to catch her breath.

The three Tarcs positioned into a semi-circle around her, trapping her against the wall.

Grunts blew from their dot-like nostrils as their chests heaved up and down from the exertion of running in the heat. They lumbered toward her, making her aware how much smaller she was compared to them and their bulky physiques... that made them slow and clumsy... Van dashed at the middle Tarc.

She dropped and somersaulted between his bowed legs.

Her game plan: outlast them. Let them kill each other. Then her fight would be against one, not three or eleven, increasing her odds at winning.

Van scrambled to run away. Her head jolted, yanking her body backward. Searing pain ripped across her scalp, like her skin was tearing from her skull. She smashed to the ground; the impact caused her to lose her breath.

The Tarc clutched a clump of her hair and used the force to hold her down, along with his knee pressed into her chest. He drew back his fist.

Unable to pull away, Van scrunched her eyes closed and braced for the blow.

"Oof," grunted the Tarc.

She heard a thud. The pain in her scalp released, and the pressure on her chest let up. She opened her eyes. The Tarc who hit another player in the throat was grappling with the Tarc who had her pinned down.

Van leaped to her feet and dashed away. All around her, Tarcs battled one-to-one. By the time she reached the opposite side of the surt, her opponents had whittled themselves down to seven. Her plan was working.

The sound of wood sliding against the clay wall echoed throughout the arena.

Two Tarcs closest to a thick iron-studded door stopped fighting and hurried away as it inched upward.

One player muttered an expletive and then, "Vinegarroon."

Two reddish-brown, hairy appendages pointed outward from the opening, followed by the head of a creature. Van thought *spider*.

As the rest of its body emerged, she changed her assessment to *scorpion*. One the size of a house with a long, whip-like tail.

Six of its eight legs lifted and tapped against the earthen ground, propelling the creature into the surt. Its front two legs, three times longer than its walking legs, moved like antennas and had thousands of underside hairs.

In a swoop, the vinegarroon used one of its front legs like a broom and brushed the Tarc standing closest to the door into its triangular mouth.

The six remaining players rushed the scorpion-creature, attacking it head-on with their fists.

Two jumped onto its back. The vinegarroon shifted its body back and forth. The players held tight and punched the creature.

One player jumped onto the scorpion's broom-like appendage as it attempted to sweep him. He gripped tight and bounced up and down, using his feet to break the creature's leg.

The creature twisted and bucked. Its pointed tail curled forward and jabbed at one of the Tarcs clinging to its back. It pierced him in the chest, going through his uniform, but unable to fully penetrate the Tarc's thick skin.

The player caught the scorpion's tail in his grip. He curled his other hand into a fist and pulled it back, ready to strike. He paused. The Tarc's arm dropped; his face slackened. His body went limp, and he tumbled off the creature's back.

The scorpion snapped its tail at the other rider, nicking him in the neck. That player slumped and rolled off the scorpion's back.

Van made a mental note to stay away from the vinegarroon's tail.

The scorpion stomped its walking legs, crushing the two motionless Tarcs lying on the ground. One of them made a noise before dying, meaning the venom in the creature's tail paralyzed its victims, rather than kill them.

Van kept far from the vinegarroon and the battling Tarcs. Her mind spun with ways to defeat the creatures.

The scorpion demolished another player.

Think! What powers did she have? Van had an advantage in the dark. No chance of that with the sun's contrary brightness shining into the surt.

The ampoule! Alden said it would give her protection. With trembling fingers, Van fumbled in her pocket. She smelled vinegar and looked up.

The scorpion squirted a clear liquid out of its mouth, splattering one Tarc as the other two continued to rush and punch the creature. The liquid burned through the player's uniform. He screeched as the affected skin on his face turned bright red and blistered.

Another splash of liquid shot from the vinegarroon's mouth, aimed at the other two players.

They ducked and darted with amazing agility.

Van snapped off the top of the ampoule and raised it to her lips. A sharp whack on her back knocked her forward. She face-planted on the ground. The ampoule flew from her hand.

Van lay face down on the hot dirt floor of the surt, watching the liquid drain from the vial. Her back throbbed where the whip-like tail of the vinegarroon had slashed her.

A sickening warmth coursed through her veins.

She didn't have the strength to haul herself back onto her feet. Each muscle felt like it weighed a ton. She tried to lift her head, and it dropped with a thud as her strength gave way to the venom. Her cheek rested against the ground, numb and unable to feel the heat. Drool trickled out of her opened mouth. Her eyes already drying from being unable to blink.

From her position, she had a full view of the surt's fighting floor. The vinegarroon and Tarcs kept each other busy, allowing Van to be ignored for the moment. She hoped by the time one of her opponents became the victor, her paralysis would wear off.

Globs of fire shot from the vinegarroon's mouth. The wet areas lit up in flames. Van knew from school that surt meant "charred appearance," now she knew how the arena got its name. It made sense. Ferox told her the matches had been going on for months.

The Tarc, partially covered with the creature's acid-spit, went up in flames. He frantically patted himself and fled without direction.

Van watched him run straight into the inferno caused from wet areas on the dirt floor. She wondered if the Tarc's skin would... if it would... *what?* Her mind blurred and she could no longer hold her train of thought.

She tried to focus as a shadowy human-shaped figure formed out of thin air near her.

A hallucination?

Its arms reached for Van. Its legs struggled to take a step closer.

It came into clarity, taking on a solid form. Thick, black goo covered its body, restraining its movements. It made incomprehensible sounds as if trying to speak.

Her mind went to Solana's dark master. The Balish princess had entered a demon into the match to ensure Van's death.

The demon tossed a floppy, black object about the size of a dinner plate at her.

Van tried to roll away from the approaching danger, but the venom had worn off only enough for her to lift her head.

The disk smacked her in the face. Then flopped to the ground.

Perhaps it wasn't real.

She lifted her hand enough to skim her fingers over it. The super-thin, pliable plastic was cool to the touch. She curled her fingers to grip it. It crumpled as real as anything in this world.

Her mind cleared. The demon dissipated. The disk remained clutched in her hand.

Whatever the demon had tried to do, it didn't work. Van was unharmed. Perhaps because of a side effect of the venom. Or maybe from her being in an altered state of consciousness.

Van fought against the venom's remnants and struggled to her feet.

The last remaining Tarc threw a deadly punch to the head of the vinegarroon. The creature spasmed and then laid silent.

The Tarc twisted, searching the arena for Van. He locked eyes with her and marched across the surt.

Van trembled. She clutched the plastic disk in a tight fist, angry at being in the match, annoyed at the unfairness of it, and furious she couldn't tap into her power. Weakened from the venom and without magic or weapons, she couldn't win a physical fight against the Tarc.

When he reached about ten feet from her, in a fit of frustration, Van gritted her teeth and hurled the disk at him.

It spun through the air, smoothed itself out, and stretched into a circle large enough to encompass the Tarc. It landed on him, a direct hit.

He disappeared.

The black disk lay on the ground, retracted back to its original size.

For a few seconds, there wasn't a sound in the arena.

Then the crowd burst into a tumultuous roar of shouts and hoots as it sunk in.

Van won the death match.

CHAPTER

THIRTY-ONE

Was the crowd cheering? Or were they angry shouts?

All Van could decipher in her state of astonishment was a convoluted, roaring noise.

She didn't know how long it took for the head gaming official to collect her. A minute? A half-hour?

He gripped Van's wrist and raised it upward. "The winner, Vanessa Cross!"

"Where'd he go?" she muttered, referring to the Tarc that disappeared into the black disk.

The gaming official chattered on. About what—Van couldn't discern. She withdrew into herself as if still numbed by the vinegarroon's venom.

He stopped prattling and lowered her arm.

Van's body wriggled back and forth as he repeatedly nudged her.

"Come," he said. "The match is over."

The gaming official led her out of the surt. A handful of guards joined them at the exit and accompanied them as they walked past the onlookers—congratulating her? Yelling at her? All their voices blurred into a clamor.

209

The official shoved her into a horse-drawn carriage. They traveled past more gawkers formed on both sides of the road. Bystanders waved as they traveled through the crowded fair. They stopped at the palace's main entrance. The driver opened the door.

Van didn't budge. Based on prior experience, she knew the water protestors loved hanging out in this spot. She warily gazed out the door.

A palace guard yanked Van out of the carriage.

"Come now," he said, as if speaking to a small child.

Guards surrounded her as they walked up the main stairway. Van twisted around and searched the crowd for protestors, but she didn't see any.

They shuffled Van through the palace and dropped her off at the girl's suite.

A woman clutching a duffel-shaped leather satchel waited for her. She introduced herself as the palace healer. Van didn't catch her name.

After sitting Van on the couch, the healer examined her.

"Does this hurt?" The woman pushed her fingers into a spot on Van's abdomen.

Van mumbled answers to multiple questions. She thought of her step-mother, the palace healer who had betrayed the royal family—Ferox's family—long ago, before he was born. With mild shock, she put together, Genie knew Ferox's parents.

The healer recommended Van take a shower.

Afterward, with Van wrapped in a towel, the healer treated Van's injuries. Patiently coaxing Van when she cowered from treatment. The woman wedged her fingers into the side of Van's mouth to open it, and squirted in several drops of liquid, same way as you would a reluctant pet.

"That ought to fortify you. Bring you back to yourself a bit, then." The healer snapped her bag closed. She left Van with a pill jar, a gel tube, and instructions on how to use them.

Van retained nothing the healer said.

Once alone, Van threw on clothes she grabbed from her back-pack, pulled her damp hair into a ponytail, and plopped down on the couch. She breathed in and took a moment.

A silver glare caught her attention. Chafing dishes. On the dining table, along with baskets of baked goods. The royal family had sent a celebratory buffet to her suite. By now, they must know her team-mates had snuck out of the palace. Did they send the buffet to torment her?

Her teammates. She needed to rescue them from the rebels... find the Runestar.

The medicines took effect and cleared her mind so she could focus on the situation at hand. Too bad she had no idea what to do next or how to find the Runestar.

"Van!" Ferox came bounding into the living area.

Van leaped from the couch.

He wrapped her in a big hug, careful not to touch the wound on her back.

"I was so scared for you." He cuddled her. "I'm so sorry you got caught leaving the palace. I did everything I could to help you in the match." He rocked her gently. "I got you the ampoule, paid a Tarc to sacrifice himself to help you survive—the one who punched the other in the throat at the beginning of the match. I wish I could've done more." He released her and gazed into her eyes. "Are you okay?"

Van glided her fingertips over the stubble on his cheeks. Then, wrapped her arms around him, needing the feel of his solid body pressed against hers.

"I'm here. I'm here. I got you." He cradled her. "My family, the court—they wanted you put back in the dungeon. Claiming you're a flight risk. I fought them. I wouldn't allow it. They respected my wishes and agreed. Thank the light we're on good terms."

A flash of irritation burned through Van when he spoke of his family. Ferox's family believed his relationship with her made him look weak in the eyes of the Balish citizens. No way did they have good intentions about keeping her in the suite rather than in a cell.

What if they hadn't agreed? Whose side would he have chosen? What Van really wondered—*does he love his family more than me?*

She pulled out of the hug. "Ferox, my team—"

He nodded rapidly. "Alden told me about it. I've had my people searching for the Runestar nonstop."

"And?"

Ferox shook his head glumly.

"What are we going to do? I have to meet the rebels at midnight."

"We'll deal with them together," said Ferox.

Van stepped back. "No. I don't want to get you involved."

"The protestors know Lodians are here," said Ferox. "They stormed the palace once and will no doubt try again. That, along with the assassin, put us on double lockdown. We can't leave using a passageway door to sneak out. Guards are stationed everywhere now. There's not an inch of grounds unguarded."

Van dropped back down on the couch, exhausted.

"Wait. I have an idea," said Ferox. "I'll be right back." He dashed into her bedroom and back into the passageway.

Van relaxed into the couch. *Ouch.* The birch tar tincture the healer rubbed onto her injury from the vinegarroon's tail needed more time to work. Her whole body ached.

She forced herself to think about something pleasant. *Ferox.*

Her heart fluttered. She imagined them getting married in a beautiful spot in the woods. Trees decorated with twinkling lights, draped ribbons, and big, white bows. Ferox, standing at the altar, looking proud and handsome. His love for Van shining in his eyes.

After the wedding, they would split their time between Lodestar and Balefire with their two much-loved children. A boy who'd have Ferox's firm jaw and broad shoulders. And a girl, blond like Van...

The looming darkness of the curse crept into her fantasy of their future. They'd never be able to have a son. With Ferox, a Bale as the father, the curse would grow stronger. Van would die giving birth to their firstborn. A girl who would inherit Van's Anchoress bloodline along with the curse, doomed to suffer the same fate as Van.

She slammed her fist into the cushion. Her knuckles ached from the punch. She shook her hand, frustrated about having incredible power and feeling so helpless.

Did she even need her magical Anchoress bloodline? Maybe if she could get rid of it, the curse would go too. Then she and Ferox wouldn't have to worry about the differences in their cultures or his family impeding their relationship.

But... that would leave the Lodians unprotected during Dishora.

She smacked both her fists on the cushions this time. Not only hurting her hands but also waking up the injury on her back.

"Hey." Ferox returned, interrupting Van's downward spiral. "Put this on." He tossed Van a robe and a headscarf. "We need to hide your blond hair and your clothes."

"What's wrong with my clothes?" Van looked down at herself. Jeans, sneakers, t-shirt—*ah, right*—no one here dressed that way.

He had already changed into robes and a turban. Under his arm, he held a six-foot long cloth scroll.

Van glanced at him as she pulled on the robe. "No fake mustache?"

"I have to look like an official with high enough rank for *this*." He unrolled the scroll—only it wasn't a scroll—it increased in size, into a rectangle of woven fabric designed with gold, black, and red intertwining triangles.

It hovered a couple feet above the floor.

Van's jaw dropped. "Is that a—"

Ferox grinned. "Magic carpet? Yes."

THIRTY-TWO

"Thuxeor gave it to me on my thirteenth birthday." Ferox placed his foot on the magic carpet and pushed down. "Not unusual to see at least one of these this time of year." The carpet supported his weight. "You ready for this?"

"I'm in!" said Van, impressed.

Ferox rolled it up. "We can take off from the balcony in my rooms."

They dashed through the passageway back to Ferox's suite. He yanked open the double doors to his balcony and unrolled the carpet. It rose to knee level.

Ferox grasped Van's hand. "Climb aboard."

Van sat, legs crossed. The carpet molded to her butt like memory foam.

Ferox knelt behind her, placed his hands on her shoulders, and pushed his knees downward in a jerking motion. The carpet zoomed forward. "Hang on!"

"Woo-hoo!" cried Van, too elated about the magic carpet ride to worry about drawing attention to them.

Ferox steered the carpet higher. Van's stomach lurched. Her fear of heights returned with a vengeance and escalated as they headed straight for a turret.

The carpet's side swiped the stone as Ferox veered away.

"Do you know how to drive this thing?" Van shouted over her shoulder.

"I've never taken her out before." Ferox directed the carpet higher, and they zoomed around the palace, then over the festival.

Van was glad for her headscarf, otherwise the wind would be whipping her hair every which way. She peered down. People meandered past the rows of pointed tent tops looking like colorful dots with their turbans and headscarves. Dusk had settled in and twinkling lights of the fair sparkled like little fallen stars. Several people pointed to the sky as she and Ferox soared above the crowd.

They glided away from the fairgrounds and flew over the palace, darting between the turrets as Ferox got the hang of steering the carpet.

Van laughed and hooted. Happy the carpet ride created an intimacy between her and Ferox, allowing them to bond over a shared, exciting adventure.

Ferox leaned down and said into her ear, "I've been meaning to ask where you got the dot matice. Great idea bringing it into the match with you."

Van twisted to stare at him. "What's a dot matice?"

Ferox frowned. "The black disk you used to take out the last Tarc." He sounded concerned, as if worried Van had brain damage.

"I didn't know that's what it's called." She faced front again.

"Did you get it at Lodestar?"

"That demon tossed it at me." Now Van wondered about Ferox's mental capacity. "You know, during the match in front of everyone."

"Van..." Ferox paused for a moment. "There was no demon in the surt. Only Tarcs and a vinegarroon. Are you sure the healer checked you over?"

Van twisted around again. "You didn't see it? Humanoid, covered with black goo?"

Ferox stared at Van, looking grave. He shook his head.

Van knitted her brow, unable to make sense of it. "Well... where did that Tarc go? What happened to him?"

"He's not dead, if that's your concern. Dot matices make an opening through solid matter, like walls, in emergency situations or when you need a quick escape. They're paper-thin and foldable. Easy to tuck in your pocket for travel." Ferox shrugged. "You sent him somewhere. Probably the last place you were thinking about."

"Geesh. I'm glad I wasn't thinking about my suite. But... it's magical. So, how did it work in the surt?"

"Dot matices are charmed objects. A gray area since the council allows magic for transportation. Only unauthorized magic wasn't allowed in the match. You impressed everyone by finding a loophole."

"I didn't find it! It was—ugh, never mind." Van turned and faced front again.

Ferox swerved the carpet, sending them soaring over a wooded area.

A loud *pop* like a gunshot startled Van. Then came another. And another.

Multiple streaks of sparkles lit the night sky. A smokey scent reached Van's nostrils.

Fireworks.

She giggled in relief and covered her ears. Van loved fireworks, but not this close.

Ferox dodged the bursts and streaks. Still, a spark landed on the corner of the carpet. Van crawled to the edge and used her palm to pat it out.

Ferox shifted, causing the carpet to tilt.

Van wobbled. Her heart raced as she and clutched the fabric, saving herself from tumbling over the side.

"Close one," said Ferox. "Sorry."

They swerved around the bursting sparkles and traveled away from the fireworks.

Van rubbed her singed palm, making a point to glare at Ferox.

"I've got the hang of it, now." Ferox grinned.

She settled back into her spot and sat cross-legged in front of him.

Ferox turned serious. "Let's go do some rescues."

The fun of the ride faded. "I don't know where the rebels are holding my team. I don't have the Runestar. I don't even know how to find it."

"I got this." Ferox steered the carpet toward the back of the palace. They soared over vast landscaped fields to a large multi-story stone structure.

"What is it?" asked Van. "It looks like a prison."

The front entrance had two guards stationed. Both engrossed in their own conversation and didn't notice the magic carpet whiz by high overhead.

Ferox landed the carpet on the roof. "Come on."

Van trustingly followed him through a rooftop door, though she still didn't know his plan.

They hurried down the stairway, exiting onto the first floor. The room was empty except for a large cage.

Tyger paced inside. He snorted and flicked his head as they approached.

"It *is* a prison," whispered Van.

"We were forced to use this warehouse after someone burned down our barn."

Van slapped her hand to her chest, eyes wide. "Who would do such a thing?"

"It worked for our benefit." Ferox smiled and shrugged. "A location far from the palace, less guarded."

They crept toward the cage, careful not to further agitate Tyger.

"Hey, boy." Van held her finger over her lips. "Shh."

Ferox unlocked his cage. Tyger sauntered out and shook his fur. Van cringed and covered her face, expecting the beast to burst into flames. He didn't.

"He's just stretching." Ferox gave her an amused grin.

Van blushed over her ridiculous behavior. "Now what?"

"This way." Ferox dashed across the room to a double-paned window in the back wall. He yanked it open. "We're only one story up. Tyger, go through the—"

Already catching on, Tyger leaped out the window.

Ferox clasped Van's hand. "Let's go."

They raced back to the roof and climbed aboard the magic carpet. They rose into the air and found Tyger sleeking through the grounds below, headed toward the woods.

"He'll lead us to Suixsha," said Van, catching on to Ferox's plan.

Cloaked by the night sky, Van and Ferox peered down and followed Tyger as he moved through the woods. His fur glowed—intentionally, like a night light—to help guide Van and Ferox.

They flew over an area intuitively familiar to Van. "There!" Van pointed to a spot ahead of Tyger.

Ferox lowered the carpet.

Van caught the motion of hooded figures moving through the woods. Rebels on their way to meet Van.

Tyger caught up with the rebels. He roared.

"Land!" cried Van.

"I'm trying," said Ferox. "There's no clearing."

Tyger lashed at the rebels. Some cowered in fear, others attacked.

Van saw the glint of blades.

"Land!" screamed Van.

"Hold on." Ferox descended. He steered the carpet between branches, too tight for a smooth landing.

The carpet magically adjusted its size to fit, curled at the edges to hold them in, and safely landed near the squabble.

Tyger kept the rebels busy, swatting away their blades with his enormous paws and snapping his jaw at them.

Van leaped off the carpet and rushed to her teammates, Ferox followed. They untied their friends' bound hands and removed their blindfolds, then hurried everyone back to the magic carpet.

"Get on," Van urged her teammates.

With a skeptical gaze, Paley stepped on. "It's a rug."

Ixl raised his eyebrows. "Is that a—?"

"Yes," said Van and Ferox.

"Fascinating." Kopius climbed aboard.

"Van, are you okay?" asked Brux.

"I am now," she smiled and made room for him on the carpet.

Ixl, in line to board next, paused and gazed at Van. "Nice outfit. This your new look?"

Daisy swatted him. Then they both leaped aboard.

The carpet magically expanded to fit them all.

Suixsha hadn't followed. Van saw her standing close to the fight, eyes on Tyger.

The big cat shook his body, his fur ignited. Some of the surrounding branches lit on fire. The rebels shouted and scattered.

"Tyger," called Suixsha.

His flames went out and his fur returned to normal. He sauntered to Suixsha, bent down and licked her face.

She scratched behind his ears. "Stay hidden. We meet again soon."

He flicked his head, turned, and disappeared into the woods.

Suixsha put out any lingering flames in the nearby brush, then climbed onto carpet without a fuss.

"Better than the fig?" Ferox raised his eyebrows at Suixsha.

Suixsha gave him a curt nod. "Better than fig."

"Hang on." Ferox took the carpet upward, maneuvering between the trees, and soared over the forest. "I'm taking you out of Balefire."

"Thank the light," said Daisy. "I'm sorry, Ferox. That was rude of me."

"No offense taken," said Ferox.

"This is amazing!" Paley crouched at the front. She held her chin high, hair blowing in the wind.

"Can this thing get us to Muspell?" asked Ixl.

Ferox shifted his body. The carpet veered. "I'll take you as far as possible."

The wall surrounding Balefire Palace grounds came into view. Their ride lurched and dropped in altitude.

Brux gripped the carpet. "The magic's wearing off!"

"There's too much weight," said Ixl.

The carpet vibrated and stalled.

"We're going to crash!" yelled Paley, latching onto Van.

Ferox jerked his knees, trying to get the carpet to re-start.

Van held on as they plummeted.

Ferox pushed his knees downward, harder. The carpet shuddered enough to shake everyone. The tops of the trees, a mere feet away...

The magic kicked in again and they rose higher.

"Magic carpets seem to have limited range capabilities," said Kopius, once they were on an even keel. "This one's is inside the palace grounds."

Brux looked glum. "Head back to the palace. It's the only way."

"Well, at least no one will be the wiser we left," said Ixl.

"Oh, they know," said Van. "Believe me."

"I'll sneak you back in," said Ferox. "Through the balcony in my rooms. I'll vouch for you."

They landed on Ferox's balcony and said hurried thanks and goodbyes.

Van and her team went through the passageway back to the girl's suite. No sooner than they entered, there was a knock on the door. The guys hid, Van answered.

A palace messenger handed her a scroll, bowed, and left.

She unrolled it.

"What is it?" Brux looked pale.

Van lowered the scroll. "The Balish Royal Court put a shoot to kill order on Tyger."

CHAPTER

THIRTY-THREE

Van's mouth went dry as she gave them the gist of the scroll. "The Balish Royal Court wants to question Suixsha about a missing tyger. As a courtesy, we're being informed they sent teams to hunt the dangerous beast. For our safety."

Suixsha clenched her jaw and stomped toward the door.

Ixl leapt over and grabbed her arm. "Whoa. Where are you going?"

Suixsha turned her head with a snap. "I find Tyger." Her eyes bored through him.

Paley's finger zipped to her mouth. "You should sneak through the secret passageway. Right?"

"Your anger isn't serving you," Daisy said to Suixsha. "For the good of Tyger, take a moment to breathe. Sit in quiet, return to your center, gain clarity. Then decide to act."

Suixsha paused—didn't shiv Ixl—and released her grip on the door handle.

Ixl visibly relaxed. "Facing the court is your best bet. Make an appeal to remove the kill order."

"I'll go with you," said Brux. "Tell them Tyger isn't dangerous, and that you had nothing to do with setting him free."

"We could… *leave.*" Kopius shrugged. "Get off the grounds. Tyger will find us—you. Just putting it out there."

"If we leave before Suixsha goes to court, Ferox will get in trouble," said Van. "We can't do that to him. He just helped me save all of you from the rebels."

"And leaving wouldn't be a great way to build relations between our tribes," said Brux.

Daisy placed a gentle hand on Suixsha's arm. "Tyger can outwit them for a few hours. I'm sure of it."

Suixsha nodded, resigned to waiting, but didn't look happy about it.

"Okay, now that it's settled…" Van recounted what had happened to her while they were apart. She used her fist to cover her yawn. "I've had a long day, as you can imagine. I need to catch some sleep."

"Yeah, I'm pretty tired too." Paley unsuccessfully stifled a yawn.

"I'll stay up with you, Suixsha," said Daisy. "If you want company."

Suixsha gave her a curt nod.

Brux glanced at Kopius and Ixl. "We should head back."

Kopius gave Daisy a quick kiss on the lips and then followed Brux and Ixl into Van's bedroom and the three guys scooted through the passageway.

Once alone, Van changed into a nightgown provided by the palace. She ran her hand over the smooth, lightweight cotton material and gave a nod of approval. Then she slipped between the cool sheets on her bed, thinking she would fall asleep instantly. Yet, the injury from the vinegarroon's tail itched and tingled as it healed from the ointment, keeping her awake. The noise coming from the living area didn't help either.

She slid out of bed, opened her door a crack, and saw Suixsha pacing. Daisy was fast asleep sitting up on the couch. Van thought about taking Daisy's place, keeping Suixsha company, to provide a means of conversation to ease Suixsha's mind about Tyger—and decided against it. Suixsha wasn't much for sharing her feelings and Van decided she would serve her teammate better after getting some much needed rest.

Unfortunately, sleep wasn't in the cards for Van. She tossed and turned all night, waking at the slightest noise. Finally, morning came and she got out of bed.

Suixsha still paced the living area, probably at it all night.

Daisy and Kopius were wide awake and huddled on a loveseat, looking anything but loving. Both of their jaws tight, forcefully whispering back and forth.

"How did I not hear you come in?" Van asked Kopius, as she took a seat at the dining table.

Daisy rose from the loveseat.

Kopius followed, looking grim. "You were dead to the world."

Van peered at them as Kopius took a seat at the table, and Daisy entered the kitchen. "Everything okay?"

Daisy nodded. She grabbed a peach out of a pretty hand-painted bowl and sat at the table.

Kopius's eyes turned to the living area. "How're you today? Didn't get much sleep, did you?"

Suixsha paused, glanced at him, and resumed pacing, looking like a magnificent beast trapped in a cage just like Tyger.

Paley emerged from her bedroom, rubbing her eyes. "Morning." She stumbled into the kitchen, grabbed a frosted red-berry scone from a platter on the counter, and took a seat at the table next to Daisy.

Van twisted around to face Suixsha and said, "You know, I've been wondering what made you enter the Jaychund games to begin with."

Suixsha stopped. "Because games Lodian. I do anything to work against Balish after what they do to my people."

Kopius bobbed his head. "You're looking for justice."

"Go justice," blurted Paley, raising a fist in the air. "Right on."

"The Alga massacre solidified King Nequus's status as a great leader," Daisy said to Suixsha. "Getting out the truth will put you in danger."

Suixsha shrugged.

"She's right. A survivor of the massacre in the palace makes Ferox's father look bad," Van said to Suixsha.

"His father status is based on lie," said Suixsha, cheeks flushed. She continued pacing again.

"So you've told him." Paley popped a piece of scone into her mouth.

"Ferox's father cemented the Tarcs alliance with the Balish," said Van. "Gave Godreel a secret to hold over the royal family."

"This talk about Ferox, his family." Suixsha's nostrils flared. "What about my family? Tyger need me." She paused as if running something through her head. "I going." She stormed toward Van's bedroom.

Kopius and Van leaped from their seats. Daisy, closest, rushed over and blocked Suixsha from entering Van's bedroom and subsequently taking the passageway out of the palace.

Without missing a beat, Suixsha spun around and stomped toward the door of the suite.

Paley's eyes followed Suixsha as she hurried past the table. "What're you doing?"

"Should already gone," muttered Suixsha. "Not waited."

"Wait! Don't leave," cried Van.

Suixsha tore open the door. Ferox, looking serious, stood face to face with her, flanked by about twenty bulky palace guards.

He appeared startled. "I came to escort you to the court meeting."

"It now?"

Ferox nodded. "It's now. I'd like to sit with you during the questioning. If that's okay."

"It okay," said Suixsha, still steaming. She pushed past him and his guards, and stormed down the hall.

Before Ferox turned to leave, he winked at Van. "See you later."

Van insides experienced a thrilling jumble.

"So now what?" Paley took a bite of scone. "We sit around and wait?"

"Morning," said Brux. He and Ixl entered the living area through Van's bedroom.

"Well, look who decided to get up," said Kopius.

"Good morning." Daisy lit up the room with her warm smile.

Brux grabbed a scone and sat at the table. Ixl made himself a bowl of oatmeal, as did Van. They all moved to the dining table, and the newcomers got updated about Suixsha.

"How're you feeling this morning?" Brux asked Van.

"Happy all of you are back safe, thanks to Ferox." She squinted at Brux, not liking the dark circles under his eyes. "How are *you*?"

He shrugged. "Feeling a bit drained, to be honest."

Ixl turned to Paley. "You?"

"Meh." Paley pushed away a partially eaten second scone.

"You've been eating a lot." Van peered at her friend. She noticed a pallor to Paley's skin.

"Excuse me, miss perfect," snapped Paley.

"I didn't mean... sorry," said Van. "It's just... the sickness you suffered last year. I think it's making the Twin Gemstones pull harder on your energy to keep you here. That's why you're eating more... and a bit crabby." Van turned to Brux. "And it's why you're feeling drained."

"I'm not crabby," grumbled Paley. "I'd just want some time to search for my birth parents. Does anyone care about that? *No.*"

"Maybe I'm drained because it's exhausting being your protector," said Brux matter-of-factly.

Van raised her brow. "*Excuse* me?"

"This obsession you have with Ferox... it's becoming a problem."

Brux pushed away his uneaten scone. "You care more about him than your own people."

"Oh, okay." Van threw her hands in the air. "Let's get this out in the open. Say what you really want to say."

Brux leaned back with sealed lips. He folded his arms across his chest.

"Brux, I'm feeling a bit edgy, too," said Daisy. "But I'm afraid your passion for Van might be turning to anger. Please try to center yourself."

"I guess I will since I have little choice in the matter."

"I'm so sorry the Elementals picked you as my protector," said Van. "What a horrible thing to have happened to you. Don't worry. I'll make it a priority to get my Items so you can be free of me and go do what you want."

Kopius and Ixl's eyes bounced back and forth between them as if watching a tennis match.

The door to suite swung open. Suixsha swept in.

Ferox accompanied her. He held back in the hallway to speak to the head guard, then came inside the suite.

"What happened?" Daisy rose from her chair to greet them.

"Tyger free," said Suixsha, relief glowed in her entire demeanor.

"What—how?" asked Ixl.

"On our way to court, there was an attempt on my life," said Ferox.

Van rushed over to him. "Are you hurt?" She placed her hands on his cheeks. The others be damned if it offended them.

He gently clasped her hands and lowered them, shaking his head. "Thanks to Suixsha's quick action. She captured him before he could do any harm."

"The assassin?" asked Paley, wide-eyed.

Ferox nodded. "Palace officials believe it was the assassin disguised as a palace guard."

Daisy and Kopius glanced at each other with worried frowns.

"I'm okay," Ferox reassured everyone. "As Suixsha's reward, they revoked the kill order on Tyger. He's free to roam wherever he likes."

"Lockdown over. Team free to go check seal," said Suixsha.

"Is that true?" Brux asked Ferox.

Van bristled over Brux questioning Ferox. Then Ferox's expression made her stomach churn.

"All of you are free to go." Ferox met Van's eyes with hesitation. "Except you."

THIRTY-FOUR

"Why can't Van leave?" asked Brux, baring his teeth.

"She's still under court orders to finish the Death Games." Ferox looked grim. "Once a player begins, they're obligated to play to the end."

Ixl marched over to Ferox. "She already played in your damn games. She won, remember?"

"How long until the next match?" asked Daisy.

"Next week," said Ferox.

"We can't stay here fooling around playing these games," said Ixl. "We've got a mission to complete. And a deadline."

"The delay will cut us close to the end of the Alignment," said Brux.

Paley chewed on her cuticle. "We'll only have two weeks to complete the mission."

Ferox gently clasped Van's arm. "I'll get you out of it. I'll do whatever I have to."

"I won't put you in a bad position with your family," said Van. "Or ruin peaceful Lodian-Balish relations."

Brux's cheeks flushed. "Now is the time I think you should do just that."

Ferox scowled at Brux. "I'll handle it."

"You better," growled Ixl.

"So… did I hear correctly?" asked Kopius. "The rest of us are free to go check the seal?"

"Go," said Van. "Finish the mission. I'll stay."

Ixl seemed to weigh the pros and cons. He nodded. "It's what my mother would do if she were here. There's no sense in all of us sitting around waiting for the next match."

"I'm not leaving Van," said Brux.

"If Brux stays, then I stay." Paley crossed her arms.

"I'll watch over her," Ferox said to Brux.

"You're doing a bang-up job of it so far," said Brux.

"We go," Suixsha said to Ixl, Daisy, and Kopius. "I show you way."

Ferox tore his glare away from Brux and said, "Grab your packs. I'll take you to the supply room so you can stock up before you go."

Van, Brux, and Paley watched as the others left the suite.

"It feels weird seeing them use the door," said Paley.

"I like the passageway better." Brux turned from the door and took a seat in the living area. "More privacy."

Van walked toward her bedroom.

"No leaving without us." Brux leaped off the couch.

"I'm just going to the bathroom," lied Van. Paley's moods, Van could deal with. But she and Brux had lingering tension that made hanging out in the living area awkward for her. She planned on ducking into her bedroom to hide until time smoothed things over between them.

Brux rested back down on the couch.

Paley plunked her butt next to him. "So what are we gonna do?"

"Want to sneak back into the Hall of Records?"

Van came rushing out of her bedroom. All words between her and Brux forgiven. She wanted to search for a way to remove her

Anchoress curse and look for any information about the Runestar. If she found it, the rebels would stop trying to provoke a Lodian-Balish war to draw out Goustav's heir. As their leader, Van could order them not to kill King Nequus or Ferox.

"I do," said Van. "Paley, maybe we'll find something about your parents."

Paley jumped up. "Let's go."

"I'll show you where I found the parchments that mentioned the curse," said Brux, his way of extending a peace offering to Van.

She gave him a nod. "Deal."

At Brux's insistence, they took the secret passageway down into the sub-levels and found the secret door leading into the Hall of Records.

Van gasped at the rows and rows of storage shelves. Stuffed with boxes, books, and bundles of parchment papers. "No wonder you didn't have time to look through everything."

They each went their own way and explored the expansive network of rooms.

Van meandered along the rows in awe at the vast information at her fingertips. She came to a room filled with museum-quality glass display cases, exhibiting ancient items from the Dark War. Weapons, statues, bowls and utensils, scrolls uncurled and pinned down. All protected in airtight glass displays to ensure the objects didn't deteriorate.

Strange place for a museum. But then again, Balish customs were altogether odd.

She came to a display case filled with headdresses from the Dark War, marked "enemy headpieces." Warriors wore them in battle and in celebrations to identify themselves and their tribes. She noticed an eagle headpiece alongside one designed with moons and stars. She recognized the eagle mask as Goustav's from a memory engram Amaryl had sent her a couple of years ago. Van squinted. The display was mislabeled.

She shrugged and meandered to the next room. Cluttered

tables, each with its own piece, filled the room. One table had a parchment clasped open by a wooden frame. Another a painting held upright by an easel with a scattering of brushes and vials of paint on the table. Others had worn leather-bound books, tin and glass cups, or wooden boxes. The tables had a scattering of small hand-held tools, bottles filled with liquids... Van had entered the restoration lab.

She passed a table with a couple of thin, oversized texts. *Goustav's True Reflections by Omazz* titled the book on top. Van grabbed a pair of white gloves stained with splotches of paint lying on the restoration table. She tugged them on so she wouldn't pass out from a memory engram.

Excited to learn more about her ancestor, she flipped open the book. The reason for its size became apparent. It was a pictorial book with stunning, hand-painted images being painstakingly restored, along with pages of text. Omazz, the author, was the palace scribe in Goustav's time. The king, on his deathbed, recounted his life to Omazz for historical records—*a biography*. After Goustav's death, Omazz added his own take on the king's musings for accuracy of record.

Van called to Brux and Paley, who came rushing in.

"I find it hard to believe the Balish are interested in restoring Goustav's true history." Brux took the text from Van. "If it's an accurate account of his life, it'll show him in a terrible light."

"Probably why the Hall of Records is in the sub-levels and off limits to the public," said Van, as she removed her gloves.

Paley peered over Brux's arm to view the text. "I wish I could read the language of the ancients. But, I can follow along with the pictures. Just tell me what it says."

"Can we please talk about how gorgeous these pictures are?" Van swept her hand over the image on the opened page.

Brux clasped Van's wrist to prevent her from touching the text. "We can read it. *Read.*"

"Getting a memory engram would be so cool." Van wriggled her wrist from Brux's grip, restricting her annoyance to keep the peace. "I could witness what was going on back then."

"Stay with us. For now." Brux cradled the book and flipped to the beginning.

Expert brushes, strokes, and faded colors depicted an image of Goustav battling demons with Amaryl by his side.

"Their tribes worked together even after Goustav killed Amaryl's mother, Cordelia," said Paley. "I gotta hand it to her. That must've been tough."

"Amaryl had to put her people first." Van could relate. "This shows the beginning of the Dark War. Even with her four Items, Amaryl tried to defeat the demon army and couldn't."

"Because she didn't know how to use them," said Paley. "Maybe we can find something to help you figure that out."

Brux turned to the next page.

"That's her, going to Mt. Altithronia," said Van. "To ask the Elementals how to harness the Item's collective power."

"We could do that, right?" Paley peered intently at the image.

"With Amaryl's husband and protector away fighting in the war, Goustav volunteered to accompany her," said Brux. "On that trip, they grew closer. Omazz wrote, Amaryl opened up to Goustav and spoke to him about her husband. She described Rowen's markings that identified his tribe and confessed that Goustav looked similar to Rowen—same gait, height, physique."

Vibrations emanated from the pictures. Van didn't even need to touch them. "Goustav realized he had encountered Rowen during his attack on Cordelia, in the same part of the woods they were soon to pass through."

Paley reached over Brux's arm and turned the page. "Look! They kissed! They *did* have an affair."

An image showed Prince Goustav embracing the young Queen Amaryl.

"They had a child together, so..." Brux raised his brow and turned the page.

"Omazz says a noise in the woods started them," said Van. "They broke apart and continued on their journey. No affair, at least not yet."

"Goustav waited while Amaryl climbed the mountain and met with the Elementals." Brux read Omazz's commentary. "When she came back down, she had become distant, focused only on defeating the demon army. When Goustav asked why she had turned cold, Amaryl told him the kiss was wrong. He caught her in a moment of weakness and longing for her husband."

"She had gained her full power," said Paley. "She didn't need him anymore."

Van furrowed her brow. "It wasn't like that. The Elementals had warned Amaryl about keeping the Anchoress bloodline pure."

"Ah, that meant no fooling around with Goustav," said Paley.

They perused the next image.

"She used the four Items of Creation and defeated the army of darkness with Goustav by her side." Paley pointed to Goustav's face in the image. "Look at his expression. She tore his heart out."

Brux carefully turned the page. "With the war over, Goustav returned to Balefire Palace. His brother Manik told him about plans for his wedding to the Lodian Princess Zurial, a five-day event, one for each year they had fought the war, now known as the Dark War. It would celebrate a new era of peace between their tribes."

Paley gazed at the image. "Goustav didn't like that idea. Again, his expression tells all. For him, the war with the Lodians wasn't over. He's only pretending to agree with the peace pact and the wedding. Look at him." Paley pointed her finger at the picture. "You can tell he's secretly plotting against them."

Van tsked. "Goustav believed Zurial enchanted Manik using her witchy ways. He took matters into his own hands. Gathered followers. Many Bales held onto the old ways. They blamed the Silver Tribe —the Lodians—for protecting the terrigens who morphed into demons and rose to their world. They didn't blame Goustav for releasing the demons."

"Goustav planned to kill Zurial before she married Manik. To free his brother from the Lodian witch's spell, and make it look like an accident," said Brux, reading the ancient writing. "Although the shadow army had been destroyed, the echo of Goustav's misuse of the Staff infected him."

Paley shivered. "He slipped further into darkness. His soul damaged by the act of unleashing an army of darkness into the worlds." She took a step back from the table, looking haunted by her own brush with being controlled by a demon.

"But Zurial was pregnant," continued Brux. "The magic binding the blood oath Goustav made with his brother prevented him from harming Manik's bloodline. That included any of Manik's children. Goustav had to wait until after Manik's baby was born."

"Goustav and Amaryl were constantly placed together for events leading up to the wedding ceremony and again throughout the cele-bration. Causing his infatuation with her to grow." Van didn't read this in the text. She knew it in her heart. "Her disinterest and mere tolerance of him ignited his rage."

Brux turned the page. The picture showed Goustav in the garden, making love to Amaryl. Both naked except for Goustav's eagle headpiece.

"Whoa! Hot stuff." Paley grinned at Van. "I guess that's where you came from. Looks like Goustav was right, she lusted for him."

"He's wearing the traditional headpiece of the warrior," said Brux. "Identifying him as a Sand Tribe prince."

Van recalled the memory engram sent to her by Amaryl a couple of years ago. Of the masquerade ball when Amaryl and Goustav made love in the garden... Amaryl's shock as her lover removed the mask. Van connected the image to the eagle headdress in the display case from earlier titled "enemy headpieces."

She took in a sharp breath. "Goustav's not wearing his own headpiece. He's wearing the headpiece of Amaryl's husband, Rowen." Van trembled with ire. "Goustav *tricked* Amaryl into having an affair."

THIRTY-FIVE

Brux's lips drew tight. "Amaryl gave herself freely to Goustav, under the impression he was her husband."

"He knew from their time in the woods... Rowen's physique, colorings... Goustav looked like her husband," said Van, with a distant gaze. "Amaryl was expecting him back from the war..."

"I would be so mad!" said Paley.

"Omazz wrote a note here," said Brux. "Goustav believed Amaryl cast a spell on him too, as her sister had done to his brother. Perhaps in retaliation because he killed her mother."

"His ego flared, infected by the darkness, led him to believe he could do anything, including a rebellion," said Van.

"The plot came to fruition the moment Zurial gave birth to Mehal," said Brux. "Since Goustav's pact only included Manik's direct bloodline, his sister Magdalene, as head of security, was the first person murdered at the beginning of the rebellion. The next order of business was to eradicate the royal Lodian bloodlines."

"Many were visiting Balefire to support Zurial during her childbirth," said Van.

"Oh yuck," said Paley. "That picture is gross."

"It's the midwife who tended Zurial," said Brux. "She was one of Goustav's followers. He instructed her to kill Zurial after the baby was safely born. That's a depiction of the midwife cutting Zurial during labor to make her bleed out."

Without thinking, and completely absorbed in the story, Van turned the page.

Oh, no! Her eyesight grayed around the edges and turned to black...

Goustav dismounted his horse. He and his men were in the woods... Tipereth Forest.

Through Goustav's eyes, Van watched a snarling shadow beast tear apart Amaryl's husband, Rowen.

Amaryl screamed.

Goustav grabbed his Staff from the horse's holster.

The Quasher, done with Rowen, turned its red stare to Amaryl, who stood to face her fate.

It pounced.

Fear gripped Goustav, terrified for his beloved's life, he pointed his Staff. A fiery rope shot from its tip, lassoing the creature mid-flight, binding the beast and anchoring it to the ground.

From where had this creature come? He wondered. Perhaps a piece of darkness remained after defeating the demon army.

Amaryl rushed to her husband's lifeless body. She knelt by him. Her hunched shoulders heaved as she wept.

Although desperately wanting her attention, Goustav gave her time to mourn, as he was merciful. He re-holstered the Staff onto his horse, pulled the Coin from his pocket, and waited.

Finally, Amaryl stood, wiped her cheeks with her fingertips, and turned to greet her savior.

Goustav saw a glimmer of desire in Amaryl's eyes upon seeing him. His excitement grew, hoping the longing was for him, but feared, instead, it was for the Coin he held between his fingers.

Annoyed by this thought, he casually flipped the Coin into the air and caught it in his palm. "Looking for something?"

He ran his eyes over Amaryl's body, and he grinned. Her figure had become fuller, curvier, sexier... more womanly... causing his yearning for her to escalate.

Goustav stopped flipping the Coin and slipped it into his tunic pocket.

He sauntered over to her husband's mutilated body. "So sorry about your husband." He nudged Rowen's lifeless body with the toe of his boot. Not sorry at all. "Where is the baby Mehal?"

"Safe." The rims of Amaryl's eyes were red from grief.

"Where is the baby?" Goustav asked more forcefully.

Two of his men grabbed Amaryl and held her by the arms.

Goustav tensed as several of his men crashed through the brush on horseback.

One of them carried baby Mehal and said, "They left him alone in the woods, my king. We found him not far down the path."

Amaryl's family disgusted Goustav, not for dropping the baby in the woods, but for leaving Amaryl behind. Something he would never do.

Satisfied, Goustav took out the Coin and began flipping it again. "We seem to be finding many things in these woods. The Coin... the baby... the Lodian queen." Flip... flip. "What would you do to get this back, my pet?" Flip... flip. "It can be yours once again. I will gladly give it to you."

Amaryl remained stoic.

The shadow beast struggled against its fiery constraints, growling and snapping. Never taking its eyes off Amaryl.

An overwhelming desire to protect her raged inside Goustav. "I will give you everything you could ever hope for, anything you desire. Once Manik hands me his throne, which he will, I will officially take my place as king, raise my brother's son, and rule with mercy and greatness. With you at my side, my Balish queen."

He stopped flipping the Coin and closed it in his fist. His heart surged with hope when Amaryl lifted her eyes to meet his.

"There is no longer any reason for you to deny me this, now that you

are widowed. Come, it is time for you to show respect to your future husband and king. Kneel to me."

Goustav filled with joy when Amaryl strolled toward him, finally ready to accept her destiny as his wife.

Amaryl stopped several feet from him. Her spit splattered his face. "I will never kneel to you!" Her lips twisted with fury as she spoke in ancient tongues.

Goustav assumed she was cursing him using Lodian magic. He sniggered and wiped her spittle from his face.

His men guffawed along with him.

"You are upset now, my pet. That is understandable. Women are of weak constitution, after all. There is plenty of time for us to get to know each other better. With the death of your husband, you are now free to be my bride."

Over time, she would come to accept his love.

"Take her back to Balefire, put her in my chambers," he said to his men. "I will take care of the shadow beast."

Goustav turned his back on Amaryl to grab the Staff from his horse. Something came rushing at him from behind, an enemy, or the shadow beast, somehow broken free.

By pure warrior's instinct, he swung around, ready for battle, his weapon raised.

The sharp tip of the Staff plunged into Amaryl's chest.

Goustav's eyes widened in surprise at seeing Amaryl standing before him. His gut wrenched at how easily the Staff punctured her delicate skin, glided into her chest, and went straight through her heart. An act he desperately wished he could take back.

She had lunged at him, wielding a dagger, most likely pulled from a hidden pocket in her cloak. Still, the puny knife was no match for his sinewy skin, his massive body, his military uniform adorned with armor from the royal mint. He could have withstood any cuts or jabs she made before he disabled her.

He stood face-to-face with Amaryl, one last time, as if a prelude to a lover's embrace.

A spear of pain shot through his own heart. His insides broke apart from regret as he watched blood dribble down the sides of Amaryl's mouth.

The same sense of regret flickered in Amaryl's eyes—of the life they could've had together—increasing the depth of his pain. Goustav had destroyed the one woman he would ever love.

The horrible shadow beast struggled against its bindings, making one last attempt to break free, snapping and growling until the light faded from Amaryl's eyes. After her death, it quieted, sank into the earth, and went back to the bowels of darkness from which it had come.

Goustav's heart shredded to pieces. As he, along with his men, witnessed the end of the Anchoress bloodline.

Van's eyes snapped open. "Wow."

She wriggled to sit up and didn't feel any aches. Her head didn't even hurt from hitting the floor. Brux's warm embrace entered her awareness.

His blue eyes stared down at her. "I caught you."

"We were ready for it this time." Paley chuckled.

Van recounted her memory engram with them.

"Deep down Goustav must've had an inkling that Amaryl's full figure was because she just had a baby," said Paley. "His baby."

"Especially with his ego." Van gave Paley an eye roll. "But, nope. He didn't have a clue. At least, not then."

"Goustav's egotistical desires led him to commit the most brutal massacre in the history of the Living World," said Brux. "To this day, its repercussions are still being felt."

"I remember when Amaryl showed you the same memory, from her point-of-view," said Paley. "Goustav and his men witnessed her death. It's the reason so many people today don't believe the Lodian's Anchoress exists."

"Well, I do exist." Van's scorching desire to retrieve the Staff had intensified since getting Goustav's memory engram. Although not part of the mission, it was likely near the third seal, as the Cup was near the second seal.

Van had relived Goustav's attachment to the Item, how it energized him, fueled him with strength and power. Having that kind of power would give Van the ability to right all wrongs.

"Don't you see?" Brux jarred Van from her thoughts. "Descendants of the group of men who witnessed Amaryl's death make up the core of the Anti-Manik Rebels."

"And Magdalene's death originated the belief that death of a royal twin is a bad omen," said Van. "Ferox told me the Balish believe it splits the royal bloodline, which precedes a great battle for power."

"It's also why the Balish discourage intertribal marriages," said Brux.

Paley scrunched her face. "That means Solana killing her twin brother is why the Balish believe Solmor is coming?"

Brux nodded. "Devon's death coincided with demons coming to the Living World. It's not that strange of a belief since many of us Lodians believe demons on Living World soil is a sign the Escalation to Dishora has begun."

"It's not like it was a coincidence," huffed Van. "Solana brought the demons here with the help of her dark master to help her kill her brother."

"She nailed it," said Brux. "Two prophecies set in motion by one murder."

"Despite Solana being murderous and evil, when I read Manik's text a couple of years ago, he advised us to live in peace. We need to listen to his warning." Van mentally underlined her priority of building Lodian-Balish relations. The best way to keep peace was by cooling her and Ferox's relationship so as not to upset his family—and for her to finish the Death Games.

They left the restoration lab, wandered into the storage room, and separated to read through scrolls, parchments, and texts that caught their interest. Brux looked for clues about the Runestar. Paley searched for something about her parents. Van about the counter-curse.

Brux said from somewhere among the rows, loud enough for them to hear. "The River of the Damned runs through Muspell. It has something to do with the location of the third seal. You guys find anything yet?"

"Nope," shouted Paley. Her voice seemed far away.

"I found something about the counter-curse," cried Van. "It has to do with the Temple of the Cross, or the Old Mound, as the Balish call it. It's pretty vague. I can't figure out—"

"Hey, guys," Brux came rushing over to Van clutching a scroll. "It mentions the three seals that bind the worlds..."

"We know, I heard you. The River of the Damned." Van glanced at him and then continued to scrutinize the passage in the text.

Brux waggled the scroll. "They bind the worlds, yes—the *three* worlds."

"Three?" Van had trouble translating the book at the fair, the passage describing how the worlds were bound. Now she knew—the seals bound *three worlds, not two!* "Brux, are you okay?"

He wobbled. His skin turned pale and beaded with sweat. "I need to sit down..." He crumbled to the floor.

Van's eyes darted around the storage room. "Dammit, Paley! Where are you?"

CHAPTER

THIRTY-SIX

"I'm going to throttle her." Van clenched her fists.

"Paley... must've... moved out of range," croaked Brux.

Van struggled to heave him up from the floor. "Come on."

"Just... leave me..." Brux could barely stand.

"Once you get closer to Paley and her Twin Gemstone, you'll feel better."

"We don't... don't know where she is."

"I have a good idea." Van gripped Brux around the waist to keep him stable. "We'll take the secret passage. It'll be faster."

They slowly made their way through the twisting and turning corridors.

"I'm feeling better. Wherever you're taking me, it's the right direction," said Brux.

Van leaned him against the wall for support. "Wait here for a sec." She peered through several nearby peepholes. "Here it is." She pulled a lever, a panel slid open.

Brux followed her inside. "What's Paley doing in the wizard's lab?"

"She went to the All-Seeing-Eye to find out about her parents, since she found nothing in the Hall of Records."

"That little spitfire," said Brux, in good cheer now that his health had returned.

"Hello," called Van. She hoped Thuxeor wasn't there. She didn't have the energy to deal with his questions or judgy stares. "Paley?"

They crept across the wizard's lab to the All-Seeing Eye.

Van's irritation escalated with each step. "I'm going to give her a piece of my mind—*Paley!*"

Their friend lay unconscious on the floor next to the table with the Eye.

Brux knelt down and cradled her head in his lap; Van shook Paley's shoulder.

Paley roused.

"You were too far away from Brux's gemstone," Van barked at Paley before her friend fully regained conscious. "What were you thinking?"

"She might've fainted from what she saw in the Eye," said Brux.

"It's one thing to have a fire in your belly about finding your parents, and another to risk your teammate's life by wandering off," said Van.

"S-sorry." Paley rubbed her head.

"The drain from the gemstones almost killed Brux." Van's tone softened as she fully took-in Paley's condition. "You don't look that great either."

"I'm okay," said Paley.

"It's all right. We'll both be fine now." Brux helped Paley to her feet. "What did you see?"

"The Eye showed me my parents... and brother and sisters. I saw a family with kids."

"You don't look too happy about it," said Brux.

Paley shrugged. "I didn't know them. They wouldn't know me. But, I'm pretty sure I'm Balish..." She sniffled. "Which means they definitely gave me up. Didn't bother looking for me."

"I'm so sorry." Van wrapped her arms around Paley.

Brux caressed Paley's back. "Are you good?"

Paley nodded. "Sorry. I won't wander off again."

Van peered at the Eye, resting on the table in the same place as their earlier visit. "So, it showed your parents, huh?"

Paley nodded.

"I have something I want to ask," said Van.

"It's easy. Just hold your hands over it like this." Paley held her palms over the glass orb, then stepped aside.

Van mimicked her gesture. "Who is the Balish spy in Lodestar?"

The gray, wispy smoke within the Eye swirled, turned into different muted colors, and then formed a picture of scenery. A graveyard.

The orb showed four cross-shaped tombstones on an unkempt mound in the woods under the night sky. Grassy and overgrown in some spots, in others worn down to the mud. One cross was intact and dripped with fresh blood. The adjacent tombstone, broken off at its base, lay on the mud-splotched ground, splattered with blood from the other cross. The third tombstone lay unbroken on the ground, knocked over, also streaked with blood.

Light from the moon highlighted the fourth cross, undamaged and standing upright. It would've been identical to the other three except it was made of gray granite instead of white and had no blood on it.

Paley scrunched her face as she peered over Van's shoulder. "What's it mean?"

"I dunno."

"Ask it something else," said Brux.

Van held her palms over the orb. "Where is the Runestar?"

The graveyard image faded into a gray mist and swirled. The smoke re-settled and presented them with the same image.

Van planted her hands on her hips. "This is so annoying."

Brux looked bewildered. "We're supposed to go to an old cemetery?"

Van blew out a sharp breath. "Lemme try again." She fired off another question at the All-Seeing Eye. "Tell me what happened to the other team."

The image blurred, turned to gray smoke that became brownish-white. Then the smoke morphed into fine sand that filled the orb.

Van stepped back, startled.

"Did you break it?" asked Paley.

"This thing is stupi—" Van paused as footsteps approached.

"Thuxeor! Come on." Brux dashed toward the back of the wizard's lab.

Van and Paley followed, and the three of them hurried through the passageway door.

As they scurried down the secret corridor, Paley said, "I forgot to tell you, I think I saw Kopius sneaking around the passageway on my way to the lab. I didn't talk to him—"

"That's impossible," said Van. "They're well on their way to Muspell."

"If you felt anything like I did," Brux said to Paley. "The drain from the gemstones could've made you see things."

As soon as they slipped into Van's bedroom, they heard their teammates' voices in the living area.

"We had to come back," Daisy told them.

"My call," said Ixl. "Rebels in the back, protestors in the front. It's too dangerous for us to leave without palace security's protection."

"Ferox help," said Suixsha.

"He's working on getting us an escort," clarified Daisy.

Van, Brux, and Paley told them about what they found in the Hall of Records, and Van of her memory engram from Goustav.

Brux described the images in the All-Seeing Eye. "Any idea what they mean?"

"It means you broke it." Kopius paced the room, appearing preoccupied, which seemed to make Daisy tense and fidgety.

"What's going on with you two?" Van asked Daisy.

"I'm going back to the guy's suite." Kopius marched toward the door. They were no longer on lockdown, so he didn't have to use the passageway. "I need to—I need some alone time, to think about... our situation."

Daisy hesitated. Then she rose and followed Kopius out of the girl's suite.

Her scream echoed into the living area. Van and the others rushed over.

The door to the guy's suite was wide open. Daisy stood trembling near the doorjamb. Kopius, along with a palace guard, knelt over a lifeless body.

"He went in looking for you, Kopius" said the guard, his voice quavering.

Blood pooled on the floor, seeping from a head wound.

"He was only inside a few minutes." The guard's crumbled forehead beaded with sweat. "No one came in or out of the suite."

Kopius knelt by the body and placed his fingertips on the man's carotid to check for a pulse.

Van glimpsed hearing horns. *Alden.*

Paley gnawed on her cuticles. "Was it an accident?"

"People of his status don't die by accident." Kopius twisted to look at his teammates. "They die by being stabbed in the back."

CHAPTER

THIRTY-SEVEN

"This means the assassin is still at large." Ixl's eyes darted around the girl's suite, like he expected to spot the intruder hidden in the decor.

Van could hear activity in the hallway, as palace officials and guards handled the situation in the guy's suite.

"How did the assassin—what did he use to... you know... Alden?" stammered Paley.

"Looked like a bash to the head," said Kopius.

"I hope he's going to be okay," said Paley.

Ixl threw her a grim look. "He seemed pretty dead to me."

Paley turned to Suixsha. "If the assassin is still here, then who did you capture?"

"Palace guard." Suixsha stood next to the dining table. Van rarely saw the girl sit.

Brux cocked his head to the side. "I wonder if the guard was trying to kill you and not Ferox."

"You suggesting there's two assassins?" asked Ixl.

Kopius shook his head. "If an assassin wanted to kill Suixsha, then she'd be dead. The attempt outside the courtroom was a blundering effort by a low-level guard."

Suixsha shifted from side to side.

Daisy placed a delicate hand on Suixsha's arm. "He didn't mean to imply you're not a skilled warrior. We all appreciate you."

"Why would a guard want to hurt you?" asked Paley.

"I know truth about Alga massacre," said Suixsha.

"Paid by whoever wanted to keep the king's secret quiet," said Van.

Ixl narrowed his eyes at Kopius. "Why are you so sure it was the assassin who attacked Alden and not another guard?"

Kopius gave Ixl a shifty look and pulled a playing card out of his pocket. "I found this tucked into his robe."

"You stole evidence?" asked Paley, wide-eyed.

"The Hierophant." The hair on Van's arms stood on end. "That's a tarot card."

A knock at the door startled them.

Brux opened it.

"Due to the incident that took place in the other suite, the palace is on lockdown again," said one of several guards. "Security in and around the palace has doubled for everyone's safety."

"The boys will remain here until further notice," said another guard.

"No problem." Brux sounded relieved about the team staying together.

Everyone liked the arrangement until a day passed. And then another, and another...

"It's been over a week." Ixl paced. "They're keeping us cooped up in here like caged animals."

"We can't attempt another escape," said Daisy. "We're lucky they didn't throw us into the dungeons after the last one."

"We're pushing Ferox's benevolence to the limit," said Kopius.

"I know," growled Van. "If you try again, I'll stop you myself."

"Time's running out," said Ixl. "We need to finish the mission—"

A fist pounding on the suite's door put a stop to their escalating argument.

Ixl, closest, tore it open, ready for a fight. Or to make another break for freedom.

The guard, ignoring Ixl, stared over his shoulder into the suite. "Vanessa Cross. If you'll come with me."

Brux stepped between the door and Van. "Why? Where're you taking her?"

"It's time for the second match," said the guard.

Kopius leaped from the couch. "We're going with."

The guard held up his palm. "Just the player."

"We want to support her," said Daisy.

"Can't we watch?" asked Paley.

"Guests of the palace are deemed in danger of the assassin and must watch the match from their rooms," said the guard. "Prince Ferox authorized a gemscreen to be brought to your suite for viewing."

Van's teammates said all the right things before she left. *You got this. Wish I could enter with you. You've faced worse. Good luck.* Still, her stomach twisted in knots.

The guard escorted Van to a back door in the palace where a handful of guards waited for them. The group rode by horseback over the landscaped grounds, out of the sight of fair-goers, and unbothered by lurking rebels. They traveled through a winding path in the woods and into another meticulously landscaped clearing. From the grassy field rose a colossal cement building with no windows, at least eight stories high, and freshly painted for the games.

At the building, they dismounted. Van wrapped her arms around herself to keep from quivering, dreading the horrible challenge awaiting her.

With shaking legs, she entered the structure with the guards.

Troubling thoughts raged through her mind—*if it wasn't for the curse, if I had my Items, if the Creator didn't hate me...*

She and the guards walked in silence along the inner perimeter of the building. They veered onto a ramped hallway that led downward to a perpendicular corridor spanning around a curved inner room.

A gaming official stood waiting for Van's arrival in front of a closed u-shaped wooden door. Other players, each with their own gaming official, waited at doors spaced about a hundred feet apart until the curvature of the wall extended far enough to take the rest out of sight. The guards handed off Van to the official and left.

"In this match, you'll be playing pitz," said the official, as if Van knew the game. "It's time for you to don your gear."

He flicked his head at a bench and table pushed against the curved wall. On top of the table lay a helmet, arm pads, knee pads, fingerless gloves with metal spikes, and... rollerblades.

"Magic is not allowed in this match," said the official.

Van sat on the bench and pulled on her knee pads. "What about weapons?"

"Hand-held, non-energy, non-magical weapons are allowed."

Hutriel, the Tarc who sat next to her at the welcome dinner and Solana's pal, hovered by a nearby door. When he caught Van staring, he sneered and twirled his spiked club.

"Why does he get a club?"

The gaming official looked down his nose at her. "That's none of your concern."

Van secured her helmet. "Isn't it, though?" With trembling fingers, she tugged on the rollerblades and snapped closed the buckles, giving her a snug fit.

"You dare question Hutriel?" asked the official, unable to hide his contempt for her.

"Yeah, I do." Her ankles wobbled, barely able to keep her balance as she stood on the blades.

"He won the club in his first match," said the official with attitude. "You're lucky to have the spiked gloves, given to you by the prince himself. You didn't win them, yet you have them."

Van fanned her fingers and appreciatively gazed at the spikes poking out of her gloves. She bet Ferox had something to do with the type of game played in the second match, too. Choosing one where Van had an advantage over the bulky Tarcs, who wouldn't do well skating around a rink on rollerblades. She was smaller, could skate faster, and her experience with ice-skating every winter on the island made her confident she could transfer the skill to rollerblading.

Van's eyes darted to the gaming official. "I won my first match. Where's my prize?"

"The vial of vinegarroon venom?" he asked.

"Well? Where is it?"

"It won't help you in this match."

"How about I be the judge of that?"

"No poisons allowed," snapped the official. "Prepare to enter the rink." He stepped toward their entrance.

"Wait—what are the rules? How do I play pitz?" Van waved her arms to keep from toppling over as she clumsily followed him.

The official scoffed. "Don't drop the ball."

"A bit more, please," said Van, too nervous to use a sarcastic tone.

"Throw the fiery eye of the sun into the hoop and you're done playing. Meaning you instantly leave the rink and earn a spot in the final. The match is timed. Any survivors at the end buzzer are also allowed to move onto the final match. Violence is not only condoned but expected."

A buzzer echoed off the walls, loud enough for the entire building to hear. All the doors in Van's peripheral vision slid upward, including her own.

"The second match has begun." He stepped aside. "You may enter the rink."

Van twisted around as she step-rolled through the archway. "Wait, what's the goal of the game?"

The official pushed a button next to the door, taking him out of sight as it slid down.

He answered Van just before it slammed closed. "Don't die."

CHAPTER

THIRTY-EIGHT

Van teetered on the short ramp leading into the rink. She gripped the rail, barely able to stand upright on her rollerblades and totally unprepared to play pitz.

Tarcs zoomed onto the oval cement track of the roller rink.

Spectators, seated behind a plexiglass wall to protect them from flying objects, spanned the arena. Since the palace was on lockdown, Van assumed most of them had traveled to Balefire City to see the event.

With dread, she released her grasp on the rail, rolled onto the track—lost her balance and crashed to the floor.

A Tarc careened at her, wielding a stone baton. He swooped down and swung at Van. The stone whacked her side so hard it lifted her off the floor for a second.

She hustled to stand upright, hip aching, grateful the Tarc who clubbed her kept skating and didn't stop to pummel her to death.

Van stuck to the outer rink and moved in sync with the other players while she adapted to the rollerblades. She quickly got the hang of it. The rolling technique of the wheels wasn't too different from a blade sliding on ice.

The myriad of players streaked around the rink. Van saw a few hip checks and the baton-carrying Tarcs swing at passing skaters, occasionally hitting them. She kept to herself, trying not to draw attention while she deciphered the game's rules.

A basketball-sized hole made from a protruding piece of cement slowly slid along the wall above the players and below the onlookers, counter-clockwise toward the skaters.

Okay, that's the hoop. Where's the fiery eye of the sun? Van figured it had to be some kind of ball. Her best strategy, based on the limited information offered by the gaming official, was to stay out of the way, go for the ball, toss it in the hoop, and get removed from the match.

A blast sounded and Van saw a clear sphere filled with fire shoot from a cannon-like metal cylinder sticking out from the wall under a large, square digital clock with a red time display. The timer began counting down from 3:00:00 to 2:59:59 to 2:59:58—hours, minutes, and seconds. The match would last three hours.

A Tarc wearing a red leather vest dotted with rivets and spikes caught the fireball. He glanced at the hoop—on the other side of the rink—too far away to make the shot. Instead of holding onto the ball and waiting for the hoop to align with him, he whipped it at the skater in front of him.

As if expecting it, the player twisted around and tried to catch the ball. He fumbled and dropped it.

The fiery eye exploded as it hit the floor and burst into flames, rocking the arena. It incinerating the Tarc who fumbled the ball, and the skaters on both sides of him. The player who threw the ball miscalculated the duration of the blast radius, skated into it, and got taken out too.

Other players continued zooming around the rink.

Van's chest heaved from exertion of the continuous skating. She forced herself to clear her thoughts, calm her trembling legs, and favor her uninjured hip. Rule: don't let the flaming ball hit the floor. *Check.*

Boom! Another fiery eye blasted into the playing area.

Hutriel caught it. He neared the rotating hoop, took a shot, and missed. He skated at a rapid pace away as the ball rebounded off the rim—it didn't explode.

It only blows up when it hits the track.

Van cursed under her breath as the fiery eye hurtled toward her. Her palms grew sweaty as she reached up and snatched the ball mid-air.

Holy—it was hot! A singed leather smell came from her gloves. No wonder the other players didn't hold on to what was literally a ball of fire and wait for the hoop to pass.

She reacted to her burning hands by tossing the ball over her shoulder without aiming it at anyone or even looking for the hoop.

A blast came from behind when it landed. Van risked twisting around. She had thrown it in such a high arc the Tarcs had time to distance themselves to avoid the blast.

"You wasted it," snarled a nearby skater. He bashed Van in the shoulder with his spiked fist and soared past.

Van spread her arms for balance as she spun around. The other players shot by at speeds upward of twelve miles per hour, taking swipes at her with their fists or batons. With each hit, her body lurched. She smashed to the floor.

As Van lifted herself upright, she screeched in pain as a skater rolled over the splayed fingers on one of her hands.

Boom—another fiery eye streaked into the rink.

Skaters rushed past Van, clobbering her with blows to keep her down. Each bash, bone-crushingly painful. She crouched on the floor and covered her head with her arms.

Van peeked out and saw players volley the fireball from one to the next, coming closer and closer to her.

Hutriel's eyes darted to Van. His raised is club and skated faster. When the fiery eye reached him, instead of passing it, he lobbed the ball into the air a short distance with his free hand, rushed forward, and caught it. He did this again and again, headed directly at her.

He winced from continually grasping the fire-hot ball. The other players steered clear, giving Hutriel a clear shot at her, also giving Van time to scramble upright onto her blades.

Hutriel approached and flung the ball at her.

Van gripped her hands together, outstretched her arms, and whacked the ball back at him as she had done a million times playing beach volleyball. She merged back into the flow of players and skated away. Her lower arms tingled from the impact of the fireball. Her injured fingers throbbed.

Hutriel reflexively whacked the ball forward using the smooth part of his club with so much force and it zoomed far over Van's head.

Another player snatched it and took a shot at the passing-by hoop. The ball rebounded off the rim, straight back at the Tarc skating behind him.

It slammed into the Tarc's chest and bounced forward onto the floor. It burst into flames, incinerating the player directly in Van's path.

She tried to stop and didn't know how. She narrowly steered around the disintegration zone. Some of the splattering fire pelted her arm and burned through her shirt sleeve like hundreds of needles stabbing her skin. The putrid scent of her burned hair filled her nostrils.

Another fireball soared into the rink, caught by a player ahead of Van. He tossed it backward.

Van kept alert and easily avoided the blast.

A Tarc hip checked her as he flew past.

She stumbled. Fuming, hip throbbing, she picked up the pace and chased after him. When Van got close enough, she swung her spiked fist, using her uninjured hand. Her arm, too short to reach his head, caused her punch to land on his lower back.

The Tarc twisted around and raised his fist over Van's head.

She ducked, avoided his punch, and continued skating in sync with the other players.

Tarcs tossed the fiery eye around the rink.

At the far side, two of them began punching each other, getting into a rolling fistfight. The other players took advantage of their distraction. The ball quickly bobbed from skater to skater, getting closer to the fighters.

Their eyes widened in surprise as the closest player soared by and smashed the ball at the fighter's feet. A burst of flames engulfed them.

Rule: don't get angry and punch each other because if you slow down or fall, another player will disintegrate you using the fireball. This explained why the Tarcs weren't randomly beating each other —and her—to death.

Hutriel whizzed by, clipping Van. She wobbled as the other players lobbed a ball toward her in a coordinated effort.

A nearby Tarc hurled it at her.

Van regained her balance and swatted away the ball.

She doubled-down on her strategy of getting the fireball into the hoop and taken out of the match.

A ding sounded. The first hour had passed. Van's confidence rose. She could get through this.

Another fiery eye zoomed into the rink from the cannon.

Then another.

And another.

They kept coming.

She swerved to avoid the explosions erupting around the track. Her injured fingers swelled and throbbed with pain. It hurt to breathe, probably from cracked ribs. Yet she batted all the fireballs that came soaring at her. Van hit so many the heat had consumed her shirt sleeves and her forearms reddened with burns. She tried several times to get the ball into the hoop and failed.

The clock dinged again. Two of the three hours were down. The rapid-fire fireballs had taken a good number of players out of the match. Only a handful remained.

A door to the rink slid open. Out ran a—*white ram*? At least that's what it looked like with its curled horns, long coat of fur, and four hoofed feet.

"What the?" muttered Van.

It dashed around the rink, zipping this way and that, looking for something to butt its head against.

It collided with Hutriel. He went flying and pinged against the side of the rink. His club skittered across the floor.

Van continued skating, dodging the fireballs, the other skaters, and, now, the ram.

The fiery eyes continued to storm the rink.

Van had no time to aim the balls bombarding her. She used her forearms to slam them as far away as possible. She pushed the pain of her blistering burned skin aside and focused on staying alive.

None of the remaining players attempted to get a ball in the hoop. They had the same revised goal as Van, survive long enough to beat the clock.

Explosions erupted around her on the track. She ducked to avoid a soaring fireball, dodged a strike by the ram, and kept skating.

Fiery eyes had swallowed most of the players. One remaining Tarc wielded a machete and headed straight for Hutriel, who had barely gotten his bearings after receiving the blow from the ram.

The machete-wielding Tarc came within range of Hutriel and raised his machete in a move that suggested a fly-by strike.

Hutriel twisted around mid-skate, bent at the waist, and elbowed his assailant. He wrangled the machete from the player's grip and in one smooth swoop, Hutriel lopped off his opponent's head.

The ram dashed toward the decapitated head. It used the tip of its horn to pick it up and toss it in the air. When the head dropped close enough, the creature rushed to meet it and head butted it back upward.

Hutriel came barreling at Van, skating counter-clockwise.

The ram bunted the decapitated head upward again. It plummeted, aligned to land directly on Van.

The ram rushed toward her. A fireball veered down. Hutriel careened at her.

Van clasped her hands and pulled back her arms, ready to bash the fireball at Hutriel's feet and take her chances with the ram.

The severed head landed in front of her with a thud.

Her rollerblade caught on its hair, causing her body to jerk just as she hit the fireball. It flung away at an odd angle. Van crashed face-first and spun across the floor from the momentum of her skating.

Hutriel skidded to a stop and raised his machete over Van, who lay sprawled on her stomach.

He swooped it downward.

Van closed her eyes and braced for impact...

Van waited for Hutriel's machete to slash her neck. Nothing came except silence. Commotion from inside the rink, gone. For a moment, Van thought she might be dead.

She cracked open her eyes and saw the u-shaped wooden door, the same one she had used to enter the match. She laid on the floor outside the arena in the same position as on the rink. Van breathed a sigh of relief. Somehow, she had gotten the fiery eye into the hoop. As rules dictated, it had taken her out of the match.

Van tried to push herself up. Her broken fingers and cracked ribs ached. The burns made her skin feel like it was on fire. She flopped back down and rested her cheek against the cold, hard floor, staring at the wooden door she had entered nearly three hours ago.

She had no desire to move. Breathing hurt, she couldn't flex her injured fingers, and her body felt bruised everywhere. The revolting smell of her singed hair and burned skin nauseated her.

Footsteps echoed down the ramp.

Hopeful it was a medic, Van sucked up the pain and sat herself upright.

A breeze swept her arm, touching the sensitive areas of her exposed burned skin.

The air distorted, about five feet away from her, forming the shape of an adult human. The well-defined area became wavy, then clouded, as if someone was trying to materialize.

At first, Van thought another player had scored a hoop and the magic transporting him out of the rink had gone faulty. Then, she got an eerie sense the creature came from an otherworldly place, one of darkness. She scrambled to her feet. The hair on her burned arms raised, adding to her pain.

The figure took shape enough for Van to recognize it as the same humanoid demon that had appeared to her in the first match. She raised her fists, though doubting she'd be able to fight this creature while wearing roller blades.

It filled-in with a black ink-like goo and stretched its arms, reaching for Van. The figure didn't step forward as if stuck in place, but reached with both its hands and made strained whining sounds.

Van stepped back, sure it wanted to snatch her, to drag her down with it into its place of darkness.

The person walking down the ramp got closer. The black, gooey demon turned into transparent squiggly lines and disappeared.

The man from the ramp marched straight at Van and clutched the front of her shirt. "Where is he?"

"R-right there." Van pointed to the empty spot where the demon had formed.

The man's cheekbones were so high they pushed his brown eyes to mere slits. His face elongated so much it appeared distorted, like he wore a mask.

"Stop playing games with me, child," he said in a smooth, controlled voice. "Where is he?" The man gripped his other hand around Van's neck.

"D-din't you see it, just now. It was right in front of me," sputtered Van, choking.

"I saw nothing." He tightened the grasp on her neck. "I checked the suites. He wasn't there."

She pried at the creepy man's fingers. "W-who are you looking for?"

The man shook her. "The Magician."

Van responded with visible surprise.

He noticed and relaxed his grip.

Van breathed easier.

"I am the Hierophant," he explained.

Van's jaw dropped. "You're the one who killed Alden."

"I have come for the Magician." His grip tightened again. "Tell me where he is."

"I don't know... who that is," said Van, gasping for breath. "All I know is he's an assassin sent here to kill my boyfriend... the prince. The palace is on lockdown because of him."

"His presence here has nothing to do with the royal family," said the Hierophant, with a hint of annoyance. "We must settle the score, him and I." He released his grasp.

"How would I know who he is?" Van rubbed her neck.

The Hierophant rose his razor-thin eyebrows. "Because, my dear, you traveled here with him."

"I don't know any assassins. Who do you think I am?"

"I know who you are, Vanessa Cross." He gave a single stroke to the goatee on his pointed chin. "I have no reason to harm you. The assassin code is to only kill for a price, or those who betray us."

"Alden betrayed you? The Magician, too?"

"Alden unfortunately got in my way. The Magician... he was my student. He left to go on a special task and never returned."

"You teach in Salus Valde?" asked Van, catching on to why this assassin thought she knew the Magician.

"The location of our training is a highly guarded secret and very much off-the-books. We are not affiliated with Salus Valde, Lodestar, or the Grigori."

"Yet, I'm supposed to know where he is?" Curiosity overtook Van, and she wondered if she might actually know him. "What's his actual name, not his assassin name?"

"A teenager named Kopius DeTata."

Van's face slackened. "Kopius is an assassin?"

"You *do* know him." He wrapped his hand around her neck again and squeezed. "Where. Is. He?"

Voices trailed down the ramp from the outer corridor. Palace guards, coming to collect Van.

Her eyes darted in their direction. The hand wrapped around her throat released. When her gaze returned to the Hierophant, he was gone.

Van rubbed her neck again. Less to comfort herself and more to help process this latest information.

She pieced together that Alden had walked in during the Hierophant's search of the boy's suite, looking for Kopius. He left his calling card in Alden's pocket to let Kopius know he was coming for him. Yet, Kopius said nothing about it to the team.

Kopius's dangerous past as an assassin-in-training endangered them all. Why would Uxa allow him on the mission? To protect Daisy?

Or to kill Ferox?

CHAPTER

FORTY

The palace healer, flanked by guards, glided down the ramp to the holding area near the rink's door.

During the healer's examination, she rubbed salve on Van's open wounds and bruises, and dropped medicinal tinctures under Van's tongue. She finished by wrapping Van's damaged fingers and cracked ribs in bandages.

"Sorry, I can't do anything about your hair," said the healer.

Van glanced at her, unsure if she was teasing or serious.

The healer gave Van an ampoule and some extra salve. By the time the guards brought Van back to her suite, her wounds had already begun healing from the medicines.

Van noticed Kopius right away, like a red flag in the middle of the living area, even as Paley descended on her with a hug.

"You did great," said Paley, lacking her usual enthusiasm.

The others offered their congrats.

"I knew you could do it." Ixl puffed his chest with pride.

"I'm dreading to see what my hair looks like." Van pulled a singed piece in front of her eyes.

"It looks fine," said Brux, looking peaked.

Paley handed Van a ponytail holder. Van furrowed her brow, concerned about Brux and Paley's health status. Yet, she needed to keep an eye on Kopius. He looked different to her now. More dangerous. His eyes shifty and his demeanor deceptive.

"Hair no matter." Suixsha stood just outside the living area looking in, watching, like an eternal sentinel.

"It matters to me." Van pulled her hair into a ponytail using her good fingers.

"Only dragon matter," said Suixsha.

Van gave her an eye roll and plunked down on the couch, occupied with her own thoughts about the team's precarious circumstances. She needed to tell them about Kopius, but felt he deserved for her to speak privately with him first.

Her teammates rousingly rehashed her performance in the game. Van added her perspective into the conversation, but decided not to tell them she saw the demon since no one had seen it in the first match. She wondered if it had been a residual hallucination from the vinegarroon venom brought on by stress from the roller derby.

"You survived two matches," said Ixl, jarring Van from her thoughts. "We're not taking a chance with you playing a third." He stood. "We're leaving."

"We already tried to leave," said Daisy. "We didn't get very far."

Given Daisy's preoccupation lately, Van figured she had also discovered her boyfriend's drop-out assassin past.

"I'll go see Ferox." Van got up from the couch. "He can help us sneak out."

"No, we're not asking him for help." Brux leaped from his chair. "He sat by and did nothing while you got thrown into the games. We can't trust him."

Van gaped at him. "Ferox saved you from the rebels." Anger heated her gut. Why was Brux being so difficult?

"That guy is all talk," said Ixl. "We don't need him."

Ixl too? Van had to clear her head, disengage from her anger to avoid making a poor choice. She took a deep breath. *Bring in the cool dragon.* She released her breath. *Out goes the fiery anger.*

"You're being a bit tough on the guy, don't you think?" Kopius leisurely leaned back on the couch.

Van peered at Kopius with mixed feelings. Given the Hierophant's attack on Alden, Kopius's presence put them all in danger, including Ferox. Still, with the Hierophant after Kopius, Van worried about her friend's safety.

Daisy raised her hand as if voting. "I trust Ferox."

Relieved to have at least two teammates on her side, Van glanced at Suixsha. "What about you?"

Suixsha's sharp eyes turned to Van. "You need master three control of Self. Tongue, hand, desire. If you not learn how handle passion, it will tear team apart."

"You're saying going to Ferox is a bad idea?" asked Van.

Suixsha remained stoic. "I say fight between friend can scorch the earth."

"Hi Ferox." Paley gave a halfhearted wave from her seat on the couch, looking pale and tired.

Ferox bounded into the living area, entering their suite from the secret passageway. "Van!" He wrapped her in a big hug.

Van's mind eased, knowing Ferox wasn't in danger from the Hierophant. She didn't believe Kopius wanted to hurt him either, or he would've made his move by now. But she still kept Kopius in her line of vision as a precaution.

"Thank the light you're okay." Ferox continued to grasp Van in a hug, as if unwilling to let her go.

Brux cleared his throat, and Ferox released her.

"You come with a plan to get us out of here?" asked Brux.

"All winners are bound to play in the third and final match of the Death Games, including Van, unfortunately," Ferox said to the team.

"When is that?" asked Ixl.

"The second matches are finishing in a couple of days," said Ferox. "The last match is scheduled for next week."

Brux stomped over to Ferox. "Forget the games. We're leaving. Now."

Van tensed when Ixl and Kopius rose from their seats and flanked Brux; Suixsha stepped closer.

"Brux." Van placed a calming hand on his arm.

He shook it off. "We're going to check the third seal, whether you like it or not," he barked in Ferox's face. "The Alignment's going to end soon. We have to get moving for Van's sake."

Ferox held up his hands in mock surrender. "Listen, I don't want Van playing in the final match either. I agree. I came to help you get out of the palace."

"What about your family?" asked Van.

"My family is just trying to do the right thing." Ferox addressed the group. "They worry about my security... my future." He turned to Van. "Even Solana is worried about your safety. She doesn't want you to risk going to check the seal."

"No, she wants me to play in the games so I'll get killed," said Van.

Ferox pulled his lips, irritated by her comment.

Paley rose from her chair, looking ill with dark circles under her eyes. "What happens after we leave and Van doesn't enter the final match?"

"I'll take full responsibility for helping you escape and any repercussions," said Ferox.

"No!" said Van. "I won't have that. I'm not going."

"I stay," said Suixsha. "Play game in Van place."

Van shook her head. "I won't allow that either."

Ferox looked into Van's eyes. "I want you to leave. Go back to Lodestar. The games are too dangerous."

"Agreed," said Brux.

"Might be a good idea for us to use the Coin to find the seal." Ixl stared Ferox down.

Ferox said to Van. "If the Staff is nearby, it might be a good idea for you to get it in case you're here outside the Alignment."

Sweat beaded on Brux's forehead. "You want Van to retrieve the Staff—why? So you can take it?"

Ferox scowled.

"Ferox is right." Van couldn't deny feeling drawn to the Staff by her innate Anchoress homing device. Whenever someone mentioned the Staff, her desire for it increased, triggering a pulse inside her like an addiction. "It can protect me from the Quasher."

Ferox said to Brux. "I'm not sure the Coin can do that."

"How about we take the Coin anyway, just in case it does," said Ixl.

"You're so concerned about Van's welfare." Brux wiped his forehead. "Why don't you prove it? Give her the Coin."

Van said, "I'm sure he has a good reason—"

Ferox reached into his pocket and pulled out a dazzling gold disc.

Paley and Daisy gasped at its beauty.

He handed the Coin to Van. "Here. Gladly."

"Oh, Ferox." Van gaped at the Coin. Its energy tugged at her. She took the Coin from him and wrapped it in her fist. Its power electrified her whole body. "Thank you."

Van opened her mouth to tell Ferox he wasn't in danger from the assassin—when Paley swooned.

"I don't feel so good." She collapsed.

"Paley!" Daisy crashed to her knees and cradled Paley's head in her lap.

Paley groaned.

Brux's skin had a pallor. "I-I need to sit down."

"What's happening?" asked Ixl, tense and alert.

"I'll send for the palace healer at once." Ferox moved to dash away—

Kopius grabbed his arm. "Don't bother."

Van helped Brux to a nearby chair. Daisy and Ixl helped Paley to the couch.

"The Twin Gemstones are draining their energy," said Daisy.

Ixl shrugged. "Looks like they're not coming with us to Muspell."

"I can go," said Paley, so softly it was almost inaudible.

"Ixl's right," said Brux, meekly. "We're too weak. We can't risk slowing them down."

"Stay close to each other until we return," said Kopius. "I'm reasonably sure you'll make it."

"I'll have the council send you back to Lodestar straight away," said Ferox. "No harm done to intertribal relations."

Brux shook his head. "I'm staying. I'll let the palace healer check us over, just in case something can be done. Like Kopius said, we'll survive."

"He said *reasonably sure.*" Van gave Brux a stern look. "You need to go back."

Ferox looked grim. "If you stay, and Van doesn't return, one of you will be required to enter the final match in her place."

"No matter." Paley crossed her arms. "Like Brux said, we're staying."

"I'm coming back. No one is entering in my place." Van handed the Coin to Ferox.

"What—no."

"Take it," said Van. "If we don't return before the final match, come find us. Bring me back."

"How're we going to find Muspell?" asked Ixl. "The River of the Damned?"

"We don't need the Coin," said Van. "We have Suixsha. It's one reason Uxa sent her with us. She knows the Pusiel region."

Suixsha gave a curt nod.

Kopius clapped his hands together. "We leave, check the seal, and come back before anyone notices we were gone."

"Sounds like a plan," said Daisy.

"I'll watch over Brux and Paley," Ferox said to Van. "Make sure nothing happens to them. You make sure nothing happens to you."

Van nodded. "How are you planning to sneak us out?"

Ferox grinned. "By stealing a fig, of course."

CHAPTER

FORTY-ONE

The team, minus Brux, Paley, and Ferox, filed through the door in Van's bedroom into the secret passage.

Van wanted to get to Muspell for more than checking the third seal. Her Anchoress sense told her the Staff was there too. She felt an undeniable pull, as if the Item were calling to her—creating a need, if unfulfilled, would drive her mad.

Ferox had given them back their weapons confiscated by the palace guards when they entered the palace along with directions through the passageway. They easily found the designated door leading to the backside of the palace's southern wing. Ferox arranged to have the guards distracted while Van and her teammates scurried across the grounds and found the fig he had parked near the allocameli corral.

Ixl tore open the door. "Get in."

Suixsha hesitated. "Walk is—"

"Nope," Kopius brushed past her. "Much too inefficient to walk." He leaped in.

"Sorry," Daisy said to Suixsha. "He's right. We're on a tight schedule."

Van and Daisy jumped inside.

Ixl held the door of the mo-rind open for Suixsha.

She stepped over and peered inside.

"Any day now." Ixl tapped his foot.

Suixsha climbed in and took a seat.

"It's a snug fit, but it's okay," Daisy said to her, making room on the curved bench seat.

Ixl piled in and closed the door behind him. He scowled at Kopius messing with the instruments on the dashboard. "I got this, amigo."

"Fine." Kopius slipped out of the driving chair and moved onto the bench seat. "Must be nice being Uxa's son."

"It has its perks." Ixl commandeered the driver's seat. "But I know how to drive this because I watched the guard when we came here." He fiddled with the controls, then pulled the metal lever.

The fig shuddered, let out a bang-poof from the exhaust, and rose higher.

"If my mother could see me now!" Ixl put the fig in gear and it took off.

They drove along the perimeter road of Balefire's grounds. Ferox kept his word, and no guards bothered them along the way. They left Balefire City without a hassle and headed deep south toward Pusiel.

THE LATE AFTERNOON sun filtered through the porthole-like windows. Van gazed outside as they hovered over the scorched desert land. On the horizon, an orangish-brown volcano came into view. A handful of black-winged animals flew around its peak. Birds, big ones if Van could see them from this distance.

Daisy rested her head on Kopius's shoulder. Her cheeks flushed from humidity permeating the inside cabin, straining the fig's air conditioning.

Suixsha bent her head and peered out a window. "Muspell

ahead. Known for jewel and lustrous gem. Is location River of Damned."

"We don't need to bother with Muspell." Kopius looked cramped and uncomfortable. His skin dewy with sweat. "Only the river." His eyes darted to Suixsha. "You know how to get there, right?"

"I know where is." Suixsha turned to Ixl. "Stop fig."

Ixl twisted around. "Why? We're almost there."

"Park now," said Suixsha. "Leave fig, walk rest way."

"It's too hot outside for that," said Van.

"People more help if walk into village," said Suixsha. "It more..." She looked as though struggling to find the right word in English. "Respectful."

Ixl settled the mo-rind into a makeshift sandy parking spot on the outskirts of Muspell. Most of the team was happy to exit the cramped space until the door opened and the desert heat whacked them in the face.

"It's like a being inside a furnace." Van squinted at the dune covered horizon. It took a moment for her eyes to adjust to the bright sun. The only man-made structures, as far as she could see, lay ahead of them in Muspell.

"So much freaking sand," muttered Ixl, breaking into a sweat that made his facial scars look like they were melting.

"Smells like rotten eggs." Daisy wrinkled her nose.

Kopius used his hand to shade his eyes and gazed into the distance at Muspell. "It's sulfuric acid coming from the volcano."

"Manipura," said Suixsha. "Too much fume deadly."

"I saw birds flying around it," said Van.

Suixsha glanced at her. "No bird fly over Manipura."

"How can the people who live here stand the stench?" Ixl waved his hand in front of his nose.

"Villager use to it," said Suixsha.

"I wonder if the other team made it this far," said Daisy. Despite the heat, she and Kopius walked close together, as if they couldn't bear being more than three feet apart.

With every step toward the village, the sand's heat burned through the soles of Van's boots. Her chapped lips stung from the breathless desert wind and she feared they'd split open. Van felt fatigued from the humidity, but otherwise okay. She was grateful for the healing tinctures administered by the palace healer after the last match, and that Ferox arranged for them to steal an air conditioned mo-rind for the journey. She couldn't imagine walking the entire way from Balefire to Muspell. The trip would've taken weeks and caused them to perish from the high temperature.

The team became more and more ill-tempered as the desert heat took its toll.

"We need to cool down." Daisy's fine hair matted against her head and neck from sweat. "I think I can help." She raised her arms high, reaching for the sky, and closed her eyes. The surrounding air swirled, shifting the sand.

The temperature dropped about ten degrees. A breeze picked up, strong enough to cool them, light enough not to kick up much sand.

Daisy came out of her trance and lowered her arms.

Kopius raised his brow. "That's new."

The team's attitude markedly improved, experiencing a more pleasant walk thanks to Daisy's newfound ability "to connect to the power of mother nature," as she called it.

As they entered the village of Muspell, the planted trees along the pounded dirt roads provided shade and Daisy's breeze faded away, no longer needed. Although the regional weather was humid, the air in the village was less oppressive from the town's strategic landscaping.

They passed cement buildings, rectangular or square in a variety of sizes and heights, many with tiny triangular windows and clay-tiled, pitched roofs. The villagers kept to themselves. No one greeted them or looked their way. Men and boys wore white, loose-fitting robes with distinctive headcloths. They wrapped the ends of the headcloth around their neck, and, most, also their nose and mouth. Females, young and old, wore bright solid-colored garments with veils. The women accessorized with jeweled necklaces and gorgeous chained headpieces.

The village was ripe with bustling trade. Shops in the marketplace displayed bins stacked high with fruits, meats, clothes, and household items. All allowed by King Nequus's relaxed regulations. Yet, most people weren't interacting with anyone outside their present company. Those who exposed their faces held serious expressions. None smiled.

Occasionally, Van saw groups of several families gathered together outside shops where the men held intense conversations with each other while the children and women stood patiently waiting to the side.

Van pretended to be interested in clay vases sold by a woman wearing an attractive cerise veil. Behind the table, a cluster of men engaged in a discussion. Decorative ropes entwined with two threads, one white and one colored, held the men's headcloths together. A passionately chatting man had a colored thread the same cerise as the woman selling the clay items. Van assumed this meant they were together, perhaps husband and wife.

"He's not fit to lead," said the husband. "We agree on that."

"The young prince allowed the mud-lovers to put a magic potion in our water," said another with a bright blue thread. "Our water! We drank it with no choice. Gave no consent. We must seek justice."

"The magic bewitches our minds," said a third man.

"He's dating the witch who poisoned us with her spell," said the husband. "The Lodians are trying to control us."

"We must wonder why the palace is cooperating with them," said one with a yellow rope entwined in his headcloth. "Are the royals' minds being controlled by Lodian magic?"

"Our *Sanctus Novus* tells us we are a superior tribe," said the one with a bright blue thread. "It is our right to rule all the Living World. Underking Mador would agree."

"So would Prince Merloc," said the husband. "He's a true leader. His desire to attack Salus Valde is well known. He wants to take troops through the portal into the Earth World and kill the terrigens. That would solve many of our problems."

"Balish soldiers need the Grigori and their magic to get through the portal," said the one with the yellow rope.

"Bah," said another. "They would risk becoming corrupted by the terrigens?"

"Prince Merloc and his followers are strong enough to repel the corruption," said another.

"If we can protect ourselves from the poisoned air of Manipura, they can do that," said the husband.

"They will have special talismans and wear protective goggles," said one. "I will make sure of it."

"Bah," said the one with a yellow rope, shaking his head. "They will have nothing to do with the likes of you."

The men chuckled.

"With the increase in demon activity in Earth World, they know as well as we do the Grigori can't do their job," said the husband.

Van's stomach dropped. Mention of increased demon activity confirmed the spy in Lodestar leaked information to the Balish palace. It's the only way these men would know about it.

"You buy?" asked the woman wearing the cerise veil. "Three pecs."

Even if Van wanted to buy the vase, she had no Living World money. She shook her head and left the table.

She had learned a lot from eavesdropping. Despite the increased trade and out-of-boundary travel allowed by King Nequus, these people proved what Van sensed all along—an antagonism brewed beneath the harmonious facade of the Balish people. This confirmed the intel Uxa had given Van. She hustled to catch up with her teammates.

Suixsha had finagled a holstered dagger from a vendor in exchange for one of her tribal bracelets.

"Like you need more weapons," said Kopius.

"Not for me." She handed the dagger to Daisy.

Daisy waved her hands. "I don't need a weapon."

Kopius took the blade from Suixsha. "I'll make sure she takes it."

Ixl glanced at Van. "Where were you?"

"Just looking around," she said.

He frowned. "Don't wander off again."

"Yeah, okay." Van turned away, thinking he sounded bossy, like his mother, and Brux.

They continued through Muspell on their way to the River of the Damned, passing by more carts and wares. Van wished she had money to buy some of the unique pieces of jewelry or a souvenir.

She glanced in an alleyway and saw two villagers taunting a monkey-looking critter with a gray, furry body and lengthy, black-ringed tail. The men had the animal cornered. Its white face had large, black eyes—opened wide from terror—surrounded by a smokey black mask.

"Lemure," said Suixsha. "Different from lemur in your world."

"Probably a related species," muttered Van.

Daisy marched past them toward the villagers. Van followed.

The men whipped the creature using long, pliable sticks. The lemure shrieked in pain with each whack.

"Go away," one man snarled at the critter.

The lemure cowered in the corner, whimpering.

Daisy stomped right up to the men. "Stop it this instant!"

"It can't go away. You have it cornered," shouted Van, fuming.

The men raised their whips and lashed the poor critter, again and again. Blood oozed from the critter's slash marks, making its gray fur turn muddy-red.

Daisy fell to her knees and cried in pain. "No." She screeched every time the whips hit the lemure, as if enduring the pain, too.

Ixl and Kopius rushed to her side.

"Villager no like lemure," said Suixsha. "Animal thought to be spirit of dead come take them to place you call hell."

Van grabbed one of the men's arms. "Stop it. Right now!"

The man snarled and shoved Van backward. She lost her footing. Ixl caught her before she hit the ground.

Kopius shoved the man against the wall. "You don't touch her."

"Hey." The other man paused his whipping. "What're you doing?" He jutted his jaw, dropped his stick, and marched over to a small barrel in the alley. He picked it up, went to the lemure, and doused the shaking animal with a yellowish, slick liquid—*oil?*

"What are you doing? Stop it." Van took a step toward the man; Kopius held her back.

"Mind your own business," snarled the man Kopius had pushed against the wall, as the other lit a match.

Ixl rushed over and tackled him. The match fell from the man's fingers and landed in a splash of yellow oil. The highly flammable liquid burst into flames and trailed straight for the drenched lemure.

Van bounded over. She frantically swiped her feet across the oily trail in the dirt, trying to rub away the path before the fire reached the critter.

Daisy's whimpers grew louder. She remained crouched on the ground, arms wrapped around herself.

The man Ixl had shoved against the wall snatched Van by the back of her shirt and tossed her away from the oily trail.

Van landed on her back with an *oof*. The man came at her. She kicked upward, smacking him in the gut. He went hurtling backward into Ixl, who clutched the man and used his momentum to slam him down hard.

Van rolled onto the trail of flames, trying to snuff it out using her body. Spots on her pants and shirt ignited. The fire raced past her, getting closer and closer to the cowering lemure.

Kopius found a bucket and had filled it with dirt from the road. He dumped it on Van, then ran aside the flaming strip, spilling soil on it along the way.

It worked. The dirt extinguished the fire before it reached the lemure.

Van groaned as her clothes continued to smolder in spots, setting off her skin's memory of being burned in the roller derby.

Suixsha rushed toward the men, twirling two tomahawks, one in each hand.

Not daring to mess with her, the villagers dashed away.

Kopius doused the rest of the fire using his dirt filled bucket.

Van got up, spit crud, and winced as she brushed off her clothes.

"You're hurt." Ixl bent to peruse her singed legs. He took a salve out of his backpack.

"Forget about me," said Van, as Ixl rubbed the salve on her leg and arm burns. "How's the lemure?"

Daisy and Kopius had already approached the quivering critter.

It used its little tongue to wet its paws, then used them to wipe the oily liquid and blood from its fur. As it cleaned itself, its masked black eyes snuck peeks at them.

"It's scared," said Daisy.

"Maybe leave it alone." Kopius stepped back.

"Is it okay?" asked Van.

"Sh." Daisy closed her eyes. A serene look came over her face.

"She's seeing if her connection to nature will allow her to communicate with the animal," Kopius whispered to Van.

"Oh." Daisy's blue eyes popped open in surprise. "It's—"

Before Daisy finished, the lemure began to change form...

CHAPTER
FORTY-TWO

The lemure buckled and bulged as it morphed from an animal into a stunning woman.

Her white-gray hair cascaded to her waist, contrasting with her smooth, dark skin. A black mask that looked tattooed framed her brown eyes, the same way as when she was a lemure. Her outfit comprised a full-length black cloak worn over a black corset bodysuit with rose and gold over-lacing, and black platform heels. She wore her cloak wide-opened, exposing her long, slender legs, not a mark from the attack on her. Around her neck hung a fabulous multi-tiered necklace with rose-colored gemstones set in gold. Other than the necklace, her clothes seemed out of place in a village where people dressed fully covered.

"I must repay you for your kindness," she said through her see-through mesh veil that was attached to a black triangular headpiece with decorative rose and gold accents.

Van gazed, stupefied by the spectacular woman. Her teammates, also mute.

"I am the Enchantress." She was all white-gray hair and silky legs. "Come." She waved her hand for them to follow.

They each introduced themselves as they trailed behind the Enchantress like rats to the Pied Piper.

The Enchantress led them into a nondescript cement, multistory building on the edge of town that blended into the surrounding structures.

Van welcomed the cool, dry air in the Enchantress's ground-floor apartment. She admired the colorful tapestries, sweeping mesh curtains, bright vases, and cute animal statues that decorated the Enchantress's living space. Pleasant scents of vetiver and bergamot infused the air. A harp's strings vibrated in the corner, playing music with no musician. The room exuded an ambiance of peace and comfort.

They settled around a coffee table in the living room. Daisy and Kopius took seats on the couch, Van and Ixl on ottomans. Suixsha chose not to sit and took a sentinel post between the side of the couch and Van.

"I don't understand," said Ixl. "Why'd you let those men abuse you?"

"My purpose does not require physical strength." The Enchantress settled into the only chair in the room, a high back Van hadn't noticed before. She draped her cloak over the armrests, crossed her ankles, and sat with a straight spine, looking like a model torn from the pages of a fashion magazine. "I have miraculous courage and exist to serve an incorporeal cause. Therefore, according to the laws of the Universe, I receive a spiritual effect."

Van could've sworn she wasn't facing the Enchantress when she sat down. All her teammates now faced the mystical woman. Or were the seats arranged this way the whole time? Van couldn't remember.

Kopius grimaced. "They whipped you and tried to set you on fire."

The Enchantress turned to him and smiled, displaying sparkling white teeth. "And you saved me. You were the spiritual effect."

Kopius gaped at the woman, appearing dazed like Van.

"I am at your service," she said. "What do you seek?"

"What makes you think we're seeking anything?" Ixl squirmed, clearly uncomfortable in the Enchantress's lair, perhaps trying to resist the lull of the intoxicating aromas and music.

"Only those who must visit Manipura come here," said the Enchantress.

"Right." Ixl shifted on the ottoman. "Because of the stench."

"In Muspell, many people cover their nose and mouth by wearing a veil or scarf to prevent their breath from contaminating the sacred flames of Manipura," she said. "We villagers do not mind the scent of the holy fire."

"Your mesh veil isn't offering much protection," said Kopius, apparently snapping out of his stupor.

"The Enchantress's breath does not contaminate the fire," she answered pleasantly. "I wear a veil out of respect for the traditions of Manipura."

"Please tell what best way to River of Damned," said Suixsha.

"Ah. The river," said the Enchantress. "It travels through the deepest parts of Manipura. Through the place where lustrous gems are mined from the walls. Valuable stones, once used mainly for spiritual practices. To help those who worship the sun gain fiery passion, vitality, and energy. Sadly, now most people wear the gems as jewelry for their beauty alone."

"We're not interested in any lustrous gems," said Ixl.

"That is good news, indeed," said the Enchantress. "Dragons live and play in the volcano. Lava forms the stones, yet the dragon's fiery breath turns them into lustrous gems. Dragons are playful and friendly by nature. But become fierce if anyone attempts to steal their treasures."

Oh, Van mouthed. That's what she saw flying around the top of the volcano—*dragons*. Suixsha was right, they weren't birds.

"Just curious," said Kopius. "If the dragons protect the gems, how do you mine them?"

"The miners of Manipura have a precarious job," said the

Enchantress. "They work among the fire and dragons in certain parts of the volcano at certain times of the year. The dragons have gotten used to them and remain pleasant as long as the miners do not overtake their bounty."

Van noticed a teakettle with one cup on the coffee table. Although it provided a diversion to the depressing conversation about working in the hellish mines, Van didn't touch it.

"To get to the river, travel through the valley at the edge of the village between the backbone of the hills. Walk due south, through the Dead Forest. Now," the Enchantress gripped her fingers around the armrest. "Tell me, what is it you seek?"

They looked from one to the other, unsure if they should reveal the details of their mission.

Finally, Daisy said, "We seek the third seal."

"Ah," the Enchantress lifted her brow and relaxed her hands. "The structural point that binds the worlds. I will give you directions to the seal. But first," she turned to Van, "you must drink the laurel tea."

"Why me?" asked Van.

"You sat on the rose-colored ottoman," said the Enchantress. "The kettle appeared with one cup. The cup is for you."

"Laurel leaf give vision." Suixsha appeared uneasy, which made Ixl even more ill at ease.

Van stared apprehensively at the kettle.

"I'm not sure—" said Ixl.

"The tea is a gift from the spirit world," said the Enchantress. "A high honor."

Van sighed. She saw no other way out of it, poured the tea, and took a gulp.

Her head became even more muddled. She closed her eyes to help her concentration.

A vision took form in her mind. Not like the connection she had with Jacynthia, where they could converse with each other. This was more like a generic memory engram.

A woman materialized who looked like Amaryl—no, Zurial—no, Amaryl, wait, no Zurial...

"The cycle is repeating," said the woman. "War is being created when none is necessary."

"It can be avoided—just—just don't do it," said another female entity, *my... mother?*

"Those who worship an altar of fire feed the flames of hatred," said a male spirit that looked like a mix of Goustav and Manik. "Desires for pleasures of the Self become so strong, they revere the falseness that gets them what they want."

"Go to the triangular rock formation outside the north-facing edge of the volcano," said the Amaryl-Zurial hybrid. "This points to the entrance that will lead you to the third seal."

"Fear is sweeping the land," said the spirit that looked like Van's mother. "It is taking over."

Van attempted to speak, to ask them a million questions. No words came out. The spirits faded away.

"No!" Van reached out to grab the vision, to keep her mother there, and accidentally knocked the teacup off the coffee table.

It smashed on the tile floor, shattering to pieces.

Van's eyes shot open. "Oh! I'm so sorry." She bent down to pick up the shards.

Daisy leaped up to help.

"Sit," commanded the Enchantress.

Daisy obeyed.

Among the broken glass, Van found a bright yellow pill. She held it up.

"The spirits have given you a gift," said the Enchantress, delighted. "Take the pill. Use it when you need it most."

Van glanced down, ready to continue cleaning up the broken pieces, but they had disappeared.

She held the oblong pill between her fingers and scrutinized it. "What does it do?"

"Cools your heat," said the Enchantress.

Van didn't understand the advantage of the pill, nevertheless, she tucked it into her pant's pocket.

"What happened?" Ixl asked Van. "Are you okay?"

"You went away for a bit," said Kopius.

"The tea gave me a vision," said Van. "Spirits told me the exact location of the third seal."

The Enchantress gave them a brief nod. Their time with her had come to an end.

Van and the others thanked the Enchantress for her hospitality and left her apartment.

Suixsha led them through Muspell to the valley at the edge of the village between the backbone of the hills.

They moved onward, headed deeper south into the Dead Forest.

FORTY-THREE

The team entered a forest filled with what Van first thought were dead trees, hence the name Dead Forest.

She shook her head, still feeling fuzzy from drinking the strange tea, and looked again. The trees weren't dead, they just looked dead with their black bark and gnarly, leafless branches resembling claws. These trees didn't provide a cooling effect like the leaf-filled ones in town and the late afternoon sun oppressively heated the forest.

The sounds of their bodies scraping against the bark and branches as they passed the trees echoed through the otherwise silent woods. Van's feet sunk ankle-deep into the loose sand, not hard-packed like the streets in the village, getting granules into her boots. She tugged at the neckline on her shirt, finding her clothes too constrictive for the desert land, and wished she had dressed in loose-fitting robes like the townspeople.

The sway of a distant branch caught Van's eye. She halted and squinted in that direction.

She saw nothing. Van figured the lingering effects of the tea and the heat played tricks with her mind until Daisy also stopped.

"Um." Daisy stared into the woods where Van had seen the movement.

The hair on the back of Van's neck rose.

The others stood still.

Suixsha's eyes held their focus. She gripped the hilts of her tomahawks and slowly drew them out of their holsters. Then, paused. She relaxed and slid them back.

Tyger gracefully squeezed through the trees.

Van let out a relieved breath.

Suixsha reached up and scratched behind his ears. He rubbed his nose on her shoulder.

"Good to see you." Daisy smiled and patted his side.

The team continued through the forest. They came to a clearing along the river's edge.

Van spread her nostrils at the stench, much stronger than in Muspell, and tried to breathe from her mouth. It didn't help. Her lungs strained like they were resisting being incinerated with every breath, more so than in the village or the woods. But what made her stomach churn were sounds coming from the river. Crackles, like breaking glass.

Van inched closer to the edge, heat blasted her. She winced and stepped back.

Glowing orange-yellow goo sluggishly flowed from the volcano. The waterless river sizzled and smoldered, giving off rising wisps of gray smoke.

"Oh, come on." Ixl threw his hands in the air. "The River of the Damned is made of *lava*?"

"Look on the bright side, mate." Kopius pointed to a rock formation on the volcano. "There's the triangle. It's directing us to the entrance of that cave."

"How do we get in? The river is flowing the wrong way." Ixl gazed at the slow-moving lava, absentmindedly running his fingers over the portal burn scars on his face.

Van figured his scars held the memory of being burned, same as the skin on her arms. Her heart went out to him. "There's a way," she said. "We just have to find it."

Tyger shifted, getting antsy. He made squeaky, throaty noises and his eyes focused on the top of the volcano.

Kopius looked up. "The river's not our only problem."

Dragons soared around the top of the volcano, dropping in and out of the crater as if playing. Some dipped down the side of the volcano, inching closer to them.

Daisy stroked Tyger's back in a comforting gesture.

"Good idea to keep him calm," said Ixl. "No need to for him to set the Dead Forest on fire."

"I go. Heat no bother me," said Suixsha. "I bring Tyger. You stay here."

Tyger rubbed his face against Suixsha's head.

"It can get up to two thousand degrees inside a volcano," said Kopius. "Before you find the seal, your throat will close. Your clothes will incinerate and you'll be cooked from the inside out. It's a one-way trip for you. Tyger should be okay since he can turn into fire."

"I'm the Anchoress. This is on me. I'm going in," said Van. "Maybe my blood magic will protect me."

The call of the Staff intensified inside every cell in Van's body. The pull became more like a yank. She knew it was hidden inside the volcano. It was her destiny to retrieve it.

Kopius clasped Van's arm before she took off. "Hold up. Why not test your theory before running into an inferno?"

Van nodded. She cautiously stepped toward the edge of the river. After about two minutes, her throat closed, and the heat fried her skin. She dropped to her knees, coughing.

Ixl grabbed her and pulled her back to safety. Van caught her breath, although her skin continued to fry, like a deepening sunburn.

"Sorry, amigo," said Ixl. "Seems you're not heatproof."

"I try." Suixsha stepped closer and closer, making it to the river's edge. After some time, she walked back to the team with nothing more than her skin beaded with sweat. "I good."

Ixl ran his fingertips over his scars again.

Daisy placed a hand on his back. "Are you okay? You keep rubbing your face."

"I didn't realize," said Ixl, looking like she had caught him doing something wrong. He shrugged. "The heat from the lava. It's irritating my scars."

"You're not going in," said Van.

"I can power through it." Ixl flexed his arms to prove his toughness.

"There must be a way we can all go," said Daisy. "Uxa wouldn't send us on an impossible task. Let me see if I can freeze the river." She closed her eyes and raised her hands to the sky.

Van held her breath, hopeful her teammate would save the day.

Daisy's palms smoldered; the lava river continued to flow.

"Daisy!" Kopius shook her, jolting her from her trance.

"Ouch." Daisy cradled her hands.

Ixl dashed over, dropped his backpack, and rummaged around inside. He removed a salve and rubbed it on her palms.

"Much better. Thank you," said Daisy. "I'm sorry I couldn't help."

"We'll find another way," said Kopius. "If the miners survive Manipura, then we can too. There's probably a network of tunnels inside from their work. We just need to find them."

Suixsha held her hand to her forehead to shade her eyes. "It look like path in cave wall by lava river. Made by miner."

"The miners probably have specialized equipment or use a spell or aren't even human," said Ixl.

Tyger belted out a roar, gaining everyone's attention. He shook and burst into flames.

Two dragons swirled in the air overhead, crisscrossing each other, getting closer and closer to them.

"They think we're here to steal their lustrous gems!" said Kopius.

Ixl cried, "Take cover! *Now!*"

CHAPTER
FORTY-FOUR

Van, Ixl, and Kopius dashed toward the forest.

Daisy and Suixsha stayed put standing on the riverbed.

Tyger growled at the hovering dragons, fur aflame.

"Wait," cried Daisy.

Van and the others skidded to a stop.

Daisy smiled at the dragons as they dropped closer. "They're curious about us."

"You sure?" asked Ixl. "It would be a bad thing to be wrong about."

"Hello," Daisy shouted to the dragons.

Van peered up at them. "Wait a minute." She strode over. Ixl tried to grab her, but Van was too fast for him. She stood next to Daisy and gaped at the scaly creatures as they softly landed. Kopius and Ixl joined them.

The dragons flicked their heads and bleated. One, a golden green baby. The other, a green adult.

"No way." Van grinned. "They're the dragons I rescued from the barn."

Suixsha relaxed her stance but held a sharp eye on the dragons. Tyger's flames turned back into fur.

Van inched closer to the dragons. She reached up and the baby dragon lowered her snout for Van to pet.

"What do they want?" asked Kopius.

Daisy smiled. "They're here to help."

"Can they fly us into the cave?" asked Ixl. "We know Suixsha can withstand the heat."

"Can you take us to the third seal?" Daisy asked the dragons.

The mother dragon stretched her neck, blurted a hoot, then bobbed her head.

"There's two dragons," said Van. "I'm going too."

"No, you're not," said Kopius. "You'll suffer hyperthermia within minutes."

"Van, use the pill," said Daisy. "The Enchantress said it will cool you."

"Brilliant!" Kopius waggled his finger at Daisy. "That's probably what the miners use."

Van fumbled in her pocket and found the yellow pill. She popped it into her mouth.

A chill rippled through her skin as the pill cooled her body. The heat from the river no longer bothered her.

"What about me?" asked Ixl. "I need one of those pills too."

"I wish we could all go," said Daisy. "But I don't think it was meant to be, or the Enchantress's spirits would've given us all a pill."

Van turned to Suixsha. "You should stay too. If I don't make it, you're the only one who can lead the team back to Lodestar."

Suixsha shook her head. "Tyger know. Show them back. He stay."

Tyger flicked his head and snorted.

The baby dragon shuffled over to Van and lowered her wing onto the ground.

"She wants you to ride her," said Daisy.

Touched that the baby came to her, Van climbed onto the drag-on's back.

The mother dragon flicked her head at Suixsha and lowered her wing. Suixsha climbed aboard.

The dragons flapped their wings, lifted off the ground, and headed toward the cave.

Van clung to the baby dragon's neck, afraid she might fall off. After a few minutes, she got the hang of the up and down motion of the wings. The breeze on her face happily reminded her of being with Ferox on the flying carpet.

The dragons maneuvered through the entrance of the cave. They entered a huge antechamber with a high ledge that looked hand-made, presumably a walking path made by the miners.

As the dragons flew deeper into the antechamber of the volcano, the air became oppressively thick from the heat. If the miners endured this during their shifts, then their working conditions were horrendous. Van glanced at Suixsha and noticed sweat beading on her skin.

"You okay?" hollered Van. "You gonna make it?"

Suixsha nodded.

Flying on the dragon, being impermeable to heat, made Van feel like the princess warrior she was. She urged the baby dragon to go faster by squeezing with her calves and heels like she was riding a horse. She steered by tugging the dragon's neck. The dragon swooped dangerously close to the lava, and then did a loop-de-loop.

"Woohoo!" shouted Van.

Suixsha yelled, "No time fun. Too dangerous."

The mother dragon gave her baby a reproaching roar.

"Fine." Van guided her dragon to fly correctly. She took a whiff and wrinkled her nose. Something was burning.

"Back!" Suixsha pointed at her.

Van glanced over her shoulder and saw her backpack smoldering. She wriggled it off with one hand and gripped the baby dragon's neck with the other. She dropped it onto the rocks below.

"Dammit." It had all her stuff. Van memorized where her backpack landed, hoping to come back later and get it. No more fooling around, she told herself.

They flew out of the main antechamber and into a tight-fitting tunnel.

The scar on Van's lower back tingled from the increased heat, as did the skin on her arms and legs where she had been burned in the second match.

They exited the tunnel into a cavern with a floor made of lava. Blasts of fire erupted in spots as if coming from submerged flamethrowers.

The dragons hovered, hesitant to cross the lava, which was not a floor at all, but part of the River of the Damned.

"The seal is straight ahead across the river," cried Van over the roar of the flowing lava that sounded like a jet engine. The heat neared inhuman levels, and she hoped the pill would continue to cool her. Van peered at her teammate to see how she fared.

Suixsha looked flushed; her chest heaved with labored breathing.

"You stay here." Van gently squeezed the baby dragon's ribcage with her calves, cuing the dragon to move forward.

Flames shot upward from the lava. The baby dragon darted to avoid them. As they got closer to the cavern's wall, a well-defined circular area came into view about eight feet in diameter with unmistakable carvings.

"The seal," Van muttered with the reverence of reaching the holy grail. She urged her dragon to fly closer to the engraving.

Small flames burned in the hieroglyphs and symbols carved inside the circle. She scrutinized the design, straining to see through the flames while moving up and down with the dragon's flapping wings. The small fires in the hieroglyphs and symbols burst into robust flames, as if intentionally trying to obstruct her view.

While Van was preoccupied studying the seal, a streak of fire reached upward from the lava below and wrapped around the baby dragon's ankle.

The dragon lurched as she screeched in pain, almost dislodging

Van, then twisted her neck and blasted the lava demon with her fiery breath.

The demon released the baby dragon's leg as it entwined with the dragon's fire, becoming one with it, using its power to grow bigger.

The baby dragon soared higher, out of the demon's reach.

More fire demons stretched upward from the lava, straining to reach them.

Suixsha yelled something from across the cavern, paused halfway over the lava, presumably on her way to help Van. She pointed at the ceiling.

The mother dragon shot its flaming breath down at the reaching demons. Those demons also absorbed the dragon's fire and grew taller.

Van and Suixsha steered their dragons higher, well out of the reach of the flaming grasps of the lava demons and convened at the top of the cavern.

"We need go." Suixsha raised her voice enough to be heard over the roaring lava and the dragon's flapping wings. "Too hot."

"I didn't get a good look at the seal," shouted Van. "You go back. I got this."

One of the lava demons grew tall enough to reach them, clutched the mother dragon's ankle, and yanked downward, jerking her. The dragon screeched in pain.

Suixsha lost her balance and tumbled down her dragon's back. She slid, her fingers frantically gripped at the scales. She dropped over the side, and reached up in time to catch a fin on her dragon's tail.

The demon continued to hold the mother dragon's leg, tugging them downward, closer to the lava.

Suixsha swayed as she hung from the dragon's tail. Her grasp loosened with each passing second.

With Van's guidance, the baby dragon swooped underneath and

snapped its jaw straight through the lava demon clutching the leg of her mother.

The demon released its grasp, as Suixsha lost her hold and plummeted.

"Suixsha!" cried Van.

Without instruction, the baby dragon flew under Suixsha, who thudded onto the baby dragon's back.

Unable to get her grip, Suixsha slid down the dragon's side.

Van reached down. "Grab my hand!"

Suixsha clawed onto the scales using both hands.

Van leaned backward, stretched her arm, and strained to reach Suixsha. She contacted Suixsha's fingers and clutched her teammate's hand.

A lava demon took a swipe at Suixsha's dangling leg.

Suixsha kicked it. The movement loosened Van's hold. Suixsha slipped from her clasp and plummeted.

The mother dragon pivoted and soared underneath.

Suixsha landed squarely onto her back, this time getting a sturdy hold.

"You okay?" shouted Van.

Suixsha nodded and wrapped her arms around the mother dragon's neck.

"It's too dangerous," cried Van. "Go back."

Suixsha shook her head. "I stay."

"Take her back," Van said to the mother dragon.

Suixsha's dragon flicked her head, turned away, and flew out of the cavern.

Van and the baby dragon headed back toward the seal. As they got closer, the lava demons grew in number. The baby dragon learned to tuck her legs into her body to prevent the demons from grabbing them.

A demon clutched Van's ankle. It immediately released its grip.

More flaming hands of the demons grabbed Van's ankles and released their hold the moment they touched her.

Van grinned. They couldn't tolerate her icy-cold legs. Their fiery clutches felt like little tickles.

Her dragon hovered over the ledge in front of the seal. The demons appeared to be confined to the lava, so she instructed the baby dragon to land. Van climbed down and rushed over to inspect the seal.

Up close, it towered over her. Flames continued to roar outward from inside the hieroglyphs and symbols in the circle. Confident the cooling effects of the pill would protect her, Van reached through the fire. She placed her palms on the engraving and felt around to see if she could find a crack.

Her cool touch caused the fire to subside, giving her an unobstructed view of the entire seal. She took a step back and craned her neck to examine it.

A bi-layered circle surrounded two superimposed triangles, one upright and one facing downward. The inner circle flowed with water, the outer, solid granite. A contained fire within the engraving highlighted the periphery of the intertwined triangles. Inside the center of the triangles was a magnificent rendering of a pair of wings.

Van gasped.

A fissure ran through the middle, separating the wings.

The third seal was cracked.

CHAPTER

FORTY-FIVE

Van placed an icy hand on each side of the crack in the seal. She closed her eyes, took a deep breath, and tried to connect to her Anchoress powers.

Nothing happened.

Dammit. She needed one of her Items. The Coin was far away at Balefire with Ferox, and the Cup, back at Lodestar. Though, hidden somewhere nearby was the Staff...

The baby dragon bleated and scratched her paws on the ground, agitated by the lava demons stretching from the river, attempting to reach onto the ledge and grasp her.

Van turned her attention back to the seal. She peered into the blackness within the fissure. A coldness emanated from it, despite the heat in the cavern.

Something moved in the darkness behind the seal.

She gasped and stumbled backward.

Van shook her head to clear it, thinking she must be mistaken. She stepped closer and again looked inside the crack.

A soulless void stared back, giving her chills, even while standing inside a volcano with active lava. Something cold and unseen reached from the fissure and touched her chest, her heart.

She leaped backward—terrified—breaking the connection.

An awareness of the cavern's heat prickled her skin. The Enchantress's magical pill was wearing off. Time had run out for Van to mend the seal.

The baby dragon roared and shot her fiery breath at a lava demon that had gained the strength to crawl onto the ledge.

Van leaped onto the baby dragon's back. They soared upward, near the ceiling, and flew out of the cavern.

When they reached the main antechamber, Suixsha and the mother dragon were waiting for Van and the baby dragon's return. Together, they flew out of the volcano.

The dragons landed on the riverbed near their anxiously waiting team.

"We're fine," Van assured them, as she and Suixsha dismounted.

Suixsha rushed to Tyger and hugged him.

Daisy checked on the dragons.

"The seal?" asked Ixl.

Van stared him in the eye, and said grimly, "It's cracked."

Daisy gasped.

Van glanced at the ground. "I couldn't fix it. Lava demons attacked us. The pill wore off."

"The crack explains why the vibration is staying low enough to keep the virus here," said Kopius.

Ixl ran his fingers over his facial scars, deep in thought. "Yeah, and it explains the Balish citizen's growing negative attitudes toward the Balish royal family and us Lodians."

"We have to go back in," said Daisy. "Mend the seal."

"I tried." Van frowned. "I'm going to need one of my Items to close that gap."

"The closest Item is at Balefire," said Kopius. "The Coin."

Van knew that wasn't true. The closest Item was the Staff. And its pull was strong. Van considered ditching Ferox, the team, and the death match to go for it.

Uxa's words permeated her thoughts.

After the Jaychund games, Uxa told Van if she behaved in an upstanding and fair manner, her actions would be recognized and properly rewarded. If she acted from a place of selfishness, it would cause her to make the wrong choice. Ego was an illusion of power, and Van's ego gave her the impulse to ditch everyone and go get the Staff, not her heart or spirit.

Anyway, Van couldn't go running off on her own mission. She had to get back to Balefire before the Balish forced Brux or Paley into the final death match in her place.

Ixl treated the dragons' leg wounds with a salve and Suixsha's minor burns and abrasions. The team thanked the dragons. After Van and Suixsha gave them special appreciation, the creatures flew to the top of Manipura, and the team hiked back through the Dead Forest.

Just before getting to the village, Suixsha whispered into Tyger's ear and he disappeared into the woods. The team hurried through Muspell and climbed back into their mo-rind.

BALEFIRE PALACE ROSE into view on the early morning horizon. The sentinels guarding the gate leading onto the palace grounds stopped their fig.

"What do we do?" asked Van. "We weren't supposed to leave. Ferox will get in trouble."

Daisy clasped Van's hand supportively.

Ixl twisted around in the driving chair. "Be cool. Ferox told us what to say."

One guard sauntered over to the porthole-like window by the driver and swirled his index finger.

Ixl unlatched the window and pushed it open.

"State your business," said the guard, as two others peered inside through the other windows and searched under and around the fig.

"We're extra help for the final match," said Ixl. "Security, crowd control."

"Papers," barked the guard.

Van's stomach did a flip.

Ixl reached into his back pocket and pulled out a folded parchment.

The guard held the document in one hand and a clipboard with papers in the other. He perused the document and compared it with his papers.

He paused. Then, flipped through pages on his clipboard.

Van held her breath; no one in the fig moved.

The guard paused again and gazed down his nose at Ixl.

"All clear," yelled one of the guards who scanned the fig.

The guard at the window shoved the parchment back at Ixl. "Move it along, then." He stepped back and waved his hand for them to go forward through the gate.

"Whoa." Van let out a breath. "That was close."

"Nah," said Ixl. "Ferox told me about the extra security. He gave me the parchment and the cover story before we left. He's an okay guy."

Kopius bobbed his head in agreement. "He had our backs."

They entered the palace using a secret passage entryway, scurried through the corridors, and made it through the panel door in Van's bedroom. They rushed into the suite's living area.

Ferox leapt from the couch the moment he saw Van and wrapped his arms around her as if she were his lifeline.

"I came over to see how Paley and Brux were doing," he said to Van. "I was about to go looking for you. I'm glad everyone made it back okay."

Van scrunched her brow. "Looking for me?"

"How are you?" Daisy knelt by the couch where her brother and Paley sat next to each other.

"Much better." Brux's color had returned. "Turns out the palace healer had a strengthening tincture. It helped me enough so I could prep before taking Van's place in the final match."

"Why were—" Van wanted to ask him what he meant, since the match was nine days away, but Paley cut her off.

"We had a great time." Paley beamed at Ferox. "Got to know each other better, played cards. One night, I even won a game."

"The seal?" asked Brux.

Van and the others told them about their journey to Muspell, meeting the Enchantress, the River of the Damned, the volcano Manipura, and about the seal being cracked.

Brux sat up straighter. "You fixed it, right?"

Van cast her eyes to the floor. "I'm still having trouble connecting to my power."

"What?" cried Ferox. "How are you winning the matches? Do you need the Coin? It might help you re-connect. You can use it to mend the seal."

Van shook her head. "No, my gut tells me I need the Staff of Fire. I'm sure it's the only Item that can protect me from the heat in Manipura while I do the repair." Was it her intuition telling her she needed the Staff's power, or her ego?

"If you say it's so, then I believe it," said Ferox. "Retrieve the Staff. Anything to help get your power back."

"Forget the games." Brux rose from the couch. "We have to mend the seal."

"Brux is right," said Ferox. "The crack means terrigens in the Earth World are morphing into demons at a rate strong enough to break it. They'll soon enter our world."

"The Alignment ends in two days." Brux paced. "I'm not sure if Van's going to make it back in time."

Van blinked. "Wait, what?"

Daisy and Ixl both corrected Brux. "Next week."

"You've got your calendar mixed up, mate," Kopius said to Brux.

"You've been gone a week." Paley snickered.

"Enchantress keep us in lair for seven day," said Suixsha.

"You didn't think to tell us?" asked Ixl heatedly.

Suixsha stared at him. "Thought you know."

Van was outright flabbergasted.

"Fascinating," said Kopius.

Daisy's jaw slackened. "I had no idea."

"If we go to the seal, what happens if Van misses the final death match?" asked Paley.

"The seal takes precedence." Ferox placed a hand on Van's shoulder. "I'll let the court know. I'll be able to use this to get you out of the final match."

"Great." Van breathed a sigh of relief. "I really don't have it in me to play another round."

Ferox made sweeping eye contact with each of them. "Clean up and take a brief rest while I gather my men. We leave at noon."

Out of the corner of Van's eye, she glimpsed a ripple in the curtain.

"Look out!" yelled Daisy.

An intruder camouflaged to blend into the curtain emerged like a blur coming into focus. He rushed at them, headed straight for Ferox...

FORTY-SIX

The Hierophant's slit-like eyes fixed on Ferox as he charged forward.

Suixsha sprung to action as Ixl leapt forward. Both wrapped their bodies around Ferox to shield him from the assassin. Brux positioned himself in front of Ferox, fists up, ready to block the coming attacker.

With the Hierophant's high cheekbones and elongated face, it was like watching a demon hone in on Ferox. Except he wasn't going for Ferox.

The assassin drew a dagger on Kopius.

Kopius blocked the jab; Daisy screamed.

They locked into a heated scuffle.

Several palace guards burst into the room, DEW handguns drawn. Two dashed over to Ferox and yanked Ixl and Suixsha off of him. The other pointed his gun this way and that, as his eyes searched to find the assailant. But in a blink, the Hierophant had disappeared.

Ferox turned to the guards struggling to hold Ixl and Suixsha.

"It's okay. I'm unharmed. You can release them. They were protecting me."

"You shouldn't be out of your suite," said one guard, tucking his gun into his holster. "This a violation of the court—"

"It's fine," said Ferox sternly. "The assassin isn't after me." His eyes darted to Kopius. "Is he?"

Kopius remained silent. He glanced at the guards.

Ferox turned to his men. "Leave me. I need to speak to my guests in private."

The lead guard bobbed his head. "My prince. We'll be right outside the door." They left the suite.

"Start talking," Ferox said to Kopius.

"I'm sorry," blurted Van. "I tried to tell you earlier—"

"You knew?" Ferox clenched his jaw.

Paley chewed on her cuticle. "Knew what?"

"I met the assassin after the second match," Van confessed to Ferox. "He told me he's called the Hierophant and was after Kopius, not you."

"You met him?" Kopius's eyes widened. "And lived to tell about it?"

Van turned to Daisy. "Did you know about this?"

She cast her eyes to the floor. "I found out, recently."

"You're an assassin?" asked Ixl. Just like that, Kopius became the enemy.

Brux seemed unsure about being impressed or angry; Paley gaped.

Suixsha stood alert and quiet. Her ears took in every word, her eyes, every movement.

"I hate school. Have no desire to enter Advanced Studies after I graduate." Kopius dropped into a chair, as if recounting the story would exhaust him. "One day a couple of men appeared, pulled me out of class. Told me they were from the Brotherhood of the Magic Circle."

"The Brotherhood recruited you?" asked Van. "I thought they were strictly an Earth World organization."

"They're in Lodestar and Salus Valde," said Kopius. "They recruited me into The Program, an assassin program. The Hierophant was my teacher. Turned out, being a hired killer wasn't for me either." His eyes shifted to Daisy. "After I met her."

She adoringly gazed back at him.

"*Daisy* was the special task." Van pieced his story together. "You left the program last year to go find her for her father, Professor Lake."

"How was my father able to pull you out of assassin school?" asked Brux.

Kopius shrugged. "Maybe it was a coincidence I ran into him that day at Lodestar. Maybe not."

"Someone recognized you at the welcome dinner," said Van.

Kopius nodded.

"Are you here to kill Ferox?" Paley continued to gnaw on her cuticle, looking confused.

"What? No!" Kopius leaped out of the chair.

"No one is here to kill Ferox," Daisy said to Paley.

"Well, that's a relief." Ferox tossed his hands in the air.

Ixl narrowed his eyes at Kopius. "If you weren't disappearing to go kill him, what were you doing?"

"I was seeing if Ferox and his family were sincere about helping us check the seal," said Kopius. "And to see if I could find clues pointing to the identity of the Balish spy at Lodestar."

"And?" asked Ixl.

"Nothing about the spy," said Kopius. "The other part is obvious."

Ferox nodded. "Of course we were trying to help."

"Why do teacher want you dead?" asked Suixsha.

"No one is allowed to leave The Program." Kopius looked mournfully at Daisy. "My teacher has come for me. I have to go. For your safety." He turned to the others. "I don't want what happened to Alden to happen to any of you."

"I guess it's a testament to how good the palace guards are that he hasn't been able to get to you yet." Ixl roughly patted Kopius on the back, assassin past forgiven.

Ferox gave Ixl a curt bob of appreciation.

"He's gotten into the suites several times," said Kopius. "But I'm superb at hiding too."

Daisy hung her head in gloom. "I'll go pack."

Kopius placed a comforting hand on her shoulder. "No."

"Why? No... I—" Daisy appeared visibly upset.

"Stay and help," he said. "You need to carry on with the mission. Mend the seal, find out what happened to the other team. Time is running out for Van. She and the team need you."

Daisy reluctantly agreed.

Kopius headed back to the boy's suite to pack, accompanied by two palace guards. He returned to bid farewell to the team and Ferox.

Tears trickled down Daisy's cheeks as she wrapped him in a parting hug.

Kopius gave her a quick kiss on the lips. "I'll be in touch."

At the fireplace in Van's bedroom, he twisted around and gave Daisy a half-hearted smile. Then dashed through the panel door and disappeared into the dark passageway.

Everyone went back to the living area and quietly processed what had just happened.

After a moment, Ixl rubbed his hands together and asked, "We still leaving at noon?"

"Just need to take care of some things and gather my men." Ferox opened the suite's door to leave. A handful of other palace guards had gathered with the ones Ferox told to wait outside.

The head guard said, "We must get you back to your rooms at once."

Ferox waved his hands to calm him. "It's okay. The assassin is no longer a threat. I'm sure my men told you that. The lockdown is over."

"My prince," said the head guard. "The rebels have breached the palace. Your life is in danger. We're under strict orders by King Mador to get you to the safety of your rooms."

Ferox agreed and stepped out of the suite.

Van dashed after him and clasped his arm. "Wait! What about the Alignment ending? Mending the seal?"

The head guard glared at Van. "For the prince's safety, he cannot travel anywhere."

Ferox placed a gentle hand over her grip. "My family simply wants what's best."

"Your family? What about me?" asked Van.

Ferox wrinkled his brow. "Not everything is about you."

Another guard said, "All guests in the palace are on lockdown until the situation is cleared. For your own safety, we ask that you stay in your rooms."

Van scoffed at his request.

"Stay put. I'll handle this," said Ferox. The guards ushered him away, leaving Van fuming.

She stomped back into the suite. "I can't believe he always sides with his family."

"Forget Ferox," said Brux. "We need to leave right now."

The team collected their belongings and gathered by the fireplace in Van's bedroom, ready to head out of Balefire Palace and never return.

They hustled through the passageway, planning to steal another fig, and found the exit to the southern grounds of the palace.

Brux cracked open the door, peeked outside to check for an all-clear, and jerked back. He slammed the door closed.

"The rebels have it blocked," said Brux.

"I don't have the Runestar." Van's shoulders slumped. "So there's nothing preventing them from killing us."

"Come on." Ixl led them down a different passageway.

They tried several more doors leading to the outside. Armed rebels or palace guards protecting the grounds blocked all the exits.

"We haven't tried this one yet." Paley pulled a lever by a peephole.

"No—" Van reached to stop her, but was too late.

The panel slid open to a room inside the palace.

"What?" Paley shrugged. "The palace is on lockdown. Nobody's here." She wandered into the drawing room.

The others cautiously followed. The panel door slid closed behind them.

"Could be worth the risk of sneaking out the main entrance," said Ixl. "We need to get out of here."

Several guards paroling the palace hallways saw them. "Rebels!" cried one.

"Halt!" cried another, gripping his DEW handgun.

Ixl dashed at the guards. To what end? Van did not know.

One guard fired his DEW at him.

Ixl dropped and rolled, dodging the blast.

Brux dashed toward the wall where the panel door was located. Another guard fired a warning shot, blowing a hole straight through the wall near Brux.

Ixl jumped to his feet to find two guards pointing their DEWs in his face. The other guards aimed their guns at the rest of them.

The team held up their hands in surrender. The guards relieved them of their backpacks and weapons. Thankfully, they had no interest in Brux and Paley's Twin Gemstones tucked away in their pant's pockets.

"Come on." One guard waved his DEW toward the door.

The guards escorted them down a stairway leading into the sublevels of Balefire.

"Not again." Van sighed as the guards locked the team in a cell.

Van thought about demanding to see Ferox, but didn't. He would be no help, and she was still furious with him.

"Ferox will pull through for us," said Daisy.

Van and the others grunted disbelievingly.

After a couple of hours, Ferox came bounding down the dungeon's stairway, looking agitated.

Van refused to acknowledge him.

"After this latest fiasco, I can't get you out of the final match," said Ferox irritably. "Why didn't you trust me and just stay in your suite?"

Van would explode if she didn't respond. She blasted, "Because when have you ever helped? You sit back all comfy with your family while I risk my life playing in the games!"

"You should've trusted me." Ferox gripped his hands around the cell bars. "Trusted my family."

"Pfft." Ixl leaned against the stone wall next to Suixsha.

Ferox addressed Van. "How are you going to win with your powers on the fritz?"

"You could give her some help." Brux shrugged, steaming. "Just throwing it out there."

"I'm working on it." Ferox matched Brux's antagonism.

"You're always *working on it*." Ixl clenched his fists. "How about doing it? Like by skewing the match in Van's favor."

"No, that would be cheating." Van flapped her hands for emphasis. "Besides, he'll never get around to doing it. Not unless his *family* says it's okay."

"Fine. You don't want my help. I'm leaving." Ferox stormed away from the cell. "Good luck in the match." He said over his shoulder before rushing up the stairs and out of the dungeon.

Suixsha placed a heavy hand on Van's shoulder. "Why you not take help offered? We need leave, mend seal. Now, no help."

"We're not going to have time to check the seal before the Alignment ends," said Paley.

"Not unless we break out of here." Van's eyes darted around the cell, searching for a weak point.

"Looks like there's only one way out, amigo," Ixl said to Van.

Van groaned and bumped her head against the bars. "I'm going to have to compete in the final match of the Death Games."

CHAPTER
FORTY-SEVEN

From the time when Van fought with Ferox through the bars of her cell, to her standing at the entrance to play in the final match of the Death Games passed faster than a wildfire ripping through a dry forest.

Two significant things happened before this moment.

One, the court allowed Van her dot matice and the vial of vinegarroon venom she had won in the first match. Giving her an advantage in the current match. This was good.

The other, Van's teammates were allowed to enter the match with her. She couldn't say this was good, only significant. She'd prefer only her life being in danger, not anyone else's.

Van had made her peace with finishing the games until she discovered a crack in the third seal. Now, competing only wasted her time. The Alignment ended in a matter of hours. Van held little hope she could finish the match and get back to Salus Valde before the Elementals released the deadly Quasher. The thought of encountering the creature made Van tremble more than facing Tarcs in the coming game.

Van and her team waited for the match to start in a noisy grand room inside Balefire Palace that reminded Van of a casino in Las Vegas.

Machines whirled and dinged, flashed gemstone powered lights, and occasionally dropped coins into a container when images lined up in a certain pattern. Gamers sat at semicircle tables with serious faced croupiers dealing cards. Others hung around rectangular tables playing games that used dice. People and Tarcs wandered about, dressed in fine tunics or robes with stylish headdresses.

"Ferox is helping you behind the scenes," said Daisy. "That's why teams are allowed in this one."

"I doubt it. Our fight was pretty terrible." Van glimpsed Ferox across the room sitting with Solana, Merloc, Underking Mador, Underqueen Sybil, Lord Godreel and other officials in a raised, cushy roped-off area in front of a big panel gemscreen.

Seeing Ferox made Van queasy. It didn't feel right entering the match while they weren't on good terms. She wished he would come over to see her off, wish her well, slip her the Coin... *something*. He didn't, which led her to believe they might've broken up.

"The council agreed to teams because they expect all of us to get killed." Ixl ran his eyes over the other contestants, all Tarcs. Each team was spaced about fifteen feet apart and corralled by their own gaming official.

Daisy shook her head. "Ferox knows we're stronger as a team."

Paley, biting her fingernails, gaped at the busy room. "Did you notice people are acting weird about this match?"

"It's the last one." Brux shifted his weight from side to side and shook his arms, prepping for the coming fight. "They're excited."

Static came from the public address system. "May I have your attention please?" asked a male voice.

The machines stopped binging and dinging; the games ceased.

"The final match in the Death Games will begin in just a moment," said the voice. "Survivors of the prior matches please gather by your gaming official with your teammates to get rules of play and entrance into the match. Although we're allowing teams this year, there will still be only one winner of the Death Games. Spectators, please see the board and place your bets accordingly."

Paley's orange-with-yellow-flames colored eyes darted to her teammates. "He means one team will win, right?"

The gaming official overseeing their group interjected, "One contestant. This match is a fight to the death."

"It's not called a final match for nothing," said Brux through clenched teeth. "The council pulled a fast one. They allowed teams and kept the rule about only one survivor."

"Now know why council agree team," said Suixsha.

Ixl sighed. "I hate being right all the time."

Brux grasped Daisy by the shoulders. "I need you to leave. I won't allow you to play, to die."

Movement in the royal viewing area caught Van's attention. Ferox rose. He had a brief back and forth with his family, and then hastily left. *Humph.* He must not have the stomach to watch her die. *Coward.*

Paley stared at Van. "You're going to have to kill us to win? How're you going to do that?" She quavered while gnawing on her cuticle with such ferocity Van thought she might chew off her finger.

Ixl shrugged. "We'll figure it out."

"If the Quasher doesn't kill us first," said Van. "More likely, the Balish Council wanted to drag out the games long enough for that beast to come and tear us apart. And, Paley, I'm not killing any of you because none of you are entering with me. That's final. I don't need any of you." She glanced at Paley. "Especially not you."

"I enter." Suixsha positioned herself next to Van. "Protect Van until end. Others stay."

"As your assigned protector, there's no question about me going with you," Brux said to Van.

She swooshed her hand like it was a magic wand. "I relieve you of your duty."

"Nope." Brux placed his hands on his hips. "You go, I go."

"That means me too," said Paley meekly.

"Gem-cams are set up in the playing area so spectators can see the contest on gemscreens in the palace." Their official reached into a box on the floor and took out a tiny clip-on gemstone. "Contestants will wear an ATG, audio transmit gemstone, at all times so the viewers can hear the event."

Ixl snorted. "So the lazy royals and arrogant Tarc king can watch in comfort from their little viewing area?"

"It's the only way to properly view the match." The official furrowed his brow as if Ixl's daftness perplexed him. "The playing field has a new expansive venue this year."

"I'd love to see one of them enter the match." Ixl titled his head to the royal viewing area.

"Members of the royal family cannot enter the Death Games." The official appeared appalled by the very thought. "It's against Balish law."

"Betting is now closed," said the voice on the PA system. "The match will begin in five minutes. Officials, please prep your contestants."

Van's stomach became nauseated knowing bets were being placed on who would die first, the order of deaths, and who would emerge the champion. She wondered who Ferox placed his bet on to win.

"Once you enter, you are magically locked in until all other contestants are dead," said the official.

"Sounds like a plan." Ixl rubbed his hands together, obviously blowing off nervous tension. "Woo! Let's go!"

The official pressed his lips together at Ixl's outburst. He cleared his throat and continued. "The goal of the match is to hunt and kill all other contestants. Collect as many items of value—jewels, gold, magical objects, and weapons—as you can along the way." He puffed out his chest in pride, as if it were an honor to compete. "One can become wealthy by winning the Death Games."

"Is magic restricted?" asked Daisy.

"What about weapons?" asked Brux.

"Only winners who collected weapons or magical items in previous matches may enter with them," said the official. "Contestants can also use weapons and magical items found in the playing area. The winner gets to keep everything they carry out. An exit will not appear until all others who entered the match are dead and there is but one survivor. One winner."

The official reached into his pocket and took out a dot matice. For a moment, Van thought it was hers and wondered how he got it.

"The match will be played in the Dunes of Dolor." The official shook the dot matice, causing it to unfold and increase in diameter. "They say it's a place made by the Creator in a fit of anger. Chosen by the princess herself." He tossed the dot matice onto the plain wall near where their team waited.

The black disc flopped and wobbled as it enlarged midair before sticking to the wall in a U-shaped opening. The other officials did the same.

"One dot matice per team, none may enter the match in the same place." The official handed Van her ATG, then Suixsha. He motioned to give one to Ixl. Van grabbed his arm, stopping him.

"No one else enters. Just me and Suixsha." She threw Ixl a pleading stare. "Uxa would never forgive me if I let you enter."

"It would make my mother proud." Ixl attempted to snatch the gem-clip from the man.

The official clenched it tightly in his hand. "No ATG, no entry."

"I'm going." Brux flexed his hand at him. "Give me one."

"No," snapped Van.

The team had come to an impasse. All eyes turned to the official.

"It's the winner's choice whether to allow the assistance of a team."

"Enter match mean certain death." Suixsha turned to Daisy. "You need stay. Need watch over Tyger for me."

Daisy hesitated. "I..."

"Please," Suixsha said so uncharacteristically it made the appeal more poignant.

"She will," said Brux. "I've already told her she's not going."

A tear formed in the corner of Daisy's eye. She nodded.

"Don't follow us," warned Van. "Suixsha and I go alone."

Brux, ignoring Van's plea, turned to Paley. "I need you with me. You in?"

Paley, although trembling, raised her chest, flipped her hair, and, in a dramatic attempt at bravery, dashed toward the entrance at full speed.

"No, you can't—" the official raised his hand and raced to block her, though not fast enough to stop Paley's charge.

Paley smacked into the solid blackness with a crack. Her head snapped back, and she crashed backward onto the floor. Blood oozed from the massive gash on her forehead.

"Paley!" gasped Daisy.

Van and the others rushed over and knelt by her side.

Paley opened her eyes half-way and seemed to have trouble focusing.

The official huffed. "Like I said, you can't enter the match without wearing an ATG."

"I-I wanted to help..." Paley lost consciousness.

"She's in no shape for the match," said Daisy.

"Looks like Brux and Paley are a no-go," said Ixl.

Brux nodded, looking resigned to his fate of staying behind thanks to the Twin Gemstones.

"I'm still in." Ixl straightened his shoulders.

Van glared at the gaming official. "He stays too." She held up her palm to stop Ixl's rebuff.

Ixl's cheeks flushed. He snorted as he came to accept his entrance into the match was not under his control.

Brux went to Van and gently clasped her hands. "We both know the Balish want the Staff. I know you feel compelled to retrieve it, like it's a lost part of your soul. If it's near the location of the final match, which I believe it is, I know you'll go search for it. But remember, we can't rule out that Ferox plotted with Solana, and probably

Merloc, to make you a participant in the games to provoke you into retrieving it."

"I have no intention of getting—"

Brux squeezed her hands for emphasis. "It's no coincidence Solana picked this location for the final match. I'm sure of it."

"It's time to enter the playing area," said the official.

His words gave Van the same dread as if he was ushering her off a cliff.

Van and Suixsha stood side by side in front of the dot matice-made entrance.

Suixsha leaned over and whispered, "Wit and friend only get you so far. In end, only strength and power keep you alive."

The official urged them to walk through the opening.

Together, they strode into the black entrance, ready to face their fate in the Dunes of Dolor.

CHAPTER

FORTY-EIGHT

Van and Suixsha cautiously entered the playing area, ready for the final match in the Death Games.

The blazing desert wind singed Van's skin. Glaring sun beat down from a clear blue sky, causing Van to squint. She surveyed the rock formations, tall as buildings, along the sandy, dune-filled terrain.

"Should've brought sunglasses," croaked Van, through chalky lips. She swallowed to soothe her dry throat.

Suixsha walked beside her without a drop of sweat.

"Where're the other contestants?" Van asked. "Never mind," she added, hearing clipped voices coming from an entrance behind them.

They whipped around, fists up, ready to defend themselves against an attack.

Ixl and Daisy bounded out of the dot matice-made doorway just before it disappeared.

"Didn't want to miss the Dunes of Dolor." Ixl grinned. "Sounded like so much fun."

Van placed a hand over her heart, touched. Then, wrinkled her forehead, angry at them for volunteering to come on this suicide mission with her. "How?"

"Knuckle sandwich." Ixl pounded a fist into his palm.

Daisy threw him a look and said, "Brux distracted the gaming official while we grabbed ATGs from his box."

Suixsha stared at Daisy with cold eyes.

Daisy waved her hands like they were white flags. "Brux promised to look after Tyger. I trust him. He's good with cats, all animals, really. Besides, we're all going to make it out alive. I know it."

Suixsha's lips flattened. Her eyes narrowed.

"Listen." Ixl attempted to cool things down. "Van needs all the help she can get. You agree? We have the same goal. Find a way out and get to the seal before the Alignment ends."

"I'm sorry, Suixsha." Daisy's hands fell to her sides. "But together we're more powerful. You know that. We can't let the Balish or the Tarcs diminish that through fear."

Van hoped the entire Balish community heard every word on their gemscreens.

Suixsha's faced relaxed as she released her anger. "Brux okay you go?"

"The choice was mine," said Daisy. "Not his."

The team trekked forward, keeping alert for other contestants.

"This area is enormous." Daisy scanned the landscape. "Where are they?"

"They here," said Suixsha, with a keen glint in her eyes.

"Look for hidden weapons and magical items." Ixl dropped to his knees and began digging in the sand.

Van paused, hands on her hips. "Really? You think there's a hidden weapon *right there*?"

Ixl dug his fingers through the sand like a sifter. "You never know."

Van appreciated his enthusiasm. Her agitation came from her throbbing feet, swollen from the heat. She worried it would slow her down and hinder her ability to fight. Suixsha appeared unaffected by the extreme conditions, increasing her annoyance. Van couldn't even beat Suixsha in the Jaychund games, in ideal conditions. Now Van had to kill a bunch of Tarcs, figure out how to get the team out alive, and mend the seal. All within a few hours before the Elementals released the Quasher.

"Hey!" Ixl leaped to his feet. He stared at the shifting sand in front of him. "I think I shook something loose."

The tip of an animal's snout poked from the sand. Followed by an angular feline-like head, except with an elongated jaw.

He jumped back.

"Tatzelwurm," said Suixsha. "It aggressive, attack anything that move."

"Your digging drew its attention," said Daisy.

"Mi mala." Ixl craned his neck and backed away as the wurm's snake-like body emerged from the sand. It rose to its full height of at least seven feet. Four stubby legs protruded from its body. It flicked its forked tongue at him. "If I hold still, will it go away?"

It leaped straight at Ixl.

"Nope." He ducked.

The tatzelwurm soared over his head and landed behind him. It rose onto its hind legs and let out three short shrieks.

Several other tatzelwurms popped up from the ground.

As one wurm ascended, a chain mail jacket and a short blade rose from the sand with it. The items tumbled down.

Van lured the creature away, dropped and rolled when it leaped at her while Ixl snatched the chain mail and blade.

Ixl used the blade to jab the creature trying to seize Van in its jaws. "Its scales are too thick. I can't pierce them."

Suixsha and Daisy held still. The wurms didn't bother them. Daisy closed her eyes.

The tatzelwurm twisted around toward Ixl. Van dashed away.

Ixl fiddled, putting on the jacket. The wurm lunged at him with an opened jaw. It snapped down around Ixl's middle, just as he had secured the jacket. The creature clamped his midline and lifted him.

His chain mail protected him from the creature's bite. Ixl hacked at the wurm. His blade bounced off its scales. He jabbed the dagger into the wurm's eye.

It shrieked, releasing its jaw. Ixl crashed to the ground. The wurm slithered into the sand.

"Ixl okay?" called Suixsha.

"Heck ya!" Ixl patted his chain mail jacket, full of adrenaline.

Van stopped and faced the wurm chasing her, knowing she couldn't outrun it forever. As the wurm lowered its head with an opened mouth, she greeted it with a flying roundhouse kick to the snout.

It jerked backward from the force and yelped. The wurm shook its head, and instead of attacking, it burrowed back into the sand.

"If you punch them in the nose, they'll leave," cried Van.

"Cowards." Ixl grinned.

Daisy opened her eyes. "If you stay still, they won't bother you."

Van and Ixl did as told and the wurms calmed. They lost interest in the humans and dived back into the sand.

"Looks like we're in the clear," said Van. "We need to be quiet and walk lightly."

Sounds of clanking of armor caught Van's ear. She saw the tops of their heads first, as a yoke of Tarcs came charging at them over a dune. Their thumping footsteps attracted the attention of the tatzelwurms. A handful popped up from the sand.

One of the Tarcs held a DEW handgun and blasted the wurms as they rose from the sand. Others slashed at the wurms with machetes and battle axes.

"They must've searched the sand," said Ixl, with a tinge of jealousy, as he gathered together with Van the others.

More wurms surged from the noise of the battle.

One Tarc got lifted from the ground as a wurm burst upward

from the sand. He flew high into the air and thudded onto a rocky mound.

He lay unconscious. A tatzelwurm sniffed his body.

Daisy dashed toward him, darting to avoid the weapon-wielding Tarcs and light enough on her feet not to draw the attention of any unearthed wurms.

Ixl furrowed his brow. "She knows they're here to kill us, right?"

Van and Suixsha shrugged. Van wouldn't put it past Daisy to help a wounded enemy.

The tatzelwurm scrutinizing the unconscious Tarc unhinged its jaw and swallowed him whole.

Daisy crashed to her knees next to the wurm that ingested the Tarc. The creature's narrow body bulged, so full it could barely move, never mind attack her. She frantically ran her hands in the sand and sprung to her feet, gripping a handheld DEW. She aimed and blew the head off the wurm next to her, then another and another.

Some Tarcs marched over a rocky hill carrying barrels on their shoulders, either won in a prior match, or found in the dunes. They emptied the barrels into one spot in the sand, pooling a thick liquid that looked like yellow oil, the same kind the villagers used to torment the lemure in Muspell.

The tatzelwurms paused, lifted their snouts and sniffed, changed direction and headed straight toward the oil pool. They hesitated at the pool's edge and hovered their noses over the surface. Then slithered into the yellow pond. Other wurms rushed over and dove in.

A blob rose from the oil and morphed into a featureless human form. The slick, yellow oil covering it changed to a thick, black goo.

Van's demon had returned.

It dragged itself out of the pond and lumbered in Van's direction, stretching its arms, reaching for her. It trailed a yellow-black oil slick behind it, oozing goo like a walking geyser.

The demon got closer, unnerving Van to where she couldn't hold still any longer. She dashed away just as a Tarc lit the oil pool on fire. The wurms screeched as they burned to death.

The stream of oil created by the demon's path also ignited, scaring the remaining wurms back into the sand.

Flames caught up with the demon and engulfed its body. It thrashed as it melted into the ground, leaving nothing but a fiery puddle.

Van, Suixsha, Daisy, and Ixl regrouped behind a rock formation.

Ixl rested his back against the granite, chest rising and falling with heavy breaths. "Did you see that? How the oil oozed into a stream?"

"I wonder how the Tarcs did that," said Daisy.

"A demon made the oil trail." Van wondered if her teammates suffered from sunstroke. "When it came after me. Didn't you see it?"

Ixl and Daisy looked at Van with concern.

Suixsha positioned herself against the edge of the rock and peered around the side to monitor the Tarcs.

She twisted around to face them. "Trouble coming."

FORTY-NINE

Ixl stretched his neck to look around the edge of the rock formation. "The players have gathered together as a unifying force against us. Led by—"

"Hutriel." Van peeped around the side. "He survived the second match." She racked her brain trying to figure out what to do next. "Ixl, you're the military strategist. What should we do?"

Ixl brushed his fingertips over his facial scars, deep in thought. "What weapons do we have?"

"Chain mail jacket, a short blade, and a handheld DEW," said Daisy.

"There's a military maneuver you like..." Van snapped her fingers, trying to remember. "What was it?"

Ixl lit up. "The hammer and anvil."

"Will it work?" asked Daisy.

Ixl paused and ran the scenario through his mind.

"They coming," said Suixsha.

"With the Tarcs grouped together, we can use it," he said. "Hit them from the front with the DEW. But we need some kind of weapon to sneak attack them from behind. Maybe if we look around..."

Daisy held up her palm to stop him. "We have a weapon. Me."

They stared blankly at her.

"If you mean magic," Van shook her head, "it won't work. You didn't win it in another match or find it here."

"Trust me," said Daisy. "I got this."

"Okay, then." Ixl clapped his hands. "Let's make my mother proud. Van, Suixsha, you're the anvil. You come at them with a frontal assault using the DEW and the blade, weaken their force while holding them in place."

Ixl turned to Daisy. "Me and you, we're going to maneuver behind the horde and pummel them with a surprise attack. We're the hammer. Theoretically, they won't have time to adjust to the threat coming from the rear." He paused and looked skeptically at Daisy. "That threat would be you."

"We need do it now," said Suixsha.

Van and Suixsha darted out from behind the rock, screaming, getting the horde's attention.

A yoke of Tarcs charged at them.

Van fired the DEW in rapid succession, hitting several of them, dropping them to the ground. She paused for a beat, stunned. She had just killed living creatures. Non-human Tarcs, in self-defense, but still... the negative repercussions of ending lives reverberated down to her soul.

A fast one rushed at Van.

Suixsha jumped him from behind and squeezed an arm around his throat. With her free hand, she stabbed him through the ribs with the blade.

The brutality of it horrified Van. Until she realized the odds of the two of them surviving an attack by the murderous mob of Tarcs were extremely low.

Van, again, fired the DEW. She took down several more, making the other Tarcs rushing at them pause, weary about getting blasted. But for how long?

Air swirled in multiple spots around them. Spinning so fast, mini tornados formed. Not of sand or wind, but *fire*.

At first, Van thought it was Daisy's hammer maneuver. It wasn't. "Dammit." Van continued firing the DEW, keeping the newest hazard of the game in sight.

Suixsha's ambidextrous handling of the blade came in handy as she battled any Tarc able to dodge the DEW's rays.

"What's taking Daisy and Ixl so long?" shouted Van. "I can't hold them back much longer. There's too many."

Drawn by the noise, a tatzelwurm popped out of the sand. Then another, and another.

The Tarcs scattered.

Van ducked as she blasted a leaping wurm midair.

"Where hammer?" Suixsha breathed heavily, bloody blade in hand, dead Tarc at her feet.

"Look out!" cried Van.

A fire tornado formed next to Suixsha. The swirling flames burned Suixsha's arm. She cried out in agony and leapt away from the fiery whirlwind.

A tatzelwurm shot up from of the sand, knocking Van backward. She dropped the DEW.

The wurm hovered over her, flicking its tongue. Its head darted at her, jaw unhinged.

Van rolled aside and scrambled to grab the DEW.

The wurm lunged forward.

Van pointed the gun and pulled the trigger. It clicked but didn't discharge. Sand had jammed it.

The wurm took another swipe. Van dropped and rolled aside.

It spit out a mouthful of sand and twisted around for another try. It swooped down at Van with its jaw wide open, moving faster than Van could crawl away.

She pulled out the vial of venom from her pocket and threw it into the wurm's mouth.

It closed its jaw, chewed, and swallowed. Then raised to an upright position, flicked its tongue at Van, eyes glazed. The wurm's body went limp, and it crashed to the ground, blowing sand into Van's face.

Coughing, Van scrambled to her feet.

Daisy and Ixl appeared on the top of a rock formation behind most of the Tarcs, who were now so spread out Van doubted the hammer and anvil maneuver would work.

Ixl stood guard, protecting Daisy as she stood serenely above the blood and terror. She raised her arms, palms skyward, eyes closed.

Van's hair whipped across her face as the wind picked up. It got stronger and stronger, blasting her ears with the roar of its movement and blowing particles of dirt into her mouth. The air blew back and forth, encompassing the players in a violent sandstorm.

The wind scoured Van's skin like sandpaper. She dove for cover in the nearest rock formation, tucking into a nook.

Suixsha flew in and smashed her back against the rock beside Van, blood stained and chest heaving.

With a whoosh that sounded like the roar of a beast from hell, the sandstorm ripped through the dunes.

After the wind settled and all was quiet, Van peeked out from the nook.

The fire tornadoes, players, and wurms had vanished. The sandstorm had acted like bristle brush and scrubbed clean the entire playing area.

Ixl and Daisy climbed down and rushed over to them.

"You see that?" cried Ixl. "Fierce!"

"Not magic. Just connecting to the power of mother nature." Daisy beamed.

"Impressive." Van hoped, when the time came, she could also access her power. Although, Van's power came from the magic in her

Anchoress bloodline, and wouldn't work in the match even if she could access it.

"Look." Suixsha gazed at the ground. Daisy's storm had uncovered objects hidden in the sand like treasures washed ashore after a hurricane. "There too." She pointed to a cave in one of the larger rock formations.

"Gather as many weapons as you can carry," said Ixl. "Quickly, before more players find us."

They dashed around, collecting the unearthed items.

"Hey!" Daisy called to them. "I need some help." She gripped a pull handle attached to a metal pole poking from the sand.

"I got it." Ixl tugged, then paused. "It's more jammed than I thought." He yanked again and again, flexing enough to strain the muscles in his neck and face. Finally, a steel utility cart emerged from the sand.

"That'll be useful." Van motioned for Ixl to bring the cart to where they had stockpiled their treasure trove.

Ixl wheeled it over and they tossed all the items into the cart's basket, not just the weapons. Gold bracelets ("real gold," said Van), high-quality gemstones (according to Van), a machete ("also high quality," said Ixl smirking), several knives, three DEW handguns, some lava sticks, and numerous gold and silver rounds.

Ixl clasped the handle of the loaded cart. "Now, let's go check out that cave."

CHAPTER
FIFTY

Suixsha ran her palm against the rock wall. "Wind cave."

Daisy followed her inside. "It is. Aeolian caves are chambers created by wind over time. They're common in desert areas. That's what formed these massive sandstone cliffs."

"I bet there's tons of stuff in here for us to find. Like more weapons." Ixl's eyes darted around the cave as he pulled the cart behind him.

Van perused the ceiling. "I see gem-cams. This is part of the playing area."

Ixl stopped and grabbed some DEW handguns out of the cart. He gave one to each of them.

Van gripped the steel handle of the DEW and moved forward, deeper into the cave. "Keep alert for other players, don't let down your guard."

"What makes you think Daisy's sandstorm didn't wipe out the other contestants?" asked Ixl, as they tread down a winding path between sandstone walls. "And now the viewers are waiting for us to kill each other?"

Van snorted. "It'll be a long wait."

The air grew cooler, giving them a welcome relief to the dry heat of the desert.

"Look." Daisy found a stack of gold chains and gemstone necklaces in a gap between some rocks. She held them up for the others to see.

"What's the quality, though?" Ixl smirked.

Van scrunched her face at him. "Toss them in," she said to Daisy.

The path led them to a wider hollowed formation. They explored its nooks and crannies, gathering more treasure and weapons.

Suixsha tossed a silver war hammer into the cart.

Daisy dumped in a handful of gold coins. "If we fill it any more, you won't be able to pull it."

"I dunno." Ixl tested its weight. The cart moved forward. "I think it's charmed. No matter how heavy the load, it's easy to pull."

They cautiously marched deeper into the cave, following another winding pathway, until coming to a spacious nook. The team searched the cavities in the walls and shuffled their feet in the sandy ground.

Daisy knelt down and picked up a dagger. "Wow, the decorative metalwork on this is beautiful." She dug in the sand around her and pulled up a piece of nylon material and frowned. Digging more uncovered the top of a singed strap. She tugged, trying to wrench it from the ground. "It won't budge."

Van and Ixl hustled over. Suixsha kept watch.

Ixl took the strap. Daisy and Van used their fingers to dig around the embedded object. Ixl heaved. The object erupted from the sand, sending him flying backward, landing on his butt.

He held a scorched backpack.

Van's heart sank. She knew what it meant to find that backpack. From the tears streaming down Daisy's cheeks, she did, too.

Ixl got to his feet and scrutinized the pack. "It's burned and useless." He tossed it aside, dropped to his knees, and dug around the spot where Daisy found it. "But there's probably more stuff here." He hit something and pulled up a grappling hook and line.

"Ixl..." pleaded Van.

He chucked aside the grappling hook and line and continued digging. He found an odd-shaped grimy white stick. "What? Gross." He chucked it.

Daisy sniffled. She knelt down beside him and brushed away sand in the area around where Ixl found the bone.

Van placed a gentle hand on Daisy's shoulder. "Stop." Van's eyes went to Ixl. "You, too. Stop."

"I need to know. *We* need to know for certain." Daisy kept digging.

"Why stop?" Ixl uncovered a burned jacket. He brushed sand off and saw the charred remnants of a standard issue Grigori windbreaker.

He took a sharp intake of breath as Daisy unearthed a blackened canteen with a partially singed sticker from the Naked Ape, Van's favorite beauty salon on Providence Island.

"Oh!" Daisy clasped her hand over her mouth. "This... them..." she choked as tears filled her eyes.

"It's the other team," said Ixl, his voice cracking.

"No doubt." Van cast her eyes down to the unfortunate graveyard; her words brimmed with sorrow.

A single tear trickled down Ixl's cheek. Suixsha shifted her weight from foot to foot.

"At least," Van cleared her throat, "we know what happened to them."

She had clung to the possibility of the other team being trapped or held somewhere against their will. This gave Van hope of saving them and bringing them home. Now, that hope was gone.

Ixl held up the windbreaker between his thumb and forefinger and inspected it. "It—it looks like they burned to death."

Van nodded. "That matches what the All-Seeing Eye showed me." If the Eye was right about the other team, then what did it mean by showing Van the tombstones? The thought of it unnerved her.

"Uh, it gets worse." Ixl unclipped a charred object from the jacket and held it up so they all could see it.

"An ATG? You've *got* to be kidding," shrieked Van.

"The other team played in the games?" asked Daisy. "How?"

Van waved her fist at the nearest gem-com. "You *bastards!*" Van wondered if Ferox knew about this, and could've helped them and chose not to. She needed to punch something. To release the building rage inside her. She crashed to her knees and slammed her fists on the ground so hard it caused particles of sand to get in her eyes and throat. She didn't care.

Daisy brushed away the sand and began to collect the remains of the other team. "We need to bring them back to their families."

Ixl and Van helped. Suixsha stayed on alert and kept watch.

Afterward, Daisy suggested she say a prayer.

Daisy, Ixl, and Van held hands. Suixsha remained vigilant as she made a gesture over her chest, then raised two fingers of one hand upward, in what Van figured was her tribal tradition for these situations.

"Our fellow teammates," said Daisy. "We thank you for your sacrifice and bravery. May your souls have a safe journey as they return to the light of the Creator, becoming one with peace and love. Once again, home."

They held a moment of silence.

Suixsha broke the quiet. "We need move. Stay one spot, get found. Or die by fire."

"She's right." Ixl clasped the handle of the cart and pulled. It easily rolled forward. "Be the hunter, not the prey."

The team continued deeper into the cave in contemplative silence.

Finding the remains of the other team brought their fate into a more focused reality. Van's heart tugged with the desire to see Genie and her strange boyfriend again... and Wiglaf... her classmates... even Uxa.

"Gosh, your mother must be worried sick about you," Van said to Ixl.

He shrugged. "I hope she has more confidence in me than that."

Van glanced at him. "You're every bit of the warrior your mother is, and more. I know she's proud of you."

Ixl beamed. "Thanks."

Time passed and with every step, an unseen force pulled Van in a direction that wasn't toward home. It was toward the Staff. She couldn't deny it. The ticking sounds of the grandfather clock in Uxa's home office grew louder in her mind. Reminding her time was running out.

"This match is taking too long," said Van. "I'm going to have to get the Staff. It's the only way to protect myself from the Quasher." If getting the Staff during the match and using it to win counted as cheating, then so be it. "The Staff is here, in the Dunes of Dolor. Brux was right, it's why Solana picked it as the playing area."

"You not able retrieve Staff until control anger," said Suixsha. "Ego still in way."

Van lifted her chin. "I may not be perfect, but I get things done."

"I'll help you," said Ixl.

Daisy nodded. "Lead the way."

Van veered off the passageway into a wider tunnel. "The Staff is close. I can sense it in every cell in my body." She picked up her pace.

"Slow down." Ixl struggled to keep up while dragging the cart.

Daisy waved Suixsha over to help Ixl. "We'll help you."

Van rushed ahead, no longer able to contain her magnetism to the Staff.

She darted around a bend and smacked into the black demon.

CHAPTER

FIFTY-ONE

Van's impact into the black demon sent them both crashing to the ground.

She lost her grip on the DEW handgun. It tumbled from her grasp.

The oily humanoid creature rose and hovered over her. Van braced, expecting an attack. None came. Instead, it spoke. But its words sounded distorted from the black goo covering its mouth.

Van cautiously got to her feet, keeping her eyes on the demon. She tried to interpret its utterance. "Go back?" She chewed on her lip. Why would a demon tell her to go back?

Ixl, Daisy, and Suixsha came stampeding around the corner, weapons drawn.

"We heard noise. Sounded like you were brawling with someone." Ixl held a lava stick for light in one hand and a DEW handgun in the other.

"Are you okay?" Daisy lowered her DEW. "Why do you have black ink on you?"

Van pointed at the demon. It wasn't there. "Uh... nothing. Never mind." This time, Van knew she wasn't hallucinating.

Ixl dashed back to grab the cart, and they continued deeper into the tunnel. The team entered a sizable chamber. Fiery-orange with red streaked sandstone walls surrounded them. A plethora of ten-petaled, yellow lotus flowers sprouted from rock crannies around the cavern.

"Smells like roses." Ixl wrinkled his nose.

"I see gem-cams." Daisy's eyes scanned the walls and ceiling. "We're still in the playing area."

Across the chamber, a triangle was carved into the wall above an opening.

In her mind, Van saw the outline of the triangle burst into flames. "We go that way."

"Let's move." Ixl gripped the handle of the cart.

Halfway into the cavern, Suixsha stopped.

Daisy twisted around. "What's wrong?"

"We stay," said Suixsha. "Van get Staff alone."

"Nope." Ixl continued on.

"Wait," said Van. "Suixsha's right. I have to prove to the Elemental I can retrieve it on my own."

"I'll go as far as I can." Ixl held up his hands to stop the protests. "I'll stay back. Van can complete the challenges on her own, but if it all goes to crap, I'll be there to have her back."

"I—" said Van.

"Don't bother." Ixl walked away from the cart. "I'm following you no matter what you say."

"Before you go..." Daisy put down her handgun and rummaged in the cart. She handed Ixl several lava sticks. "You don't have Van's flashlight eyes."

Suixsha bent down to retrieve Daisy's handgun when thundering footsteps caught their attention.

A handful of Tarcs stormed into the cavern, one wielded a machete, another a war axe.

Before Suixsha could rise, a Tarc swung his machete at her.

Daisy got bashed across the face by another. She dropped to the ground, unmoving.

Suixsha contorted her body in a cartwheel-style move, escaping the Tarc's swing range. The machete dinged against the side of the cart.

Daisy's attacker raised his knee and aimed his foot over her head.

A ray from Ixl's DEW hit the shoulder of Daisy's attacker and knocked him backward before he crushed Daisy's head. Ixl pulled the trigger again. It jammed. "Dammit." He tossed the gun aside and charged at the Tarc.

Van fired at the axe wielding Tarc rushing at her. His head exploded. Blood and pieces of his flesh splattered across her face and chest. His headless body dropped at her feet, his hand still clutching the war axe.

Ixl, haven beaten his attacker, rushed over and leaped onto the back of another Tarc who was hurtling toward Van, as another bent down to pry the war axe from his dead teammate's hand.

Suixsha's nimble kicks and punches impaired her assailant. He dropped the machete. She snatched it and fatally slashed his neck in one fluid movement.

As Ixl grappled with a Tarc, he cried to Van. "Shoot him."

Van's fingers went limp, dropping the gun. She remained immobilized. Stunned by her actions. The bitter, iron-like taste of Tarc blood in her mouth.

"Shoot... him." Ixl's Tarc had him in a neck hold.

Van's eyes followed the bloody axe as the Tarc in front of her raised it over her head.

As he swung down, he twisted around, blocking Suixsha's machete attack from behind and shoved her hard.

Suixsha crashed into the side of the cavern, dropping the machete, and crumbling to the ground.

Van rushed at the Tarc.

He turned and smashed Van over the head with the handle of the axe, knocking her to her knees.

Her head throbbed. Blood dripped into Van's eyes, impairing her vision as the Tarc raised the axe over Suixsha.

Van hurled her body sideways toward her gun. She grabbed it, aimed at Suixsha's attacker, and fired.

The blast flung the Tarc backward into Ixl and his attacker, knocking them both down.

The Tarc with a DEW blast in his side, landed on top of Ixl. The other rolled and leaped to his feet. He snatched up the axe as Ixl tried to free himself from the hefty weight of the dead Tarc on top of him.

The axe-wielding Tarc loomed over Ixl, grinning. He raised the axe and sliced down, mostly hitting the dead Tarc. Ixl screamed.

The Tarc raised the axe again, this time aiming for Ixl's neck.

A blast sounded. The Tarc's head exploded. He crashed down with a thump.

Suixsha stood, legs spread, gripping a rifle DEW she took from the cart.

Van rushed to Ixl and helped him push off the dead Tarc.

He sat upright, looking pale. Blood gushed from the wound on his leg.

By the cart, Suixsha bent over Daisy, who remained unconscious.

"Damn Tarc axed me." Ixl gripped his leg.

"You're losing too much blood." Van wiped her own blood out of her eyes, ignoring her dizzying headache from the blow to her head.

"You don't look... so great either," he said, with labored breathing.

Van patted her waist. "I don't have a—"

Suixsha dangled a leather belt next to Van. Bruises had already formed on her face.

"Thanks." Van tightly wrapped it around Ixl's thigh above his wound. "This should help stop the bleeding."

Suixsha went back and knelt by Daisy. She placed her index and middle fingers on Daisy's neck to check for a carotid pulse. "She alive. For now."

"Is there anything in the cart that might help?" asked Van.

Suixsha left Daisy and went to Van. She placed a gentle hand on Van's arm and stared her in the eyes. "I take care of them. You go."

Van hesitated.

"Go," said Ixl. His skin looked damp and pallid. "Only one can win."

Van's nostrils flared. "We'll see about that." She sprung to her feet and stomped across the chamber. "I'll be right back."

She sprinted into the tunnel under the flaming triangle. Her throbbing head worsened with each step. With no further flaming triangles giving her directions, the myriad of winding and splitting passageways slowed her down. She saw no more gem-cams and it gave her confidence she was on the right path.

Van continued on, tense and alert, ready for anything, and relying on her inner pull to guide her to the Staff.

She entered a small chamber and halted.

Van gaped at the being standing in its center. The woman's reddish-orange hair cascaded down to her ankles. Her golden robe sparkled with the same gleam as her bright-blue eyes.

"Welcome." The woman's rose-colored lips curved into a smile. "I am Hestia, the Fire Elemental and Guardian of the Staff."

CHAPTER

FIFTY-TWO

"H-hi," stammered Van. Even after encountering two other Elementals, she still wasn't sure how to greet them.

Next to Hestia, a serpent made of sparkly fire swirled around a sandstone post. It reminded Van of the red stripe whirling around a barber's pole.

"This is my pet, Miniel," said Hestia. "He lives here with me in the sand caves. Together we guard the Staff of Fire."

Van's eyes adjusted and realized it wasn't a post. Miniel swirled around a transparent container that held a steel rod with reddish bronze accents and a pointed top encircled with decorative metalwork.

"Your time has come to face my challenges. To prove yourself ready to handle the power of the Staff."

"I'm ready." Van hoped her blood streaked head and black goo stained clothes didn't suggest otherwise.

"I am not like my sisters." Hestia looked perturbed. "My challenges differ from Lady Loka's and Thalassa's. Passing through the Dunes of Dolor was one of them."

"I wouldn't be here if I wasn't ready." Van's head injury throbbed when she spoke.

"Very well." Hestia gave a curt nod. "You may approach Miniel. Retrieve the Staff from my pet and it is yours."

Van carefully approached the swirling creature.

"Stay away from it. Run," Brux, who wasn't there, shouted in her mind. "Go back."

Van hesitated. Fear gripped her. Then she remembered Suixsha's words about not giving up her will. To do so gives away one's power. "I'm not giving up," she replied without using words.

She got close to the shimmering fire-creature. It wasn't scary. Or hot. Miniel's beauty filled her with veneration at the magnificence of its creation. Its hypnotic, flowing movement mesmerized her.

"What it is you seek?" Miniel's mouth didn't move. Its words entered Van's mind like a hiss.

"The Staff," answered Van.

"To get it, you must walk through fire." It continuously twirled around the post.

Van reached her fingertips to the flames cast from Miniel's body. Her reality altered like a waking dream.

A thriving forest surrounded her. Van meandered between the trees, her mind foggy. She came to an altar. On top lay a shining gold wand.

The dazzling wand pulsed in rhythm with the blood pumping through Van's body.

It was the ticket to her glory. She imagined clutching the wand in her hand. With it, she would win the match. Save her friends. Be celebrated and establish herself as a worshipped leader. The wand would give her ultimate control over her destiny.

As she reached for it, a twig snapped behind her. She yanked back her hand and turned around.

A red lion shook its brilliant mane that flowed from its head like flames and held its chest high. It wore a jeweled necklace.

The lion curled its lip, revealing fangs, and growled, "What hand dare seize the wand?"

Van gritted her teeth in ire. The lion intended to block her from getting the wand, preventing her from winning, from fulfilling her destiny. The hot flames of anger grew inside her. Her passion to snatch the wand escalated and turned to rage.

"I *need* it." Van turned away from the lion, her eyes focused on the shinning gold.

"Do you?" In a blink, the lion sat between Van and the altar.

Van's mind spun with crafty ways to get around the lion and grab the wand. Possessing it meant fame, power, accolades...

That lion has no right! Van dashed forward, prepared to brawl with the lion, if that's what it took.

She leaped on the lion and wrapped her arm around its neck in a choke hold. She squeezed.

The lion easily shook her off, throwing Van to the ground.

Van jumped up and charged at the lion. Before making contact, she pivoted toward the altar in a calculated move.

The lion stopped her by appearing in her path again.

She hurled her body onto the beast. The lion tossed her off.

The same thing happened over and over until Van stepped back, breathing heavily and drained of energy. She rested her hands on her knees. "Just... let me... have it."

"One must transform within the vessel," said the lion. "Therein lies success."

A short, white pillar appeared next to Van. On it sat a plain, pearl-white urn that looked like it held cremated ashes. It gave her the creeps. Her annoyance grew. The very presence of it insulted her. Demeaned her.

Van pulled back her hand to whack it off the pillar—

She paused and lowered her arm as the sunlight caught the rounded edge just right. She gasped at the urn's enchanting beauty. So incredible with such depth and character, Van's eyes teared up. Its shape and color offered vitality and strength, also humility. Van would be content to stare at it for days. Years.

"It's... it's... *beautiful*," said Van, in admiration. Unable to resist its allure, she lifted it from the pillar.

A rush of energy flowed from the urn into Van's hands. It ran down her arms and through her body. Her heart beat faster. She raised her eyes to the sun, which glowed in the blue sky as if she were standing in the dunes, rather than in a lush forest.

Instead of being blinded by the sun's brightness, a smiling child appeared, about the age of five. Her pretty blue eyes gazed down at Van. The child's smooth, white-blond hair fell neatly against her flawless porcelain skin. The little girl wore a familiar outfit—red bowtie shoes and a white-ruffled, tailor-made dress. Van's favorite outfit as a child.

Van locked eyes with her child-Self. A deep connection to balance and peace reverberated within her, filling her with a newfound sense of empowerment and purpose. The wand no longer served her ownership of energy, neither did her attachment to the Staff.

Van turned away and placed the urn back onto the pillar. She glanced at the wand on the altar. It was nothing more than a simple stick, a dead branch from a fallen tree.

"I'm okay now," Van said to the lion, who sat next to the altar. "I don't need the wand. I want to go back to my friends. They need my help."

In a blink, Van faced Miniel. The fire animal swirled and shimmered. She stood in the same spot in Hestia's chamber as before her reality had been altered. But now, Miniel's flames were tumultuous and raging—a hot dragon. It continued to wind around the post, guarding the Staff.

Miniel's flickering flames reached for Van like the fingers of a fire demon. Now, Van could feel its heat.

Brux's muffled voice registered in the background of her mind, calling for her to retreat, for her to stay away from the creature or she'd die. Van held her focus on Miniel.

Miniel's flaming fingers scorched the skin on Van's arms, in the same spots that got burned in the second match, causing a surge of pain that triggered her anger. She wanted to lash out in rage. Fight back, matching the creature's fury, and take the Staff by force. Van brimmed with so much energy, she had the power to do it, if she so chose.

Instead, Van did the opposite. She became a cool dragon.

She understood Suixsha's advice about brute force never being a match for spiritual strength. With a clear head, Van stepped into Miniel's reaching flames. The fire engulfed her, yet she was unaffected by the heat.

Inside Miniel's fiery body, she paused. The Staff had moved, staying out of her reach. With every step, it remained the same distance from her.

Instead of lashing out and becoming violent, Van, a cool dragon, quietly and calmly retreated within her Self. She dropped to her knees and entered the child's pose before Miniel.

"What is it you seek?" asked Miniel, again.

"Nothing," said Van, with a sense of completed Self, filled with the light of the Creator and all that is good.

"What is your purpose?"

"To correct injustices. To protect the innocent and the voiceless."

"You seek to make yourself important?" asked Miniel.

Van remained in the child's pose. "I seek to use my power to create a future that benefits humanity, not myself."

"Is this your will?"

"Freedom of choice is the will of the Creator," said Van. "Because of this, I am empowered to create my future. I make my own choices. Those choices have consequences. Through this concept, I reclaim my power."

"Where comes the source of your power?"

"I release anger, which frees me from ego. This gives me a clear connection to the Creator and is the source of my power."

Van had an epiphany in her altered reality. People, including herself, make bad choices, as is the will of the Creator. The problems she's faced in life had nothing to do with the Anchoress curse, or the Creator singling her out, or Pernilla or Suixsha, or losing the Jaychund games. They were a product of her choices, her perspective of the situation, and how she reacted to it.

"Is retrieving the Staff your will?"

"It is. To protect my people."

Van released the child pose and rose to her full height. She stepped forward and reached deeper into the flames… to Miniel's heart… to the Staff…

In a snap, she was out of her trancelike state and back in Hestia's chamber.

Miniel no longer swirled in front of her, or anywhere. Van realized in her hand she grasped the Staff.

Her vision dimmed and grayed.

"Oh no."

All went black as Van lost consciousness and collapsed.

CHAPTER

FIFTY-THREE

A hag with a crooked nose and wild, fiery-orange hair sat before Van at a well-used wooden table. Cloying incense burned in a stone bowl.

"I'm sorry, my king," said the mountain witch. "I cannot help you."

Goustav's rage surged. He had taken Van to a time after he realized Amaryl's curse was real and had made him unable to produce an heir.

"But I can tell you this," said the witch. "You fathered a child before the curse. You have an heir."

Goustav's anger dissipated and turned to joy. "Where?"

"The location of the child is cloaked by magic. I see the mother... locks of golden hair—"

The witch's words became muted, pushed to the background of Goustav's thoughts. He didn't need to listen to the witch's description. He already knew. Amaryl's weight, her glow, the fear in her eyes...

His beloved had given birth to their child.

Goustav remembered the flash in Amaryl's eyes after he had run the Staff of Fire through her chest. He thought it was regret over the loss of their relationship and all they could have shared. Goustav now understood

344

that Amaryl's regret was in knowing that by cursing Goustav's bloodline, she had inadvertently doomed her own child.

"A girl," said the witch.

Of course, it was a girl, thought Goustav. The Anchoress heir's first-born was always a girl.

After losing Amaryl in such a terrible way, he never thought he could feel any worse pain. He was wrong. Sorrow over the loss of his would-have-been family gripped him with such intensity, it would reverberate through the ages.

His little girl lived without him somewhere. Not knowing her father longed to have her in his life. He wished to wrap her in his arms. To protect her, take care of her. The weight on his chest became so burdensome, for all his warrior might, he could not shake it.

Goustav struggled to expand his lungs to breathe. He tried to speak and instead sucked in a gasp that sounded like a sob. His weakened state confused him. Seasoned warriors do not express sorrow, only victory.

Yet, even as Goustav acknowledged his unyielding nature, he allowed himself to shed a single tear.

As it streaked down his cheek, a glimmer of kindness shone from deep inside his being. He would not kill the witch for her incompetence, or for witnessing him express grief.

His baby girl had entered his life moments before and she had already changed him for the better...

Goustav moved the vision forward.

Van had seen this place before, in a prior memory engram, the Temple of the Cross. The Elementals created the temple in Amaryl's honor, built on the spot where she died.

Goustav fretted about the name. He had to change it, and to let the weeds of the forest grow and hide it, or his followers would destroy the temple. He couldn't bear to let anything happen to it. It was all that remained of his beloved Amaryl.

Or so he thought until discovering they had a daughter.

Goustav wanted his daughter to find her way to him, and, in time, to take her rightful place as queen along with control of the Balish Kingdom.

He worked at a table inside the temple with the palace wizard Omazz. They had just finished creating a piece of jewelry. A brooch in the shape of an eight-spoked wheel with coordinated dashes through the prongs and forked ends that resembled the feather end of an arrow. Its shape, a symbol sacred to the ancients. One that represented a force of invincibility known as the Helm of Awe.

They encrusted each gold spoke with rubies, emeralds, and sapphires. Omazz then magically charged the brooch to find Goustav's daughter and guide her to him. At Goustav's instruction, Omazz added magical protective properties to keep his child safe on her journey home, and also to amplify her power. The piece resembled a snowflake, except for the human brown eye in its center.

Omazz waved his hand over the brooch. The eye closed. "The eye will not open unless the object is reunited with its rightful owner, your daughter, or her descendants, as it may be."

Goustav held the dazzling piece in his palm. He thought of it as a star shining in the darkness of night, certain it was as beautiful as his daughter.

He named this piece of jewelry the Runestar.

The night was clear as he walked outside the temple, newly renamed the Old Mound.

"May the winds carry this to the hand of my heir, guide her to me, and offer her protection on her journey home."

Goustav cast the Runestar into the sky to find its way to his child and guide her to Balefire, to him...

VAN WOKE from the memory engram.

She lay on the sandy floor in Hestia's chamber, still gripping the Staff. Her head ached as she sat up. She licked her chapped lips, trying to moisten them.

Hestia grandly stood before her. The Elemental's sparkling golden robe shimmered like flames. Her ice-blue eyes bored into Van.

"A change of consciousness occurs when we shift our point of view from that of victim to that of co-creator," said Hestia, all no-nonsense. "If we continue to see our circumstances as someone else's fault, then we are powerless to change them. Everything is your choice. You are the creator of your own life."

Van got to her feet, ready to take on the Elemental's next challenge.

"We must regard our lives as a product of our own choices," said Hestia. "Only then do we connect with the power of our personal will. This is done by acknowledging that your will is responsible for your actions and creates everything you have, even the things you do not want. Once realizing will is in force, we can learn to redirect it."

Van wondered if the Elemental was about to grade her test, and had trouble gauging if she had done well or not.

"By reclaiming your right to act, you enabled your will and thus embraced the Elemental Law of Choice. All beings have the right to choose. You have learned to release your anger and gained the clarity needed to use your power under the ideals of the Creator. I am pleased you have adequately conquered the third plague of human-ity, the Plague of Power."

"I'm done?" asked Van. Last year, Thalassa gave Van another test after she had finished the initial challenge.

"You may leave the sand chamber with the Staff of Fire. But you are not *done*. Your true test lies before you."

Van gripped the Staff tighter. Now that she had it, she would never let it go.

"Our future is created by our choices and is therefore constantly changing," warned Hestia. "Remember to maintain your clarity and use the Staff in accordance with the will of the Creator, or you will meet certain defeat."

In the past, the chamber collapsed, and the Elemental faded away after her parting words. Van waited for Hestia's dramatic exit. It didn't come.

Filled with purpose and strength, Van dashed toward the exit.

She glimpsed a white ball of fluff on a rock and came to a skidding halt.

"Wiglaf?" Van could hardly believe her eyes. Her bunfy sat next to an icy-looking stone formation that seemed out of place in this land of fire and sand.

"Wrrp pft peep." Wiglaf stuck his nose at the icy formation shaped like flames frozen in time.

It rose to just over Van's height. She squinted and leaned closer. It wasn't ice. Sand had converted into partially opaque glass and enclosed something... no, some*one* inside it.

Van rubbed away the grime in a spot so she could see clearly and gasped.

Inside the frozen fire stood Ferox.

FIFTY-FOUR

Ice crystals crusted Ferox's eyelashes and eyebrows. His lips, blue.

Van clawed at the structure, trying to scrape through the icy glass and set him free. Her effort proved futile and left her fingers frostbitten. She turned to Wiglaf. "How'd he get in there?"

She knew the answer to her own question. Ferox had tried to retrieve the Staff and failed.

Wiglaf peered at Van with his soulful blue eyes.

"I wish our reunion could've been under better circumstances." Van scratched Wiglaf behind the ears, happy he decided it was safe to return after her anger had frightened him away. "How are we going to get him out?"

She and Ferox hadn't mended their relationship. Brux believed Ferox wasn't trustworthy. Once defrosted, Van wasn't sure if Ferox would forcibly take the Staff from her. Or kill her for it.

"*Should* we get him out?" Van thought about leaving him frozen in the fire to reap the consequences of his own choices.

Wiglaf locked eyes with Van and waited for her decision.

It was Van's turn to make a choice. What would be in accordance with the will of the Creator?

"Freeing him benefits Lodian-Balish tribal relations..." More so, Van couldn't deny her heart still belonged to him. "But how?"

Fire, sand... icy glass... safe rescue...

Magic. Blood magic. Hers.

She pointed the Staff at the frozen fire. Flames shot from its tip and flickered over the structure, melting the glass like ice without harming Ferox.

Within minutes, the flames cleared away the container. Ferox stood motionless, in the same position, dripping wet. Then, he crumbled to the ground unconscious, barely breathing, and looking cyanotic.

"Ferox!" Tears streaked down Van's cheeks. She learned CPR in school and took action. She placed her hands over his sternum and began compressing his chest.

Wiglaf chirruped and hopped down from the rock onto a partially singed backpack lying on the ground.

Van paused doing compressions. She recognized the mustard-colored pack, *hers*! The one she dropped while riding the baby dragon.

Wiglaf pawed at the zipper. "Mrrp weep."

"How did you find this?" Van brushed off sand. "Is something in here that can help?" She unzipped it at Wiglaf's insistence and searched through her things.

She hadn't needed most of the items she packed, not with the wardrobe and toiletries provided by the palace, so she hadn't dug around inside since arriving at Balefire, only pulled clothes from the top. Van's fingers bumped against something hard, metal. She pulled it out.

Her jaw dropped. It was the Cup of Life.

"It was in here the whole time?" Right next to the yellow dress she wore at the Placement Ceremony. "Uxa snuck it in before I left?"

Wiglaf bobbed his head in confirmation.

"Why?"

Did Uxa think Van was incapable of completing the mission without it? The people back home needed the Cup to make the vaccine and cure. Was Uxa trying to make it look like Van stole it?

Whatever the reason, Van was thankful Uxa had tucked it into her pack. Thinking she didn't need it for the mission was an ego trip on Van's part. Having the Cup in the Death Games meant Van could use it to win. Maybe her teammates could fake their deaths. Or come close to death so she could get them out, then use the Cup to revive them.

Ferox might have a better idea about getting them out of the match. If he didn't murder her and take the Staff first.

Van shook her head to clear the negative thought. She cradled the Cup in her hands and created a healing potion. Then used her fingers to open Ferox's mouth and poured the liquid down his throat.

Next, she took a sip. The power of the potion surged through her veins, healing her burns and her head wound.

Within minutes, Ferox's color returned, and he breathed normally.

"Come here often?" Van gave him a hesitant grin.

He sat up and rubbed the back of his head. His eyes went to Van. He reached for her...

She flinched, expecting an attack.

He gripped her in a big, wet hug, trembling. "I'm so glad you're all right."

Van let out a sigh of relief. "How d'you feel?"

"Forget about me," he said. "We need to figure out how to get you and your team out of the match." He glanced around the chamber. "Are-are they still alive?"

Van nodded. "Barely." Her eyes locked with his. "Why did you come?"

"When I heard the match was a fight to the death with one winner, I asked the Coin to show me the best path to help you." Ferox ran a gentle finger over her cheek. "It brought me here."

Van noticed he wasn't wearing an ATG. "But how did you—"

"The Coin led me to an agreeable gaming official, who I paid well… and threatened to send to the dungeon if he didn't use one of his dot matices to get me into the playing area before the officials magically locked entry. I recognized where I was and figured it led me here to retrieve the Staff. That's when I knew the match would put you outside the Alignment. The Staff would help me protect you from the Quasher."

"I'm just glad you're not here to kill me and take the Staff."

"What? No!"

Van beamed. Elated Ferox left his cozy viewing area, his *family*, to help her, even when it meant getting thrown into the final match of the Death Games. This proved to Van he chose her over his family.

She smirked. "You didn't pass the Elemental's test."

"No, I didn't." Ferox hung his head. "While frozen in the fire, I had time to think about what I did wrong. I wanted to make right the injustice to you for being forced to play in the match. My failing was that I didn't do it solely for your benefit. Part of me wanted to make myself more important and to prove my power."

"Only the Anchoress heir can retrieve the Staff."

"I'm not looking for a fight." Ferox rose and offered his hand to Van.

She was in no mood to argue. Finishing the match still loomed before them. She clasped his hand.

"Let's use the Coin and find a way out of this match." He glanced at the Cup and raised his damp brow. "The Coin, the Staff, the Cup. Seems we'll be invincible."

Ferox's clothes were rapidly drying from the heat. He reached into his pant's pocket and pulled out a piece of folded black plastic. "Trip's on me. The gaming official insisted on tucking a dot matice into my pocket before letting me enter the playing area. He made me promise to use it if I needed to get out. So where do we go?" He held the Coin in the palm of his other hand.

Van placed her hand over his, covering the Coin. "What happens in the match if I use my dot matice to travel to Manipura?"

"The match would follow you. Magic extends the playing area to wherever the players are. Since no other players can travel, the magic of the game would eventually transport you back to the main playing area. There's no getting out of the match, other than by finishing it."

"Then, I have time to mend the seal. The Staff will protect me from the heat. You take the Coin and use it to find my teammates. Use the Cup to heal Ixl and Daisy before they die. We'll figure out how to win the match afterward."

"You're letting me take the Coin and the Cup?"

"We have to work together for the good of our people... and... I trust you."

Van gave him the incantation she used to make a healing potion and charged the Cup with her moon energy. Being royal, Ferox could tap into its power without becoming corrupted.

"After they're healed, try using the Coin and your dot matice to get them safely out of the match," said Van. "I'll use the remaining trip on mine to get back to Lodestar, to hell with the games."

"Leaving won't work," said Ferox, grimly. "For any of you. The rules of the match magically bind all contestants to finish. Like I said, wherever the players go, the game follows until only one is left standing."

"Then use your dot matice to get yourself out, you're not a contestant."

Ferox didn't respond.

"Promise me."

He met Van's eyes. "I should go with you and help you mend the seal."

Her heart tugged. She wanted him to go with her, for them to never be apart again. But... that would benefit her, not her friends. "My teammates need you to be their hero."

Van would mend the seal alone and get no glory, only the satisfaction of a task completed.

"Time is running out before the Quasher is released," she said. "Please go."

Ferox begrudgingly agreed and dashed away with the Coin and the Cup.

As Van tossed her dot matice onto the chamber's wall, she realized Ferox never agreed to leave the match.

The dot matice stuck and formed a U-shaped, human-sized opening in the sandstone.

Van grabbed the Staff and rushed in.

Wiglaf followed.

CHAPTER

FIFTY-FIVE

Heat from the lava river blasted Van as she stepped through the dot matice into a familiar cavern made from igneous rock formations inside the volcano Manipura.

Ferox told her the game would follow her, but she saw no gem-cams. Van assumed it was too hot for them.

Time was running out before the magic of the game bounced her back to the main playing area, and the Alignment ended, releasing the Quasher. Gripping the Staff, she stepped toward the River of the Damned. It flowed between her and the seal.

Dammit. She had entered on the wrong side. "Where are dragons when we need them?"

Wiglaf peered at her with his little whiskered face; his ears drooped and his fur looked matted from the heat.

Although the Staff kept her from overheating, she used the back of her hand to wipe her beaded forehead. "Step back." Van shooed Wiglaf away from the river's edge and raised the Staff. She rammed the pointed end into the volcanic rock. Again and again. Until a sizable chunk disengaged and sloshed into the lava.

"Come on." Van leaped onto it. Wiglaf joined her.

355

It swayed when she landed. Van wobbled as she caught her balance.

Wiglaf, with his four paws, easily adjusted to the rocking makeshift raft.

The lava's flow slowly carried them downriver, away from the seal.

Van energized the Staff through her hands. A stream of fire shot from its tip. She stuck it into the lava to act as a motorized rudder. The floating rock changed direction and chugged upstream.

They approached the area with the seal. Swirls of heat collected at various points on the river's surface. The whirls rose from the lava, spinning so fast they turned to fire and formed into demons.

"They're drawing energy from the cracked seal," Van said to Wiglaf. "The closer we get, the more demons will rise to stop us."

All around them, fire demons surged from the lava, flickering like beastly infernos. They stretched their fiery arms and grasped at the raft.

"They're stuck in the spot where they formed."

Wiglaf hung tight, gripping his paws into the surface of the floating rock.

Van skillfully navigated around the fire demons, thankful she had learned how to boat growing up on the island.

One demon stretched and stretched, elongating far enough to clutch onto the raft. With a snap, it detached itself from the lava and clawed at the rock as it crawled aboard.

Wiglaf hissed.

Van plucked the Staff out of the river and blasted the demon with fire from the Staff's tip. The fire entwined with the demon, consuming it.

"It didn't gain strength from the fire, thank the light."

Wiglaf gave a relieved chirrup.

Another demon clutched onto the raft, rocking it.

Wiglaf raised his hackles.

Van blasted the demon with fire, killing it before it climbed aboard. She stuck the tip of the Staff back into the river.

More and more demons rose, close enough to grip their floating rock. So many Van had to keep lifting the Staff out of the river to fight them. Unable to propel the raft against the current, it drifted so far downriver the fire demons calmed and became harmless swirls of heat again.

"One more time." Van held the tip of the Staff in the lava and propelled upriver toward the seal.

As they got deeper inside the cavern, the swirls picked up again.

Wiglaf stared at the river's edge and hissed.

Van twisted to see what alarmed him.

Hutriel stood on the river bank. He had followed Van through the dot matice, using its last transport.

"Wiglaf, go back to your animal realm."

Wiglaf shook his head and stayed hunched by Van's feet.

"Welcome to the final match of the Death Games," boomed Hutriel. "I'm the only player left." He smacked his chest. "Just me and you."

"Wrong. My teammates are alive." Van didn't mention Ferox. If Hutriel didn't know the prince had entered the match, she wasn't about to tell him.

"Are they?" asked Hutriel.

Van fumed. Then, refused to let him rile her. "Liar."

Hutriel kept pace with Van on the river's bed as she slowly floated the raft upstream. "There are no gem-cams here. My connection in the palace made sure of it."

"Solana." Van gripped the Staff tighter. For once, she wished there *were* gem-cams so everyone, including Ferox, would know Solana remained rotten. Van's ego urged her to shout out loud, "I knew it!" But she didn't.

Solana and Hutriel didn't deserve the energy she spent hating them. Negative emotions blocked her connection to Creator. Van redirected her thoughts and focused on the task at hand.

Hutriel sauntered along the river bank, sweating profusely, but able to withstand the heat, no doubt protected by a sun spell placed on him by Solana before he entered the match.

"I've come for the Staff. Be a good girl and give it to me." Hutriel outstretched his gloved hand. "No?" He snapped it back. "Well, after I take it from you, I'll go back and take the Cup and Coin from that pathetic prince you call your boyfriend, right after I kill him."

"You can't kill Ferox," cried Van. "He's the crown prince."

"I didn't kill him," said Hutriel, with a faux, wide-eyed, innocent expression. "The evil Lodian witch lured him into the playing area and then killed him in Manipura, where there happen to be no gem-cams." His manner turned serious again. "Giving cause for the Balish to conquer Salus Valde. I will oversee the invasion... while sitting on the Balish throne."

"You mean, you and Solana."

"She was right. You're not bright, are you? The princess is helping me, yes, but once I take possession of the Items and gain their power for myself, *I'll* use it to rule the Living World."

"Double-cross Solana? Who's being stupid now?"

"By right of being the winner of the Death Games, I'll get to keep the Items. I'll be part of the new Balish royal family. In the name of the Tarcs, Godreel will bow to *me*." Hutriel thumped his fist on his chest.

Van knew Hutriel's plan to seize the throne wouldn't work. Solana's dark magic would see to that. His ego hindered his ability to think clearly. Van sneered. Hutriel represented the epitome of the Plague of Power, the third blight of humanity.

"He can't reach us," Van said to Wiglaf. She directed the raft to the opposite side of the river from Hutriel. They were still far enough from the seal for the heat swirls not to form into demons. "Be ready to jump onto the riverbank. We'll walk to the seal."

A clunk came from behind. The raft dipped.

Van twisted around. Hutriel had tossed a line with a grappling hook onto the floating rock, taken from the deceased team's supplies. He yanked the line and began reeling in their raft.

Van pulled the Staff out of the lava. The raft drifted downstream as far as the line allowed.

Hand over hand, Hutriel towed them in.

Van aimed the Staff's tip at Hutriel.

He jerked the line.

Van teetered as she fired. The blast missed its mark and landed in the river.

Lava bubbled in the spot where it hit. A blob rose. It grew larger and taller until it morphed into a giant with burning black eyes, long arms, clawed fingers, and a body made of lava and flames. The fire demons had used power from the Staff's blast to join collectively and form a huge lava monster.

It roared and bashed its fists into the river, causing a wave of lava to rise in the raft's direction.

Van and Wiglaf struggled to maintain their footing while the raft rocked and tipped, dislodging Hutriel's grappling hook.

The monster waded through the lava toward them, impeded, as if walking through thick mud.

Van clutched the Staff and screamed at Wiglaf, "Go! Now!"

Wiglaf disappeared.

Van entered the warrior pose and held the Staff with both hands above her head. Her legs wobbled and knees bent to meet the challenge of the swaying raft. Her yoga practice paid off, and she remained balanced.

The monster clasped and unclasped its fiery clawed hands at Van, reaching for her, chasing the raft as it drifted downstream.

She twirled the Staff and then shot a blast of fire straight at the lava monster's chest.

It cried out in pain, then roared in anger. It pounded its fists into the river, splashing a tidal wave of lava toward Van.

Van braced for impact, expecting to be burned alive. The Staff generated a protective, transparent sphere, encircling Van. *Of course!* One of the Staff's properties was protection from fire.

On shore, Hutriel stomped his feet in frustration. His eyes fixated on the Staff. He huffed and hurried along the cave's cliff walk, unconcerned about the massive lava demon pursuing Van. He kept pace with the raft as it continued to drift downstream and out of Manipura.

Van blasted the creature again with fire from the Staff, this time a direct shot to the head.

It let out a blaring shriek and sunk beneath the surface, giving Van a moment to use the Staff as a rudder.

She directed the raft to the riverbank at the edge of the Dead Forest and hopped ashore, leaving the raft to continue drifting downstream.

Hutriel came charging down the riverbed toward her.

The lava monster rose from beneath the surface of the lava river. Its fire-claws gripped into the sand in the riverbed as it hauled itself onto shore.

Van used the Staff to shoot the monster again.

It kept coming.

The Staff pulsed in her gripped hands. She looked inside herself and connected to her Anchoress magic, linking herself to the Item.

She fired again. This time, the fire continuously streamed from the Staff's tip, enveloping the lava monster. Holding it back while it battled to break free.

Van struggled to maintain the strength to contain the creature.

Hutriel laughed.

She bristled. Was he attempting to weaken her power by laughing at her? Van refused to let him affect her. She could do this. She just needed to maintain her concentration and stay connected to—

Chimes from the odd grandfather clock in Uxa's home office rang in her mind.

With a racing heartbeat, Van realized Hutriel had a backup plan —to distract her long enough for the Alignment to end.

A guttural growl resonated through the Dead Forest.

Van held steadfast, blasting the lava monster, as she risked glancing at the woods behind her.

A fanged snout poked from between the dead trees. Its vile red eyes pierced Van's.

From the shadows emerged a snarling wolf-like creature. Darker than dark. Blacker than black. A beast that had crawled to the surface from the pits of hell.

The Quasher homed in on Van. Its claws ripped into the sand for traction as it hurtled straight toward her.

FIFTY-SIX

"You play with fire, you get burned." Hutriel snickered.

Van's body quivered, loosening her grip on the Staff. Her mind blanked as she locked into the Quasher's red stare.

The beast leaped at her.

Tyger came bounding from the forest, fur aflame. He tackled the shadow-creature midair.

Wiglaf sat huddled by the roots of a nearby tree, watching. Van's heart warmed at her brave little bunfy. He didn't to go back to his animal realm. He went to find Tyger. By doing so, he saved her life.

With Van's attention diverted, the lava monster seized the opportunity and broke free. It lumbered at her, arms stretched, fingers reaching...

Van re-directed the shooting flame of the Staff and smacked the lava monster in the chest.

It kept coming, though slower, as it fought against the thundering blast with each step.

Peripherally, Van saw the tussle between Tyger and the shadow-beast intensify. They wrestled, inching toward her. The closer the

Quasher came to Van, the more enraged and determined it became. It swiped its claw across Tyger's hindquarters.

Tyger squealed in pain and slumped to the ground.

The Quasher rushed at Van from the side. The lava monster came at her from the front. Hutriel chortled nearby.

Van shut off the fire shooting from the Staff and closed her eyes.

She touched the tip of the Staff to her temple. Van looked deep inside herself and tapped into the strength of her ancestors and the Creator. She shifted her energy to join with theirs, rather than solely relying on her own strength, and incorporated it into the power of the Staff.

She opened her jaw. A jet of continuous fire shot from her mouth like dragon's breath. Van glided her head back and forth. First hitting the Quasher as it leaped at her and then at the lava monster whose clutch was but a foot from her body.

The Quasher yipped and dropped to the ground, on fire. It rolled and screeched, trying to put itself out.

The fire from her flame-thrower breath mingled and became one with the lava monster. Van used her will to hold the creature in place.

The lava monster absorbed Van's flames, its body grew bigger and bigger. It tried to grab Van, but the weight of the additional flames made it sluggish.

The black trees of the Dead Forest ignited.

Hutriel gaped at the events unfolding in front of him.

Wiglaf disappeared.

Tyger lay on the ground bleeding, struggling to rise.

Van closed her mouth, ending the shooting flames, stunned at what she had just done.

The lava monster continued to grow and grow... to such a size it burst, causing an inferno that ripped through the area like an atomic blast.

Van winced and covered her head with her arms. The Staff generated a transparent shield, automatically encasing her, protecting her from the firestorm.

Van, unaffected by the heat, and glad her little bunfy had gone back to his magical realm, watched the blaze rage through the forest.

As fast as the blast came, it left. Leaving nothing but a smoldering, charred landscape. It made the Dead Forest look even creepier and more desolate than before. Mounds of charred debris lay among the surviving black trees, scorched and smoking. The blue sky looked bigger and brighter than before.

The Quasher, lava monster, and Hutriel were gone. With no immediate threat, Van's protective shield vanished. The forest appeared quiet except for the crackling of burnt embers.

Tyger lay unharmed by the blast. Protected by his species being one with fire, yet still bleeding from the Quasher's attack.

Wiglaf popped back. He looked up at Van with his little whiskered face, sitting on the unburnt ground by her feet.

A strained sound echoed from the scorched earth.

Van's feet vibrated. The forest floor shuddered from the intensity of the inferno's heat. She drew in a sharp breath as cracks crawled around them, then separated into fissures. The blackened ground crumbled, chunks of it slid down forming chasms.

"Brace yourself!" Van cried to Wiglaf and Tyger.

The ground beneath Tyger broke, and he plummeted.

The earth shuddered under Van and Wiglaf's feet. It gave way, and they dropped.

Van landed hard. Her breath knocked out on impact and her fingers splayed, causing the Staff to skitter away.

Her body hurt in too many places to count. She groaned. Her eyes scanned the wreckage for Wiglaf and Tyger.

Wiglaf sat upright and appeared unharmed, though covered with black soot and dirt. Tyger lifted his head and snorted. Okay, but in need of medical help.

Van hauled her aching body up and scanned her surroundings.

She had fallen into a chamber at the volcano's base. There were others…

She gaped, sickened by what she saw.

Slaves.

In man-made alcoves in the rock, one after the other along the wall, locked in by bars.

Their sallow faces spoke volumes about their abuse. Their eyes, dead and hopeless. They wore tattered, coarse linen garments on filthy bodies beaded with sweat and barely more than bones. Most were men, some women, lots were children. Well-used pickaxes, shovels, carts and other mining equipment lay stored away until the next shift.

Although the dungeons were crafted by design, jagged volcanic rock dominated the space. Lava popped and bubbled in pockets formed by the rocks, making the chamber unbearably hot.

These were the people who harvested the renowned lustrous gems that Van had seen worn by the citizens of the town and sold throughout the Balish kingdom. The Enchantress referring to their work as a "precarious job" was incredibly inaccurate. These people worked in a hell pit.

Gem-cams peeked out from crevices in the walls. It made sense. This is where the leaders of Muspell kept their slaves who mined the gemstones. Cameras prevented escapes and theft. Solana couldn't have foreseen Van falling into the hell pit, and it was too late for the Balish princess to get rid of the gem-cams, not without exposing her nefarious intentions.

Tyger, his front half sitting upright, howled with displeasure at the injustice set before him.

"Eerrp." Wiglaf wrapped his long ears around his body as he hunched into a trembling ball.

A blackened lump shifted near them, the size and shape of a large human.

Van's eyes searched the chamber's floor for the Staff. She rushed over and scooped it from the ground.

Tyger let out a low growl; Wiglaf raised his hackles and hissed.

The scorched lump stood upright.

Hutriel.

His clothes and skin appeared badly charred. He survived the fire in the forest and the fall, probably from the protective spell put on him by Solana. Talk about cheating.

Van had tried to cheat in the Jaychund games. She had lost. Hutriel and Solana would lose now.

"Here we are, face-to-face in the fiery depths of the volcano mines." Hutriel sneered. "Let's finish this."

No surprise Hutriel seemed fine with the caged slaves. Van twirled the Staff. Its tip ignited.

Tiny red lights shone from each of the gem-cams. The gaming officials had locked into the hell pit's cameras. All of Balefire was watching.

"Toss the Staff aside," said Hutriel. "Play the match fair."

Van didn't have an issue using the Staff against Hutriel. She had to win, or his next move would be to kill her teammates. He wasn't human. There were no warnings about using the Items against Tarcs.

She sent a fiery blast at him from the tip of the Staff.

He zigged with shocking agility, given his size. The fire nicked his elbow; he didn't flinch.

Right. If Hutriel could survive the firestorm, Solana's sun magic would also protect him against a graze of fire shot from the Staff.

"You're using magic. It's not allowed in the match. It's cheating." Hutriel stared at Van. "If you use the Staff to kill me, it won't count. Your teammates will still die and you won't be the winner. There will be no winner."

They circled each other. Hutriel, alert, and ready to pounce. Van moved cautiously, tensely gripping the Staff.

Hutriel feared the Staff. That meant Solana's magic didn't fully protect him against its power.

Tyger used his front paws to drag himself closer. His body flickered with minor flames, his injury draining him of the energy needed to convert his fur into a full-on fiery coat. He let out a diminished roar at Hutriel.

"Give up. Are you really going to go back and kill your team-mates? Your friends? Allow me to do it." Hutriel lunged at Van.

She ducked, zagged, and whacked him on the back with the Staff.

He stumbled forward, re-gained his balance, and faced her once again.

"The protection spell Solana put on you is cheating," said Van, with the ATGs and gem-cams in mind. Now, Ferox and his family would know their cherished princess still connected to her dark side.

"The princess's monetary support is not a spell," snarled Hutriel, not as stupid as he looked, well-aware of Van's motive to expose Solana.

The slaves cried out from their cells.

Lava streaming in from the river above cascaded down the mountain-like wall created when the ground collapsed and began seeping into their cages. They didn't have long before the lava would enter their cells and burn them alive.

A black entity plummeted into the cavern.

It rose on all fours, shook its body, and growled. The Quasher's red eyes locked on Van and dashed for her.

Wiglaf disappeared.

Tyger, his fur still not fully aflame, regained his energy using sheer will and leaped on the Quasher, again preventing it from digging its deadly fangs into Van.

The screaming slaves caught her attention. Some were on fire, shrieking as they burned to death from the lava creeping into their cells.

"Stop hiding behind your magic, witch," said Hutriel. "Toss the Staff aside. Fight like a man. Unless you're afraid."

Van kept one eye on Hutriel, the other on Tyger. She wanted to bind the Quasher with the fiery lasso from the Staff, the same way Goustav had done a thousand years ago. But Hutriel would seize the opportunity and bash in her head, and with Tyger and the shadow-beast grappling, she couldn't risk accidentally binding them together.

"Help us," cried the slaves, reaching through the bars. Children wailed.

More cells flooded with lava and their occupants burst into flames.

"Save our children," pleaded a woman. "Please."

Streams of lava inched past the bars of the remaining cells. Moments remained before magma consumed the rest of the slaves.

Tyger kept the Quasher at bay. Blood oozed from his injury. He wouldn't be able to hold back the beast for much longer.

Van faced a choice. Kill Hutriel or free the slaves.

If she saved the slaves, who were mostly children, she would part with the Staff by essentially throwing it across the chamber. Losing the match, her guaranteed protection from the Quasher, and her ability to beat Hutriel.

If Van used the Staff against Hutriel, she would win. Solana would lose. Van would get glory, status, accolades. Then, she would call for Tyger to move and use the Staff to bind the Quasher. But the slaves would die.

Van's knuckles turned white as she gripped the Staff and raised it over her head.

She had made her choice.

FIFTY-SEVEN

Van grasped the Staff, throwing arm jacked.

"It's all about power." Hutriel sounded smug in the face of his imminent death. Like he saw Van's soul and knew she would make the same self-serving choice as he would.

"It's not about power." Van pivoted. "It's about people." She hurled the Staff at the slave's cages.

It zoomed along the outside of the cells, busting the locks. The doors sprung open, freeing the slaves seconds before the lava trapped them in and burned them to death.

Van half-hoped one of the Staff's magical properties was a boomerang effect and it would return to her. It didn't. She faced Hutriel, relying on her own power and training. No magical weapons or tricks. No cheating.

Van met Hutriel's stare and her confidence faltered. She wasn't sure she could beat him bare handed.

He gloated, believing she had made a fatal mistake that ensured his win. One where he would claim victory in the Death Games and gain three Items of Creation. He would be a hero to his people, bringing much desired respect and status to the Tarcs.

Hutriel charged at Van.

The commotion with the slaves distracted Tyger for a split second. The Quasher took advantage and its fangs ripped through the cat's shoulder. He yelped and slumped to the ground, writhing in pain.

The Quasher stampeded at Van, following the same narrow passageway through the lava strewn chamber as Hutriel.

The dark beast, much faster than the Tarc, plowed over Hutriel in its relentless pursuit of Van. Its massive paw crushed his head as it stomped over him.

Its claws tore up the dirt floor as it came for Van. Its lips pulled back in a growl, exposing long fangs. Like Amaryl, Van surrendered to her fate and bravely faced the beast. Her last thought as the Quasher leaped was that Hutriel had been right. There would be no winner of the Death Games.

A rope of fire encircled the Quasher, ensnaring it, and binding it to the ground.

For a second, Van thought Goustav had returned from the grave. Back to save her like he had saved Amaryl during his rebellion.

But it was Ferox who gripped the Staff. Wiglaf hunched by his feet.

The Quasher struggled against its restraint, snarling and snapping.

"Ferox," said Van, as if the word were part of her breath.

The Staff tumbled to the ground as Ferox dashed to Van. He wrapped his arms around her, not caring about being seen as weak to his family and the palace officials who were viewing the match live via gem-cam.

He pulled back, clutching her shoulders, and gazed into her eyes. "Are you okay?"

Van nodded. She looked down at Wiglaf. "Thanks for getting Ferox."

"Meep wrrp." Wiglaf lifted his nose and wiggled his whiskers.

"I revived Daisy," said Ferox. "Told her to stay and heal Ixl and Suixsha while I—"

"What happened to Suixsha?" asked Van, alarmed.

"Hutriel found them and she got injured in the fight. I left them the Cup. They would've come back with me, but there was no time. I was sure Hutriel left them to go after you."

Van and Ferox both glanced at the Staff, lying on the ground several feet away. Ferox hurried over and snatched it up.

Van braced, unsure what he would do next. Claim it was his? Shoot a fiery net over her and take her prisoner?

"Here." He handed Van the Staff. "It's yours."

Van's heart swelled with love for him. She clutched the Staff. Its power pulsed through her, but she controlled it, it didn't control her.

Her eyes shifted as she saw movement in the air behind Ferox.

Something was taking form.

Hestia appeared.

Miniel swirled up and down her body. Every time the creature came around to her front, its eyes held steadfast on the Staff, as if eager to reclaim it.

Van now realized that Hestia had incorporated her final Elemental challenge into the match, a real-world scenario using the Staff's power. Van's confrontation with Hutriel and the slaves was her last test.

Nothing compared to the actual power surge from holding the real thing, and Van's perspective had changed from the experience. She empathized with Goustav, a man who had become addicted to the Staff's power. Leading him to overuse it to the point of insanity.

Hestia grinned and dipped her head to Van.

Van returned her nod.

Sparkles from Hestia's dress overtook the Elemental and her pet, more and more, until the twinkles turned their bodies into a shimmering fire. In a burst, they disappeared.

Ferox frowned and twisted around to see who Van had nodded at, but Hestia and Miniel were already gone.

The newly freed slaves cheered and hollered their thanks as they dashed out of the hell pit in a race to embrace freedom. They climbed up the debris from the collapse, rushed down tunnels, ran any which way they could to get out.

"They're free, but are they?" asked Van. "What will the leaders of Muspell do?"

With his head down, Ferox said, "It's their culture to enslave them."

Tyger whined.

"Tyger!" cried Van. "We're coming!"

Ferox kneeled by the wounded animal. "He's in terrible shape."

Van placed a hand on Ferox's shoulder. "Go, get the Cup. Come back and heal Tyger. *Hurry*. I'm going back to the seal."

"Take this." Ferox slipped Van the Coin. "In case you need it. I can find my way back to the others without it."

Van clutched the Coin. Grateful Ferox didn't argue or try to push his own opinion on her.

"Listen, I know going back and forth will use the last two trips on your dot matice. You don't have to go. It's your choice."

"I got this. Good luck." He dashed away.

Van held the Coin in her opened palm asked it to show her the best way to the seal. It pointed at the top of a debris mound to a fissure made by the collapse. Van grasped the Staff and sprinted toward it. Her bunfy bounded along with her.

"Wiglaf. Go back. Stay with Tyger." Van began her climb up the rocky pile.

"Pmmf." Wiglaf followed her.

At the top, Van squeezed into the rocky passageway. She and Wiglaf edged their way through the fissure and exited into the cavern directly across from the third seal. On the opposite side of the lava river. Again.

Van tucked the Coin in her pocket and used the pointed end of the Staff to break off a piece of volcanic rock at the ledge. She extended her arm toward the floating rock and said to Wiglaf, "Déjà vu."

Wiglaf leaped onto the makeshift raft. Van did the same.

She stuck the pointed end of the Staff into the lava, charged it into a motorized rudder, and used it to navigate across the current toward the other side.

Heat swirls formed. Fire demons rose from the lava.

Every time one climbed onto the raft, Van pulled the Staff from the lava, pointed the tip at the demon, and created a blow torch blast that consumed it. She eliminated one, only to have another try to climb aboard.

The raft crept downstream every time she took the Staff out of the river to obliterate a demon. She increased the speed of the process, hoping it would make a difference. Blow away a demon, slip the Staff back in the lava to motor the raft. Still, she struggled to hold their place, never mind cross the current.

"We have the same problem as before." Van watched the seal slip farther away as they drifted downstream, confused, since the Coin had pointed across the river as her best path to the seal. She couldn't risk stopping to tap into the Staff's other powers, or the Coin's. The fire demons only needed a split second to nab her or Wiglaf. "We can't get across with all these demons."

Wiglaf hissed, staring at something up the riverbank.

Van saw the black demon, who had repeatedly appeared to her, squeeze out of the crack in the seal. It dived into the lava and swam downriver toward them, unbothered by the fire demons.

Van blasted another fire creature as the black demon raised his hand from the lava and gripped the raft. She twisted and aimed the Staff at the black demon, ready to fire, but Wiglaf was no longer hissing... he was *purring*.

The black demon didn't climb aboard their floating rock. Instead, it towed them toward the edge of the river by the seal. The black demon was *helping* them!

Van continued to blow away the fire demons until the raft reached the edge. Then she and Wiglaf hopped onto the riverbed, out of the reach of the fire demons who remained confined to the River of the Damned.

The black demon crawled onto land and stood before them. It spoke with muffled words, hindered by the black goo covering its humanoid body. Male... in a shape Van recognized...

"Elmot?" she asked, stunned to see her former, and *deceased*, teammate. Elmot had died in the Caves of Wolfenden by falling into the black mud. He sunk to the bottom, never to be seen again, until now.

He nodded, apparently relieved Van finally comprehended his presence.

"It was you. You've been attempting to communicate with me in your morphed form this whole time," she said. "You gave me the dot matice in the first match to help me. I thought you were trying to kill me."

In Elmot's garbled communication, he said he tried to scare her away from getting the Staff for the good of the people.

"Because it contains the power to release demons into this world?" asked Van.

Elmot nodded. His attempt at speaking came strained and seemed painful. It made Van appreciate his help even more.

She gathered from Elmot's distorted communication that because she had retrieved the Staff, he no longer needed to block her. He wanted to help Van mend the seal.

"No one else saw you in the first match. Why?"

Van picked up the words "different frequencies" and "multi-tracks."

"It's because, as the Anchoress, I change my vibration." Van bobbed her head in understanding. "I'm able to see demons who exist at different frequencies, like the way Grigori do using multi-tracks."

Elmot nodded. He uttered more words.

Van repeated, to see if she got it right. "You're appearing to me for the last time because after I mend the seal, you won't be able to come back?"

He nodded.

Van's heart broke for him, and for her, to never see him again.

"Where have you been? Why can't you stay?"

Elmot said, as Van interpreted it, "I've been in... bad place, a horrible other world. Must warn you about impending doom. Creatures there... much worse than Balish or Tarcs... they're building a dark army."

"What place?"

"Anti-World," said Elmot.

"A third world? And creatures who live there are building an army of demons?"

Elmot nodded. He mumbled something unintelligible that sounded like, "Goob-der-on."

"Is that a name? Solana's dark master?"

Elmot nodded again, then indicated the time had come for him to go back through the crack. He would help Van mend it from the other side by distracting any demons that attempted to stop her.

"But... I'll never see you again?" Van's eyes brimmed with tears.

Elmot hung his head low.

"Ep." Wiglaf stared up at Elmot, wide-eyed, ears drooping.

"There must be something I can do? The Staff—"

He cut her off by shaking his head and communicated a sense of urgency.

"I-I miss you..."

He blew Van and Wiglaf a kiss and slid back through the crack into the dark world behind the seal.

Van paused for a moment. Then the darkness in the crack alarmed her. She looked down at her bunfy. "We have work to do."

She gripped the Staff with a renewed sense of importance, pointed its tip at the crack, and blasted it with fire.

Even with Elmot's help on the demon side, Van had trouble mending the seal. She stopped and pulled the Coin out of her pocket.

She held it in her palm and clutched the Staff. Using the power of both, she shot a supercharged ray of firepower at the crack.

It began to close.

Red reptilian eyes appeared in the blackness behind the seal and glared at Van.

Absolute terror struck her. She gasped and almost lost her hold on the Staff.

Elmot moved between the eyes and Van.

She strengthened her grip on the Staff and shot fire and light at the seal with all her might, praying the red-eyed creature wouldn't slither out of the crack.

Van exerted a tremendous amount of energy. The crack slowly disappeared as the seal mended.

She released the Staff and the Coin. They tumbled to the ground. Van bent over, hands on her thighs, and took gasping breaths. She couldn't stop shuddering.

Her and Wiglaf's eyes met, widened in fear, as they comprehended who they had just seen.

Solana's dark master.

FIFTY-EIGHT

Van and Wiglaf made their way back to Ferox and Tyger, who waited for their return in the hell pit.

Ferox wrapped her in a big hug.

Tyger let out a short barking roar and flicked his head, full of vitality.

Wiglaf hopped over and raised his face to Tyger. The big cat bent down, and they touched noses.

"He's fully healed." Ferox reached up and pet Tyger's side. "The seal?"

"Mended. I'll tell you about it after we get out of here."

Van asked the Coin for the best path to leave the chamber. It advised them to climb out, straight up the fallen debris from the collapse like many of the slaves had done. The lava from the river continued to ooze down its side, slowly filling the cavern.

Ferox tipped his head toward the Quasher. "What happens with that? Will the lava consume it?"

The beast struggled against its bindings, snarling, clawing. Its eyes never strayed from Van.

"It can't exist on this plane without my Anchoress light

balancing it. Once I go back to Providence Island, its connection to me will fade. It'll sink back into the earth and wait for me to return."

As they scaled the rocky mound created by the collapsed terrain, careful to avoid the streaming lava, Van thought she'd be tired from mending the seal, but she had steadily re-gained her energy and easily clambered up the debris.

With the Quasher bound and Hutriel dead, there was only one danger left.

"How does the match end if we refuse to murder each other?" asked Van.

The only players remaining were Van and her team: Daisy, Ixl, and Suixsha, with the unexpected addition of Ferox. As the Balish crown prince, Van had to make sure he survived or the Balish would blame her for his death and use the incident to invade Salus Valde. Plus, Van was pretty sure she loved him.

"The gaming commission will send creatures to challenge us until all but one is dead," said Ferox. He, Van, Wiglaf, and Tyger reached the surface. They stood on the riverbed next to the Dead Forest.

"Go," pleaded Van. "Ask to be taken out."

He shook his head. "I'm not leaving you."

Van huffed. "Okay, then, let's figure out how to get back to the Dunes of Dolor. We don't have any dot matices left, no figs, no magic carpets..."

"So." Ferox raised his brow. "Walk?"

Van grinned. "Suixsha would be so proud."

Tyger belted out a roar, getting their attention.

"Werp eep." Wiglaf sat on Tyger's back. His fur cleaned and gleaming white.

Tyger flicked his head and snorted. He lowered his body to the ground.

"Um... that's an idea," said Van.

Ferox gave Van a leg up getting onto Tyger's back. Ferox climbed on after her.

Once they mounted, Tyger raised and took off.

Ferox wrapped his arms around Van from behind, the Staff horizontally tucked under both their arms. They held tight to the scruff of Tyger's neck and bobbed along with his gait. Van protected Wiglaf between her arms as she leaned forward and gripped tight. Tyger soared through the remains of the Dead Forest.

"Do you know where you're going?" Van shouted into Tyger's ear, her words carried away by the wind breaking over her mouth.

Tyger grumbled and flicked his head.

Of course he did. He could sense Suixsha's presence and hone in on her location.

Muspell and the sandscape of the desert zoomed by in a blur. Before she knew it, tatzelwurms popped up from the sand behind them in the Dunes of Dolor. Tyger left them in the dust with his super speed. The entrance to the wind cave came into view. He slowed down and navigated through the tight passageways.

Tyger sauntered into the cavern where Daisy, Ixl, and Suixsha waited for their return. He lowered his belly to the ground, allowing Van, Ferox, and Wiglaf to dismount.

Tyger bounded to Suixsha. He rubbed his nose on her head and licked her face. She joyfully wrapped her arms around his wide neck in a hug.

Daisy rushed to Van. "Your time in this world, the Alignment—it's ended! The Quasher—"

Van shook her head to stop Daisy's fretting. "The Quasher is back in Manipura. Ferox used the Staff to bind it."

"Wow." Ixl stared at the Staff clutched in Van's hand. "Can I touch it?"

Ferox moved between Ixl and the Staff. "Best if you don't."

Ixl nodded and stepped back.

Van told them about her encounter with Hutriel, the Quasher, and how she used the Staff to set free the slaves.

"Viewer see power of Staff," said Suixsha. "Now more trouble."

"My family, the officials... they'll be afraid at first," said Ferox. "They'll instate more restrictions—"

"Lemme get this straight," interrupted Ixl, his eyes darted to Van. "You threw the Staff away, so anyone could pick it up? No offense, Ferox."

"None taken," he said, without animosity.

"By saving those slaves, I acted in accordance with the will of the Creator," said Van. "I made an altruistic choice that benefited humanity, not myself. I couldn't let Hutriel bully me into thinking I'm powerless. I wasn't afraid to confront him without the Staff. Just me and my power. If I can't do that, then I have no hope of facing a demon army during Dishora."

"Without the Staff... you could've... what if you *died*?" Ixl asked Van.

"Ferox, Brux, and Daisy would've looked after the Lodian people and the Items of Creation." Van would've been at peace with them taking her place, getting her glory.

"Seal?" asked Suixsha.

Van told them about Elmot's return as a black demon.

"Even with Elmot's help from the other side, I had to use the power of the Staff *and* the Coin to mend the seal." Van's eyes went to Ixl. "He validated what your mother and my father suspected years ago. The three seals bind *three* worlds. The seals can crack and allow demons to rise from a dark place, a third world, called the Anti-World."

"My mother was right," said Ixl, with a distant gaze. "She's always right."

Van's shoulders tensed. "They're building an army."

"We don't know for certain the place Elmot mentioned isn't part of the Earth World," said Ferox.

"It's possible, but I'm sure he would've told me if that were the case." Van wasn't angry at Ferox's contrary nature. He acted based on his beliefs, which differed from hers, and she respected his viewpoint.

"I didn't know Elmot well," said Daisy, who had met him before her team had set out on a mission two years ago. "Still, I'm sad he had to return to that dark place."

"What we do now?" asked Suixsha. "No play game forever."

"So." Ixl clapped his hands. "Back to us killing each other."

Tyger growled and stepped closer to Suixsha.

"No one's killing anyone," said Daisy.

Ferox paced. "The magic boundary will stay in effect until all contestants but one survive."

Ixl shrugged. "So, this is where we live now?" He leaned back against the wall of the cavern, pulled a dagger from his belt, and began cleaning his fingernails with it.

"Use the Coin to find the best way out," Ferox said to Van.

"Already on it." She held the Coin in her palm. The pentagram pointed at the cart.

Wiglaf stared at them, sitting atop of the loads of gold, jewelry, weapons, and other items the team had collected during the match.

"Weep mrp," he said, ears tall and straight.

Ferox ran his hand along the rail of the cart's basket, deep in thought.

"Let me know when we start killing each other, okay amigos?" Ixl scraped the tip of the dagger under his fingernail.

"I have a better idea." Van grabbed handfuls of gold and jewelry from the cart and tossed them on the ground.

"Wha—wait a minute." Ixl tucked the dagger back into his belt. "What are you doing?"

"Empty it." Van threw out a ruby the size of a football.

Ferox hastened to help. "Even the weapons?"

"Everything," she said. "Take it all out."

Daisy, Suixsha, and Ixl accepted the call to action and began unloading the items. They worked together and emptied the cart.

Van ducked behind a broad rock formation and rummaged through her backpack.

"Now what?" Ixl called out to Van.

She stepped from behind the rock wearing the relatively clean yellow chiffon dress she wore at the Placement Ceremony. Her hair and skin, splotched with black goo, dirt, and dried blood.

"You look beautiful!" Daisy beamed, along with Ferox.

"You taking us to a dance?" asked Ixl.

"Get in the cart," said Van.

"Nice." Ixl bobbed his head, grinning. "I get it. The dress is your way of flipping them off."

"Yup. Now get in." Van looked at Tyger and Wiglaf. "You too."

Van stayed outside the cart and handed Ferox her backpack and the Staff.

"Are we all going to fit?" Daisy's question was immediately answered as the cart magically expanded to fit them all, even Tyger.

"Cool." Ixl jumped out and grabbed weapons. "There's room for these." He handed two war axes to Suixsha, a handheld DEW to Daisy. He kept a rifle DEW and handed Ferox the smallest dagger with the shortest blade.

Ferox waved it away. "Keep your puny dagger. I've got the Staff."

"Let's take the remains of the other team," said Van. "Leave the gold and jewels."

Ixl did as told, then leaped back in.

Van tugged the cart's handle. It easily pulled forward, no matter the heavy the load. It contorted and shifted size as they squeezed through narrow pathways, similar to how the magic carpet adjusted size to accommodate its passengers. She walked out of the wind cave, expecting the exit to appear.

Nothing happened.

She continued to pull the cart across the desert, headed toward the spot where they had entered the playing area. A few tatzelwurms popped up from the soft treading of Van's feet and the light as air cart. Ferox took care of them with fiery blasts from the Staff, scaring away other wurms from bothering them.

Finally, the familiar black U-shaped door appeared.

A handful of Anti-Manik Rebels stormed through the dot matice toward them. Dressed not in their hooded cloaks, but in leather and chain mail combat wear and wielding war axes, swords, and morning stars.

Van's teammates bounded from the cart. Tyger burst into flames.

Ferox raised the Staff; Daisy touched his arm and said, "You can't use it against them."

Ferox paused.

Van snatched the Staff from him. "She's right. You can't use it."

"No." Daisy clutched Van's arm.

Ixl aimed his rifle, ready to fire. Suixsha gripped a war axe in each hand.

"They're humans," Daisy pleaded with Van. "Using it against them will corrupt your soul."

"Trust me." Van yanked her arm away and pointed the Staff at the charging rebels.

She connected to its energy and blasted the ground in front of the charging men. They skidded to a halt, jaws dropped, eyes widened.

The rebel's weapons tumbled from their hands. They dropped to bent knees and bowed their heads.

"My queen," said their leader. "You have shown yourself to us as we always knew you would."

"What's going on here?" Ixl lowered his rifle.

The leader looked up and addressed Van. "The Balish officials promised us Goustav's Staff if we killed you and your team."

"And?" asked Ixl, still confused.

Van kept her stare on the rebels and said, "They believe only Goustav's heir can harness the power of the Staff." She and her teammates knew this was incorrect, but went along with it.

The leader bowed his head again. "I have witnessed your great power, my queen. It is our duty to worship you as Goustav's heir, the rightful Balish monarch." The leader raised his eyes to Ferox, yet spoke to Van. "Once the Runestar is found and confirms your identity, we will put you on the throne."

Ferox shifted his shoulders, obviously not comfortable with this threat to his family.

"According to rules of the match, you must fight to the death," said a male voice coming from the public announcement system tied into the gem-cams and ATGs.

The rebels clutched their weapons and leaped to their feet, eyes searching the desert, ready to fight any oncoming threats to their newfound queen.

"They mean we fight each other." Ixl raised his rifle and peered through the scope.

Van placed a hand on his arm; Ixl lowered his DEW.

"Get back in the cart," she said to him. She looked at the others. "Get back in. All of you." She said to the rebels, "Get in."

The rebels hustled to comply with the command of their queen.

Before the first one stepped aboard, Van stopped him. She said to their leader, "I want your word you will not harm Prince Ferox, or any of his family members, when we get back to the palace."

The rebels hesitated and grumbled.

Van held them up. "Your word," she demanded.

"You have it." The rebel leader gave her a curt nod, and they climbed aboard.

The cart magically expanded to fit them all.

Van clutched the cart's handle in one hand, with the other she held the Staff. Her yellow chiffon dress ruffled in the light wind. She pulled the magical cart with everyone in it across the Dunes of Dolor toward the location where the dot matice doorway had appeared.

"I won," Van shouted to the rock ledges that presumably held hidden gem-cams. "I'm the winner of the Death Games. Open the door. The match is over."

"You must fight to the death," said the voice of the unseen official. "There can only be one winner of the Death Games."

"The rules of the match are very clear." Van flashed a winner's grin. "I get to keep whatever I can carry out. That includes the cart and everything in it."

CHAPTER

FIFTY-NINE

The desert sun beat down on them.

Van remained tense and watchful, ready for another surprise attack as she hoped for the exit to appear and end the game.

Not a sound came from the others in the cart.

The pause stressed Van enough to wonder if one of the Staff's properties was blasting a doorway in time and space. One she could use to run away from it all.

She was fairly certain the Balish Royal Court wouldn't allow Ferox to die. They always made a big deal about not harming the royal family, and Ferox was their crown prince. But then again, Solana wanted control over the Balish kingdom, and she was on the other side, plotting and conniving.

Van jumped, startled, when the black U-shaped doorway appeared.

She proceeded forward and entered the casino room in Balefire Palace. The unseen announcer said, "This year's winner of the Death Games... Vanessa Cross!"

Excitement electrified the casino. Some of the crowd cheered.

The royals seated in the roped off area looked displeased. Maybe over Van winning, or the subsequent loss of their bets, or perhaps at Ferox for blatantly breaking their laws. Probably all three. Money changed hands among the spectators as they cashed out bets.

A handful of guards and the palace healer rushed over and hustled Ferox away. Onlookers crowded around Van and her team. They gawked at the Staff; Van swatted their hands away to keep them from touching it. They also gaped at Tyger, who barely fit between gaming tables. Wiglaf, not one for crowds, disappeared back to his magical animal realm.

Van's beaming gaming official said, "After much debating among the leaders, they declared you can keep whatever you carried out in the cart."

The Balish Council and the Balish Royal Court had permitted all of them to leave the playing area—*alive*—based on a loophole in the rules.

"Congratulations!" The official's cheeks puffed from his big smile, causing Van to assume he got a cash bonus for his player winning.

To the relief of the onlookers, Suixsha, along with several nervous looking guards, escorted Tyger out of the casino so he could run free on the grounds of Balefire. The rebels were also escorted out of the casino.

With the palace healer away treating Ferox, a different healer waited in a roped off area with an oversized cot and medical supplies, ready to treat the winner. She was a jennet. A female assimilated from the Tarc's takeover of the Kezef region.

Her long, mule-like face fretted over the number of patients—Van, Ixl, and Daisy—crowding her small space. "I was only expecting one, and a Tarc at that."

She calmed when none of them needed much in the way of medical care since they had already healed themselves using the Cup.

Underking Mador stopped by the medical area. "Congratulations! How are you all faring?"

They muttered their okays.

"I want you to rest easy knowing the remains of the other team are being priority shipped to Lodestar," he said. "And the three Items of Creation are locked away in a heavily guarded room in the palace."

"Are you certain they're secure?" asked Van warily.

"Yes, very secure." Mador rubbed his hands together excitedly. "The palace requires all guests to stay for the Winner's Celebration Gala tonight, especially the winner." He winked at Van.

"Can't wait," she said, pleasantly, for the sake of tribal relations.

After he left, Van and her teammates agreed they'd stay at Balefire for as long as politically correct and not a moment longer.

The healer cleared them, and guards escorted them back to their rooms. Per usual, they piled into the girl's suite where Brux and Paley waited for them. Everyone hugged. Their relief and joy palpable.

"We watched the entire match from the gem-screen set up in the living area." Brux pointed at the flat panel gemstone on the wall.

"Except the part where you disappeared off screen." Paley fanned out her fingers. "I have no fingernails left."

Van rested her hand on Paley's shoulder. "Thank you for your heroic attempt to enter the match with me. It seemed a suicide mission. I'm so proud of you."

Paley shrugged. "First time I try being a hero and not the sidekick and look what it got me."

"You're all healed?" asked Van.

"All healed." Paley smiled.

Suixsha entered the suite. Paley rushed over and gave her a quick a hug, anything longer and Suixsha might've punched her.

"So glad you made it! And Tyger, too," gushed Paley. "How did he find Van in time to protect her from the Quasher? That was incredible."

Suixsha stared wide-eyed at Paley and didn't answer, perhaps suffering from shock over a different kind of attack—one on her personal space.

"It was a favor from Lilla," Daisy answered for Suixsha. "Paying back Van for freeing the dragons. Every time you aid an animal, you win her support. She also helped Wiglaf find Tyger and Ferox."

Brux patted Ixl on the back. "You made your mother proud."

"Man, you should've been there." Ixl punched the air. "What a ride."

"I wish I was," said Brux, then he asked Van, "We watched you go off camera. You got the Staff. Did you check the seal, too?"

"Seal's fixed, amigo," said Ixl. "We've got bigger problems."

Van filled them in.

"Elmot?" Paley's eyes welled with tears. "I hope he's okay in that dark place."

Brux rubbed his chin. "I think you saw Solana's master demon."

"I'm sure of it." Van nodded. "I've been so worried about a Balish invasion of Salus Valde, now that seems small compared to what's coming. The need for our tribes to unite has never been greater." The importance of what Manik wrote in his text about not fighting with each other hit home.

"Shouldn't be a problem with Ferox on our side," said Brux. "Seriously. He put himself in the match. You're alive, thanks to him. He proved himself a great leader. I officially step back." Brux amusingly bowed. "I give you my approval to date."

Van gazed at Brux. Her heart warmed. She hadn't known his acceptance of Ferox was important to her until that moment. "Thank you."

Efore and Ebus entered the suite and congratulated Van, Daisy, Suixsha, and Ixl, but mostly Van. They brought a light snack of cut vegetables and dip.

"Rest, get showered," said Ebus. "Then, get ready for tonight's Winner's Celebration Gala. Please be downstairs in the sitting room at eight p.m. sharp."

Efore's eyes ran up and down Van, still wearing her wrinkled yellow chiffon dress. "I recommend you change out of that."

THE GALA BEGAN with a ceremonial dinner.

Van, wearing a smokey green dress, sat in a special throne-like chair at the head table called the "winner's seat."

Lord Godreel sat to her right and Underking Mador to her left. Seating scattered her teammates throughout the head table, alternating with the royals. Ferox sat at the end, far away from her, probably as punishment for entering the games. His family would no doubt blame Van for bewitching him and endangering his life. She gave them credit for restraining themselves enough to keep from throwing her in the dungeon again.

Someone dressed her in a sash with "winner" plastered on it and plunked a crown on her head. Guests gave Van more attention at this event than at her welcome dinner, making it clear the Balish and Tarcs prioritized violence, strength, and winning over all else. Van kept her ego in check by refusing to believe the fanfare.

"I waited all year for a good gaming season," bellowed Godreel. "I disapproved of your little trick. Me and my people, we wished to see *more blood*." He smashed his fist on the table, rattling the silverware and glasses. "In the end, I am pleased with the effort the royal family took to enhance the viewing experience of our Death Games." He stood, loudly scraping back his chair. "To Underking Mador, my ally and good friend, for hosting this event."

He and others in the room raised their cups.

"Here, here," the crowd shouted back at him. Everyone took a sip.

Godreel sat; Underking Mador stood. He raised his cup and cried, "To King Nequus!"

"King Nequus!" The guests raised their cups and drank.

Godreel leaned into Van and loudly asked, "What's that you're eating? Grass?" He guffawed.

"Salad," said Van. "It's delicious."

"Hah. Bunfy food." Godreel sniggered at his own joke.

Van tolerated the crude Tarc and counted the minutes until she and her teammates could head back to Lodestar.

The gala included a nod to the end of the demon illness and a stop to putting the magical vaccine and cure in the water supply. Van caught glares thrown at her from some guests, still untrusting of the Lodian witch. However, with Van's mending of the third seal, the illness would be gone for good.

Van overheard someone say the water protestors had dispersed and left the palace grounds. Empathy for the Balish people consumed her over how they must've felt about a magical treatment and cure for the demon virus being put in their water supply without their knowledge or consent. Despite it being done for their benefit, it took away their choice, forced them to take the treatment against their will, which took away their power. It was an incorrect action on Van and the Balish Council's part. No wonder the people were outraged.

However, Underking Mador informed Van the rebels still lurked, ready to defend their queen, waiting for her command.

"They won't attack us unless you give them word," said Mador jovially. "You won't, will you?"

Van shook her head, grinning, surprised to find she enjoyed talking to the underking. She found him pleasant and charismatic. Hard to believe he was Merloc's father. "I'm only seventeen. Can I be a queen? Shouldn't I be a princess?"

"Seems the rebels are in it for the long game." Mador gave her a wink.

A messenger interrupted them, delivering a scroll to Van. She uncurled the parchment.

Ferox left his seat and rushed over.

"It's from Alden!" Van said to him. "Congratulating me."

"Don't be mad," said Ferox. "I haven't had a chance to tell you yet. He's doing well and is expected to make a full recovery."

"I'm just glad he's okay." Van closed the scroll.

"I wanted to let you know I requested a meeting with the Balish Council to discuss the end of slavery in Muspell."

"That's great!" Van went to plant a kiss on his lips, then thought it better not to incite rage among those at the gala who were against their relationship. "Thank you."

"It's a first step to ending it in the rest of the kingdom."

Ferox hovered around Van for the rest of dinner and during the mingling of guests afterward. They brushed fingers out of the eyeline of guests, and whispered sweet nothings to each other when no one else was listening.

"Besides really wanting to kiss you," whispered Van. "I'd like to visit Alden before I leave."

"I'll arrange it."

"The kiss or Alden?"

"Both." Ferox grinned and zipped away.

Despite being elated over her and Ferox's relationship, Van couldn't shake her lingering terror at seeing the red eyes behind the seal. And Elmot's confirmation of a third world and the existence of a demon army headed by Solana's pal, the master demon, made Van even more wary of the Balish princess and her fiancé, Merloc.

Ebus edged his way through the crowd and found Van. He brought her to a spot by the door where he had gathered her teammates and then escorted them back to their suites. He advised them to pack and be ready for their departure first thing tomorrow morning.

"Gladly," muttered Ixl.

Van went to her bedroom. There was a brand new backpack waiting for her on the bed. Her singed backpack lay on the floor. She had little to pack. While folding her yellow chiffon dress, she heard a knock on the main door to the suite.

Efore arrived holding a bouquet. She handed the flowers to Van.

"Thank you. They're beautiful."

"They're for Alden," said Efore. "The prince has arranged for you to visit him in the medical wing. If you will follow me."

Efore led Van through the palace and into a quiet, sparsely decorated wing. She stopped before an unmarked door. "I'll wait."

Van peeked in and saw Alden in a sterile-looking room, lying in a bed made with crisp white sheets.

Alden saw Van and lit up. He snatched his ear horns from the nightstand and wrapped them around his ears.

Van entered the room. "I hope those are high thread count sheets."

Alden chuckled.

Van handed him the bouquet.

"Yellow? I'm mildly disappointed they're not pink." He smirked.

Van laughed. She sat in the guest chair next to his bed. "How are you feeling?"

"I'm right as rainbows," he said cheerily. "I heard you survived an encounter with the Hierophant, too."

"He approached me in disguise," said Van. "I didn't see his actual face, so he didn't harm me."

"I don't think I saw his true identity either. I think I startled him with my unexpected magnificence."

They chuckled.

"I want to hear all about the final match," he said. "Tell me everything."

Recounting the match included Van's retrieval of the Staff of Fire. Their conversation turned to Goustav.

"You know, magic blocked Goustav from ever finding where the Lodians hid his child, Astrid," said Alden. "It deeply saddened him."

"Is that why he banned magic?" asked Van.

Alden nodded. "Except for necessities like transportation, medicines, communication, and other infrastructures. The surviving royal Lodians thought it best for Amaryl's baby, the Anchoress-in-waiting, to be raised on Providence Island. They wanted to keep her birth and identity a secret from Goustav and the ruling Balish party, to prevent Goustav from taking her."

"And Astrid needed to be kept safe from the Quasher." Van shivered, remembering her most recent encounter with the shadow beast still bound in Manipura. "Goustav's Balish blood tainted her Anchoress bloodline, causing the Elementals to end her protection from it."

"True," said Alden. "Amaryl's cousin Regina Lake and her husband, Romet, raised the child as their own. On paper, they kept Astrid's royal name Cross, out of respect for Amaryl. But socially the girl was known as Astrid Lake."

Van bobbed her head. Now she understood why, a couple of years ago, most people had believed Daisy was the secret Anchoress heir.

"Goustav never spoke of Astrid or told anyone he had a child with Amaryl. He didn't want to put his daughter's life in jeopardy from his own people. He knew her powers as Anchoress heir were a threat to Mehal's throne. When Mehal got older and took his place as king, the environment would become even more dangerous for Astrid."

"He must've been in great pain knowing he couldn't have children when he really wanted them. Then, finding out he had a daughter with the love of his life and he could never be with that child." Van shook her head. "He had gained all the riches, land, and control. Still, his greatest desire was to be with his daughter."

"The one thing he wanted more than anything else, he couldn't have. Fulfillment of the curse." Alden gave a wistful flick of his wrist. "He secretly held hope that someday Astrid would come to him."

Van was moved by how much Goustav loved his daughter *and* Amaryl.

"The Anchoress is the true owner of the Runestar," said Alden. "This was not done intentionally. Goustav's heir happens to also be the Anchoress heir. He designed the brooch to magically find its way to her. To *you*."

Van knew Astrid had received her father's gift. Her recurring dream of a little girl catching a falling star was a memory engram. Van had witnessed Astrid catching the Runestar.

But how did Van get the memory engram? It came as a dream, not by touching an object. "Why don't I have it?"

Alden shrugged. "Your guess is as good as mine."

Van had a gut feeling the Runestar was never lost or stolen. Those rumors protected the Anchoress lineage, perpetuated the lie the Anchoress bloodline died with Amaryl. Assuming the Runestar stayed in her family for generations meant Van's mother, Aelia, had it in her possession when she died.

It was reasonable to believe Van's father, Michael, inherited it for safekeeping until Van came of age and learned of her identity as the Anchoress heir.

Van recollected what she knew about the night her father passed away. His last act before dying was to get a necklace—her mother's *locket* necklace—to Van.

The necklace... the Runestar.

Van took in a sharp breath as the realization hit her.

The Runestar didn't have to return to its owner. It never left.

It was hidden inside her mother's locket necklace.

CHAPTER

SIXTY

Van and her teammates gathered in the main hall, the same place where they entered Balefire Palace over thirty days ago.

For the sake of peace, Van said goodbye to Solana.

"See you soon," said the Balish princess.

Van narrowed her eyes, taking Solana's words as a threat.

"My sister means next year, we'll see you back here for Quinduana." Ferox gave Van a sultry gaze. "I hope."

"Merloc's family hosts a fabulous masquerade ball at Windermere Castle," said the princess.

Van stared Solana straight on. "Wouldn't miss it for the worlds."

No matter how much Ferox tried to mend her and his sister's relationship, it would never happen. The Escalation to Dishora had begun. Van was certain Solana was on the wrong side.

Ferox clasped Van's hand. He whisked her away to a cozy nearby alcove for some private time before they parted ways.

"Merloc was the one who blocked my letters to you." Ferox caressed Van's cheek. "In his mind, he was protecting me. Didn't want us to get together. He thought you cast a spell on me. It's unac-

395

ceptable for him to interfere in our relationship. I'll see to it he goes before the council."

"Is your family mad at you for entering the match?" Van placed her hands on his chest. His body heat warmed her palms. "Or are they blaming me for that, too?"

Ferox grinned and bobbed his head. "Yeah. They're blaming you. They're sending me for a psych eval and to Thuxeor for a spell removal." Ferox placed his hands around Van's waist and pulled her closer. "At least now they know our relationship is serious and real. Right?"

Before Van answered, she had to ask him, "Did you know about the other team being used as practice in the Death Games?"

"No." He grimaced. "I didn't. Godreel won't be granted title of Underking of Kezef for that. I'll make sure of it."

"Will he keep your family's secret?"

"I think he will. Our army is bigger and stronger than his, and he knows it. Godreel will stick to his goals of ascending to a higher title and making life better for his people."

"Getting back to your question." Van's heart whirled. "Yes. Serious and real."

She leaned in for a kiss, and joked, "To advance tribal relations."

Van had foolishly been afraid a war between their tribes would ruin their relationship. A war would have repercussions much deeper than her romantic affairs. Avoiding one was the best way to preserve cultures, friends, and families.

They pulled apart and simply stared into each other's eyes.

Van couldn't enjoy it. She thought of so many things that could go wrong and take this wonderful guy from her. "What about your family? And the council? I'm worried the three Items will cause our tribes to fight with each other. Manik warned against it. Goustav too."

"My officials fear knowing your tribe can use the Items to obliterate ours. Storing the Items at Lodestar will keep Salus Valde safe from an invasion, and will make solidifying our relationship a priority with the council and my family."

To Van's surprise and relief, Ferox and his family were allowing her to take the Items back to Lodestar without a fuss. All the tribes would be safer with the Items secured in the Celestial Tower. After seeing Goustav's vision where he used the Staff to break a seal and release demons from the Anti-World, Van wanted it kept far away from Merloc and Solana.

"You haven't told me why you never mentioned to your family you had the Coin."

"My father is a drunkard." Ferox scowled. "My sister is in a state of redemption. I don't know who I can trust in the court. I wanted to protect you from my family and my people. If the council believed your tribe had both the Cup and the Coin, they were less likely to cause trouble."

Van took the Coin out of her pocket. "Take it."

Ferox waved it away. "No, you keep it."

"Are you sure?"

He grinned. "Rules of the game, you keep what you carry out."

Van gave him an alluring grin. "I carried you out. That means I get to keep you."

"Damn right."

They kissed more.

Then Ferox clasped Van's hand and placed it over his chest. "My heart... it's taken. I don't want us to see anyone else."

"Me either," breathed Van. "I'm yours."

"You're mine," whispered Ferox.

His breath brushed against Van's lips, sending thrilling tingles throughout her body.

After more smooching, Ferox promised to see her soon.

Van's heart soared with delight.

"I'll gladly accompany you back to Lodestar," said Ferox. "You sure you don't want me to?"

"Stay. It wouldn't be right for the crown prince to leave during the Death Game celebrations." They were scheduled to run for several more days.

Van and Ferox's relationship had grown stronger after their ordeal in the match. The choice Ferox made to enter had reinforced his feelings for Van. She hoped his interests would remain aligned with her and peace among the tribes, not with Solana, his family, and war.

During the past month, Van learned how to release her anger, apply her will, and control her power. But she couldn't control her heart. She and Ferox remained locked into a trajectory, like Zurial and Manik, Amaryl and Goustav, and her parents. None of those relationships ended well. She constantly worried she and Ferox were hurtling toward a doomed romance, too.

They wandered out from the alcove, said their goodbyes, and Van re-joined her teammates gathered at the sidewalk in front of Balefire's main entrance, the Kupalle festival long over. A mo-rind hovered, ready and waiting for them.

"I was about to send a search party for you." Brux opened the fig's door for Van.

She smiled and jumped in. Van had a newfound acceptance of Brux's protective influence over her. She was glad Grigori rules required him to remain Van's protector until she came into her full power. Having him around meant he would always have her back. At the same time, Van's growing power made Brux's safeguarding less needed each year.

Ixl, Paley, and Daisy climbed in. Brux held the door for Suixsha, who hesitated.

"I—"

"Prefer to walk," said the team in unison, chuckling.

Suixsha grinned. Tyger flicked his head, enjoying the teasing.

Van slid out of the fig, saddened to say goodbye to Suixsha.

"Won't you come back to Lodestar with us?" asked Van.

"Uxa remote debrief me," said Suixsha.

"It's not that... I'll... I'm gonna miss you." Van's eyes watered.

Suixsha's face softened. She placed a gentle hand on Van's shoulder. "We learn lesson from those closest to us. Once learned, they no longer needed and leave our life."

Suixsha nodded, turned away, and began her journey back home with Tyger by her side.

Van climbed back into the mo-rind and closed the door. Ferox's man revved the engine. The fig rose higher, and they zoomed away from Balefire Palace, back to Salus Valde.

SIXTY-ONE

Back at Lodestar, Uxa and Fynn appeared frazzled about Van and her teammates going over the thirty-day window of Alignment.

"Balefire said you were fine. Still, we worried." Fynn nervously rubbed his hands together. "We were about to contact your families."

"I am happy you are back." Uxa glided over to greet them. "Especially you, son." She and Ixl hugged. "Are any of you in need of medical?"

"Nope," said Paley.

"We're all good." Van narrowed her eyes. "And you know why."

"Putting the Cup in Van's backpack was a huge risk," said Brux.

"I thought the Cup might save your lives. We have experienced too many deaths."

"But... our people, they needed the treatment, the vaccine," said Daisy.

"We had enough stockpiled to last more than a month." Uxa exuded confidence and calm. "I trusted you would return with the Cup and you did, along with the Staff and the Coin. Great job, team."

Fynn eyed the Staff. "That's one amazing rod."

They all spoke at once.

Uxa halted them. "I will debrief each of you before you are sent home. Van, you are first." She gave Fynn a nod.

Fynn escorted the others out of Uxa's office.

Van sat in a high-backed chair and began recounting what happened over the past month.

"I'm wondering about Kopius," said Van, when it was her turn to ask questions. "You assigned him to our team, knowing he was a dropout assassin. Why?"

"His skill set, experience, and closeness with Daisy made him an asset." Uxa clasped the Staff with a gloved hand as she leaned back against her desk.

"You knew my Anchoress homing device would lead me to the Staff? Is that why you agreed with the Brotherhood's decision for me *not* to retrieve it?"

"Yes," admitted Uxa. "And another reason why I decided to give you the Cup."

"It came in handy." Van nodded, thankful for Uxa's foresight. "I did as you asked. I found out where the new demons in the Earth World are coming from." Van informed Uxa of Elmot's return and his eyewitness account of a third world, the Anti-World. "There was no virus mutation. It lingered here from the crack in the seal."

"As you know, your father spoke to me about ancient parchments he read in the Hall of Records containing passages hinting of a third world." Uxa's gaze glimmered with reminiscence. "We hoped it might be a metaphor or a mythical place. The language of the ancients is difficult to translate and therefore open to inter-pretation."

Van couldn't help glancing at Uxa's neck to see if she wore Aelia's locket necklace. Uxa was secretive about important information, supposedly for security reasons. But Van still couldn't shake the possibility of Uxa being the Balish spy.

"The potential for war in the Earth World is escalating," said

Uxa. "The terrigens' violence and negativity will feed the red-eyed demon. Despite mending the seal, it will continue to push upward, trying to break free of the Anti-World and rise into ours."

"Balish beliefs are strong," said Van. "Acknowledgment of a third world takes away their power. That's why the royals altered history, confiscated all written words, and banned books. Except those printed by the Royal Balish Press. They destroyed written evidence that proved Goustav was responsible for releasing demons by using the Staff."

"The Balish find it inconvenient to believe in the Anti-World. They hide the truth in the sub-levels of Balefire Palace, in the Hall of Records." Uxa pushed from the desk and stood. "Now, we must place the Staff in the Celestial Tower along with the Cup and the Coin."

They began their walk up the winding stairway with one thousand one hundred and twenty-two steps.

Van paused once they reached the landing at the top. "I want you to approve Ken for Advanced Studies Grigori Support. I want him to attend class with Paley."

"I'll see what I can do." Uxa opened the heavy white marble door into the tower.

Sunlight trickled into the cylindrical room through the elongated, elaborately braced windows on the funnel-like ceiling.

Inside, Van halted again. "And Myles. How you treat him is unjust."

Uxa remained silent.

"You need to set him free. Holding him against his will is wrong." Van crossed her arms.

Uxa gave her a curt nod and handed her the Staff. "I'll work with the Brotherhood to make it happen."

Van clutched it and hesitated. She hated parting with the Items, even while knowing they'd be secure in the tower.

"We must use the Items when needed and only for a brief period or their immense power will eventually corrupt the user's mind." Uxa extended her hand toward a statue of a man wearing a flowing toga that looked like flames. "Please surrender the Staff to Hephaestus, the Guardian of Fire. He will keep it safe."

The sun's rays illuminated him out of the four evenly spaced statues facing outward in a circle around a snake mosaic on the floor. Over Hephaestus's wavy, shoulder-length hair, he wore a plain headband with a triangle design on his forehead. Positioned in a partial warrior's pose, he was half-sitting, half-leaping out of a nondescript throne. His right arm raised, his hand clasping an object that wasn't there. Two thick branches wound with leafy vines acted as the back legs to his throne and ran upward to support the top of the backrest.

Van took a fortifying breath and walked over to the statue. She placed the Staff in Hephaestus's hand.

The statue made a soft rumbling sound as it slowly turned away from her. The circular mosaic on the floor depicting two snakes swallowing each other's tail came to life, moving in a figure eight. When Hephaestus faced inside the circle, the statue stopped rotating and the serpents halted, once again becoming a motionless mosaic.

Van pulled the Cup of Life out of her backpack. She placed the Cup in the curled fingers of the woman sitting on a throne carved entirely of seashells. Yemaya, the Guardian of All Water. The statue turned, the figure-eight snake mosaic came to life again. Once Yemaya faced the inner circle, she stopped moving, as did the serpents in the mosaic.

Van carried out the same action with the Coin of Creation. She placed it between the outstretched hand of Gaea Mater, the Guardian of the Earth. The statue rotated, the snakes again moved in a figure-eight. All motion stopped once Gaea Mater faced the inner circle.

Van and Uxa left the tower and made their way back down the winding stairway.

"It is time for you to go home to your step-mother," said Uxa.

Van didn't argue.

～

A FEW DAYS after returning to Providence Island, Van walked alone in the nature preserve, enjoying the serenity offered by the woods. She sat on a rock in Astrid's Hollow and gazed at the beautiful grassy clearing surrounded by an abundance of leafy trees.

The blissful tranquility refreshed her. Chirping birds and the soft rustle of leaves in the light wind were the only sounds. The name of the hollow now held deep meaning to Van, a special place in her heart. The hollow was, after all, named after her ancestor.

Van thought about her recurring dream where she witnessed Astrid catching the brooch designed in the shape of the Helm of Awe as it fell from the sky. It happened right here, in the hollow. The Runestar had reached its rightful owner.

Thuxeor had claimed the Runestar wasn't lost. Did that mean the necklace was somewhere on the island? In Mt. Hope Manor? At Balefire?

When Van told her teammates about the Runestar being hidden in the locket of her mother's missing necklace, Ixl had commented, "Whoever has the necklace is the Balish spy in Lodestar. Otherwise they would've turned it in to the Lodian Consilium."

Van agreed.

She renewed her vow to track down her mother's necklace. Finding it would uncover the Balish spy and prove her lineage as Goustav's heir to ensure the Anti-Manik Rebel's loyalty.

Her thoughts drifted to the seals. Something about them bothered her. She had checked two of the three. At both seals, she retrieved a nearby Item of Creation. If there were three seals and each seal had a companion Item, it stood to reason the first seal, the portal between Lodestar and Providence Island, also had one.

If that were the case, why couldn't Van sense it? And wouldn't there be an Elemental guarding it?

She wished Jacynthia would reappear soon so they could talk. Van's spirit guide hadn't returned over the past thirty days. But Van had used Jacynthia's advice about clearing her anger, given to Van before she set out on her journey. This enabled Van to connect to the power of the Creator and allowed her to complete her mission.

By mending the seal, Van had, again, thwarted Solana's master demon's rise to the Living World. Solana and her dark master might've lost this round, but they weren't out of the game. According to Elmot, they were building a demon army in the Anti-World.

Her stomach ached thinking about the coming struggle for power, one much fiercer than Van originally thought. The darkness that seeks the light wasn't the Balish seeking to take over Salus Valde and the Earth World. It was a legit army of demons not generated by terrigens. All tribes must put aside their differences and work together if they wanted to save their world during the next Dark War.

It was coming, incited by a kind of evil not seen for a thousand years.

Van needed to be ready. They all needed to be ready.

Solana's dark master was coming for them.

READ THE FIRST CHAPTER OF BOOK 4, ECHOES OF FATE

Her boyfriend's family wanted her dead. Simple fact.

Vanessa Cross tore through the tangled canopy of Providence Island's trees. Behind her, Paley Ash's footsteps pounded against the forest floor in a relentless rhythm, the only proof Van hadn't taken flight. Wind whipped her hair, branches slashed at her arms, stinging, but ignorable. She couldn't slow down. The Brotherhood agents were closing in.

The Balish royal family didn't just dislike her. They wanted her gone. Eliminated.

Van shoved her doubts aside, focusing on the weight in her pocket. The stolen gem pulsed with possibilities both thrilling and terrifying. This wasn't about power. It was about *potential*. One she couldn't fully grasp yet, one that made every risk worth taking.

The gem was theirs, if she and Paley could just lose their pursuers.

"Van, wait!" Paley gasped behind her.

Adrenaline spiked through Van's system as she glanced over her shoulder. Sinister tendrils crept through the branches, writhing in pursuit. She could almost feel the Brotherhood agents' breath on her neck.

A twig snapped nearby. Van halted, dragging Paley behind a massive oak. They pressed against the rough bark, holding their breath as silence thickened around them.

"Donovan, take the east path," a gruff voice commanded. "We'll cut them off before they reach the amphitheater."

Footsteps crunched through the underbrush, growing fainter. Van's brain shifted into survival mode. The amphitheater. The Summer Love Masquerade. Risky, but their only chance.

"This way," Van hissed, tugging Paley's arm. "And lose those flimsy sandals. They'll get us caught."

Paley kicked off her shoes without argument, wincing as her bare feet met the forest floor.

"Van, if they catch us with this thing, they might not let us go—"

"They won't," Van cut her off. Her voice came out harsher than intended, so she softened her tone. "Trust me."

The girls burst from the treeline into a familiar clearing beside the amphitheater, nearly colliding with a group of costumed revelers. Twinkling lanterns swayed in the breeze, casting a romantic glow over the scene, while base-heavy music filled the air. A banner fluttered overhead: *Summer Love Masquerade Bash!*" Masked dancers twirled and laughed, unaware of the girls' plight.

Van's eyes swept the crowd, desperate for allies, when she spotted a table of discarded masks. "Quick," she said, snatching two and tossing one to Paley.

As they slipped them on, Van spotted two men in dark suits forcing their way through the crowd. "Blend in," she whispered.

Van searched frantically for a way out. The gem stirred in her pocket like a binding oath, tethering her to something she could never escape.

"Van," Paley's voice trembled. "What is that thing really? Why is it worth all this?"

Van hesitated. How could she explain herself without sounding pathetic? "It's a powerful crystal—a Prismheart. Uxa and the other Elders keep it hidden from everyone. It's not right."

Paley's yellow contacts caught the light behind her mask as she searched Van's face. "Since when do we just take things?"

A commotion erupted near the refreshment table. One agent had cornered two of their classmates, demanding to see their faces.

"We need to move," Van said, searching the crowd until she spotted a makeshift fencing area. Hope flickered when she recognized two familiar figures: Hannah and Jacob.

As they approached, the ring of steel on steel stopped. The couple lowered their blunted practice swords.

"Hey! Looks like fun." Van forced a casual air she didn't feel. "Any chance we can borrow some gear?"

Hannah's eyes narrowed behind her mask.

"I don't know, Cross," she said, her voice loud enough for the costumed revelers around them to hear. "This requires staying on your own two feet. Think you can manage that without your protector holding you up?"

Van's blood turned to ice. Hannah had just exposed her status in front of students who knew nothing about the Anchoress. The whispers Van had endured in the halls at Lodestar—*tainted blood, weak leader, liability*—threatened to spread beyond their elite circle.

Jacob crossed his arms, his expression darkening. "Yeah. Or are you just looking for an excuse to get close enough to critique our form?"

"No, I—" Van faltered. The rejection cut deeper than expected. "I was just asking."

"Save it," Jacob snapped. "We don't need your 'guidance.' Why don't you go find Brux? I'm sure he can give you a piggyback ride back to Marble Hall."

They turned away, dismissing her without a second thought. The sting solidified her resolve. She didn't just want to *use* the Prismheart anymore. She needed to prove them all wrong.

A rough hand clamped down on her shoulder. "You there," a deep voice growled. "Let's see your face."

Van's pulse raced as she met Paley's terrified gaze. They had nowhere left to run. No more chances.

A crash of shattering glass pierced the air, followed by shouts and laughter. Van whipped around toward the commotion. Her heart leaped—a group of freshmen stumbling away from an overturned refreshment table. The Brotherhood agents immediately changed course, shoving through the crowd.

"Now." Van's fingers dug into Paley's arm. "Move!"

They slipped away from the party, discarding their glittery masks as they plunged back into the dusky woods. Van sent a silent thanks to the chaos-causing freshmen, even as guilt pricked at her conscience. How many times had she lectured younger students about responsibility? And here she was, a thief in the night.

Each branch lashed against her like punishment, reminding her of the stolen crystal and the consequences of getting caught.

Paley's ragged breathing filled the air as they stumbled through the underbrush. "Van," she gasped, "where are we going?"

Van slowed their pace and turned to face Paley in a small clearing.

"There's something I need to tell you." She slipped a hand into her pocket, fingers closing around the Prismheart. Its energy hummed against her skin.

"I tried to achieve aerochrysalis over the summer," she admitted, her voice dropping lower. "Failed. Every single time."

Paley's brow furrowed. "Aero-what now?"

"Aerochrysalis," Van said, longing creeping into her voice. "A magical transformation that lets you soar through the skies. I thought my Anchoress powers alone would be enough, but..."

Paley's eyes widened. "I've never heard of that before. Why keep it secret? I could've helped."

Van turned away, her cheeks burning. The thought of Paley's pity twisted nausea through her stomach.

"Looks like someone could use some help," a familiar voice teased.

Van looked up sharply. Brux emerged from the darkness, moving with practiced stealth. His genuine smile sparked an unwelcome flutter in her chest. Despite her feelings for Ferox, something about Brux still stirred a reaction she refused to examine. The awareness only frustrated her more.

He approached, cradling a sleek metallic contraption. "Behold the Luxpherium Shell," Brux announced with a flourish. "Borrowed from the university, courtesy of my father's badge. Not quite aerochrysalis, but it'll give you wings. So to speak."

Van studied the exoskeleton, a storm of emotions wrestling within her—relief, annoyance, grudging gratitude. Always ready to step in, she thought, unsettled by how much she depended on Brux.

"It's this damned island," she blurted, desperate to preempt his judgment. "We're stuck between worlds here, Earth and Living. Nothing works right."

Brux's smile faded. "Magic flows through everything, Van. You just have to tune in. Maybe it's time to get out of your head and open your heart."

She scoffed, but his words hit home. This wasn't just about magic. Ferox's face flashed in her mind. Every failed attempt at aerochrysalis had been for him: to prove her strength, to protect him, to break the curse that loomed over their relationship. The fear remained. Their love was ill-fated, and aerochrysalis was supposed to be the key.

Van touched the streamlined contours of the suit. "This could be my chance."

She faced her friends, her decision crystallizing. They deserved to know the truth. All of it.

"Actually, there's something else." Her voice grew serious. "This flight training isn't just about proving myself or showing off. I need to get to the Temple of the Cross during the Alignment, to find a way to break my curse. If I can win over Ferox's family at the masquerade ball, show them our relationship could be the key to lasting peace between the tribes, it changes everything."

Brux frowned. "Van, this is all moving really fast. Stealing the Prismheart, the suit, and now this mission to the Temple. What's gotten into you?"

Van hesitated, then met his eyes. "I found out something. About Anchoress traditions I didn't know before."

"What traditions?"

"Every Anchoress has to choose her mate by her twenty-first birthday," Van said quietly. "I have less than three years, Brux. What am I supposed to tell Ferox's family? 'Let's unite the tribes, but by the way, I'll die giving birth to his daughter, which will cause an inter-tribal incident'?"

Paley gasped. "Choose by twenty-one? Van, you never told us about the deadline."

"Because I just found out!" Van's voice rose. "Uxa mentioned it in passing, like it was something I should already know. Every decision I make now affects whether I can convince his family to accept our relationship and whether Ferox and I have any chance at a real future."

"So this is about both missions," Brux said. "Win over his family for tribal peace, and break the curse so you can actually have that future."

"Exactly. And I need to reach the Temple of the Cross during the Alignment to find a counter-curse. If I can break the curse, I can offer his family a real political alliance instead of a doomed romance."

Her voice sharpened. "It's dangerous, I know. But I can't keep living under this death sentence. I won't spend my life waiting to die in childbirth like every other Anchoress. And honestly? I'm sick of everyone tiptoeing around it like it's inevitable."

"Of course we're in," Paley said. "You don't even have to ask."

"The Temple is where my father searched for answers," Van continued, her tone growing more commanding. "Where my mother died giving birth to me. If there's a counter-curse anywhere, it's there. And unlike my father, I can intuitively read the ancient writings on its walls."

Understanding crossed Brux's face. "That's why you need to master flight. To reach the Temple."

"No more relying on missions to take us there. Or scrambling for transportation. I need to get there myself when the time is right." Van's jaw set. "The Alignment gives us our window."

"What do you need from us?" Paley asked.

"Trust," Van said bluntly. "I need people I trust completely. People who won't hesitate when things get dangerous. They will get dangerous."

Her attention returned to the Luxpherium Shell. It was a masterpiece of gossamer-light metal fibers interwoven with enchanted gemstones that caught and scattered light. Its core needed only the Prismheart to surge to life, channeling celestial magic through every strand.

"I can't believe you pulled this off," Van whispered, awe and apprehension mingling in her voice as she examined the suit more closely.

Brux's expression grew serious. "Tell me you have the Prismheart. Without it, this thing's just a fancy paperweight."

Her hand flew to her pocket, palm closing around the crystal's warmth.

Anticipation thrummed through Van as she pulled on the Luxpherium Shell. The cool metal fibers sent a shiver across her skin as the suit became a welcome exoskeleton. The Prismheart throbbed with an ethereal energy in her grasp, its power radiating through her fingertips.

Holding her breath, she snapped the crystal into the heart of the suit.

A surge of energy erupted through her. The Prismheart synced with her heartbeat, its rhythm reverberating through the metal like a second pulse. The Shell stirred to life, its gleaming surface shifting and molding to her every move.

Brux handed her a multi-track, worry gleaming in his eyes.

"It's now or never," she muttered, willing herself to rise.

For a breath-holding moment, nothing happened. Then, ever so slowly, her feet lifted off the ground. Van let out a startled laugh as she wobbled in the air, arms flailing for balance like a newborn bird.

"It's working!" Paley cried.

As Van steadied herself, she cautiously pushed higher. The initial wobble gave way to a smoother ascent, each moment bringing more confidence. Soon, she was soaring, relishing the rush of wind that whipped through her hair and tugged at her suit.

The island stretched out below her, a patchwork of forests, fields, and clustered rooftops. She had never felt so free, so powerful. Far below, Paley and Brux ran to keep up, their voices crackling through the multi-tracks.

"This is incredible!" Van shouted, dipping low to savor the moment.

"Be careful," Brux called.

"Oh, how sweet of you to worry about my well-being," Van teased through her MT, grinning as she climbed higher.

"I'm obligated to bring that suit back intact," he shot back, his sarcasm dry enough to make her laugh.

Paley's excited voice burst through. "Van, you should see yourself! Oh, look! I can see Venus right behind you!"

Van smirked, unable to help smiling at her friend's enthusiasm.

"It's also called the Evening Star," Paley continued eagerly. "Ken mentioned it during ASG Support. It's visible in both the morning and evening skies because of its brightness."

"Fascinating, Paley," Van replied, half-listening, her focus fixed on the horizon. The thrill of flight consumed her thoughts, drowning out her ex-boyfriend's astronomy trivia. She imagined herself soaring toward the Temple of the Cross, no longer bound by earthly limitations.

"This is exactly what I needed," she said into her MT. "I'll be able to reach the Temple in no time. No guards, no restricted paths."

Concern edged Brux's response. "Just remember, mastering the suit is only the first step. The Temple's full of passages and crypts. Your father searched for years and found nothing."

"I know. But this gives us options we didn't have before." Van banked into a smooth turn, reveling in the suit's responsive control. "I'm going to fly over the masquerade bash. Everyone should see what's possible when you refuse to accept limitations."

Brux's voice came through the MT. "I'm not sure that's the best idea. It might make them resent you more."

Her exhilaration faltered before irritation flared. "They'll love me," she snapped, brushing away his doubt with a flick of her hand. "Once they see what I can do."

A pang of guilt rose at Brux's silence. Van shoved it aside. This was her moment to shine.

"I wonder how high I can go?" she murmured into her MT.

"Why don't you find out?" Paley teased, a playful energy in her voice.

Van grinned. "I'll fly to the roof of the Celestial Tower—the highest point on the island." She angled upward, exhilarated by the rush of wind against her face.

An eagle glided beside her, and she grinned. "I fly just like you, but can you do this?" With a teasing smirk, she executed a flawless backflip, the Luxpherium Shell responding to her every movement.

As she righted herself, something unsettling caught her attention below. A line of black, military-style buggies parked ominously at the Complex. "That's new," she murmured, making a mental note to investigate later.

A gust of wind buffeted her, stronger and colder than anything natural, carrying with it the faint scent of sulfur. Van adjusted her flight path, squinting as the surrounding air rippled and distorted like heat waves rising from hot asphalt.

"Weird," she muttered, trying to make sense of it.

The shimmering air coalesced into an undulating, translucent shape. It struck—ethereal claws raking across her suit and shredding the mesh like brittle parchment.

Van gasped, more from shock than pain. "What the—?"

"Van, what's happening?" Alarm shot through Brux's transmission.

"Something's attacking me," she replied. "It's made of air, I think. But solid somehow."

The air demon lunged again, its form constantly shifting. Terror coursed through Van. This was no ordinary foe. Nothing from Advanced Studies had prepared her for this type of attack.

"I got this," she sputtered into her MT, forcing bravado into her voice. She swiped at the creature. Her hand passed through its ghostly body.

The demon's strikes intensified, each blow sending shockwaves through the Luxpherium Shell. Desperation surged as she fought an enemy she could barely see and couldn't grasp.

"Be careful!" Paley shouted. "What is that thing?"

"I don't know," Van snapped. "But I'm not letting it win!"

"Stay focused!" Urgency sharpened Brux's voice. "Keep your heart clear, or the Prismheart will fail!"

Van was already lost in the frenzy of combat, her movements growing more ruthless. The Prismheart flickered erratically as she struck out with a final, desperate blow.

The demon dissolved into thin air. In that instant, the Prismheart's rhythm faltered. Horrifying clarity struck Van as gravity began to reclaim her. It wasn't about winning the fight. The demon's true purpose wasn't to kill her. It was to make her *hate*. To make her lose control.

"No!" she cried, vertigo overwhelming her. The suit was dead. The Celestial Tower loomed ahead, its stained-glass dome growing larger with terrifying speed. Everything slowed as she hurtled toward it, each colorful pane becoming clearer, more distinct.

With a deafening crash, she burst through the dome. A kaleidoscope of glass shards exploded around her, catching the light and transforming her fall into a dazzling, deadly spectacle.

The ornate mosaic floor rushed up to meet her, its intricate patterns swirling in her vision. Four shadowy statues seemed to reach for her, silent witnesses to her failure.

Then came the impact—a bone-jarring thud that shattered through every part of her.

The world became a universe of pain.

AFTERWORD

Enjoyed *Helm of Awe*? Let's stay connected!

Be the first to know about updates, releases, and exclusive content! Sign up for my newsletter at:

<u>DLArmillei.com</u>

Follow the *Anchoress* Series @anchoressseries
Dive deeper into the adventure and connect with other fans of *Anchoress*!

FACEBOOK GROUP:
HTTPS://WWW.FACEBOOK.COM/GROUPS/ANCHORESSSERIES/

INSTAGRAM:
HTTPS://WWW.INSTAGRAM.COM/ANCHORESSSERIES/

TIKTOK:
HTTPS://WWW.TIKTOK.COM/@ANCHORESSSERIES

Connect with D.L. Armillei @DLArmillei

Learn more about her, her writing journey, and upcoming projects:

FACEBOOK:
HTTP://WWW.FACEBOOK.COM/DLARMILLEI

INSTAGRAM:
HTTPS://WWW.INSTAGRAM.COM/DLARMILLEI/

X (TWITTER):
HTTPS://X.COM/DLARMILLEI

BOOKBUB:
HTTPS://WWW.BOOKBUB.COM/PROFILE/D-L-ARMILLEI

GOODREADS:
HTTPS://WWW.GOODREADS.COM/DLARMILLEI

AMAZON AUTHOR PROFILE:
HTTPS://WWW.AMAZON.COM/D.-L.-ARMILLEI/E/B06XD25WT4/

Thank you for being part of this journey. Your support keeps the magic alive!

About the Author

D. L. Armillei (Donna) is a *USA Today* and international bestselling author who began her storytelling journey at just four years old. Unable to read or write at the time, she presented her mother with a "story" in "cursive," hoping to hear it read aloud. Instead, her mother lovingly tucked the pages away, promising they'd read it together once Donna learned to read and write.

Today, Donna crafts immersive, imaginative stories with emotional depth. Her flagship *Anchoress* series—a young adult epic fantasy—invites readers into a richly layered world of adventure, spiritual self-discovery, and empowerment.

A Massachusetts native, Donna now splits her time between living in her home state and Florida.

9 780998 672090